Ben-Oni:
Son of Sorrow

Ben-Oni:
Son of Sorrow

A Message of Hope for an Anguished World

by
Agnes Scott Kent

The rise and fall of the
House of Rothschild

Published in Nashville, TN, by Thomas Nelson. Thomas Nelson is a trademark of Thomas Nelson, Inc.

Thomas Nelson, Inc. titles may be purchased in bulk for educational, business, fund-raising, or sales promotional use. For information, e-mail: nelsonministryservices@thomasnelson.com

All Scripture quotations are taken or adapted from the King James Version of the Bible.

ISBN-10: 1-5955-4447-X
ISBN-13: 978-1-5955-4447-6

To all Christians who
love the Jews

Contents

Preface		*ix*
Chapter 1	Dr. Benjamin Rothschild	1
Chapter 2	Unexpected Invitation	8
Chapter 3	Snatched from Death	13
Chapter 4	Warm Welcome	20
Chapter 5	Strong Bonds	26
Chapter 6	Pastor Martin Luther von Ludwig	32
Chapter 7	Changed Life	38
Chapter 8	Home Foundations Tremble	47
Chapter 9	Sinister Situation	60
Chapter 10	Secret Shelter	68
Chapter 11	Dire Tidings	80
Chapter 12	Crossroads of Destiny	93
Chapter 13	Home Foundations Crash	106
Chapter 14	Battle of Wills	116
Chapter 15	Rendezvous with Death	129
Chapter 16	Fearful Plot	143

Chapter 17	Hastened Vows	151
Chapter 18	Ben-Oni, Son of Sorrow	170
Chapter 19	Friends from Afar	177
Chapter 20	Mission of Mercy	186
Chapter 21	An Ally	198
Chapter 22	The Ransom	206
Chapter 23	Dachau Encounter	216
Chapter 24	Victorious Prisoner	229
Chapter 25	The Fugitive Safe	241
Chapter 26	A True Daughter of Israel	245
Chapter 27	Let My People Go!	257
Chapter 28	A New Vision	271
Chapter 29	Home—at Last!	288

Bibliography *303*

Acknowledgments *304*

Author's Preface

If *Ben-Oni* is to be understood and its purpose appreciated, a reading of this preface is imperative.

A person with supersensitive nervous temperament should not attempt to read this book, for it presents reality in stark and horrifying portrayal. The chief setting of the book is Nazi Germany, under the awful rule of Adolf Hitler. Its essential theme is the hideous suffering of the Jews under his wicked regime.

A word of explanation concerning the character of the story: While all of these are entirely fictitious—as in the companion Jewish stories, *David*, *Rachel*, and *Zonya*—they have their prototypes in real, well-known, and extremely vital men and women, though they are by no means identical with them either in their personalities or in their activities. Thus it will readily be seen that Pastor Martin Luther von Ludwig is inspired by and very largely drawn from Pastor Martin Niemoller; Dr. Hollister Steele derives from the distinguished and lovable Dr. Howard Kelly of the famous Johns Hopkins University and Hospital of Baltimore, Maryland; and Miss Keturah Zelde from Miss Henrietta Szold, the founder and honorary president of Hadassah, the women's division of the Zionist Organization, and one of the chief organizers of the wonderful Hadassah Hospital in Palestine.

Heinrich Starkmann (strong man) and Konstantin von Wolfmacht ("might of a wolf") present composite pictures of such notorious Nazis as Himmler, Goering, Goebbels, Streicher, Rosenberg, Hiss, and their ilk. The black shadow of another Nazi—the arch-Nazi of them all—a terribly real and a terribly sinister personage—pervades much of the story and furnishes the background for its major theme: the triumph of light over darkness. This Nazi is Adolf Hitler.

The four apostate sons of Pastor von Ludwig, the saintly minister of Christ, are representative of the thousands of German youths—many of them from the most godly German homes—who were deliberately commandeered by the National Socialist Government for consolidation into the Nazi movement—where they were insidiously indoctrinated with Nazi totalitarian ideology and trained to become, eventually, full-fledged members of and political leaders within the Nazi Party.

Pastor von Ludwig's beloved only daughter, Margarete, the heroine of the story—Gretel, as she is popularly and affectionately known—portrays German young womanhood of the finest and truest and most noble order. Her striking and winsome personality is a blending of the personalities of close German friends we have long known and admired and loved.

As for the hero of the book and its leading character, Dr. Benjamin Rothschild: while he himself is completely fictitious (we must stress this point), he is representative of the actual and famous Rothschild family of Germany, which family, in turn, represents the very highest type of German Jewry. In thus constituting the Benjamin Rothschild of this story, a member of this brilliantly distinguished house, and giving him the family name, our objective is to demonstrate the astounding fact that even a Rothschild was not exempt from Nazi fury and outrage. Even a Rothschild could be dragged, by the evil power of Hitler, from his pinnacle of fame and fabulous fortune, to the very depths of penury and despair. In this case imagination is not overstrained. An actual Rothschild, one certain Count von Rothschild—so we read at the time in the press—had a considerable portion of his vast holdings impounded by the Nazis. And countless other Jews of previous great wealth were ruined, as their entire fortunes were confiscated by the National Socialist Government; while they themselves and their families became victims of physical and mental torture, thousands of them even to the point of death.

If, then, this book, *Ben-Oni*, is such a gallery of horrors as we have suggested, the question very naturally arises: Why resurrect them? Why perpetuate them in anguished memory? What possible justification is there for such a story as *Ben-Oni* to be written at all? An explanation, we believe, is therefore due the reading public. Essentially, it is as follows:

A few close friends who very kindly reviewed the book

have all, without exception, insisted, "It is timely." For one thing, the story centers largely within Berlin, and Berlin assuredly was front-page headline news within our generation—very much so. The author herself, during the entire writing, has had, over and over again, assurance of mind and heart that it is a God-given message for the predicted "perilous times" in which—beyond all possible doubt—we find ourselves living in this our own lifetime.

In a very wonderful book, *Discoveries of God* by H. E. Govan of the Faith Mission—sent to us by our cherished friends, Mr. and Mrs. J. H. MacFarlane of the Faith Mission in Canada, during a period of serious crisis in our writing—commenting on the thrilling story of Gideon as recorded in Judges, chapters 6 and 7, the author presents this striking thought: "Our surest hope of success lies in the consciousness that God is on our side . . . All Gideon's hope of victory must rest on the certainty of divine commission." In all humility we affirm that we have had this same certainty of divine commission—that, consciously, we have been under divine compulsion and empowering for this prodigious task.

The outstanding purpose in view in the construction of *Ben-Oni* is sevenfold. We list the seven strands of this purpose numerically, not in order of importance, for that would vary according to the reader's viewpoint; but solely for convenient possible reference. These seven motives are as follows:

1. Historical foundation. The story has its historical background in one of the most critical periods of the twentieth century—the decade immediately preceding the outbreak of World War II. This book includes a graphic review of the trend of events, and of the chief personages involved therein, which directly led up to that monstrous horror.

2. To give solemn warning to our present generation. We in America have grievously turned away from the Christian principles so faithfully established by our godly Founding Fathers. In consequence thereof, "It could never happen here" is—though a popular one—an altogether unfounded boast. It *could* happen here, and it *will* happen here—even such frightfulness and agony as happened in Germany and all of Europe and, indirectly, in devastating reverberation throughout the world—it could happen, and it will happen, even here in our own beloved United States of America, unless we return to God, as it will happen in all other nations that defy Him. In the last analysis, the root cause of World War I and World War II—as it will be also of World War III if and when it comes—was departure from God's holy Word and God's holy law, and from God Himself. And just as surely as He used godless heathen nations of old to chasten His own chosen people, Israel, when they departed from Him, so surely may He use even godless Russia to chasten the nations of today who hold Him in contempt—except they repent and return.

3. *To foster a clear understanding and appreciation of Germany.* To distinguish between the true Germany and the false; between the Germany that cherishes the principles and purposes of Martin Luther, and the Germany so tragically deluded and debased by Adolf Hitler; between the Germany beloved of God and faithfully following God, and the God-rejecting Germany. To hope that former enemies of Germany may overcome all bitterness and prejudice with forgiveness and magnanimity; their erstwhile hatred with Christlike love.

4. *To urge love and deepest sympathy for the Jews.* To give an authentic understanding of God's purpose for and through Israel. To emphasize His evaluation of them: *For thou art an holy people unto the LORD thy God; the LORD thy God hath chosen thee to be a special people unto himself, above all people that are upon the face of the earth.* To recall God's covenant with Abraham: *In thy seed shall all the nations of the earth be blessed.* To remind ourselves, as Christians, that our Lord Jesus Christ was born, according to the flesh—a JEW. Also to remind ourselves of our Master's own assertion: *Salvation is of the Jews.* To arouse the Church to its responsibility for proclaiming Christ among His Jewish brethren.

5. *To make us realize the extent and enormity of Jewish persecution and suffering.* To deplore anti-Semitism in every form, as well as all other interracial prejudice and hatred. In the knitting together in unity and loving accord of the hearts of four leading characters in this book—Dr. Rothschild, a Hebrew; Pastor von Ludwig, a German; Dr. Steele, an American; and

Dr. Reginald Trevelyan, an Englishman—we have joyous demonstration of the fact that God *hath made of one blood all nations of men for to dwell on all the face of the earth,* as these four representative men are indeed *all one in Christ Jesus.*

6. *Advent testimony.* Our Savior ere His departure gave faithful promise: *I will come again, and receive you unto myself; that where I am, there ye may be also.* And the Word of God abounds with signs whereby the approaching time of His return might be discerned: *upon the earth distress of nations, with perplexity . . . men's hearts failing them for fear; evil men and seducers waxing worse and worse;* departure from the faith; as in the days of Noah, the earth corrupt before God and filled with violence.

During our own generation, from the evil days of Adolf Hitler even to the present "perilous times," surely these portents and many more have multiplied and converged with startling rapidity and have extended throughout the world. In view of this undoubted fact, we do well to heed anew our Master's own words of admonition and of hope—the only possible hope for our weary, sin-cursed and strife-torn earth—even the glad hope of the near coming of the Prince of Peace:

When ye shall see all these things, know that he is near, even at the doors . . . When these things begin to come to pass, then look up, and lift up your hearts; for your redemption draweth nigh.

7. *To show forth the power of faith.* The story of Ben-Oni, Son of Sorrow, is proof and demonstration of the glorious fact that *this is the victory that overcometh the world, even our faith.* The faith of this Hebrew Christian—*being much more precious than of gold that perisheth, though it be tried with fire*—came through even the seven-times-heated burning fiery furnace of affliction, strong and radiant, joyful and triumphant. Truly such a faith as Ben-Oni's will *be found unto praise and honor and glory at the appearing of Jesus Christ.*

Chapter 1

Dr. Benjamin Rothschild

Herr Doktor Benjamin Rothschild sat meditatively before his handsome desk in his private consultation office on *Unter den Linden*, Berlin. The hour was five thirty on a Saturday afternoon in early October, 1929.

Outdoors a soft, autumnal rain was falling, but the rays of the brilliantly setting sun shone through it, touching the tops of the linden trees with a golden glory. The dazzling light penetrated the heavy plate-glass western windows of the office, richly illuminating the gilt-framed oil masterpieces on the paneled walls, the copious brass appointments of the hearth and desk, and the gold-embossed volumes within the broad walnut shelves lining the luxurious room.

But it was upon the face of the distinguished surgeon himself that the golden rays conspicuously focused, giving to his striking features a luminous effulgence and lighting up his fine, dark eyes with a peculiarly soulful beauty.

A fire of charcoals was burning cheerily upon the hearth, directly opposite the desk. For the October air already was tinged with frost, and the good *Herr Doktor* loved his warmth and comfort.

He sighed wearily and leaned back in his massive walnut desk-chair, resting his aching head within his uplifted, folded arms against the crimson velvet cushion. All of Dr. Rothschild's days were heavy ones, but today had been exceptionally so.

It had begun with an emergency call from the hospital at 4 a.m. A young man and his car, both badly smashed in collision with a truck on the Kürfurstenbrücke, following a night of carousal. Poor fellow! Dead before they could get him to the operating table. "Too bad, too bad!" the sympathetic surgeon reflected sadly. "His own fault, though, entirely," he was compelled to add. Dr. Rothschild had known the boy intimately since babyhood. He had brought him into the world, in fact. Such a fine child he had been, of such excellent, respected parents. And such a promising youth—until the wrong sort of companions got hold of him. Again the tender-hearted servant of humanity sighed heavily. The whole thing had exerted an unnerving effect upon him all day.

Among the steady stream of patients there had been, this afternoon as always, members of leading families not only of Berlin, but of other cities throughout all Germany. There had been the usual sprinkling of travelers from France and other continental countries, from Britain and even from America. One man had brought his wife for consultation all the way from California. For Dr. Benjamin Rothschild, by reason of his brilliant skill in diagnosis and in surgical procedure, was world-famous.

Slowly and stiffly the tired surgeon withdrew his arms from his head, leaned forward in his chair, and pressed the desk buzzer. Instantly from an adjoining room his office nurse appeared—still crisp in her white linen uniform and eagerly alert for her chief's orders, despite the weariness which she, too, showed after the long, exacting day at her post. As she stood tall and erect and perfectly poised before Dr. Rothschild, her flaxen hair, blue eyes and fair complexion were in striking contrast to the surgeon's dark coloring. For nurse Carlotta Schultz was a German—a pure Aryan. And Dr. Benjamin Rothschild was a Jew.

"Ja, Herr Doktor?" The nurse's tone as she responded to the summons from her high commanding officer was one of utmost respect, blended was pardonable pride in his prestige and a genuine warmth of personal regard—after nearly twenty years of service as his professional right hand. She had come to him just shortly after he began his career, in his midtwenties, and had continued with him during all of his steady rise to the pinnacle of world renown, which, at forty-five, he now held securely.

"Have I seen everyone, Fräulein Schultz?" he asked her in his vibrant, deliberate, slow voice.

"Yes sir! They have all gone. Herr Heine was the last."

"Ah, that is well! For you, Nurse Lotta, I am glad." The famous surgeon relaxed his professional air to one of frank comradeship. "You look tonight so very tired," he added solicitously. "You have had a trying day, *nicht wahr*?"

"Oh, never mind me! I am quite all right. But yourself, *Herr Doktor*, you are the tired one. You have been going steadily since four o'clock this morning."

Dr. Rothschild shrugged his shoulders deprecatingly. "Yes, but I am strong," he countered playfully as he flashed his wonted captivating smile. "You see, Nurse Lotta, you are a woman. A woman has not the iron constitution, the nerves of steel of a man. But anyway"—here the playful mood swiftly gave place to seriousness—"for me, what does it matter to be tired? But you, Nurse Lotta, you need sleep. Go right home, just as soon now as you can. Have a happy evening with your friends. Then over the weekend, take a good, long rest. You need it. And you deserve it," he added warmly.

Nurse Carlotta Schultz flushed with genuine delight at this generous tribute from her chief, who, she knew from long experience, was also her friend. "Thank you, *Herr Doktor*," she said simply. Still she stood at respectful attention. "Is there anything more that I can do for you, sir, before I go?"

"Just one thing, please, Fräulein Schultz." Again the surgeon's tone became strictly professional. "Will you call up the hospital? Find out how little Hedwig Hildenkranz is responding to the serum. Leave word for the superintendent that if the temperature rises at midnight, she is to call me up at the house. At once I shall come. The child's condition is critical."

"Yes sir."

Nurse Schultz turned toward the doorway. But Dr. Rothschild detained her further. "Ah, just a moment! I almost forgot. Still one other call I would like, if you will, please."

"Certainly, sir! What message?"

"Get the university. Find out if Joseph is still at his *verein*. If you can contact him, please remind him that both he and I promised his mother we would be home by six if possible, in good time for dinner at seven. You see, Nurse Lotta," he explained, laughing happily—his tone again becoming entirely unprofessional—"this is to be quite a gala night at our house. Mrs. Rothschild and I are celebrating our twentieth wedding anniversary. Very quietly, however. Just the family and a few of our old friends."

"Ah, I am so glad for you, *Herr Doktor*! I congratulate you and Mrs. Rothschild with all my heart, and I wish you every joy for many, many more years to come."

"How very good of you! Thank you, Nurse Lotta, most sincerely for us both. Your felicitations mean much to us. Mrs. Rothschild and I are deeply touched," he continued with warmth of genuine gratitude, "by your many kindnesses to us all." He shook hands with her cordially. "And now," he urged, "you hurry home. I shall be staying only a few minutes more. Good night!"

"Good night, *Herr Doktor*, and every happiness!"

Left alone, Dr. Rothschild walked to one of his western windows and looked out. The rain had stopped. The golden glow had faded to a dismal gray. It was fast approaching twilight. *Unter der Linden*, however, already was brilliantly illuminated. The handsome bronze streetlamps were all alight. Myriad lights, too, were blazing from the steady stream of motors rushing up and down the famous thoroughfare. Throngs of pedestrians were hurrying homeward. Among them, now and then, appeared German soldiers, haughty and fear-inspiring in their gray and red, long-skirted military greatcoats, with high-spired helmets and swords of gleaming steel.

And now the long day was ended, and it was time for him, too, to go home. Home! The magic of the very word had never ceased to thrill him—in all these twenty years that Rose had made his home indeed a bit of heaven upon earth. Home to him meant Rose supremely. But after Rose there were the boys—Joseph and Moische, their hearts' chief pride. And all the sweet, tender memories of their precious little Sharon!

How glad he was that he could leave his office early, tonight of all nights. His weariness was quite forgotten. He was exhilarated, alert, electric. For he was going home! To Rose!

He returned to his desk and sat before his telephone. He took down the receiver and called, first, his chauffeur.

"That you, Fritz? I shall be ready within ten minutes. Come right over."

And then the surgeon of world renown called the number

most familiar to him—the one best loved in the whole Berlin directory.

"*Prinzessin* 4-0377, please."

A moment of eager listening . . . And then suddenly his face became luminous as he heard from the other end of the wire the one dearest voice. His own voice, always sonorous and rich, was very soft, very tender, as he replied.

"Ah, Rosalie!" (He pronounced it Rōscź-al-lay.) "It is you, my own? . . . Yes, yes, right away, already. I have just called Fritz . . . Dinner at sharp seven? Yes, yes, surely. In less than half an hour I shall be there . . . You will believe it when you see me? Röslein! How can you be so unkind? And on our wedding day! But this time I mean it, truly . . . The patients are all gone? Yes, everybody. I am clearing up my desk. Five more minutes only, and I start . . . Here is Fritz now, honking for me. Just twenty minutes more, heart's dearest, and I will be with you. *Leb wohl!*"

Dr. Rothschild hung up the receiver, gathered some papers into his briefcase, arranged the fittings on his desk in perfect order, then walked over to the closet for his hat and coat. But before he could don them, he heard the familiar soft knock upon his office door.

"Come in!" he called—this time, however, with a shade of impatience in his tone. Once again, Nurse Carlotta entered.

"I am so sorry, *Herr Doktor*, to detain you, but there is another caller. He is not a patient, but he says he has a personal errand that is urgent. Will you see him? Here is his card." As she extended it, she watched the surgeon's reaction closely.

The frown of annoyance on his face gave way to a look of surprise and then to one of distinct satisfaction. He smiled with unfeigned pleasure as he read the visitor's name aloud.

G. HOLLISTER STEELE, MD
Southeastern Hospital
Baltimore, Maryland

"Ah, Steele of Southeastern!" Dr. Rothschild exclaimed in delight. "He is a man I have long waited to meet. One of the most brilliant young brain specialists, Fräulein Schultz, in the United States. Certainly I shall see him. Show him in at once."

He replaced his coat and hat within the closet and then turned with eager expectation toward the doorway. A man of fine appearance and bearing—thirty-five or thereabouts, tall, immaculately groomed, aristocratic—entered. The next moment the two distinguished surgeons, Dr. Benjamin Rothschild of Germany and Dr. Hollister Steele of the United States of America, were eagerly shaking hands in Dr. Rothschild's private office.

"Dr. Steele! This is a most unexpected and welcome visit! I am delighted—absolutely so!" Dr. Rothschild exclaimed in perfect English.

"Ah, Dr. Rothschild! The delight and privilege are mine, I do assure you. I long have coveted the opportunity of meeting you."

"And I of meeting you. Although I feel, Doctor, I already know you well. I follow your work, through the journals, with keenest admiration. You have made to our profession most valuable contributions."

"Thank you, sir! Your commendation of what I have tried to do is highly gratifying. But I must acknowledge, Dr. Rothschild, whatever measure of success I may have achieved, I am indebted for it very greatly to your inspiration and example. You realize, of course," he added laughingly, "that you are a beacon light to all the rest of us."

With his characteristic humility Dr. Rothschild tossed the adulation off lightly. "Ah, well!" He smiled winsomely. "We are always glad if we can be of some little help one to another. But come, lay off your coat and sit down. I want to have a good talk with you."

Dr. Steele demurred. "Thank you, no, not now. I must not detain you. I just called in to arrange for an appointment later."

"That's quite all right. My patients have all gone."

"Then you were hurrying away yourself, were you not?"

"Should I be hurrying when a famous colleague arrives all the way from America? And from *Southeastern*? Come, my dear Dr. Steele. Certainly you will sit down at once. There is so much I have to ask you about. Your latest paper on cerebral tumor. Your brilliant postoperative work. You—but here, let me have your hat and overcoat."

He carried them over to his closet and then drew up two large, comfortable armchairs before the glowing fire. Within a moment the two professional gentlemen were settled down in them. And for one of the gentlemen, at least, everything outside the world of surgery was entirely forgotten—even Rose and the wedding anniversary celebrating awaiting them.

Chapter 2

Unexpected Invitation

"And now," Dr. Rothschild began quite leisurely, "tell me first of all, when did you arrive in Germany?"

"I landed in Hamburg just at ten o'clock this morning."

"Ah, indeed! And what brings you to the Fatherland, Dr. Steele?"

"Three very important errands, Dr. Rothschild, all centering on yourself."

"Myself?"

"Yes, Doctor. It is purposely to contact you that I have come all the way from Baltimore, Maryland."

"To contact *me*?" The astonishment in Dr. Rothschild's voice was humbly feigned. He was quite accustomed to people coming to contact him from far greater distances than Maryland. "Ah, you have me curious! And your three reasons are . . . ?"

"First of all, if it is agreeable to you, I greatly desire to get from you some advanced instruction. I am eager to study your technique. Would you be willing, perhaps, to have me attend a few of your student clinics?"

"Why not? I shall be honored. Whatever aid I can give, I give you gladly. All the resources of my hospital—my operating theater, my library, my laboratory—are fully at your disposal."

"How very generous! Thank you, sir. I am most grateful."

Dr. Rothschild's face beamed happily. Again he could be of service to humanity. "And now your second reason? That is . . . ?"

"My second reason in coming to you, Doctor, is purely a personal one. I wonder," he continued, forcing a wistful smile, "if you would be good enough to take me on also as a patient?"

"A patient! You are needing treatment yourself, is it, Dr. Steele? I am so very sorry." Dr. Rothschild looked at his guest intently with professional scrutiny. His keen eye at once detected that all was not well with the man before him. The handsome chestnut hair was prematurely graying; the face was thin and pale and strained; the fine blue eyes were sunken and haggard. "Indeed," he exclaimed sympathetically, warmheartedly, "I shall be only too happy, my friend, to do everything within my power to help you. How long have you been ill? Just what is it that is wrong?"

"I do not quite know, Dr. Rothschild. For nearly a year now there as been a loss of grip on myself—a paralysis of willpower, of initiative, of any desire whatever to hold on."

"Nerve overstrain."

"Yes, partially. But there is some underlying cause; no one, thus far, seems to be able to locate it. However, Doctor, pardon me! I did not mean to bother you with all this just now. Perhaps you would kindly give me an appointment. I shall greatly value your opinion."

"With pleasure, Dr. Steele. Come here at five on Monday. We shall have a thorough checkup and get right after things."

"Thank you, sir, with all my heart. You give me new hope."

"Well, do not worry, my dear friend. We soon shall have you all fixed up, as good as new . . . And now that makes two reasons for your traveling all the way to Germany. So the third . . ."

"My third reason is the most compelling of them all. I have the great honor of being entrusted with the commission of conveying to you personally a most important invitation. On behalf of the American College of Surgeons, I am authorized to bring you their very cordial greeting and felicitation together with their earnest hope that you may be persuaded to consider a call to the United States as president of this fraternity, to fill a sudden vacancy. As their highly privileged representative, I am happy to offer to you now, Dr. Rothschild, this, their most urgent proposal.

"Your headquarters would be in New York City. Your field would be nationwide and unlimited. As to your staff and equipment—and your emolument—you would be entirely free to command whatever resources and compensation you might desire. Our one absorbing concern is that you come to us."

"Dr. Steele, I am profoundly moved. No honor that has ever come to me do I regard as highly as this honor from the United States of America. I would greatly welcome the opportunity it affords of having some little part in the wonderful professional achievement represented by your American College of Surgeons. But—without taking any further time whatsoever for more consideration of the question—I know at once and decisively, my dear friend, that I must decline this very signal honor which so graciously you have presented to me.

"My reasons are rather difficult to define. At least, it may be difficult for you to understand them—and for our fraternity in America to understand them. But to myself they are completely clear and convincing. Let me try, please, if I can do so, Dr. Steele, to explain to you my exact position.

"In brief, it is simply this: I could never leave Germany. My roots are planted here too deeply. As perhaps you know, the Rothschild family in its widely diversified branches has been interwoven into the very life of Germany for many generations. I myself am one of the lesser branches of our family tree, but even I personally, by the grace of God, have become identified with the Fatherland. My home has been constructed with a view to permanency. My sons have their future here. My church is here—my pastor—all my richest spiritual ties. My lifelong friends are here. And, of course, my hospital is here. All of my strongest personal and professional interests, therefore, are here—in Germany.

"Moreover, in addition to all this, there is another and a most compelling reason why I cannot leave. This one is still more difficult for me to define, or probably for you, an American, to appreciate. The word *patriotism* perhaps best covers it. I love Germany! Our glorious Rhine—our mountains—Berlin—our other beautiful cities—our romantic history and traditions—our wonderful German home life: I cannot express to you, Dr. Steele, the deep love I have in my heart for the Fatherland. It is more than a love. It is a passion. It is the very breath of my being. For all of my country's faults and failures—and no one knows them better or deplores them more deeply than I—and for all its present terrible depression and distress, for me ever to have to leave Germany would cost me, I am confident, my very life blood.

"And so, my dear Dr. Steele, please convey to your most highly esteemed American College of Surgeons my profoundest appreciation of this distinguished honor they so graciously would confer upon me; but, at the same time, please try to make clear to them the reasons, as I have set them forth to you, why it is impossible for me to accept it."

As Dr. Rothschild ceased speaking, Dr. Steele gazed at him silently with fullest respect and admiration, too moved at the moment for reply. At length he answered thoughtfully:

"My dear Dr. Rothschild, I believe I understand you perfectly; and I want to assure you that I respect profoundly your decision and your reasons for it. Your devotion to your native country is very exalted, very noble, very beautiful. But we shall console ourselves with the hope, at least, of a visit from you soon—one of considerable length, we trust—and frequent visits and many clinics in the years to come."

"I trust sincerely that it may be possible. Thank you, Dr. Steele, for your ready understanding and your very kind consideration. And now, tell me, have you a reservation in Berlin?"

"Yes, at the Kaiserhof. Is that a good hotel?"

"One of the very best. I can recommend it highly. However, Dr. Steele, I know of a better place for *you*." There was a twinkle in Dr. Rothschild's eye. "You need home comforts," he added, "and proper care—which you could not get in a hotel."

"And where, then, might I find them?" There was a wistful, almost pleading note in the traveler's voice.

Dr. Rothschild extended his hand toward his guest with his warmhearted, genial smile. "Well, if I might suggest it, Doctor, if you think you could be happy there, we all—my wife and I and our two sons—would be most honored to have you make your home with us for as long as you are in Berlin."

"Dr. Rothschild! You are most generous and gracious. I can think of nothing more delightful. I do indeed accept with deepest gratitude—that is, if you are sure I would not be any . . ."

The Hebrew host cut off Dr. Steele's final word with his rich, full-throated laugh. "Perfectly sure. You won't be any trouble whatsoever. Besides," he added mischievously, "you are my patient now—or soon will be. Though if I am not mistaken, you will not be spending much time at the house yourself. You will be happier, I take it, at the hospital."

Dr. Steele pleaded guilty. "Well, I must confess, Doctor, operating rooms, ordinarily, do hold greater charms for me than drawing rooms."

"That is settled, then. But now we must be starting. We will stop at the hotel for your luggage and cancel your reservation. Come." But suddenly Dr. Rothschild recalled something. Abruptly he rose from his chair and rushed to his desk. "Excuse me, Dr. Steele, one moment, please. I have to phone my wife." He looked at his wristwatch guiltily.

Again he called "Prinzessin 4-0377" and again his eyes became luminous, his voice tender.

"Rosalie? Just now it is I am leaving. I shall explain everything, dearest, when I get home. I am bringing with me a friend from the United States of America. He has just arrived in Germany. You have heard me speak of him often—Dr. Hollister Steele of Southeastern in Baltimore . . . What is that? Yes, it is an honor indeed. Prepare for him, *liebchen,* our best. We welcome him gladly . . . Yes, certainly. In just twenty minutes, surely. Right away we are starting. *Auf Wiedersehen!*"

He hung up the receiver happily. "And now, my friend, we go. I fear we are a little late for dinner. My wife says when I get talking, I forget to eat. But I must apologize to you. However, very soon now we shall be home."

The two surgeons helped each other into their overcoats and started for the street door. But before they could reach it, through the long hallway, there was a sharp, insistent ringing of the emergency bell outside. While Dr. Steele stood quietly apart, Dr. Rothschild quickly flung the door wide open.

Chapter 3

Snatched from Death

A sad sight—but by no means an unaccustomed one—met his keen professional gaze. A man in his early thirties, a son of poverty, judging from his thin, shabby coat and ragged cap, his broken shoes and his red, ungloved hands, stood upon the doorstep, a shawl-wrapped little lad of three within his arms. By his side, also shawl-enfolded, stood the mother, silently weeping.

"Dr. Rothschild, sir?" the father asked with utmost embarrassment and awe. And then he broke down and wept. "O sir," he pleaded piteously, "it's our little boy—our Heinie—our only child. He's very sick."

"Come in my good friends, come right inside," the world-famed surgeon answered in his kindly, confidence-inspiring tone. He closed the door and then, taking the little fellow out of the father's arms, quickly he carried him to an inner office. Beckoning the parents to follow and to take chairs nearby, he very gently laid the suffering child upon the examining table. Dr. Steele, standing within a concealing alcove, watched intently the pitiful little drama which ensued.

The man and his wife both sat down awkwardly, the man twirling his cap in his hands, the woman wiping her eyes with a corner of her shawl. Dr. Rothschild, with fine tact, spoke to them reassuringly. "And now, my friends," he said cheerily, "let us have a look at this little laddie and see what we can do to get him well again."

With his deft skill the surgeon made a swift examination of his tiny patient. Clearly the child was seriously ill. Dr. Rothschild questioned the father quietly. "How long has your little boy been sick?"

"He was took early yesterday morning, sir."

"And what did you do for him?"

"We wrapped him in blankets and kept giving him hot drinks."

"Didn't you call a doctor?"

"Yes sir, we did, sir, late last night—a German doctor."

"And what did he do for Heinie?"

"He gave us a prescription for the apothecary. But it took all the money we had, sir, to pay the doctor what he charged us. There was none left for medicine—or for food," he added bitterly.

Dr. Rothschild's eyes flashed anger.

"And so"—here Heine's mother took up the sorrowful tale—"we couldn't do nothing more. He kept getting worse and worse. We thought he was going to die." Again the shawl was screwed piteously into the little woman's eyes.

"Yes," the father resumed, "we almost gave up. But just an hour ago, sir, a Jewish neighbor came in, and she said to us, 'You take Heinie right to Dr. Rothschild—the man they call "the children's friend." He'll cure him if anybody can. And he won't worry you about paying him, neither, not till you are able to.' You are our last hope." He looked at the greathearted man imploringly.

Dr. Rothschild's eyes looked straight into his. They were kind but deeply serious. "Our hope is in God alone," he answered gravely. Then, laying his arm compassionately around the crumpled shoulders, he added quietly, "I am glad you came to me. But I wish you had come sooner. Your little boy is very, very ill. But God helping us, we still can save him."

He walked quickly over to Dr. Steele and said in an undertone, "Doctor, we must get this child to the hospital at once. It is pleuropneumonia. His condition is extremely critical."

Again he addressed the father gently—albeit, this time, commandingly. "I think it will be best for us to take your little Heinie to the hospital. There he can have the necessary care. Come, we must go at once. My car is at the door."

But at the word *hospital,* both the father and the mother showed instant consternation. "Hospital?" the man queried in a frightened tone. "But I told you, sir, we have no money!"

Dr. Rothschild replied with tenderness. "Money? What

means money when a little child is sick? To save his life, to get him well, that is all that matters. Do not worry one bit, my dear friends, about the money. You will not have to pay one single *pfennig*. God has provided everything."

Dr. Rothschild himself carried the sick child to the car, the others following. Fritz, the faithful chauffeur for many years—well accustomed, therefore, to patient vigils, for his very irregular master—was at instant attention. Deferentially, he held the door open while the patients entered the luxurious limousine. Dr. Rothschild carefully lifted little Heinie into his mother's arms. Then he and Dr. Steele seated themselves in front with Fritz. The doors were closed, and the high-powered, handsome car sped like an arrow down *Unter den Linden*.

Everyone was silent and reflective. Dr. Steele's reflections were strangely mingled. Keen interest in the beautiful city of Berlin—deep sympathy for the pathetic little German family in the car, particularly for the child so dangerously ill—proud satisfaction in the happy prospect of close association with Dr. Rothschild within his hospital, even within his home! But underneath all of these immediate ruminations were the constant stabbings of memory—those inescapable, persistent thoughts that always brought back the heartache. Oh! Would it never heal? Would there never be surcease from all the bitter pain?

Dr. Rothschild's voice aroused him suddenly from his reverie. "We are almost there! This is the *Wilhelmstrasse* we are turning in to. The hospital is on the next block."

The next moment the car drew up before an imposing ten-story limestone building, brilliantly lighted. As they ascended the broad steps leading to the impressive entrance—above which a magnificent bronze lamp was suspended by a heavy square-linked chain—Dr. Steele's admiring glance noted the name of the great institution clearly chiseled in large block lettering upon the marble lintel over the doorway. He read it with wonder:

SHARON ROTHSCHILD MEMORIAL HOSPITAL
FOR SICK CHILDREN

As they passed through the massive bronze doors, Dr. Rothschild leading, with little Heinie again within his arms, Dr. Steele's keen intuition sensed the almost electrical effect the Jewish surgeon's presence immediately produced upon the hospital. The secretary at the information desk stood quickly at attention. Nurses and orderlies passing through the lobby drew themselves up in deferential attitude, a happy light in many eyes. Visitors exchanged significant glances with one another as they gazed after the important and magnetic personage.

Quickly summoning an orderly, Dr. Rothschild placed the sick child upon a wheeled stretcher and covered him with a blanket very tenderly. He instructed the orderly to take him swiftly to a private room while the switchboard operator called Dr. Eisenleben.

Left alone, Dr. Steele gave free rein to his eager curiosity. First, he reflected upon the inscription above the entrance: Sharon Rothschild Memorial Hospital for Sick Children. "Sharon Rothschild!" he repeated to himself. "What a lovely name!" *Who could she be?* He wondered. Someone who was dead, obviously. What relation was she to Dr. Rothschild? Was it he who had erected this great plant? And did he still control it? Dr. Steele had heard of the Rothschild Hospital in Berlin. But he had never visualized such an imposing place as this. Nor had he ever known that the hospital was a memorial.

At the extreme end of the lobby there was a huge fireplace of terracotta ornamental brick. A pine log was burning redolently upon the hearth. Above the heavy walnut mantel there hung a life-size portrait, done in oils, within a handsome gilt frame. Dr. Steele walked toward it to obtain a closer view.

He saw it was the picture of a lovely, laughing child—a girl, distinctively Jewish, of about ten or eleven. A connoisseur of art, he was enthralled by the sheer beauty of the masterpiece. The child was clad in an azure-blue frock of shimmering silk made in Empress Eugenie style, with high waistline, shirred lace bodice, low neck, short, puffed sleeves, and voluminous flowing skirt that swept the ground. Dainty silver slippers peeped out beneath the deep hem. Her hair, a tangle of silky curls, was of lustrous black. Her eyes, too, were black, with sunny twinkles in their depths. Her cheeks, beautifully rounded, were a blending of rich olive and wild rose. Pearly teeth gleamed behind the sweet, laughing lips. A magnificent Collie dog was bounding toward her playfully. Behind her stood her Shetland pony.

And then he saw the nameplate. It was a small, bronze plaque beneath the portrait. It read simply:

SHARON ROTHSCHILD

Dr. Steele's wonder deepened. So this was Sharon Rothschild—this delightful little girl! But she was dead. How very, very sad. He gazed upon the portrait, fascinated. And then he marveled. It was in her memory that this magnificent hospital had been established. But just who was she, anyway? What relation to Dr. Rothschild? Could he ask his host about her? Or might not his question touch some too-tender memory?

And then suddenly he had his answer. For on the eastern wall, at right angles to the fireplace and the portrait, he observed a large, bronze tablet. Inscribed upon it in clear, raised lettering was the whole pathetic story. The visitor read it, profoundly moved.

And then his eyes became riveted upon the last two lines of the inscription. "The LORD gave and the LORD hath taken away. Blessed be the Name of the LORD." He was frankly astounded by the statement. Did Dr. Rothschild really mean such a thing as that, or was it merely a pious platitude? Could anyone genuinely bless the name of the Lord for causing sorrow?

But here in Dr. Rothschild, Dr. Steele recognized—with perplexity but with chagrin, he was forced to admit to himself—an entirely different spirit from his own. What amazing forgiveness and beneficence the man had shown! He had deliberately translated his grief into the vast humanitarian enterprise this wonderful hospital represented.

From his contemplation of the tablet, Dr. Steele turned once again to Sharon's portrait. He was gazing upon it intently when Dr. Rothschild reappeared at his side. The visitor felt instantly a sense of intrusion upon holy ground. He was visibly embarrassed as he sought for fitting words.

SHARON ROTHSCHILD MEMORIAL HOSPITAL
FOR SICK CHILDREN

THIS HOUSE OF HEALING
WAS ERECTED IN 1925

TO THE GLORY OF GOD

FOR THE ALLEVIATION OF SUFFERING
OF ALL CHILDREN WITHIN THE FATHERLAND
REGARDLESS OF RACE, CREED, OR CIRCUMSTANCE

IN SACRED AND TENDER AND EVER-IMPERISHABLE MEMORY

OF

S H A R O N

DEARLY BELOVED ONLY DAUGHTER
OF
BENJAMIN AND ROSE ROTHSCHILD

BORN IN DRESDEN	NOVEMBER 17, 1913
DIED IN BERLIN	DECEMBER 25, 1924

THE LORD GAVE AND THE LORD HATH TAKEN AWAY
BLESSED BE THE NAME OF THE LORD

But Dr. Rothschild quickly put him at his ease. "Our little daughter, Sharon, Dr. Steele," he said simply. And then he added quietly—with a shade of sorrow in his tone, albeit with entire strength of control—"She died five years ago of spinal meningitis. On Christmas Day. A most engaging child. I shall tell you more about her later . . .

"But come!" he suddenly commanded briskly. "We must

certainly be starting now at once. I am ashamed for the way that I have had to treat you, Doctor. You must be altogether starving! I had strict orders to be home for dinner at seven." He chuckled. "And here it is nearly nine already! Fortunately, Dr. Steele," he added laughingly, "I have a very patient wife. She has need to be patient—putting up, as she must do, with my idiosyncrasies. But we shall be home very soon now, I promise you. Just *one* moment more of delay, Doctor, if you will be so kind," he pleaded. "I must call Mrs. Rothschild to tell her we are really on our way at last."

"Rosalie . . . I am calling from the hospital. An emergency, darling. But we are just now starting. Only half an hour more and we shall be there. *Leb wohl!*"

He turned quickly toward his new friend from overseas, smiling joyfully. "And now we are on our homeward way at last!" he exclaimed. He took Dr. Steele's arm and hurried him from the hospital and into his waiting car.

Chapter 4

Warm Welcome

As the beautiful limousine bowled smoothly homeward, the two gentlemen, enjoyably relaxed within its deep, luxurious comfort, at once became engaged in mutually delightful conversation—each quickly recognizing in the other a kindred spirit.

"And now, do tell me, Dr. Rothschild," his companion inquired eagerly, "how did you leave your little patient? I am very much interested in this case."

"Thank you, Dr. Steele. It meant a great deal to me having you come with us to the hospital. Well, I am happy to report that I believe the little fellow is really going to pull through. I left him with Dr. Eisenleben and two of our finest nurses. They got him into an oxygen tent immediately and started right in with the penicillin—with most gratifying response. Dr. Eisenleben agrees with me that his chances of recovery are now excellent. But our Heinie had a very close call. Only fifteen minutes more and it would have been too late."

"It was a good thing, then, after all, that I detained you as long as I did, Doctor."

"Yes, I am sure it was by divine appointment. I am a firm believer myself, Dr. Steele, in God's ordering of every slightest detail of our lives—provided, of course, that we keep ourselves within the center of His will. Do you not agree with me in this?"

"Well, I must confess, Dr. Rothschild, such an aspect is rather outside the areas of my personal experience. And what about the parents? Were you able to quiet them?"

"Happily, yes. When I assured them there was good hope for Heinie's recovery, they got themselves in hand. I arranged for them to stay in the hospital through the night, within quick call. It will comfort them and it will have a quieting effect upon the little patient to know that they are near."

"An excellent idea."

"And then," Dr. Rothschild continued, "as soon as Heinie's condition is favorable, one of our social service specialists will take them home and will investigate conditions there. She will report directly to me and recommend how we best can help them."

As the two surgeons continued their conversation—following their brief stop at the Kaiserhof for Dr. Steele to cancel his reservation and for Fritz to collect his luggage—each exchanged with the other a rich fund of professional knowledge. Much of what they said would have been quite unintelligible to the average layman, but to themselves it was both profitable and enthralling.

Gradually the crowded streets of downtown Berlin receded and the car approached the outskirts of the city. Dr. Rothschild glanced out of the window as they turned a bend in the beautiful wooded road they were now traversing. "Ah!" he exclaimed happily, "we have reached the *Wahnsee*. We shall be home now in just ten minutes." He glanced at his watch and laughed guiltily. "Half past nine! Really, Doctor, this is perfectly outrageous—the way that I am treating a hungry man. But we shall soon be there at last, and dinner will surely be awaiting us, I promise you."

"Shall I have time to change, Dr. Rothschild? I am still in travel togs only."

"That is quite all right, Dr. Steele, to dine just as you are. We live very informally—purposely so, indeed. I do love to feel that my home is the one place where I can relax completely from rigid social conventions whenever I please. Oh! I forgot to tell you about the little festivity we are having. It is what we Jewish people call a "togethering"—just a few hours of happy fellowship with friends of ours. My wife and I are celebrating our twentieth wedding anniversary."

"How very delightful! But I fear I am intruding . . ."

"Not at all! Not at all! You will add greatly to our pleasure. We have planned for a very quiet evening—only my wife and myself and our two boys together with our closest friends, the von Ludwig family. I never can bear a crowd or a fuss. Just a quiet, happy evening at home with a few congenial spirits—I certainly prefer it to any ostentatious gathering."

"I entirely agree with you, Doctor. And I am honored indeed to be included within this happy company."

"We are honored in having you, Dr. Steele. You will find the von Ludwigs most delightful people, I am sure. A German family. Pastor von Ludwig, especially, I know you will greatly admire. Perhaps already you may have heard of him—Pastor Martin Luther von Ludwig of Charlottenburg."

"Yes, certainly. He is one of Germany's important churchmen, is he not?"

"Yes, he is the most outstanding leader of our German Lutheran Church. He is undoubtedly a great man in his vigorous, fearless defense of the true Christian faith against the liberal thinking—the so-called 'higher criticism'—which has been making such alarming inroads into our German spiritual life during the past half century. Except for such stalwarts as von Ludwig, Protestant Germany would be completely destroyed. I have been a member of his church for a number of years."

"Doctor, you are a member of his church? I do not understand. I thought you were a Hebrew."

"So I am. But I am a Hebrew Christian. So are all my immediate family, Christians."

"That astonishes me, Dr. Rothschild! You have opened an entirely new avenue of thought. I did not know that Hebrews ever were Christians—except, of course, in the first century of the Christian era."

"Assuredly they are—increasing numbers of them. You have never met, then, Dr. Steele, any Christian Jews?"

"No, I believe you are the very first. Though perhaps that is my own fault—and misfortune. I must confess, I rarely ever go to church myself—at least not anymore," he added sadly. Dr. Rothschild's keen ear detected a catch in his voice. Wisely, for the present, he changed the subject.

At length the car turned off the road, passed through imposing bronze gates and bowled slowly up a curving driveway illuminated by a double row of handsome bronze lampstands. Giant oak trees bordered either side of the drive behind the lamps. At the end of the drive, the car drew up before a granite mansion. A flood of warm, soft light streamed from several windows.

"Ah, here we are! Home at last!" the master of the mansion exclaimed joyously. "Welcome, Dr. Steele! Welcome to the House of Rothschild!"

So imposing was the size of the dwelling, so palatial its exterior, that as he ascended the broad steps toward the massive door, Dr. Steele fully expected to see it opened by none other than a liveried footman. But suddenly, to his amazement, it was, instead, flung wide by one of the most beautiful women he had ever seen. As she stood for an instant floodlit in the doorway, his quick eye focused in delight upon the exquisite picture she presented.

She was attired in azure-black silk. Her beautiful arms and hands were eagerly outstretched in welcome. The clear-cut Jewish features, the black hair and eyes, the radiant smile were almost identical with those of the lovely child of the portrait in the hospital—Sharon Rothschild. The likeness was startling.

Like a very sunburst of light and laughter, she bounded out upon the tessellated terrace to meet her husband's fond embrace. Without a trace of self-consciousness in the presence of their guest, demonstratively, yet with queenly dignity, she drew her diminutive stature up on tiptoe and flung her arms around Dr. Rothschild as he caught her to his heart.

"Welcome, my beloved! Welcome *home*!" she murmured happily in a voice of rich contralto charmingly blended with a curious little throaty gurgle on an ascending scale. Her tone held not the faintest shadow of reproach for her husband's extreme tardiness. Dr. Steele stood aside in respectful—and wistful—silence as he observed this beautiful domestic scene. His host, suddenly recalling his presence, turned toward him apologetically. Fondly grasping his arm, he presented him to his wife.

"Rosalie, *liebchen*, this is my good friend I told you I was bringing home with me—Dr. Hollister Steele of Baltimore, USA. And this, Dr. Steele, is my wife Röslein." His voice, his face, radiated unconcealed pride and joy.

With her delightful ingenuousness Mrs. Rothschild seized Dr. Steele's extended hand with both of hers. In English as perfect as her husband's, she exclaimed, "Ah, Dr. Steele, you have come from overseas! From America! You are welcome to our beautiful Germany—our Fatherland! And *most* welcome to our home! Quickly! Come inside, both of you!" she commanded imperiously. "Outdoors it is much too cold." With her piquant combination of dignity and naïvete, as simply as a child she linked arms with her husband on one side and with Dr. Steele on the other and led them vivaciously across the broad terrace and through the welcoming doorway. Inside the foyer she turned to Fritz, who was following behind them with the luggage. "Take the bags upstairs, Fritz . . . Benny, darling, will you show Dr. Steele to his apartment? And hurry down quickly, both of you. I am sure our friend from America must be absolutely starving!"

"Oh, no indeed, not at all!" her guest insisted.

"But why did you wait for us, Rosalie? I told you not to. I am always telling her, Dr. Steele, that she must never wait for such an erratic person as I am."

"Yes, but I never obey him, Dr. Steele. I always wait dinner until my husband comes—no matter who may be here. I serve refreshments if he delays too long. But dinner—no. That always has to wait—for *him*."

Dr. Rothschild led the way up the handsome staircase, richly carpeted with Persian runners. His guest followed in delighted wonder as the palatial mansion opened to view before him. Midway up the stairs there was a platform with palms and ferns and priceless statuary—at the rear of which was a high colonial mirror, flanked on either side by lavish stained-glass windows.

The upper gallery was square and extensive, with a number of doors opening upon it from the three sides beyond the staircase. Dr. Rothschild ushered his guest through one doorway and led him down a lengthy corridor to a remote wing of the great house. At the end of the corridor, he opened another door.

"Welcome, my friend!" he exclaimed warmheartedly, as he invited his guest into the elegant apartment and made sure that everything was in perfect readiness for his reception. "This is your sanctum sanctorum, Dr. Steele; we call it 'Medics' Barracks.' Make yourself completely at home in it."

"How can I ever thank you sufficiently, Dr. Rothschild, for all your great kindness toward me?"

"You do not need to thank me. Just your being here is all the thanks we want. It is indeed our joy to have you, Doctor, in our home . . . And now I shall leave you for exactly fifteen minutes. I shall come back for you then—and at last you will have *food*."

Left alone, Dr. Steele eagerly inspected the sumptuous quarters that had been assigned to him by his gracious host. Their spaciousness and luxury gave him at once a delicious sense of tranquility and peace. Private sitting room, bedroom, dressing room and bath—all were furnished richly, yet in perfect harmony and with exquisite taste. He breathed a deep sigh of relief. Ah! Here he could fully rest—as he had not been able to rest for many stormy months. Again he sighed, this time hopefully. Yes, here, perhaps, he could even fight through to new self-confidence—to *victory*.

Chapter 5

Strong Bonds

As Dr. Rothschild, returning promptly, conducted his new friend downstairs to the waiting family circle, strains of music filled the mansion. Piano and pipe organ were being played in unison, each by a master hand. Dr. Steele quickly recognized his favorite composition: Wagner's *Tannhäuser*.

"How exquisite!" he exclaimed in delight.

"Yes, they do play rather well together. It is my wife and our younger son. You are fond of music, Doctor?"

"I love it!"

"Good! Then I can promise you a feast of it this evening. We are all musical—I the least of the family—and the von Ludwigs are very gifted. Their little daughter is exceptionally so. She has really a remarkable voice, although she is only sixteen . . . Ah, my kind, patient friends, here we are at last!"

As they entered the living room, the music came to a harmonious conclusion, and Mrs. Rothschild, together with the lad at the piano and an older boy, advanced to meet them—while the other guests, rising from their chairs, waited respectfully.

Placing an arm lovingly around each one, the Jewish mother proudly presented her two sons to Dr. Steele. Fine-looking lads they were, both of them, tall and lithe and clean-cut and strong. Both were dark and pronouncedly Jewish in appearance. The older son resembled his father; the younger one was strikingly like his mother and his dead sister. Both of them were winsome to a high degree. They advanced toward their guest with entire ease and well-bred charm, extending their hands in frank, wholehearted boyish welcome.

He greeted the lads warmly, and they responded with equal warmth. They all would be fast friends soon, he was sure.

Dr. and Mrs. Rothschild turned toward their other guests, and Dr. Rothschild presented his colleague from America.

"My dear friends, I want you all to welcome one of my distinguished fellow surgeons, Dr. Hollister Steel, just come from Baltimore, Maryland. And these dear people, Dr. Steele, are our very close German friends, the von Ludwig family: Pastor Martin Luther von Ludwig, Frau Hildegarde von Ludwig-Arnheim, their four fine sons—Bernhardt, Bruno, Karl, and Kurt. And this," he added proudly, placing his arm in fatherly affection around a lovely young girl, "this is their dear daughter, Fräulein Margarete von Ludwig—our own little sweetheart, Gretel."

They all shook hands cordially in eager greeting of the American guest. Dr. Steele quickly noted that everyone present spoke to him in excellent English—to his vast relief, for his German, though understandable, was by no means fluent.

Deftly Mrs. Rothschild assigned the places at the table; and soon all were standing behind their chairs, according to the manner of a Jewish home, while Pastor von Ludwig invoked God's blessing. Then they seated themselves around the hospitable board, and the wedding anniversary festivities began.

At the head of the table Dr. and Mrs. Rothschild sat side by side in tall-backed armchairs, a strikingly distinguished couple. With the soft candlelight gleaming upon her beautiful face and her shimmering blue silk dinner dress, Mrs. Rothschild was a picture of loveliness. Again Dr. Steel thought of the exquisite portrait in the hospital—of little Sharon. Somehow that portrait would always hold for him a haunting fascination.

The feast went forward happily from course to course with delightfully informal merriment. Halfway through dessert, as the candles in the seven-branched candlestick were burning softly, suddenly a brilliant burst of light appeared in the doorway; twenty other candles gleaming upon a three-tiered frosted wedding cake, which one of the maids bore to the table upon a silver tray and sat down before Dr. and Mrs. Rothschild. Amid joyous mirth it was cut by Mrs. Rothschild and distributed to all. And then it was eaten with the delicious coffee which was served at the lower end of the table from a handsome brass samovar, presided over charmingly by Gretel.

The happy party lingered long around the festive board, loath to disturb their joyous fellowship. But at length Mrs. Rothschild gave the signal for them to withdraw to the cozy living room, where soon they were devoted to the hour of music. At last, when all had presented their various renditions, an intense stillness pervaded the beautiful room, even as it pervaded all the closely intertwined hearts within it. And then Pastor von Ludwig rose softly and conducted evening family devotions. Reading the Ninety-first Psalm in profoundly reverent tone, he then offered earnest prayer, invoking God's blessing upon them all, particularly upon the distinguished Hebrew couple—his own dearest friends: Benjamin and Rose Rothschild.

Finally, to crown the entire happy anniversary evening, the devoted friends stood together in a circle, hands and voices joined as they sang their parting song: "Blest Be the Tie That Binds."

And then the von Ludwigs donned their outer garments; and amid a final chorus of felicitations to the joyful Hebrew husband and wife—still lovers after their twenty wedded years—and merry shouts of "Auf Wiedersehen" among them all, at last, near midnight, they started forth upon their homeward way.

A few more loving good nights within the Rothschild family circle; and ere long Dr. Steele found himself again in his inviting apartment. He was escorted thither by his gracious host who, before he left his guest, made sure that he had everything needful to induce quiet, comfortable repose.

Alone at last, Dr. Steele sank wearily into a deep armchair. His emotions were strangely stirred. He had spent a most delightful and exhilarating evening. In an atmosphere of beauty and high culture, he had quite lost his earlier depression of spirit. But now, alone and physically tired, there was a swift and keen reaction.

Clare's face came persistently before him—Clare's and dear little Elinor's. "Oh, where were they tonight?" again he wondered sadly.

He groaned deeply. The vivid contrast between the sweet tranquility of Dr. Rothschild's life and the sorry wreck of his own weighed upon his spirit like a pall. Dr. Rothschild had anchorage; he did not have it. Dr. Rothschild was firmly established; he was not. Dr. Rothschild's life was perfectly coordinated; his life was chaotic. Supremely happy . . . because his life—here in Germany—was so absolutely secure.

Meanwhile, downstairs Dr. and Mrs. Rothschild, alone together at last, still lingered at the ruddy fireside.

"Twenty years! Ah, my Rosalie, to think of it—that you and I have been together twenty years! You have been happy, heart's dearest?"

"Happy? Oh, so happy, never could I put it into words! God's angels in heaven could not be possibly one-half so happy as you have made me, beloved.

"O, Ben dearest, sometimes I feel I cannot bear it! Our Sharon, our beautiful, beautiful little Sharon—our only daughter! Oh, oh . . . !" The impassioned words ended in a moan.

Tenderly Rose Rothschild's husband kissed away her tears, his own eyes moist, his voice choking with his own deep emotion. "*Mein liebchen*, he murmured, "we must not grieve. The Lord gave, and the Lord hath taken her away—our precious treasure. But remember, love, even out of this great sorrow—our only one amid all the joys—God has wrought marvelous blessing. Because of our Sharon, thousands of other little lives have been spared. *Her* hospital! Oh, what it has meant to children throughout all Germany!

The long-wedded lovers sat for a few moments longer in a silence more eloquent than words. The logs were almost burned away. At length Rose broke the reverie.

"Ben!"

"Yes, heart's dearest?"

"Did you not notice it again this evening?"

"What should I notice, my love?"

"At dinner—and afterwards. Especially afterwards."

"You mean . . . ?"

"Why not? Certainly. Joseph and Gretel, of course."

"Well?"

"Well, *what*? He could not keep his eyes away from her all evening."

"You think it is becoming serious, perhaps?"

"Not 'perhaps.' Positively. And not 'becoming.' Already it has *become*. And very, very deep."

"Well, my darling? And so . . . ?"

"You would approve, Benjamin?"

"Why not? I think it is very beautiful. We could not ask a lovelier wife for our dear son than Gretel."

"You feel it would be . . ."

"Suitable? Eminently so, I am confident. Our two families already are so peculiarly close. Assuredly I feel that it would be quite wonderful. Do you not believe so, Rose?"

"You forget, Benjamin." There was a shade of sadness in her tone. "The von Ludwigs are pure Aryans. We are Jews."

"Aryans? Jews? But what has that to do with it? Should that make any difference? It has made no difference with the rest of us. Martin von Ludwig is an Aryan; I am a Jew: we are devoted to each other. The von Ludwig boys are Aryans; ours are Jews: they are inseparable. You and Hildegarde are closest friends—she an Aryan, you a Jewess. Is that not true?"

"Yes, certainly. Between our two families there is a friendship nothing in the world could break. But *marriage*, Ben—that is different. You see, I am thinking in political and social terms. And the von Ludwigs are Germans, and we are Jews. And there *is* discrimination, Benjamin—you know it."

"Among the unintelligent, yes, there always will be. But no enlightened, broad-minded, democratic man or woman—Jew or Gentile—would ever entertain a racial prejudice. So when the happy day does come, I am sure we can pray God's blessing upon our dear Joseph and Gretel with perfect confidence. Are you not satisfied, dearest Rosalie, that this is true?"

"I—I try to be. Only . . ."

"Only what? Something certainly is troubling you. Tell me, my darling, exactly what it is!"

"It is—oh, I know you will think me foolish, dearest—but I just cannot get *him* out of my mind day or night. He *frightens* me!"

"*Who*, Rose? Who frightens you?"

"That man Hitler!" She burst into sudden tears. "Oh, Benjamin," she moaned, "he does frighten me so terribly. He is so rabid against the Jews."

Dr. Rothschild looked at his wife in blank amazement. His

tone, as he retorted explosively, registered abysmal disgust and scorn. "HITLER? *ADOLF HITLER?* That mountebank? That charlatan? That monstrosity? Rose! Rose! Whatever in the world are you dreaming of? Put that man out of your thought instantly and absolutely! His ravings are unworthy of one intelligent consideration. He is a megalomaniac!"

"But I am telling you, Ben, he is gaining *power*! And he hates the Jews. He is dangerous, I *know* it. My woman's intuition—"

"Your woman's intuition, Röslein, must be corrected by your husband's common sense! Now, put that wretched man completely out of your mind, once and for all. Do not let him spoil our happy day—and all our happy years. And you can dismiss forever, *mein liebchen*, every slightest shadow of disturbing doubt. For I assure you, the responsible leaders of government will never accord Hitler recognition. To them he is simply 'a festering mushroom growth upon the body politic'—one that must be disposed of as painlessly and speedily as possible. So there is not the slightest cause for fear, my precious Rosalie. It is utterly absurd. Adolf Hitler will never be allowed to gain control in Germany."

Chapter 6

Pastor Martin Luther von Ludwig

Sunday morning dawned clear and cold. It was shortly before nine when Dr. Steele awoke feeling, for the first time in weeks, relaxed and refreshed.

He drew aside the heavy draperies at an eastern window and involuntarily gave an exclamation of delighted surprise at the beautiful vista which invited his gaze—a view hidden from him the previous evening by the enveloping darkness.

The window looked out upon a lovely park enclosed within an ivy-covered high brick wall, divided at intervals by massive bronze gates. Giant oak and elm and beech trees, interspersed with spruce and pine, extended their brilliant foliage over the whole broad area. Carefully nurtured flower beds, still blooming with late fall flowers, bordered the winding driveway. Beyond the park, viewed in the distance from the eminence of the mansion, there extended the great city of Berlin, its domes and spires gleaming in the sunlight.

When, within an hour, Dr. Rothschild came to escort his guest downstairs, he exulted frankly in his manifest improvement. "Ah, Dr. Steele, good morning, good morning! I do not need to ask you how you rested upon our German soil. Already you look a different man!"

"Good morning, Dr. Rothschild! Yes, thank you, I feel a different man. I rested amazingly well—the best sleep, really, that I have had for months."

"Admirable! That is good news indeed, my friend. And now, I am sure you are ready for some breakfast:"

"But I have had, already, a most delightful one. Your excellent Fritz brought me a tray of hothouse grapes and coffee—

by your gracious order, so he informed me. Thank you very much, sir!"

"That was merely an appetizer! Let's go downstairs and see what Olga will offer us."

As, once again, they descended the richly carpeted stairway and passed through the foyer and the conservatory into the adjoining breakfast room, Dr. Steele's artistic soul thrilled with fresh delight. The brilliant morning sunshine streamed in through the plate-glass windows, lighting up the tastefully appointed breakfast table with a warm, inviting glow. The perfume of the rare conservatory flowers filled the air. Lovebirds with gayest plumage were singing in their gilded cages.

"Come, all of you," Mrs. Rothschild invited. "Please come to the table quickly. Olga has made for us some of her famous *apfel pfannkuchen*; we must eat them piping hot." They took their places around the delightful breakfast board, and Dr. Rothschild reverently invoked God's blessing upon His bountiful provision and upon His holy day.

The morning meal proceeded forthwith, the atmosphere one of highest refinement, albeit of gladsome cheer and mirth. But toward the end of the repast, Dr. Rothschild suddenly became serious. "Dr. Steele," he addressed his guest, "every Sunday morning we always go, as a family, to Pastor von Ludwig's church in Charlottenburg. If you care to go with us, we shall be very happy to have you. But please do not feel obliged to go unless you would really enjoy it. After your long voyage perhaps you might prefer to remain quietly at home and rest. Do just as you wish."

"Thank you, Dr. Rothschild, for your consideration. But I feel quite rested now, and I really would be happy to go with you. I should greatly enjoy hearing Pastor von Ludwig preach."

As Hollister Steele passed through the sacred portal later that morning, his emotions were strangely stirred. It was years since he had entered a church. All that had happened during the intervening time came flooding back. The tide of memory was almost overmastering. Again Clare's face rose vividly before him. In the plaintive voluntary the organist was playing, he was sure he heard her voice . . . A lump gathered in his throat . . . his eyes became moist . . .

Sternly controlling his feelings he glanced about him curiously while the congregation continued to assemble. He studied the quaint interior with increasingly keen interest.

It was different from any church he had ever seen before. Almost everything within it was entirely white—except that the white walls were decorated with richly illuminated texts. But all the appurtenances were white, even to the choir stalls and organ. Old-fashioned, high-backed white benches on either side of the broad center aisle served as pews. A broad white gallery, very low-ceilinged and running completely around the edifice, also was filled with white benches. At the front of the church, facing the center aisle, rose a high, white pulpit reached by a narrow winding staircase, also white.

By the time Pastor von Ludwig began his sermon, Dr. Steele was feeling tired and depressed. But within five more minutes he completely forgot his weariness, forgot his sorrows, forgot even Clare—so enthralled did he become in the majestic grandeur of the Sabbath discourse. The man of God was lofty, eloquent, dynamic. With scarcely a perceptible gesture other than the occasional emphasis of his sensitive hands, with no conscious effort whatsoever after dramatic effect, yet by sheer force of the spiritual power controlling ever fiber of his being, quietly, steadily, convincingly, he held his hearers spellbound.

His theme was Martin Luther and the Protestant Reformation.

"Beloved," he began, "once again in the history of our great Lutheran Church, we have come to another Reformation Festival. The thirty-first of this month of October in this year of our Lord, 1929, marks the 412th anniversary of that tremendous event in Wittenberg which proved to be the foundation stone of Protestantism . . ."

In logical sequence and with exact historical verification, Pastor von Ludwig carefully built up his argument and then drove home his impassioned, powerful appeal.

"In his glorious warfare for truth and righteousness, Martin Luther dared to stand alone against all the mighty power of Rome. He dared even to oppose the pope. He dared refuse obedience to the edict of the emperor. Yes, he dared assail Satan himself and all his demon hosts. . .

"At this, another season of the Reformation Festival, the inspiration of Luther's sublime faith, of Luther's God-empowered and Christ-centered life should challenge us anew to strive to emulate his magnificent example.

"Martin Luther stood up for his convictions, undaunted and undismayed. He assailed the very gates of Rome—the very gates of hell. Can we who call ourselves evangelicals and Lutherans—we who have reaped the abundant blessings of Protestant Christianity which have come to us from God through the consecrated channel of His faithful servant, Martin Luther—can we, dare we, do less than keep alive in Germany the glorious heritage of the Protestant Reformation, the sacred reverence for the inerrant and the infallible Word of God, the loyal and loving devotion to our Lord and Savior Jesus Christ? God helping us, we, too, shall stand! And to Him shall be all the glory and the praise, world without end. Amen."

A profound stillness followed the conclusion of the service—a stillness that could be felt. The holy hush was broken by the organist's softly modulating into the magnificent Tersteegen hymn: "God reveals His presence: Let us now adore Him." As the congregation sang and the organ swelled in crescendo, the dome of the venerable and stately church reverberated with the exquisite harmony.

Once again the congregation stood—this time for the benediction while the beloved pastor pronounced in his most tender tone, even such a tone as the one wherewith a father would caress his own dear children. His hands uplifted over his people in blessing, he seemed to pour down upon them from his lofty pulpit all the love of his great, warm heart.

The worship of the morning at last completed, the devout, God-fearing German folk, many with their Bibles again beneath their arms, wended their way out from the sacred edifice, down the wooded hill to the white picket gates, passing through which they dispersed to their several godly homes.

By contrast with the Rothschilds' palatial mansion, Dr. Steele found the von Ludwigs' comfortable dwelling modest in the extreme. But far above mere dimension and material furnishing, both houses possessed in common the one essential quality that makes a home: the atmosphere of love. Dr. Steele was quick to sense this fact in the gracious welcome accorded him by the whole von Ludwig family when they returned from church.

The dinner that followed shortly thereafter bore evidence—as did everything within the house—to the careful frugality of the excellent German *hausfrau*. The hour spent in the dining room was indeed a merry one—with the six lively lads and Gretel keeping up a steady stream of laughter and vivacious conversation, amid which the more serious reflections of their elders could make but little headway.

But Pastor von Ludwig's coveted opportunity for holding scholarly discourse with his distinguished guest came later, when, following dinner, he drew him apart to his secluded study on the top floor of the house.

"And now, Dr. Steele," his genial host began when they were comfortably seated beside the big, old-fashioned porcelain stove, "I want to hear more about your wonderful America. So please begin where you left off last night."

"We have always prided ourselves upon being 'the land of the free and the home of the brave,'" Dr. Steele began, "but I fear we have to confess with sorrow and dismay that the great foundation stones of freedom our forefathers laid so faithfully are sadly rocking today."

"Yes, I fear that is only too true,"Pastor von Ludwig replied. "And yet, despite all the tragic inroads of criminal and communistic and atheistic propaganda, America in its essential soul still stands—and always shall stand, please God!—as the world's greatest exponent and exemplar of liberty."

"I trust so indeed. Certainly liberty is the genius of our country. It is for liberty and democracy that her sons have bled and died and will continue to bleed and die if ever war must needs arise again—which God forbid! But Germany, Pastor von Ludwig? Surely Germany is now not far behind the United States in her strivings toward democracy?"

"I deeply value your sympathetic concern,"he said thoughtfully. "For although our two fair countries, unhappily, were enemies in the deplorable World War, and although we two men stand here today as representatives, respectively, of the victor and the vanquished nations, it is comforting to me to hope that as individuals, as men of mutual goodwill and faith, you and I might yet be friends."

He extended his hand appealingly, pathetically. Dr. Steele seized it in a warm, heartfelt clasp. Their friendship was sealed for life.

While the afternoon stole toward evening, Dr. Steele pressed his host for information concerning Prussian totalitarianism . . . the Kaiser . . . the ruinous first World War . . . and Germany's urgent need for a democratic leader to unite the nation.

"How about that amazing young Austrian," Dr. Steele began, "who recently has come so meteorically to the forefront of popular acclaim? I understand he claims to be Germany's deliverer. I refer, of course, to Adolf Hitler."

Like a lightning flash, a look of horror swept over the gentle face of the minister of God. The sweet, sensitive mouth was contorted sharply; the starry eyes were dark with sudden passion. He choked with violent emotion. "Adolf Hitler? God forbid! Hitler has a tremendous following among disaffected groups. He is a blatant demagogue, an anti-Semite, a wild fanatic, an egotistical monstrosity. But certainly, I, for one, could never take his ravings seriously. No,"—he voiced his conviction cautiously, meditatively—"no, my dear friend, I make bold to affirm that we need never be at all alarmed, really, by reason of 'the Housepainter of Austria'—Adolf Hitler."

But even as the saintly minister of Christ uttered his confident words, Dr. Steele was quick to detect within his voice an underlying, hidden note which he tried resolutely to suppress. Was it—the quest from America could not but wonder—was it an unwelcome, involuntary note of fear? Dr. Steele said nothing. He could only wonder.

Chapter 7

Changed Life

The cuckoo clock upon the study wall chirped five.

"Five o'clock already!" Dr. Steele exclaimed in surprise.

"Yes. Dr. Rothschild gets back about six, and soon after that, Mother will be calling us for *abendessen*. And then our Sunday evening service is at eight. If you prefer not to come with us, please do not hesitate to say so.

"But I do want to come indeed! I want another of your wonderful sermons, Pastor von Ludwig."

"Thank you. You are very kind. Well, all that I tried to say this morning, and all that we have been discussing this afternoon sums up to just one deplorable fact: The confusion in your country and in my country—the political and economic crises, the increasing lawlessness and crime, the breakdown in social standards and in family life, the deepening strife even within the Church—all these maladies spring from the one common source: departure from the Word of God.

"The Lord Jesus Christ is barred from tens of thousands of our homes, from tens of millions of our hearts. Within our universities, within our seats of government, yes, within our very pulpits even, He is being crucified afresh today. His name is held in levity and derision. His claims are scorned. His love is spurned. He is now, even as truly as in the days of His flesh, despised and rejected of men. Our present evil generation, just as assuredly as His own when He walked upon the earth, is defiantly proclaiming: 'We will not have this Man to reign over us.'

"And in your own great United States of America, I fear, my friend, the situation is essentially the same. The modern generation has grievously departed from the moorings established by your saintly founding fathers. Do you not agree with me, Dr. Steele, that this is the appalling truth?"

The surgeon's reply was given with visible disquietude. "Really, sir, I am greatly embarrassed. But I must confess that I am not conversant with current theological discussion. My own interests have centered in other fields of thought."

"But, Dr. Steele, you are yourself, of course, a Christian?" The sudden question was put with the long-practiced gentle directness of the faithful minister of Christ.

The man of science, completely thrown off his guard by the surprise attack, was undeniably chagrined. He flushed as, lamely, he stammered his reply: "What, I? A *Christian*? That would depend upon your definition, would it not, sir?"

"My definition is a very simple one. By 'a Christian,' I mean a believer in the Lord Jesus Christ—one who has accepted Him as his personal savior. In that sense, Dr. Steele, are *you* a Christian, might I ask?" The pastor's voice was solicitous, tender, fatherly. His guest winced under his quiet, searching gaze. His reluctant reply, when at length he made it haltingly, was fully revealing.

"Oh, yes, certainly—er—at least—that is—I have always considered myself a Christian. Why, of course! I belong to the Protestant Episcopal Church! I was confirmed and took my first communion when I was only ten. And long before that, I believe I was baptized—or so they tell me, anyway. But I can't remember that. I must confess, though, that I haven't gone to church very frequently. My parents never approved of making church attendance compulsory when I was a child, and since I grew up, my life has been such a particularly busy one. I really have not had time to go to church, you see."

The man of God looked grave. "Yes, I see quite clearly—exactly where you stand." This he murmured to himself alone. Aloud he said with utmost solicitude, "Ah, my dear young friend! Please do not feel that I am too intrusive into so very personal, so very sacred a matter. I am a minister of the gospel, and, as such, it is distinctively not only my prerogative but my God-commanded duty to concern myself about the souls of men. And I confess, dear Dr. Steele, I am profoundly concerned for your soul's welfare. So I trust you will forgive me when I tell you very frankly that I perceive your understanding of spiritual truths is, at best, a hazy one. Will you permit me to explain?"

"Certainly, sir."

"Well, then, it is not a question of 'going to church' or of church membership or office—not even in the great Protestant Episcopal Church. It is not family connection or precedent. It is not even baptism or confirmation or communion that makes one a Christian. It is solely and essentially a matter of individual personal relationship to the Savior of the world. Every soul of man must answer for himself the one inescapable question: 'What think ye of the Christ?' And this is the question, my dear friend, that God is asking *you* and that you yourself must answer: 'What think ye of Him?' Do you believe in Him as the only begotten Son of God, who gave His life for your salvation? Do you, Dr. Steele, *believe* in the Lord Jesus Christ?"

"Why, certainly! Definitely so! I have always believed in Jesus Christ, ever since I can remember."

"Yes," the faithful servant of the Lord persisted gently, "but in just exactly what sense do you believe in Him, I wonder?"

"Well, I have, of course, always accepted the historical fact of His existence. I have always had the utmost respect for Him and for the Church. And I believe, undoubtedly, that we all should try to pattern our lives after His as the most perfect example, particularly in its unselfish, sacrificial aspect."

A solemn stillness followed. The shadows within the little upper room began to lengthen. The golden afterglow of sunset fell upon the faces of the two men, both profoundly bowed in thought. The surgeon's strongly featured face was drawn with perplexity and doubt. And with his ever-present grief. The face of the venerable pastor was illumined with a heavenly radiance—with a tenderness as lovely as the fragrance of springtime violets. But his voice, when at last he broke the tense silence, was tremulous with yearning. Lovingly, he placed his hand upon the shoulder of the younger man.

"Oh, my son," he urged him pleadingly, "will you not bear with me as a father if I speak very, very plainly? I am immeasurably distressed for you. I long unutterably for your salvation. *And you do not know the way!* It is not enough to believe intellectually in the historic Christ. It is not enough to respect Him for His illustrious influence upon the world; not enough to admire His perfect life; not enough to take Him merely as our pattern and example. It is not enough even to emulate His sacrificial spirit. No! No! No! A thousand times, *no*! Not any one of these things nor all of them put together could ever save a soul. No, my son! No! Only by our acceptance of the Lord Jesus Christ—the Lamb of God who died upon the cross to make atonement for our sin—only by wholeheartedly receiving Him as our own personal Savior, our Redeemer, can we be born again as sons of God and have His gift of eternal life. 'For God so loved the world, that he gave his only begotten Son, that whosoever believeth in him should not perish, but have everlasting life.'

"To believe in the Lord Jesus Christ in this way implies the commitment of our soul and our eternal destiny to His omnipotent, omniscient keeping. It is to entrust ourselves to His unerring, loving guidance throughout all of the hazardous, perplexing mazes of this present life. It is to know the peace that passeth all understanding—the peace *of* God because we have peace *with* God through the reconciliation accomplished by His Son at Calvary.

"All this is what it means to be a Christian. Can you say, then, my dear friend, in the light of this wholly scriptural definition, you know assuredly that *you* are a Christian—that you have thus received the Lord Jesus Christ?"

Dr. Steele shook his head sadly. "No sir. According to those terms, I fear not."

"But do you not desire, dear Dr. Steele, to be a Christian?—to be born again?—to become a son of God?"

"How could I?"

"It is so very simple. There is but one condition. That is set forth clearly in God's Word: 'As many as received him, to them gave he power to become the sons of God, even to them that believe on his name.' That is all that God requires: that you receive Jesus Christ, His only begotten, well-beloved Son. Oh! Will you not, dear man, receive Him—even now—as your Savior and your Lord and King?"

Dr. Steel's face worked convulsively. "I would really like to," he answered wistfully, "only . . ."

"Only what? What is it that is troubling you, my friend? Can I not help you?"

"You have raised difficulties."

"Intellectual difficulties, you mean?"

"Yes."

"Can you state them to me?"

"Well, as I said, I have always taken it for granted that I was a Christian in the generally accepted sense of the term—a person who belongs to the Church and who lives a respectable life and all that sort of thing. But you give it now an entirely different meaning. However, you keep appealing to what you call 'the Word of God.' Do you mean by that, the Bible?"

"Certainly."

"My difficulty, then, is exactly at this point. You do not mean, Pastor von Ludwig—surely, with all your exalted scholarship you cannot mean—that you accept the Bible as authoritative, as infallible?"

"Absolutely so, every jot and tittle of it! For the Bible is the very Word of God! Do you not also thus accept it?"

"Hardly. I am quite willing to concede that it may *contain* the Word of God—it probably does. But as to the claim I have sometimes heard advanced that the entire Bible *is* the Word of God, that it is inspired and inerrant—pardon me if I speak very frankly; I would not for anything in the world, my kind friend, offend your sensibilities—but to me, as a scientist, such a supposition is absurd."

"But just why, Dr. Steele?"

"Because there is so much in the Bible that is absolutely untrue to fact."

"For example?"

"Well, for example, the miracles that are accredited to Christ. Healing leprosy instantaneously. Giving sight to a man who was born blind. Even raising up the dead to life. It is ridiculous! Preposterous! Why, the most mediocre physician could demonstrate that such a thing is altogether and utterly a biological impossibility!"

The man of God who was rooted and grounded in the faith was unperturbed. He met the skeptic's sudden heated argument with his gentle smile. In confident tone he replied quietly, "A biological, a human impossibility—yes, entirely so. I grant it without question. But with God all things are possible. And Jesus Christ is God manifested in the flesh. All power is given unto Him in heaven and in earth. He is the Creator of all things. 'Without him was not anything made that was made. In him was life; and the life was the light of men.' No, Dr. Steele, the miracles performed by Christ present no difficulty whatsoever when we recognize Him as the Lord of life and glory. Accept the Word of God—the written Word and the living Word—by faith."

"Yes, but where faith is contradicted by reason—where we cannot see—what then?"

"Faith transcends reason, even as the sun transcends the candlelight. Faith is a vastly higher faculty than reason. It is the evidence of things not seen. Where we cannot prove, we can believe." Even as the intrepid minister of the gospel patiently developed his argument, even as he quoted Tennyson's glorious poem, a new light began to dawn upon the doubter's face. His drooping shoulders lifted, his expression softened, his whole bearing became alert. "I think," he said eagerly, "I think I begin to understand, Pastor von Ludwig, what you mean. It is not that 'seeing is believing' but, on the contrary, that believing is seeing."

The pastor's voice became very tender. "Only believe," he repeated softly. "Believe on Him, the Lord Jesus Christ. He is the author and finisher of our faith. Will you not receive Him as your Savior even now? Never mind the intellectual obscurities; they will vanish as mists before the sun when the Sun of Righteousness shines within your soul. Satisfy your heart's desire for rest, for joy, for assurance of salvation—by inviting Christ to enter in."

But Dr. Steele shook his head sadly. One last bulwark of resistance was yet remaining to be broken down.

"Yes, but how can I?" he asked mournfully. "How can I invite *Him* to come into my heart? My heart is not fit for Jesus Christ to enter. There has been *sin*."

"Ah, my dear friend! That is the glory of the great Evangel—the glory of the grace of God. Where sin abounded, 'grace did much more abound.' Christ died for our sins. 'The blood of Jesus Christ his Son cleanseth us from all sin. If we confess our sins, he is faithful and just to forgive us our sins and to cleanse us from all unrighteousness. Behold the Lamb of God, which taketh away the sin of the world.'

"That is the marvel of the gospel. From the moment that we accept the Lord Jesus as our Savior, from that very moment we are created anew."

A deep stillness reigned. The two men gazed through the western window upon the glory of the setting sun, each for several moments apparently oblivious of the other. The presence of the Holy Spirit filled the room, vividly realized by them both.

At length the pastor broke the silence. He repeated the pleading invitation: "Come! Just as you are!"

Deep chords of recollection suddenly vibrated within the surgeon's breast. A vivid memory picture rose before his consciousness: the picture of a white-haired, sweet-faced, saintly old lady sitting in her old-fashioned rocking chair, her open Bible on her lap, with a small boy kneeling beside her. It was the beloved little grandmother of his childhood—and himself, a child of six.

Even so long ago she had first sung to him the song: "Just as I am—without one plea," her favorite hymn. She had urged him then, even as a little lad, to come to Christ. And again and again she had continued to urge the growing youth. But again and again he had resisted. And then she had died. And all too soon his grandmother's hymn and his grandmother's tender pleading became buried beneath the weight of the succeeding years—years of study and of fame, years of sinning and of sorrow. But now it all came back to him in poignant remembrance. He heard again the beloved little grandmother's gentle voice—and in her voice her heard, once more, the pleading of the Spirit of the Lord.

The last barrier went down. Contritely and in tears he knelt, together with the man of God. In broken tones of mingled sorrow and triumphant joy he made complete surrender: "O Lamb of God, I come!"

A few moments later a soft knock sounded on the study door.

"Welcome!" the gracious host responded. The door opened quietly and Dr. Rothschild, back from his visit to the hospital, entered. Great was his amazement, greater still his delight, as he quickly comprehended the scene that met his gaze: his two friends, both with radiant faces, kneeling by the western window—the white head close beside the dark one, the arm of the faithful pastor thrown lovingly around the shoulders of the newborn babe in Christ.

The two men rose from their knees. Advancing towards Dr. Rothschild with hands outstretched, they gave him warm-hearted reception. His response was a glowing one.

"Dr. Steele!" he cried exultantly. "Ah, my good friend, what has happened? You are a different man. Ah, yes, yes! I *understand*! I rejoice for you with all my heart that you, too have found the Savior."

"Yes," Pastor von Ludwig echoed, "we do indeed rejoice, dear Dr. Steele, to welcome you as a brother beloved in the Lord. Praise God from whom all blessings flow!"

In the now waning light, the three men stood for a moment in silence, hand clasped in hand. All distinctions in their respective backgrounds—all differences in age, in wealth, in social rank, in experience, in nationality—all were completely obliterated. They stood there in their essential splendid manhood, three sons of God—a German, an American, a Hebrew—all one in Christ Jesus, by faith in His redeeming love.

And then, as always, his thoughts flew homeward to America—to Clare . . . to little Elinor. But they were no longer agonizing thoughts. The bitter poignancy of all the long preceding days was gone. In its place there was a sweet serenity, a tenderness, a deeply abiding peace. He recalled the vivid words of his wonderful new friend, after he had shared the agony of his wife's estrangement and his lonely years in an empty house: "You hold within your own hands the key to the entire situation. And that key is faith."

And it shall come to pass, that before they call, I will answer; and while they are yet speaking, I will hear.

The very first moment of their arrival home, even as they entered the doorway, Dr. Rothschild espied upon the great oak table in the foyer a cablegram. He lifted it and read the address: "For you, Dr. Steele, from America . . . from Baltimore!"

Quickly seizing it from his host's extended hand, Dr. Steele opened it apprehensively. As he did so, he trembled and his face turned pale, then relaxed, then brightened. With unrestrained, ecstatic joy, he thrust the cablegram back into the hand of his sympathetic friend: "Read this! Read this!" he cried.

> MOTHER DIED IN MIAMI LAST TUESDAY MORNING FOLLOWING SUDDEN HEART ATTACK. ELINOR AND I ARE HERE IN HOTEL STAFFORD. UTTERLY DESOLATE AND ALONE. CAN YOU FORGIVE EVERYTHING AND LET US ALL COME HOME? SUCCESSFULLY RID OF MR. B_ _ AT LAST. LOVING ONLY YOU FOREVER.
>
> —YOUR HEARTBROKEN CLARE

"My wife is coming back to me!" he shouted triumphantly. "I'm going home! Home to Clare and little Elinor. *Home!*"

Chapter 8

Home Foundations Tremble

Seven years later, in 1936, ominous political events began enveloping Europe. Germany became the focal point of the evil center. And, mysterious beyond all comprehension, it was within one man above all others that the evil was concentrated. That man was Adolf Hitler. He it was who, in maniacal fury, wrought untold infamy and grief upon his suffering nation. By every diabolical strategy, he grasped ascendancy over the entire political, economic, and social life, with resultant chaos, confusion, terror, and anguish among all people.

Hitler was born on April 20, 1889, in a home characterized by poverty which was alike chronic and acute. Atmospherically it was dreary and depressing. Adolf's youthful years were characterized by a series of invariable frustrations. He developed an inferiority complex, a persistent gloominess of spirit, a sense of fatalism. "Failure dogs me," was his constant, bitterly impassioned complaint.

Shortly after his mother's death, Adolf decided he would go to Vienna and there try anew to realize his golden dream of success in art. But the ill-kempt, uncouth, awkward, and abashed lad failed miserably in every examination.

As a sense of degradation gnawed at his soul, Hitler resented the occupation of Germany following the devastating World War I. He hated trade-unionism, Marxists, and, as a result of the propaganda of Karl Luger and other racial-strife mongers, he developed a burning hatred of Jews. The root cause of this fierce hate was, ostensibly, jealousy. To see the beloved country of his adoption go down in ruin and dishonor had such a prostrating effect upon him that he was "crazed with fury and grief." He later confessed, "I buried my face in covers and pillows." Through many a sleepless night he was in a violent frenzy—in a state bordering dangerously close to insanity—until, at last, like a light emerging from a black fog, a wonderful vision slowly dawned within his warped and fevered soul. Gradually it assumed definite shape and then flashed upon his consciousness in ecstatic radiance.

He himself—Adolf Hitler—would be Germany's Deliverer! He would save it from all who had crushed and desolated it so wickedly. He would rescue it from the deadly economic morass into which it had been plunged. He would liberate it from all its evil enemies: the alien armies, the Communists, the Jews. Chiefly, the Jews. They above all other people had been the curse of Germany. And, transcending every other exalted purpose, he would, first and foremost, deliver Germany from that degrading Treaty of Versailles—in accordance with the terms of which the proudest nation of all Europe had been humbled to the very dust; stripped of all its former military grandeur; occupied by a triumphant and vindictive army; denuded of all its colonies and colonial resources; weighted down with such an intolerable burden of reparations as would crush it economically for centuries. But from all these cruel injustices and indignities, and many more, Germany would be freed completely. Its soul would be restored. Its rightful "place in the sun" as the leading nation upon earth would be achieved.

It was a Wednesday evening in November 1934 within the Rothschild mansion. The entire family—father, mother, and the two fine sons—were gathered happily around the dinner table. They were enjoying a rare treat—an informal meal alone, by themselves, without the usual guests and with no servants in attendance. Such family gatherings were becoming increasingly infrequent. For Joseph was now in the medical school of the University of Berlin, diligently working for his degree in surgery, and most of his late afternoons and early evenings were given up to research in the laboratories, or in the library. Moische, too, was spending many evenings away from home—at the Berlin Conservatory of Music, practicing in preparation for the public appearances at the Conservatory concerts which he was soon to make as an acknowledged pianist. This was the goal toward which his longing eyes had gazed for years. And Dr. Rothschild was frequently out upon his professional calls, or possibly at the hospital for an emergency operation; while Rose Rothschild, with her vivid charm, was in constant demand at social or charitable gatherings.

As the evening wore on and they gathered around the fireside in the living room, they became more grave. Gradually their conversation turned into serious channels. They spoke with deep concern of the troublous times upon which their beloved Fatherland had fallen since Adolf Hitler had gained power as chancellor—the political and economic confusion; the sense of unrest and bewilderment which, more and more, was now prevailing throughout all Germany. And then very reluctantly, very cautiously—in bated tones almost of apprehension—they talked together of that strange, upsurging movement which, like a terrible miasma, undoubtedly was wrapping itself around German life, choking the very atmosphere they breathed: even *anti-Semitism.*

"In our enlightened age, and after all the contribution our Hebrew people have made to Germany in every field for generations," Dr. Rothschild exclaimed with unwonted heat, "it is incredible, it is absolutely unbelievable, that such a feeling as this—such terrible antagonism—could exist against *us.* But it is coming. Yes, I fear that it is surely coming."

Nearly two years later, Mrs. Rothschild was alone in her boudoir, trying to choose from her extensive wardrobe the gown she would wear for the dinner she and Dr. Rothschild were invited to that evening. A soft knock sounded on her door.

"Come in, please!" she called sweetly.

Ermingarde entered hesitatingly, obviously troubled and abashed. Ermingarde was one of Mrs. Rothschild's upstairs maids—one who had been in her employ for over seven years. She was clad in street attire and held a suitcase in her hand.

"Why, Ermingarde!" exclaimed her mistress in surprise. "You are going out? You did not tell me. Is anything wrong?"

"There's a lot that's wrong, ma'am! Yes, I am going out. To stay. I—I'm leaving, ma'am. For good."

"But why, my dear girl, *why*?" Mrs. Rothschild queried in consternation. "You have given me no notice whatsoever. What is wrong? Why are you leaving me like this—so very suddenly? And after all these years! Have you not been satisfied, Ermingarde?"

Ermingarde began to weep piteously. "Oh, yes, ma'am!"—the words were sobbed out brokenly—"I've been perfectly satisfied. Satisfied with my wages and with my work and with the way you all have treated me. I couldn't ask for better treatment anywhere. I couldn't ask for a finer home. And if I searched the world over I couldn't find a kinder mistress, dear Mrs. Rothschild, than you have been to me—only I—I—"

"Only *what*, Ermingarde? What is it that is *wrong*?"

"All right, ma'am," Ermingarde sobbed, "I will tell you all about it. Oh, but please do not be angry with me for saying it or for leaving you! Dear lady, I don't want to leave you. Oh, I want to stay! I do, I do! But I can't. I have to go. I cannot help it. It is my father that is making me walk out. The whole trouble, ma'am, is this: *You are Jews!*"

"ERMINGARDE!"

"Oh, please let me explain, ma'am! When I came to you seven years ago, I did not understand it would ever make any difference, your being Jews. If I had understood, I never would have come. And I can't understand it now, why it should make any difference. But my father says it makes all the difference in the world. My father is a Nazi and an officer in the Gestapo. And he says that I have got to leave your house, that I must not work for Jews another day. He is warning me that if I stay I will be right in line for terrible trouble soon. Because he says it was the Jews who made us lose the war; and for that reason every Jew has got to be put out of Germany. Our new Fuehrer, Adolf Hitler, says so."

"Ermingarde! Oh, *Ermingarde*!"

"Oh, my lady, please forgive me! Oh, I did not mean to frighten you! And I have hurt your feelings too, and I didn't mean to do that either. Dear Mrs. Rothschild, I wouldn't hurt *your* feelings, not for all the world I wouldn't. You have been so very, very kind to me, all of you. I don't care if you *are* Jews. It doesn't make one bit of difference to me. Anyway, *you* can't help it: you were *born* Jews. But I like you just the same. I only wish that I could stay with you forever. But my father says that I have got to leave. I have been trying to put him off for a whole month. But he's mad now and he says he won't stand for my staying another hour even. He has just come for me. He is waiting for me at the gate. He insists on my going home with him. Right *now*. At *once*. He told me to tell you he will come himself tomorrow for my wages and my trunk. Oh, my dear lady! I am so terribly sorry. But I have got to go. I do not dare to disobey my father. My father is a Nazi and a Gestapo! And *he* does not dare to disobey the Fuehrer!"

The mistress of the mansion almost never came into the domain of the kitchen after the evening meal. But obeying a certain inward impulse, she did visit one Saturday evening at almost twelve o'clock.

To her dumbfounded astonishment, there, in the middle of the floor, stood a man. He was tall and striking in appearance and, undeniably, "pure Aryan." Moreover, he was impressive in full-dress military uniform of a Nazi officer. Lena was in his arms! Staid, middle-aged, unglamorous Lena—hitherto never once even remotely suspected of a romance. *Lena,* in the embrace of a *man*! It was a shock indeed.

Mrs. Rothschild screamed. And Lena screamed at the sudden, unexpected sight of her mistress. Both of them were electrified by the tremendous, swift surprise. Their commingled screams, in piercing crescendo, brought Dr. Rothschild rushing in from his library across the foyer.

The Nazi, quickly releasing Lena, stood with folded arms, defiantly confronting the master of the mansion. Dr. Rothschild answered his rude stare with equal, unconcealed antagonism. The Aryan and the Jew were in sudden and violent collision.

At the same instant the two women—mistress and willful servant—stood face-to-face, each taking cautious measure of the other. Under Mrs. Rothschild's continued sad gaze, Lena averted her eyes, her shoulders drooping guiltily.

Dr. Rothschild quickly regained his self-control and took the situation strongly in command.

"Who are you, sir?" he questioned the Nazi sternly. "And what are you doing in my home at this late hour?"

"Who am I? the officer retorted rudely, his whole bearing still more defiant. "If you want to know it, sir, I am Captain Ulrich Reitzmann—a Storm Trooper in the Army of our glorious Fuehrer, Adolf Hitler. And what am I doing in your house? I'll tell you, sir, what I am doing! I am here to take away from your grand house—my wife whom I married two months ago."

"You have been married for *two months*? But why did you never tell us this before? Surely, Lena, we had every right to know of it when you were living in our home. *Why* did you not tell us?" Lena quailed before Dr. Rothschild's stern, reproachful eyes.

Her military husband answered for her—arrogantly, masterfully. "I left Lena here to find out all that we Nazis desire to know about the Jews. Just *what* we want to know—and *why*—you lowdown dogs, all of you, will realize soon enough!" With that they turned and were gone.

The Rothschilds stood for a moment thus, and then—impelled by a swift, keen intuition—they both walked toward the outside door. Opening it, they peered after the two sinister figures retreating down the driveway. Screening themselves from view, they watched the two intently as they paused for several moments beside the massive bronze gates.

"Benjamin! Look!" Rose cried in sudden consternation. "Oh, just look what he has done!"

"I see! Yes, yes—I see! Röslein, oh, my darling! No, no, beloved, do not look at it! It is too horrible!"

Rudely chalked upon the two gateposts was a devilish design. Drawn in lurid red, outlined in black, it blazed forth its evil portent ominously. It was an emblem that rapidly was extending throughout all Germany, even that same emblem of Nazi totalitarianism and Jew-hate: the terrifying swastika.

Still more ominous, below the swastika there was chalked in brilliant yellow a large *J*. had it been drawn in letters of fire, its dastardly significance could not have been more clear. It proclaimed to all beholders: "Here in this house live *Jews*."

From that night things moved forward with startling rapidity.

Before daylight the next morning, without calling even the

faithful Fritz to the task, Dr. Rothschild himself went out to the gateposts with a stepladder and cleaning outfit and labored feverishly to eradicate the hideous emblems inscribed thereupon: the swastika and the telltale *J*.

But in vain. For of whatever nefarious ingredients the chalk had been composed, it was absorbed within the porous brick indelibly. Nothing short of a mason's hammer and chisel could obliterate the fiendishly emblazoned proclamation that here in this house dwelt Jews.

By seven o'clock the mason had been summoned and set to work. But before he could chisel out half a dozen chips, he was suddenly interrupted by a strident "*Halt!*" He turned upon his ladder and looked down in the direction of the voice.

In front of the gates stood a Nazi officer. Peremptorily he demanded that the work cease at once and that the man depart. And then he strode up the driveway to the palatial mansion and pounded furiously upon the massive front door with the butt of his revolver. Dr. Rothschild himself opened it, trembling with fear. For, stealthily peering through a window he had witnessed the whole alarming situation.

"Your name!" the Nazi demanded angrily.

"Benjamin Rothschild."

"A Jew?"

"Yes sir."

"Very well, then! You will leave those identifying signs upon your gates untouched!"

Dr. Rothschild shuddered. For by this time, as he and every other Jew in Germany well knew, Adolf Hitler—now the newly self-appointed president as well as chancellor of Germany—had swiftly seized the powers of absolute dictator. In consequence thereof, the strain in every Jewish home throughout the land had become a thousand-fold intensified. And Benjamin Rothschild no longer dared deceive himself: the House of Rothschild would be no exception.

Nor were his fears without foundation. That his dwelling was now set forth to all beholders as an abode of Jews, rapidly became known with most painful certainty to the entire family. Before the day was over they were under boycott.

First of all, they were deserted by their milkman. Next, that selfsame afternoon, it was their laundryman. Always prompt to call for the household laundry on the appointed day, this time he did not appear. And finally, the hamper sent from the Rothschild home the week before was returned by a messenger boy. Attached to it was an envelope containing the weekly bill. Across the bottom of it was this penciled notation: "Please remit immediately by check. Further services discontinued."

Most distressing of all, even their postman failed them. Very briefly he stopped at their front door the following morning. With frightened glances right and left, quickly he voiced his sad farewell. Then quickly he turned and fled—that he might not have to witness Joseph's consternation as he perused the piercing words:

> *Notice is hereby given that from this date forward all Jews residing within Berlin must call for their mail at the City Post Office. Future house deliveries to all non-Aryans are officially cancelled.*
>
> *By Order of Adolf Hitler.*

***

On a Saturday midnight in May, in the year 1936, high up in his tower study, Pastor von Ludwig sat alone. Alone and deeply sorrowful. Full often now was he alone and sorrowful. For the dear companion of the many happy years of wedded life—his beloved Hildegarde—no longer blessed his heart and home. For she was now in the Father's house above.

Karl and Kurt, the two younger boys, were away in Jena, in one of the Nazi Youth training schools—commandeered and sent thither by order of Adolf Hitler.

As for the elder two—Bernhardt and Bruno—they were worse than absent. That is to say, although betimes they were present in person because they still maintained residence within their father's house, in spirit they were as far away as the antipodes. For between them and their saintly parent, gradually but surely there had grown up an impenetrable wall of ice—an ice composed of sad misunderstanding on their father's part and of arrogance and willful disobedience and disrespect on theirs.

Their attitude toward him now was one of open, supercilious contempt and cold disdain; of insolent, overbearing defiance; of irreverent and oft-times blasphemous mockery of all that he—and they themselves of yore—held dear.

In the ever-widening gulf between Pastor von Ludwig and his sons, his one great consolation was his dearly beloved only daughter—his precious "Margarete" as invariably he called her. To everyone else she was always "Gretel"—but to her father, her full and proper name seemed more dignified, more fitting. She still, and more than ever, was the apple of his eye, the deepest comfort of his lonely heart. She was the one remaining family tie—the one fond link that bound him ever more closely to her mother in Heaven.

But even the dear solace of Margarete's presence was sadly infrequent now. For no longer was she domiciled within her father's home. She was now living in the nurses' residence of Dr. Rothschild's hospital. For Gretel's dream of years at last was being realized. She was in training to become that which, from childhood, she had longed to be—a registered nurse.

Dr. Rothschild quietly observed and studied her. And after her mother's funeral, and after the first shock of sorrow had been assuaged, it was he himself who approached Gretel with the offer for which secretly, over many years, she had been longing.

"Gretel, my little sweetheart," he said to her gently one evening, as she and her father were visiting in his home, "you took care of your dear mother so beautifully. With proper training you will make a wonderful nurse. How would you like to come into my hospital someday and pursue the three years' course?"

Her response was ecstatic. "Oh, dear Dr. Rothschild, *could* I? Oh, I would love it! Better than anything else in all the world!—But no, I'm afraid not. I could not leave my father."

"Certainly, Gretel, it would not be possible for you to leave him just yet. You must take very tender care of him, dear child. Your father has had a fearful shock, and he is not too strong. And besides, you have not yet finished your Gymnasium. But when the time does come that you are fully released from your present duties, if then you still desire to obtain nurse's training, I shall be most happy to get you embarked upon your course."

Thus had it come about. As soon as Gretel completed her academic studies, and as soon thereafter as arrangements could be made for Klara Kronin to take up residence within the manse and assume full-time duties as housekeeper for Pastor von Ludwig and the boys, the delighted girl entered the Sharon Rothschild Memorial Hospital as a student-nurse. She then was twenty-one.

The love that knit together the hearts of the masters of the two houses—the Jewish surgeon and the German minister—even as the love of David and Jonathan, strong and faithful, beautiful and true. The same warm endearment had entwined the hearts of the mothers of the two homes also. And, in their boyhood years, before the cruel swastika had intruded its black shadow, the mutual attachment of the sons of the two households had been equally devoted.

But the strongest bond of all that united the two families was that heaven-sent, wonderful love between the elder son of the Hebrew family and the only daughter of the family that was pure Aryan. For Joseph Rothschild, a Jew, loved Margarete von Ludwig, a German, even as she loved him, with a love that was stronger than all the hate within wicked Nazi hearts throughout all Germany—with a love that was stronger than death.

Even as the fair spring flowers grow underground before their first appearing, softly, gradually, imperceptibly, until they burst forth suddenly in all their glowing radiance, and fragrance: even thus it was with the early dawning of the boy-and-girl love of Joseph and Gretel—a love as sweet and pure and beautiful as the flowers of a heavenly May morning. Each was unconscious of the feeling within the other's heart—though amazedly aware of the warm glow within their own—until instantaneously the age-long wondrous miracle burst into full view before their enraptured eyes in all its radiant loveliness and joy. Joseph was then but eighteen; Gretel only sixteen. A Jewish boy and an Aryan girl. In *Germany*.

The miracle had transpired two years before the death of

Gretel's mother, on the very evening—that never-to-be-forgotten happy evening in the Rothschild home—when their two families, together with Dr. Rothschild's distinguished guest from America, Dr. Hollister Steele, had celebrated Dr. and Mrs. Rothschild's twentieth wedding anniversary.

It was following the merry celebration dinner and during the hour of music in the living room, when Joseph and Gretel had quietly slipped away from their elders and from all the other boys, to their favorite cozy nook—the window-seat behind the palms upon the gallery, halfway up the staircase. There for a while they sat in silence, looking down through the balustrade upon the delightful scene below: Dr. and Mrs. Rothschild, radiantly joyful, the center of the group of admiring and devoted loved ones. And then Gretel exclaimed impulsively: "Oh, Joseph! Aren't they *wonderful*—your father and your mother?" There was a wistful tone in her voice.

Joseph rose to his feet and gazed down upon his parents proudly. "Yes," he replied in an outburst of boyish enthusiasm, "they are wonderful, Gretel! They are the most wonderful father and mother any boy ever had! And isn't my mother beautiful tonight?" he added eagerly.

"She is always beautiful. I think, Joseph, your mother is the most beautiful woman I have ever known. And right now, in that blue silk dress and looking so completely happy—oh, Joseph, she is *sweet*!"

He turned toward the charming girl in quick appreciation of her sincere, warm-hearted tribute to his so dearly beloved mother. He stood for a moment close beside her. And then slowly he bent over her as she sat gracefully poised upon the window seat, her arms extended, her hands grasping the edge of the deep-red velvet cushion, her dainty silver slippers peeping out beneath her billowy skirt. "I know someone else who is sweet!" he murmured softly.

Gretel bent her head downwards to hide her swift emotion. Her heart pounded wildly for very joy.

"Someone in a *white* dress," he continued in tender tone.

"Oh, Joseph, no—you mustn't—!" she whispered shyly.

"Someone whose eyes are just like stars tonight," he went on daringly. "Someone whose hair is like shimmering, golden moonbeams. Someone . . . oh, Gretel, you are lovely, *lovely*!"

Joyfully she lifted her glowing face toward his. Their gaze met in fascinated wonder. Instantaneously each read the marvel in the other's eyes.

Joseph sat down beside her and very gently took her hand. "I love you, Gretel," he said simply. "Do you love me, dear?"

"Yes," she answered softly. "I have always loved you, Joseph. Ever since I can remember."

He placed his arm around her tenderly. "Do you believe, dear, that you and I could be like them? That we could get married and be as happy as they have been? As *your* father and mother have been? Could we, dearest Gretel?"

"Oh, but Joseph! We shouldn't talk about that yet—about getting *married*! We are much too young, both of us."

"We are too young yet to be married, Gretel, but we are not too young to love each other, dearest. And so we are not too young to make plans for our marriage when the happy time does come."

She smiled up into his imploring eyes—a smile of glad content. "Well, since you put it that way, Joseph, yes, dear, I *promise*. Someday I will marry you. Because I know—*I love you!*"

Gently he drew her within his arms. "My darling! And I love you! We love each other, Gretel. Ours is the most wonderful love in all the world. Nothing in all the universe can ever break it. God has given us to each other forever." Gravely and tenderly he kissed her. Their eternal troth was sealed.

Within twenty-four hours the young Hebrew intern and the Aryan student-nurse were both made painfully aware of the difficulties that lay ahead. Scarcely had Gretel swung into her usual routine when there was a sudden disturbance in the yard where she was working. A number of her little patients began to cry. One child screamed out in terror. Looking up quickly from the crib where she was taking a baby's temperature, Gretel perceived the cause of the alarm.

A procession of Nazi soldiers, two abreast, was turning into the ward from the corridor. There were about twenty of them, with an SS Elite Guard officer at the head of the procession. He was strikingly handsome, but his face was hard, his eyes cold and cruel. In precise military stride and with an air of arrogant superiority, the Aryans marched down the length of the ward, wheeled sharply right-about-face, and marched back again to the doorway, swung through it, and proceede down the corridor.

There was not a word spoken, not an instant's pause in their tour of the ward, but they left behind them an atmosphere of extreme disquietude. Their visit very evidently had been one of routine inspection and of silent declaration of authority and might. Their eyes, Gretel noted carefully—especially the eyes of the commanding officer—had appraisingly taken in every detail of the ward: its equipment, and particularly, its patients and its nurses.

Chapter 9

Sinister Situation

The Nazis came again the following week. There was a different group of soldiers but the same number—twenty. And the same officer was commanding them. And with the same air of contemptuous disdain.

This time Dr. Rothschild himself was present. Not only was he present—and compelled, therefore, to witness the indignity—but to his now highly supersensitized consciousness regarding everything Aryan, the unannounced and altogether unwelcome invasion of his cherished hospital was a torturing experience.

For this time the Nazis came most inopportunely. They paraded arrogantly right into the very operating theatre itself just at the exact moment when Dr. Rothschild was beginning to perform a critical appendectomy. Around and around the operating table they marched, two by two, describing three complete circles. And again, upon this occasion, as before, their procession was in total silence and without an instant's pause—but with the same display of insolent overbearing and of absolutely proprietorship. As silently as they entered the room, just as silently did they depart—leaving the brilliant surgeon so shaken that he dared not proceed with the operation. Feigning illness, he handed it over to a colleague and left the theatre.

Alone in his private office after the Nazis' departure from the building, Dr. Rothschild sat limply down before his desk and held his throbbing head between his hands. He experienced a sense of sickening helplessness. He tried to think the whole thing through clearly—to evaluate the entire crisis. But his brain was in a vortex. No longer was his sickness feigned;

he really felt desperately ill. He was powerless to get himself under control.

But this would never do! None of his hospital staff must ever see him, Benjamin Rothschild—their *chief*—in such a state as this! He must send for his son. He would steady him.

When, in response to the summons, Joseph entered the office a moment later, he read instantly in his father's face something that he had never seen there before in all his life: fear. Agonizing, paralyzing *terror*.

"Father!" he cried out in alarm.

"Joseph, my son! Whatever does this *mean*? Whatever are these infamous Nazis doing? What mischief are they perpetrating? Are they going to keep on invading our hospital as they are invading our home? What evil do they purpose against us? Wherever will it end?" Dr. Rothschild paced the floor frantically.

Tenderly Joseph placed his arm around his father's shoulders and tried to calm him—although he himself was tremulous with dread. "Dearest Father, do not take it to heart. It will all work out in time."

During further visits of the Nazis, Dr. Rothschild kept a strong calm of spirit. Nor was his calmness feigned; it was real and it was fixed. For although he recognized fully the danger that now assuredly was threatening his hospital, his home, his own loved ones, and his entire Hebrew race, his faith had triumphed. Consciously he was more than conqueror in very strength—*strengthened with all might, according to his glorious power, even unto all patience and longsuffering with joyfulness.*

As the pattern of the Nazis varied, so also did their personnel. Seldom did the same soldiers appear. The officers, as well, were frequently changed. However, the commander was invariably the identical SS Elite Guard officer who had headed the procession the first time the Nazis invaded the hospital. He was the selfsame haughty, handsome, silent Aryan with the iron-featured face and the cold, cruel eyes. The identical man who had stared at Gretel so rudely on his first visit. On subsequent visits the rude staring continued, becoming each time more and more brazen. And, finally, one day he broke his arrogant silence and spoke to her.

This day he had come alone—with the purpose, apparently, of making detailed inspection of the hospital equipment. For he carried a notebook in which he jotted down frequent observations. As he came into the ward where Gretel, at the time, was ministering to a tiny patient, this child, like several others previously, screamed out in terror at the sight of him. Bent over the crib, Gretel tried to soothe the little fellow. The SS *kommandant* strode up and stood in front of them both, scowling darkly.

"Why do you let him yell like that? Make him stop it!" he demanded sharply. "I detest howling children."

"He has been very ill," Gretel replied. "And you have frightened him!" she added indignantly. Her tone was one of definite reproof. The Nazi gasped in amazement. This was altogether new in his experience as a top-ranking military Aryan—being rebuked. And by a young woman, at that! He scowled yet more fiercely. But then he looked squarely into Gretel's face, and suddenly his own relaxed. A quizzical smile curled the corners of his lips. She had spirit, all right! And, ye gods, but she was beautiful! Who was she, anyway? He must find out. He took a step nearer to her. He bent over her, ever so slightly. He smiled ingratiatingly.

"Oh, I beg your pardon, Fräulein Nurse! I'm sorry, really. Sorry that I made the youngster cry. There, there, baby, don't be frightened anymore. I won't hurt you. Come, come! You mustn't cry any longer. If you cry like that, you will never grow up to be a fine Nazi soldier." He patted the baby's head—whereupon the little fellow screamed yet more lustily. Again the SS officer scowled fiercely. He looked at the tiny face intently. And then in a sudden rage he wheeled upon Gretel.

"Is this child a Jew?" The question was almost a hiss.

Gretel tried to evade it. Her heart pounded with sudden fear. But the Nazi repeated his demand, his face blacker than a thundercloud. "Answer me at once! Is *this child a JEW!*"

Reply was inevitable. Gretel made it—slowly, reluctantly. "Yes sir. He is."

The SS Elite Guard officer exploded in most violent wrath. "Do you mean to tell me that this hospital is admitting *Jewish* children?"

Gretel's reaction to his rage and to his insulting question was equally wrathful. Swiftly an utter loathing for the man swept over her.

"Certainly this hospital is admitting Jewish children," she retorted hotly, "as well as any others who need our help. This house of healing has been established 'for the alleviation of suffering of *all* children within the Fatherland, regardless of race, creed, or circumstance.'" Unconsciously Gretel quoted the words upon Sharon Rothschild's memorial tablet.

"But never *Jewish* children!" the Nazi persisted. "That is infamous! Who is accountable for such a ruling?" he demanded furiously. "Well, never mind. You need not undertake the responsibility of informing me. We shall investigate this entire matter for ourselves. We shall track down this outrage to its foundation source! And believe me, we shall remedy it swiftly. I shall be seeing you again—soon!" Angrily he turned upon his heel and passed rapidly out of the ward, leaving Gretel's emotions shaken to their very depths.

He did see her again soon. To Gretel's consternation the SS Elite Guard officer came back the very next afternoon. She was working so diligently among her little patients in the same ward as on the day before, when in he strode in his magnificent military uniform. Again he was alone. Ostensibly his visit had as its objective a further detailed inspection of the hospital equipment for, as on the previous afternoon, he peered into drawers and cupboards and made careful memoranda in the notebook he was carrying. But it was not long before he contrived to find himself again at Gretel's side as she was bending over a little crib, gently caring for its tiny occupant.

He stood a full minute in silence, narrowly watching her every movement. The quizzical smile played about his lips. He swayed toward her ever so slightly, an eager, evil glint within his eyes.

Gretel froze with horror. A swift sense of fear benumbed her as, at last, he spoke.

"Ah, good afternoon, *mein liebe Fräulein*! I see you still are busy with your little charges. Do you enjoy your work?"

"Very much, thank you." Gretel forced the answer coldly without a glance in his direction.

"You are not working too hard, I hope?" He asked the question in a purring tone.

"Not at all." Gretel's reply was altogether ice.

The purring became mellifluous. "You must not get too tired, Nurse—? Ah, I believe I do not know your name! It is...?"

Gretel remained mute as mingled fear and anger stormed within her heart.

The Nazi's reaction to her silence was electrifying. Instantaneously his dulcet mood stiffened into military severity. He straightened up rigidly. His face grew cold and hard, his voice authoritative and austere. He whipped out his fountain pen and notebook and began to make an entry.

"Your name!" he ordered sternly.

Gretel tried feebly to parry the demand. "What is that to you? What right have you to ask my name?"

"I have every right! I am here in this hospital as the personal representative of our great Fuehrer, Adolf Hitler. Upon his authority and in his name, I must require that you give me yours." He poised his pen above his notebook awaiting her reply.

With a sickening sense of utter helplessness Gretel gave it. "Very well, then. My name is von Ludwig—Margarete von Ludwig."

"Von Ludwig!" the henchman of Adolf Hitler repeated in astonishment—in gloating satisfaction. And then again Gretel witnessed what she was destined to witness many, many times more—another of the swift, electrifying, chameleon veerings of the Nazi's mood. Instantly the military harshness vanished. Again he was the soft-spoken, unctuous courtier.

"Ah, the honorable Fräulein Margarete von Ludwig! At last I have the proud privilege of making your acquaintance. I have heard of you frequently—through your distinguished brothers, Herr Bernhardt and Herr Bruno von Ludwig. I am happy to number them as under-officers within my SS Elite Guard regiment. Most admirable Nazis, both of them. I congratulate you indeed upon your relationship to them as their sister.

"You are also related, then, of course," the inquisitor continued, "to Pastor Martin Luther von Ludwig." His tone of cold contempt expressed unmistakably his unspoken verdict: *That is truly a pity.*

"Yes, I have the honor to be Pastor von Ludwig's daughter," Gretel replied proudly.

"Ah, of course! Of course! Yes, certainly! Well, Nurse von Ludwig, your esteemed father has made himself quite prominent of late by reason of certain of his sermons. But naturally, as a loyal Aryan, you yourself must realize that they border rather dangerously upon the subversive. That is to say, they are not what you would call entirely 100 percent in harmony with our National Socialist ideology or with our glorious Fuehrer.

"But never mind!" he added quickly as he noted Gretel's mounting anger—"I would not take it too closely to heart if I were you. Your father's recalcitrant position is quite understandable. He, of course, is getting old. He adheres to a passing generation with its outmoded theological concepts. It will not be easy, at his age, to indoctrinate him with our progressive Nazi principles. But your enlightened brothers will do their best with him, I have no doubt. At any rate, even if they cannot convert him, they will be able, I very earnestly trust, to restrain him from making further foolish utterances both from his pulpit and through the press. Not only are they foolish but they are perilous, as well—perilous to himself and to his church if he persists in them."

Suddenly he stopped speaking and squinted at Gretel. "Are you ill?" he asked. "I thought you were going to faint. Really, my dear Nurse von Ludwig, you must have more consideration for yourself. Or you will be ill indeed. What time do you get off duty?"

Gretel struggled in fierce inward conflict. Should she reply to the Nazi's insolent interrogation or should she not? She hated to speak one further word to him, so intense was her loathing. But instinctively she was aware of the imperative need of extreme caution. Power was altogether on his side. He was the authorized agent of Adolf Hitler.

Sternly he repeated his question: *"What time do you get off duty?"*

She steeled herself to answer him: "Seven o'clock."

Once again the chameleon change of attitude, of voice.

Again his tone became suddenly very gentle, very ingratiating. "Ah! Seven o'clock! Very, very good! It is six thirty now. Only half an hour more, little nurse, and then you can rest. You need it very greatly. And you deserve it richly. You have worked so hard today. You must have complete relaxation." His voice became cajoling, tender. "How about a little party for two? Just you and I alone together—say at the Kurfürstenbrücke Inn. Let's make it a dinner of roast duck—with plenty of good German beer. How about it, *mein lieb Fräulein* Margarete?"

Gretel flung caution and discretion to the winds. Her wrath blazed forth in fury. Her words fell from her tight, parched lips like whipcords.

"How dare you, sir! You are insulting! No, I thank you! I never drink beer, and I never go out with men I do not know!"

Still another swift kaleidoscopic change of mood. The Nazi laughed uproariously—a hard, cynical laugh that was a curious mixture of high amusement, scorn, and injured pride.

"Aha! A little Puritan, is it? Never drinks beer and never goes out with bold, bad men she does not know! Most estimable! Well, never mind, little nurse, we soon can remedy the situation. Perhaps your excellent brothers will do me the honor of presenting me to their very proper, very charming sister and vouching for my virtuous character. Then—if still you prefer not to go out with me in public—you may perhaps be compassionate enough to invite me to your home. How about an evening of music, possibly? Your brothers have been telling me about your gorgeous voice. I am longing to hear it. I sing a bit myself. We could have some divine duets.

"And then afterwards—I hope you would not mind, there in the sacred privacy of your own secluded, sanctimonious dwelling—just a few innocent glasses of champagne, if you prefer that to our fine old German beer. Unless, of course"—his voice became a sneer—"your dear Herr Papa might perhaps object. In that case we could take you to our SS Elite Guard Officers' nightclub—your two brothers and myself. Your exemplary brothers—Herr Bernhardt and Herr Bruno—would provide sufficient and sufficiently correct chaperonage for their very meticulous, very puritanical, very delightful little sister. And so, dear Fräulein Nurse, just think it over and let me know when I come back again. For, of course, I will be coming back. *To see you.* Definitely. And very, very soon. And *often.* Good-bye for now—my sweet little Nurse Margarete von Ludwig. Auf Wiedersehen! *HEIL* HITLER!"

Chapter 10

Secret Shelter

It was a Saturday evening in Berlin some four weeks later. Dr. Rothschild was in his basement recreation room together with his spiritual counselor and closest friend, Pastor von Ludwig. The two gentlemen, seated in comfortable armchairs before the fire, were deeply absorbed in mutually sympathetic discussion of their several grave anxieties.

"It is so good of you to come to me tonight, Martin," Dr. Rothschild exclaimed in warmest gratitude. "And on a Saturday night, particularly, when you need all the rest that you can get in preparation for the morrow. I feel guilty in sending for you."

"Not at all, not at all! You promised you would send for me at any hour day or night that I could be of help to you. I do want to give you all the strength and consolation possible. Your burdens, Benjamin—as a Jew in Germany at this terrible hour—are so completely overwhelming."

"Thank you, dear friend, with all my heart. You can never know how much it means to me to have your counsel and your comfort. And I confess I do feel overwhelmed tonight. All the waves and billows have gone over me. Oh, Martin, Martin!" he groaned. "The whole Jewish situation is becoming absolutely desperate! Whatever can we do?" Dr. Rothschild buried his face in his hands and wept.

The minister of Christ was instantly compassionate. Placing his arm around the shoulder of the man so keenly suffering beside him, he held him with quiet firmness. "I know, dearest Benjamin," he said gently in soothing tone, "I know your sorrows. I long so tenderly to stand with you through them all. So won't you unburden your heart to me fully? Tell me what it is that is especially grieving you tonight. Is it dear Rose's illness?"

At the mention of the name of his beloved wife, the distinguished Hebrew wept afresh.

"Ah, my Rose! My Rose!" he cried aloud. "My precious little Röslein! For her my anguish is inexpressible. Martin! My wife is dying! Before my very eyes! Dying of a broken heart!"

"Oh no! Not that, dear Benjamin; surely not *that*!"

"I gravely fear so. There is complete nervous breakdown."

"But what are the indications?"

"Chiefly her persistent insomnia. She is sleeping naturally just now, thank God—but this is the first time without sedatives for over a month. Still more serious . . ."

"Yes?" The pastor's voice held deepest concern, with which there was mingled a wealth of sympathy and tenderness.

"More alarming to me that even her sleeplessness is her terrible depression. It has her in stranglehold. And that is so completely unlike Rose. You know how extremely sunny-hearted and vivacious she is ordinarily."

"Ah, yes indeed! Never in all my life have I met anyone who possessed such an exuberance of spirit as dear Rose. But you say that now—?" The compassionate eyes of the faithful friend and minister expressed the sorrow he could not put into words.

Dr. Rothschild moaned. "It is all gone, Martin," he said hopelessly, "completely gone—all her wonderful overbubbling joy. Rarely ever now does she even smile. And quite frequently I find her crying—crying like a heartbroken child. She is so weary—*weary*."

"Physical weariness, Benjamin?"

"Worse than that. Heart weariness. Weariness of life. There is, of course, weariness of body also. Often, complete exhaustion. For you know, Martin, that out of all our former staff of servants, only two remain—Fritz, and one of the upstairs maids, a Jewess. The others, Aryans, have all gone—forced out by the Nazis."

"But the Jewish friends that you are sheltering, do they not help her?"

"They want to, certainly. They would do anything in the world to show their love and gratitude for Rose. But through the day, when the Nazi spies are bursting in so constantly without any warning, they dare not leave their hiding places in the garret. Fritz even has to smuggle their food up to them."

"What a blessing that you still have Fritz!"

"It is a blessing indeed. Fritz is our joy. His faithfulness has been the one ray of light amid our domestic darkness. He is so very sympathetic, especially toward Rose and toward our poor Jewish refugees. He is so wholeheartedly helpful to us all. But we dare not think how soon it may be before he, too, will be compelled to leave us like all the rest."

"It is amazing to me that Fritz has stayed so long."

"It *is* amazing. But I believe I have explained to you the apparent reason. Fritz is beyond military age; thus he was not conscripted into the army as were all our other Aryan men servants."

"But still that does not explain why he has been allowed to remain in a Jewish home."

"No—except that he stands high in favor with the Nazi officials. That is very evident. The men who patrol our house are extremely friendly toward him, and we know they give him many privileges. Obviously, this is one of them—that he might stay on with us as, repeatedly, he has expressed his desire to do so."

"Well, I shall pray earnestly that he may be permitted to remain with you as long as you need him."

"Thank you, Martin. God grant it indeed. For I do not know how in the world we could ever get along without him. That is one of Rose's most acute distresses—the fear of losing Fritz."

"Quite understandably so. May God provide speedy deliverance from this and all other anxieties dear Rose is suffering. I am sure, Benjamin, that He will hear our prayers for your lovely little wife. It cannot be His will that she should break. He will hold her fast. He will hold all of you and all of your Hebrew people—His own beloved Israel—in the hollow of His hand until this present terrible calamity of Nazi anti-Semitism is completely overthrown."

The mutually strengthening and consoling conversation between the two kindred spirits went on in closest intimacy. "Martin," Dr. Rothschild continued, "in this desperate conflict between Church and State, my concern for you yourself is very great. Do you not realize, my dear friend, that you personally are in a position of extreme peril?"

The gentle minister of Christ made answer very quietly, very gravely: "Of course I realize it, Benjamin."

"Then why are you so outspoken? Why, dear Martin, are you not more cautious in your utterances? You well know the steadily increasing Nazi persecution of the evangelicals of Germany. And you are emerging, more and more conspicuously, as the foremost leader of the opposition movement. You must surely be aware of the fact that your sermons are attracting widespread attention. You of course know that the press is full of them, especially in adverse editorial review. And the press, remember—since all Jewish journalists throughout Germany have been expelled from it—is now completely Aryan-controlled. And I have observed myself that each week your pulpit discourses are becoming more and more daring—more and more critical of the Nazi government. I fear they are bordering perilously near to seditious outcry. You are openly urging defiance of the *State*! Oh, my beloved friend, do you not understand the danger?"

"Benjamin, when did I ever allow consideration for my personal safety to stand in the path of duty? And I regard it as my clear, God-given duty to warn my flock—to warn all Germany—of the present fearful peril to our Christian faith, which the National Socialist Government is undertaking, with most deadly purpose, to destroy completely. No, dear friend, I appreciate deeply and thank you with all my heart for your loving concern for my own protection, but I can never compromise in my position."

"Assuredly not! And I would be the last person in the world to suggest your compromising. All I am pleading, Martin, is that you be more prudent—more temperate in your discourse. You can be absolutely true to your convictions, true to our evangelical Christian doctrine, true to our God—without dangerously stirring up a hornets' nest; without suicidally antagonizing 'the powers that be.' So will you not try, my dear pastor, to preach and write—well, more judiciously, perhaps; more *guardedly*?

"Should any sudden emergency arise, involving immediate need of asylum, I want you, dearest Martin, to come right here at any hour, day or night. This whole house—should shelter be required—is at your disposal, and at your daughter's also. It might well be God's place of refuge for you, for no Nazi would be likely to search for an Aryan Christian minister within a Jewish home. And I gravely fear, my friend, you may have necessity to make use of it before very long."

"Sooner, perhaps, than either of us thinks! Thank you, Benjamin, with all my heart. I appreciate your gracious provision for my safety, inexpressibly. For I, too, of course, fully realize my danger. I frankly admit that in my pulpit I have taken a stand diametrically antagonistic to the National Socialist Government. And we all know exactly what that means. But as I said to you before, so say I now again—and always: *God helping me, I can do none other.*

"It is altogether probable, as you agree, that there will indeed be urgent need of sanctuary before long. I shall hold my ground until the last moment possible. But should I be forced out of my pulpit, out of the Confessional Church—even out of my home, it well may be—I shall remember with most fervent gratitude your loving invitation and, if it is by any means within my power to evade arrest, I shall flee at once to this sacred refuge."

"Thank you, Martin. This gratifies me deeply. I now feel much less anxiety concerning you. I am immeasurably relieved. And be assured, my friend, whatever crisis may arise, I shall regard it as my highest honor to afford you shelter. Should your presence within my house become suspected, and still greater security become thereby more urgently required, I truly believe I could provide for you a secret hiding place—one well nigh impregnable: a 'place prepared' for just such an emergency as yours would be."

"And where might that be found? You have me curious, Benjamin. Just what do you mean by a 'place prepared'?"

"I mean exactly that. It is a place of safety I have prepared for Jewish refugees from Nazi outrage."

"*Benjamin!* But where? And when? And how?"

"I have just completed it, Martin. It is a secret project I have been working on intensively for the past three weeks. With the exception of the people who were helping me, I have not spoken of it before to anyone—not even yourself—because I wanted first to satisfy myself that it is feasible. Now I am assured that it is entirely feasible, and I am ready to put it into operation immediately. What is more, I feel the time has come when it must be put into operation as speedily as possible. The need is not only urgent; it is desperate. You have heard, have you not, of the new Jewish Eviction Law?"

"Yes, slightly. But just what is it? I am not quite clear."

"It is the latest of those hellish Nürnberg decrees. This one is the most venomous of them all. It was proclaimed three weeks ago and becomes effective next Monday morning. By its terms all Aryan landlords are required, within thirty days, to evict all Jewish tenants—on only twelve hours' notice and without refund of rent or any other compensation whatsoever."

"How preposterous! How absolutely ruthless! This will cause untold confusion, immeasurable suffering."

"Exactly. Jews who do not own their own homes will be turned out upon the streets, completely roofless, completely helpless. Of course the purpose of this newest Nürnberg Law—and its inevitable end—is very evident: Jewish segregation within the Ghetto. There is the greatest consternation throughout the entire community of our poorer Jews, non-property holders. Already a number of our Jewish friends have come to us in deep distress, imploring our aid. They all appealed to me so piteously for counsel and for help."

"And of course with your great heart, dear Benjamin, you promised both."

"How could I, Martin? All that I can possibly do to relieve the distress of my people, even to the very limit of my resources, would be but a drop in the bucket of the tremendous need there soon will be."

Pastor von Ludwig shook his head sadly. "I fear that is only too true."

"But at least," Dr. Rothschild's face and tone brightened perceptively, "I rejoice that I shall be able to help a few, anyway, of the most urgent cases among Jews who will have to go into hiding."

The ministerial guest looked alarmed. "Into *hiding*?" he repeated incredulously.

"Yes, exactly that—for fear of arrest and the concentration

camp. Already Hitler has apprehended a considerable number of our leading Jews. I shall be happy in providing asylum for a small group, at least, of possible victims of the Nazi fury—for how long or for how short a time, God alone knows. As I believe you are aware, thus far we have sheltered just a few Jewish families in our home—five altogether. But now, with my project completed, we can accommodate a few more. Would you care to see it, Martin—our secret shelter?"

"Intensely so!"

"Remember, it is *your* shelter also—yours preeminently, indeed—the very first moment that you may need it."

"Again, my most profound gratitude, dear Benjamin."

"Come this way; here it is . . . But wait! Before I show it to you, I must first explain how it came into being. I want you fully to understand the whole situation—my motive in providing it, the way in which it was achieved, its proposed mode of operation and its intended purpose in general."

"I am eager indeed to know all about it!"

"Well then, you may remember my once showing you—some years ago—a little green cottage in the midst of our grove of spruce trees, on the northwest corner of our estate, about three hundred yards behind the house. We had built this cottage, you may remember, as a playhouse for our little daughter, Sharon. It was connected with the house by means of an underground tunnel. We had this passageway constructed underground, rather than above ground, in order not to have to sacrifice our rose garden.

"After Sharon's death her mother could not bear to see the little playhouse, or even the tunnel, ever again. And so I had the tunnel sealed at both ends; and the playhouse, with all of its tender memories, was boarded up at every door and window. And then I had more trees and shrubs—a dense thicket of them—planted around the cottage, thus screening it completely from view from the house, as well as from the roadway. By this time its very existence is probably forgotten by the public. Rose has never been near it since our darling's death. I myself had seen it only very seldom—until just a few months ago.

"But then it was that I began to frequent it—with the definite purpose of making very careful study. For Hitler's atrocities against our Jewish people were then becoming more and more appalling. Their danger was growing daily more and more acute. A strong desire to shield them from his fury took possession of me. And out of this desire there gradually formulated a possible plan for rescuing a few of the more despairing Jews, at least. The more I studied the whole situation, the more firmly it gripped my mind, the more keenly it clarified in my imagination. Jews fleeing from danger—an unknown, deserted cottage deeply hidden from sight and ken of man—an unsuspected underground tunnel—this large house with spacious secret areas for hiding Jewish refugees: Do you begin to see the connection?"

"Benjamin! I understand!" Pastor von Ludwig's tone was tense with amazement, with suppressed excitement, with profoundest admiration for his Hebrew friend—but then with sudden very dreadful fear.

"But my dear man," he pleaded, in deep solemnity, "are you *sure* about it all? Your project is superb. It is absolutely wonderful. It reveals so perfectly your great compassionate heart, your clear comprehension, your fearless courage, your intrepid daring: the whole plan is magnificent. But have you thought it through to its conclusion? Have you considered carefully all that is involved? The enormous undertaking? The grave responsibility? The fearful risk? Have you weighed the terrible consequences of possible discovery by the Nazis? Benjamin, my dearest friend! I ask you: Have you counted well the cost?"

"Martin, you yourself declared but a moment ago: 'Love counts not the cost.' And I love my Jewish brethren. If it is within my power, in any way whatsoever, to succor them in this darkest hour of their most dire extremity, God helping me, I wish to do so. As long as I possess this beautiful home and other God-given wealth that still remains to me; and as long as I can retain strength of body and mind and spirit: I do want to place them and myself all at God's disposal for aid and comfort and protection to my fellow Hebrews. Will you pray for me, dear Martin, that I may be unflinching in the fulfillment of this purpose which I am confident has been God-inspired? Oh! Will you not *stand* with me, that I may be kept true to Him and faithful to my Jewish people?"

Hot tears rushed to the eyes of the tender undershepherd

as he gripped the hand of his Hebrew brother in the Lord. "God bless you, Benjamin!" he said chokingly. "God bless you exceedingly for your wonderful unselfish love. Your devotion to your Hebrew kinsmen is completely Christlike. But oh, may he hold you and all of them in perfect safeguard! I do indeed pledge you my unfailing prayer and my fullest possible cooperation. God helping me, I *shall* stand with you unswervingly—and with all the Jews of Germany—until this present hideous calamity is overpast; until that monster of iniquity, Adolf Hitler, is completely overthrown and the sun of prosperity and peace shines once again upon our beloved Fatherland."

"Thank you, Martin! You give me new courage to go forward stedfastly. You always make me strong. I can never express how great a debt of gratitude and love I owe you."

There were some moments of profound silence between the two close friends—the one, Aryan; the other, Hebrew—a silence eloquent with deep emotion and with perfect mutual accord of spirit. At length, Dr. Rothschild spoke again:

"And now, if you will, come over here. I want to show you the shelter." He took Pastor von Ludwig's arm and quietly led him to the opposite side of the large recreation room. And then suddenly he turned a floodlight upon the rich walnut wainscoting. "Tell me, Martin"—his voice held a note of anxiety as he asked the question—"can you see anything unusual or at all conspicuous about this paneling?"

"Why, no—except that it is conspicuously handsome. Just what do you mean?"

"Look at *this* panel very closely. Now—watch!"

Dr. Rothschild pressed his fingers gently against what was, evidently, a concealed secret spring. Instantly the panel—about six feet in height and half as wide—began to slide slowly sideways. As Pastor von Ludwig gazed in astonishment, the floodlight poured into a tunnel, about three hundred yards in length, extending in a straight line to a flight of stairs at the extreme end.

"This is our underground passage," the Hebrew host said quietly. "Another secret panel door, similar to this one, at the top of those stairs, leads into what once was our little daughter's playhouse, as I was telling you. From this time forward, until all the Nazi terror is past, I pray it may be a house of hope for the few Jewish refugees fortunate enough to reach it. Another secret door, at the opposite side of the cottage, gives entrance to it from outdoors."

"Benjamin! This is amazing!" Pastor von Ludwig could scarcely speak, so profound was his emotion.

"But wait!" Dr. Rothschild admonished. "There is something more I have to show you."

He closed the panel door upon the tunnel very cautiously, switched off the floodlight, then silently led his guest to an identical secret door directly across the room.

"Watch *this* panel, Martin!" he commanded. His voice was almost a whisper. His hands trembled visibly as again he pressed a secret spring.

Tense with excitement, Pastor von Ludwig peered through the slowly widening aperture. As his host switched on a wide circle of electric lights, he gazed in speechless wonder upon the strange sight suddenly revealed to his astounded eyes.

A very extensive low-ceilinged inner room was subdivided into curtained cubicles—in four rows, with ten to a row. Each cubicle was comfortably furnished with an attractive-looking cot-bed, all freshly made up and ready for occupancy, a small table and chair, and a rack for clothing. Each of these little private compartments bespoke complete and careful preparation and a warm-hearted, sympathetic, loving welcome for whatever Jewish victim of Nazi fiendishness might have the wonderful opportunity of finding this blessed haven of safety.

"This," Dr. Rothschild said simply, "is our shelter. It was, formerly, our storage cellar. Now it is dedicated as a little sanctuary for our beloved Jewish refugees—for a few of them, at least. And for *you*, Martin—never forget that!—if ever you should have need of it. The password is 'Shalom.'"

"Thank you, again, dear Benjamin, with all my heart!"

"In this unit"—the Hebrew host continued, in explanation of his benevolent provision—"we have these forty cubicles and eight baths for our Jewish men. Opposite to it, on the east side of the recreation room, is a similar unit for the women and children. But theirs is somewhat larger than this one. It will accommodate sixty. The two units together, therefore, can take care of one hundred refugees. Only a drop in the bucket, as I said before, in comparison with the appalling total number there soon will be. But still it is a joy to believe that I shall be able to succor even so few of my beloved kinsmen.

"This recreation room"—still Dr. Rothschild continued his explanation of the shelter—"will provide the refectory. There is ample space for sufficient folding tables and chairs. They are there, as you can see, together with the table equipment, all stacked up beneath the stairs. Everything is in perfect readiness for action as soon as our guests arrive."

In silent and awed amazement the compassionate minister of Christ stood rooted in the doorway, still gazing with moist eyes upon this astonishing "project" of his greathearted Hebrew friend. But at last he found his voice.

"*Benjamin!* This is overwhelming! A miracle of mercy! And absolutely perfect to the last detail. But I am completely mystified! How ever in all the world did you achieve such a tremendous undertaking? And *when*?"

"Fritz and the two boys and I—together with some hired artisans—have all been working on it assiduously during the past three weeks, at such times as we could spare from regular duties and from sleep. Soon after the Nazi atrocities began, Fritz had blacked out all the windows and made all the secret panel doors for our own security—the two in this room, two in the cottage, and one at the top of these stairs, leading into the library . . ."

A swift shadow passed over Pastor von Ludwig's gentle face. "Benjamin," he queried thoughtfully, "is Fritz, do you believe, completely loyal?"

"Fritz? Loyal? Oh, absolutely so! Beyond the faintest possibility of doubt! Whatever, Martin, could even have suggested such a question?" Dr. Rothschild looked at his friend in blank astonishment.

The pastor returned his gaze unflinchingly. "Yes," he replied slowly—sadly: "I agree with you perfectly that Fritz is very fine. But, of course, we must remember, Benjamin—Fritz is an *Aryan*."

"An Aryan, yes. Assuredly. But never a *Nazi*! Fritz is an earnest Christian. Moreover, he sincerely loves the Jews. His sympathies are altogether on our side. He has proven that repeatedly. And, of course, Martin, you know his devotion to our family. For nearly twenty years! Time and again he has had opportunities in the business world where he could have commanded a salary much higher than we have ever paid him. But he would never leave us. He has been almost a son beloved. Why, there are confidences we have given Fritz that we could not share even with our own two boys. So never doubt his loyalty, my dear Martin. It is absolutely unimpeachable. Completely golden.

"But now, my good friend, I must allow you to go home. I have kept you far too late already. You must have sleep. You may have, perhaps, a hard day ahead of you tomorrow. You are not afraid to drive to Charlottenburg alone?"

"No, not at all! I never have the slightest fear at any hour, day or night. I am so conscious always of God's protecting nearness."

"Then may the shadow of the Almighty cover you most tenderly tonight, my dearest Martin—for I feel your danger is acute. But remember! If any crisis suddenly develops, you are to flee to this shelter immediately. Promise me that you surely will."

"If it is at all possible. Yes, I promise you—with deepest thankfulness."

"That comforts me. Pray God all may be well with you!"

Chapter 11

Dire Tidings

On that same Saturday evening—but in an entirely different section of Berlin, and in an entirely different environment from that of the palatial Rothschild mansion—another and an altogether different meeting was taking place.

During that same Saturday evening, in downtown Berlin, in the *Militärischenhalle* on *Königstrasse*, a lively program was in progress. A crowd of Nazi youths—a hundred of them, perhaps—were storming in through the opened street-door and up the broad stairway. Entering a large recreation hall at the top, they seated themselves uproariously in groups of six, at small tables placed around the walls, and ordered their steins of beer from the obsequious *kellner* attending them. Soon the place was ringing with coarse songs and ribald laughter and the noise of clinking steins. The air quickly became fetid with fumes of beer, and smoke from the many long Meerschaum pipes.

The youths, ranging in age from fourteen to twenty-one, were typically German. For the most part they were of stocky, medium build with flaxen hair and blue eyes. They wore motley attire. A few of the older ones had on gaily colored sleeveless velvet jackets, which proclaimed them as university students and members of *vereins*. Some of the others were in ordinary street suits, mostly of coarse weave with loose sack coats. The majority of them, however, wore dark belted trousers and brown, open-throated shirts. In one respect only was there complete uniformity of attire among the youths. Without exception every one of them had on his left arm a red armband bearing the symbol of Naziism—the sinister black swastika.

At a long table at the end of the room, holding themselves

arrogantly aloof from their inferiors, were eight young men in their mid-twenties, wearing smart military uniforms, with flashing sabers rattling at their sides. These were the Nazi SS Elite Guard officers.

For perhaps an hour the drinking and the noise and revelry went on. Then suddenly a shrill whistle pierced the foul air and an intense silence ensued. The officers, rising from their table, ranged themselves at even intervals across the front of the broad room and snapped swiftly to attention. And then at a peremptory command from the top-ranking officer—Herr Kommandant Konstantin von Wolfmacht—the young Nazis rose instantly to their feet and pushed the chairs under their tables. And then they marched into ordered formation at the center of the room to dismiss the group to classes arranged for special drill.

Two of the officers, however, at a signal from von Wolfmacht, remained behind. They joined him at a table after all the others had departed.

"HEIL HITLER!"

"HEIL HITLER!"

The *kommandant* greeted his fellow Nazis with a friendly handshake. "*Ach*, brothers, von Ludwig—Herr Bruno, Herr Bernhardt! *Wie geht's ihnen diesen abend?*"

"*Ganz gut, danke schön!*" The two elder sons of Pastor Martin Luther von Ludwig—both of them now full-fledged SS Elite Guard officers—made reply a bit uneasily. Was von Wolfmacht going to speak to them about their father, they wondered?

Herr Konstantin smiled at the brothers engagingly. "Could you stay on for perhaps another half hour?" he queried. "There are some rather urgent matters I must talk over with you."

The spirits as well as the countenances of Bruno and Bernhardt suddenly congealed. Then von Wolfmacht *was* going to do exactly that: speak to them about their erring father. They lowered their eyes guiltily.

"I'm afraid we realize what it is you want to talk about, sir," Bruno replied shamefacedly. "Yes, I guess we can stay a little while longer. All right with you, Bernie?"

"It suits me if it suits you." Bernhardt's gloom equaled his brother's. Both smiled sheepishly. Both were visibly embarrassed.

"Very good!" Herr Kommandan*t* von Wolfmacht beamed encouragingly. He must put the men at their ease.

"I'm awfully sorry, comrades," he began with mock compassion, "I realize exactly how you feel about all of this, and I know how hard it is for you to talk about it. But we must get together in the matter and find out how best we can handle the whole unhappy situation. For of course, boys"—von Wolfmacht's voice became stern—"you are aware of the terrible disturbance of last Sunday morning—"

"Yes, certainly," they both replied with a crestfallen air.

"—that was created in the Confessional Church," von Wolfmacht continued, disregarding the interruption, "by the man who, most unfortunately, is your own father—Pastor Martin Luther von Ludwig."

"Yes, we are aware of it," Bruno answered sadly. "We are more than sorry for it!" Bernhardt added with abject apology.

"I am sure you are," von Wolfmacht responded warmly. "And out of consideration for your embarrassment over the whole affair, I wish we might say nothing more about it. But, of course, that sort of thing simply cannot go on any longer. For weeks we have been studying the problem closely. Thus far—until last Sunday—we have said nothing, hoping against hope that your father would come to his proper senses and realize the dangerous position he was taking. But last Sunday morning's sermon was the climax of outrage and positively could not be ignored. Nor could it by any possibility be condoned. You are, of course, aware of the ugly situation it precipitated within the church—the sheer necessity of our dragging Pastor von Ludwig forcibly down from his pulpit and threatening his arrest if ever he dared to repeat the nefarious performance.

"I am terribly sorry to have to speak to you about all this. You surely understand, men, that for yourselves I have only the highest respect and regard. But as good and loyal Nazis undoubtedly you must know that your sire's diatribe on 'The Word of God and Jesus Christ' or some drivel like that—I forget the exact title he announced—such a sermon as he preached was not only recalcitrant and completely heretical to the tenets of our new National German Church, but it was politically dangerous, as well."

The sons of Pastor Martin Luther von Ludwig sat abashed and mute before the relentless tirade.

"Now, as your friend," von Wolfmacht continued condescendingly, "I simply want to give you boys kindly warning that if your reactionary parent persists in his defiant attitude, he is heading squarely into trouble. And that trouble—make no mistake about it—will engulf not only himself but his family and his entire church, as well. For under our Nazi regime, you of course understand, any and all elements subversive to the State must be dealt with drastically. Reactionaries—whether in pulpit or in pew, whether in press or in university or forum or in any place elsewhere whatsoever—will surely and swiftly be put down.

"And so—I want to talk things over with you very frankly. I want you to know that your sister *interests* me—vitally and profoundly. You, of course, understand what I mean. We Nazis do understand one another completely in these matters. So I can speak to you quite plainly.

"Your sister will make a magnificent mother of future Nazi soldiers. Therefore I have made it my firm determination that *I shall marry her myself.* And I am counting upon you two men—her brothers—to pave the way for me to do so. More concerning all this later on. But that is all for just now. Auf Wiedersehen! Remember to report for drill at seven o'clock tomorrow morning. And at ten o'clock for the Youth Parade. *Gute Nacht!* HEIL HITLER!"

On the opposite edge of the city, Pastor von Ludwig sat brooding in his study. A wave of unutterable loneliness surged suddenly over him. The presence of the Comforter was very close and very sweet; but the longing for human fellowship—for human understanding—was almost unbearable . . . Oh, for the touch of the vanished hand, the sound of the voice that was still! His own beloved Hildegarde's. If only Margarete might have been at home with him tonight! Ah, if only he could have *her* dear presence, at least, always at home! But no, he checked the longing sternly. He was selfish even to think of such a thing. Margarete's life was dedicated to her noble calling. Margarete belonged to the sick and suffering. Margarete belonged to God.

Slowly he drew himself up. And then slowly he stood upon his feet and turned toward the doorway—to seek at least a few hours' rest before he should have to arise and prepare for his morning service at eleven. But just as he was about to descend the upper staircase he heard, very faintly, the sound of footsteps on the front veranda. He paused and listened intently—then eagerly—as he heard a key turning in the lock and the opening of the house door. And then suddenly the light was flashed on in the lower hall.

Joyously he recognized the buoyant step upon the staircase. "Margarete! My darling daughter!" he cried out in delight. "Is that really you? Ah, I am overjoyed!" Gretel, all aglow with happy laughter, bounded lightly up the two flights of stairs and in an instant was clasped fondly to her father's heart.

"Oh, Father! Father darling! Oh, but it is good to see you! So good to get *home*!"

"And it is good to have you home! But my dear child, what brings you here tonight—and at this late hour?" He scanned her face anxiously.

"I just *had* to come, Father. I had such a craving for a sight of your dear face. I have not seen you in two weeks. And I do so greatly need your counsel and your prayer."

He reentered his study, deeply comforted in the unexpected presence of his beloved daughter. Again he drew her gently into his fond embrace. And then they sat down together, in precious harmony of spirit, he in his armchair and she on the little hassock where, since her babyhood, he always had delighted to have her nestle close beside him.

Anxiously he scanned her face. "You are tired, dear child. It has been a heavy day for you at the hospital?"

"Yes, rather heavier than usual today. They are putting me in the operating theatre now for six weeks of surgery. It is much more difficult than the ward duty; but once I can get myself properly adjusted to it, I know that I am going to love it—especially if I can be on hand for Dr. Rothschild's operations. I can't wait to see him perform them. They all say he is so wonderful . . . But Father darling, *you* are the one who is tired! Whatever have you been *doing*? Is there anything wrong? Come, dearest, you must tell me! Remember, I am your *nurse*!"

He hesitated. Should he tell her? Should he impose upon this precious child, already so greatly burdened, this new and steadily growing weight of sorrows Dr. Rothschild had reposed in him? But sadly he reflected: Margarete is marrying into the Rothschild family. For all the days to come their burdens must be her burdens; their sorrows, her sorrows. And their perils must be Margarete's perils also. Yes, certainly she must know what now immediately threatens. She must be warned. She must be prepared.

And so he told her. High up in his tower study, in the still solemnity of the midnight hour, he told her everything. He withheld nothing from her. Very gently, very tenderly, but with firm, unflinching courage born of a sense of stern necessity, he told her, first of all, of the imminent perils which surrounded the family of her beloved Joseph—the *Hebrew* family she was pledged one day to enter. He told her of the threat to the Rothschild's fortune. He told her of their several other multiplying griefs.

He told her, next, of the new Jewish eviction law, and of all the anguish and confusion that it would entail. And then he outlined to her the magnanimous but highly perilous plan devised by Dr. Rothschild for sheltering evicted Jewish refugees within his own palatial home—as long as that beloved home might still remain to him and to his dear ones.

Quietly Gretel listened to it all. Her grief was deep. Her grave anxiety for Joseph and his family was unmistakably apparent. But there was no outcry, no bitterness, no protest, no rebellion. She received the dire tidings with that mature fortitude which now was hers by reason of her already-long experience within the school of sorrow.

Quietly he continued to talk to her—to calm her fears, to restore her strength, to anchor her, as well as himself, within the perfect will of God.

The clock struck the hour of one—and then the hour of two; but still father and daughter held close, sweet communion, each with the other, in the deep things of the Spirit. All thought of sleep, truly all desire for it, was forgotten.

The quiet of the tower study was suddenly and rudely pierced by an ominous sound—again the sound of footsteps on the front veranda. But this time, however, these steps, unlike Gretel's gentle footfall, were rough and heavy tread.

And then again the turning of a key within the lock, the opening of the outer door, the flashing on of the lower light, and the ascent of the stairway with rapid, pounding, vindictive strides.

With swift dismay both Pastor von Ludwig and Gretel recognized the intruders upon their sacred fellowship: the two boys, Bernhardt and Bruno. They reached the top stair and burst into the tower study in an ugly mood. Before either their father or their sister could say a word, they turned wrathfully upon them.

"What! Are you still *up*? You should have been in bed hours ago!" Bernhardt addressed his father surlily. At the same moment Bruno espied and angrily confronted his sister. "*You* here? Why aren't you at the hospital where you belong?"

"I am here—*at home*—to see my father!" Gretel retorted hotly. "What are *you* doing here?"

"We are here to see him too," Bernhardt replied defiantly. And Bruno added significantly, "Yes—and it is on very urgent business."

"Well, you must keep it, then, until the morning. Father has to have his sleep."

"He can sleep all he wants to later. But he is going to talk to us *first*. No, we won't wait five minutes. We are going to talk to the old man *right now*." Dire warning was in both Bruno's and Bernhardt's tones.

Pastor von Ludwig gently but firmly intervened to avert further clash between the two brothers and their sister.

"Sit down, boys . . . Now, what is it that you have to tell me? . . . No, Margarete, my darling"—as she protested—"I am not too tired. I prefer to talk with the boys before I sleep. Now, what is it, my sons, that brings you at this hour so very urgently. Tell me at once."

"All right! We surely shall!" Bernhardt made threatening reply. "For, believe me, we *are* here urgently! We have come to warn you against attempting to preach this Sunday the sort of a sermon that you preached last Sunday morning."

"Yes," Bruno added insolently, "we are here to warn you of the consequences if you dare to try it!"

"Just what, exactly, do you mean, my sons?"

"We mean *this*." Bernhardt, as the eldest son of the godly minister of Christ, assumed the role of spokesman, of accuser of his father. "We have just come from our Nazi Youth School and from a private interview with our *kommandant*—our highest SS Elite Guard officer—Herr Konstantin von Wolfmacht. And Herr von Wolfmacht, through us, has sent to you this official message: that your disgraceful performance last Sunday morning has alerted the whole Nazi Party to the dangerous nature of your subversive sermons, and that they have got to *cease*. They are all determined that you must be silenced. Therefore, Herr *Kommandant* von Wolfmacht sends you this stern ultimatum: that if you attempt, this Sunday, any further invective against the State, you will be under immediate arrest. If you are wise, at your eleven o'clock service, you will stay out of the pulpit altogether. Promise us that you will."

"Certainly I shall promise no such thing!" the saintly father of the Nazi sons replied indignantly. "I am ordained a mouthpiece for the Lord Jesus Christ; and I shall, as always, occupy my appointed pulpit and deliver fearlessly *His* message to my people."

"All right, then. But you will promise, at least, that if you do preach, you will be guarded—that you will refrain from any pronouncement whatsoever that could possibly be interpreted as in the slightest degree subversive to our National Socialist Government or to our Fuehrer?"

"I will promise you just one thing: I promise you that I shall faithfully declare the Word of God as *He* has put it into my trust. I shall not curtail or change it by one jot or by one tittle!"

"Then be prepared for trouble! That's the last thing I have to say to *you*," Bernhardt retorted bitterly. "Remember, we have warned you: *Be prepared for trouble!*"

Bruno, with equal earnestness but with lesser degree of heat, attempted a new avenue of approach to his intractable parent.

"Will you never realize, my esteemed sire, that we are living now in an entirely new age? We have an altogether new bible:

Rosenberg's wonderful *Myth of the 20th Century*. We have new saints and apostles: our superb Nordic Supermen. We have a new *savior*: even our glorious Fuehrer Adolf Hitler. Your ministerial duty now is to teach the German people to worship *him*—to worship the Nazi State—to worship our transcendent Aryan race, of which race Hitler is our all-glorious head."

"Stop it! Stop it *instantly*! Not another word!" the horrified man of God cried out in holy anger. "Bruno von Ludwig! How *dare* you! That is absolutely blasphemous! You are exalting Adolf Hitler above our Lord Jesus Christ!"

"Well, where would *you* put him?" Bruno persisted maddeningly. "In secondary rank? Adolf Hitler must have always the *preeminence*. Once again, Dad, I plead with you: Won't you try to follow him? Won't you yield yourself to the light? Hitler is the Light of Life! I tell you, sir, with finality: all your drivel and nonsense about loving and worshipping Jesus Christ—all your ridiculous claim that *He* is the Savior of the world—is completely nauseating to me. I have a new savior: our wonderful Fuehrer—our almighty Adolf Hitler! I love and worship only *him*!"

Thus far Gretel had been a silent, horrified auditor to her brothers' outrageous tirade against her beloved father, fearing lest any intervention of her own might make it still more difficult for him. But she could bear it no longer. She turned upon both of the boys in furious rebuke.

"Bernhardt! Bruno! How dare you talk so to our father! Have you no regard for him whatever? Have you no respect? No reverence? No *love*?"

The two sons of the saintly minister of Christ laughed harshly. "Reverence . . . respect . . . *love*"—Bernhardt sneered sardonically. "My sweet sister, don't you know that all of these supposed human excellencies are quite outdated in our Nazi ideology? All of your old-fashioned virtues: love and loyalty, obedience to parents, filial piety and devotion, and all the rest of that sort of nonsense—are as alien to our Aryan way of life as is your reactionary, obsolete theology. We extol the rugged virtues: lionlike courage and daring; aggressiveness and zeal and *hate*. We abominate effeminate weakness of any sort whatever. Love is nauseating weakness; hate is manly strength, and we glory in strength."

"How dare you say such things within this house—our *father's* house! How *dare* you?"

"We dare to, all right!" Bernhardt answered with a leer. "We dare to say over and over again every word that we have said tonight. And you had better believe, my precious sister, there is a whole lot more that we shall have to say—both to you and to your fuzzy father, as well—if the two of you do not swing soon into Party line!"

"And there is something else, my charming Gretel, that we have to say to you *particularly*, right now!"—Bruno's tone was still more menacing than Bernhardt's—"We have to say just this: If you have no regard for *us*, your own brothers, perhaps you will have some consideration for *yourself*—for your own highest present interests and for your future."

"What do you mean by that?" Gretel asked coldly.

"We mean this!" Bruno answered her significantly. He paused for an instant. Then quickly he turned to his brother for advice. "Shall we tell her tonight? What do you think, Bernie?" he asked hesitatingly.

"We have to tell her soon, certainly. We are under orders from our *kommandant* to pave the way for him. So, yes, I say, we had better tell her right now—to warn her."

"To thrill her, you mean," Bruno amended.

"Well, yes," Bernhardt agreed, "both to thrill her and to warn her—in general, to bolster her morale."

"All right, then." Bruno nodded decisively. "Let's tell her all about it this very minute. *You* tell her, Bern."

"Tell me what? Thrill me and warn me and bolster my morale for what?" Gretel's tone was altogether ice.

"I have *this* to say, my dearest sister. It is something that will make your very ears tingle with pride and joy! Something wonderful beyond all believing! If only you yourself will swing into Nazi line and embrace totalitarianism as your credo—whatever your misguided parent may do or may not do—there is an amazing opportunity, a whole glorious future opening before you.

"We have been entrusted," he began impressively, "in liaison capacity, with an official message to be delivered to Gretel. The import of it is astounding to us—almost beyond our comprehension. But it is the glorious truth.

"Our SS Elite Guard *Oberoffizier,* Herr *Kommandant* Konstantin von Wolfmacht has confided in us—just this evening—that he tremendously admires Gretel, and that, after very thorough and painstaking investigation, he has arrived at the conclusion that she is the most perfect type of Aryan womanhood he has ever met. In consequence of which, *he has determined that he will marry her!"*

Gretel turned pale with fury. Her voice congealed in her throat. But she managed to choke out the anguished words: "Marry von Wolfmacht! That *monster*! Never! Never in all this world! I loathe him! From the very depths of my being I utterly *loathe* him!"

"Loathe him or adore him, what has that got to do with it?" Bernhardt now took up the cudgels. "That is another of your queer, old-fashioned concepts: that marriage must be based upon love. Love has a very minor part in a successful marriage nowadays. Wealth, rank, privilege, compatibility, companionship, mutual understanding, common aims and purposes: these, according to our Nazi ideology, are the things that really matter."

Gretel blazed her ultimatum: "Never! Never, I tell you! Never in this whole wide world!"

At the same time Pastor von Ludwig voice his outrage: "Konstantin von Wolfmacht is insulting! You may return *my* answer to his infamous effrontery! As Margarete's father, I absolutely repudiate his design of marriage with my daughter. Tell him, as from *me,* that he is utterly unworthy of her. Tell him that I hold him in supreme contempt!"

"In any case"—quickly Gretel blocked her brothers' retort to their father lest they should continue to inveigh against him—"in any case whatsoever it would be impossible for me to marry Herr von Wolfmacht or anybody else you might desire."

"Why would it be impossible?" Bruno snarled.

Throwing discretion to the winds, Gretel replied defiantly: "You know perfectly well that I am already engaged! You have known for a long time, both of you, that my heart belongs to one man alone—the only man that I shall ever marry: Joseph Rothschild!"

The reaction of her two Nazi brothers was volcanic. In vitriolic fury they lashed out at her with scorching words:

"Joseph Rothschild! That damnable Jew!" Bernhardt and Bruno both fairly choked from rage.

"You," Bernhardt hissed at her, *"you*—a von Ludwig, an *Aryan*—intend to marry a *Semite*! Are you *insane*? Have you taken leave of *all* of your senses? Have you no remaining sense of decency? Of pride? Of honor? Where is your Aryan womanhood? Are you going to degrade that completely?"

Again their father intervened.

"Bernhardt! Bruno! Stop it! Stop all of this at once! Not another word! Do you wish to kill your only sister? She cannot stand this sort of thing. I cannot stand it either. And I cannot endure to hear you speak so disparagingly against dear Joseph Rothschild. You astound me! Why, Joseph was for years your closest boyhood friend. You three lads were all inseparable. However in the world have you turned so utterly away from him?"

Bruno retorted with a sneer. "Our closest *boyhood* friend! Yes, we do admit it. He *was* our closest friend. We were inseparable. But that was years ago, before our eyes were opened to what Joseph Rothschild and all his filthy race represents. We know better now. To put it in the words of the book you champion so vigorously—we concede that it does have a few really good things in it, and this is one of them—*'when I became a man I put away childish things.'*"

In menacing, ugly tone Bernhardt gave the conclusion of the entire argument:

"Gretel von Ludwig, if you have no concern for your own honor, you have no right in the world to wreck *ours* as you are so intent upon doing. For I tell you it will be wrecked irreparably—our honor in our Aryan community and all our glowing prospects for a brilliant Nazi future—if we have to go through life suffering the ignominy of having a sister married to a Jew. So if you have any consideration whatsoever for your brothers, you will call a halt immediately to your nefarious engagement to Joseph Rothschild. And you *will* marry Konstantin von Wolfmacht!" Then they were gone.

White and shaken with anguish too awful to be borne—for his apostate elder sons—the gentle minister of Christ sank, in unutterable weariness of body, soul, and spirit, into his armchair, his beautiful silvery head bowed within his trembling hands. "Oh, my sons, my sons!" he moaned heartbrokenly. "My Nazi sons! My *Absaloms*!"

With infinite tenderness Gretel again gathered him into her strong, young arms, her own terrible grief resolutely set aside in her deep concern for his. Both were dumb in their great suffering.

There they remained for several moments—until the clock chimed four. Startled at the sound, the stricken father raised his head and resolutely pulled himself upward to his feet.

"My precious child! My own beloved Margarete!" he breathed softly as he drew her to his heart and kissed her with particular devotion. "How inexpressible is my thanksgiving to my God for you! You have been my one sweet consolation in all my sorrows. You have been my strength. Always you have been my dear delight.

"But now, my darling, we must both seek rest. Only a very brief time remains before we must face the new day—and all that it may bring. Remember, Margarete, we both shall face it bravely by God's enabling and in His all-sufficient grace and strength. You in your hospital, I in my pulpit. Go, my precious daughter, and God's peace enfold thee."

Chapter 12

Crossroads of Destiny

"Ein' Feste Burg Ist Unser Gott." High aloft from the gleaming white spire of the Charlottenburg Confessional Church, the silvery chime poured forth the grand old Luther hymn. In each slow, majestic tone there rang out the glorious conviction:

A mighty fortress is our God
A bulwark never failing;
Our Helper He amid the flood
Of mortal ills prevailing.

From every direction streams of worshippers were wending their way up the wooded hill toward the stately ancient stone edifice that crowned its summit. As the throng poured through the sacred portals on that wintry Sunday morning, in the year 1936, a sense of high excitement and tense expectancy pervaded the very atmosphere surrounding the house of God. For the memory of the previous Sunday morning, with its dramatic climax of military intervention following the pastor's daring sermon, was still vivid; and the faithful Confessional Church flock were all a-thrill with suspense as to what would be the outcome of this morning's service. But with entire quietness and reverence they took their places in the quaint U-shaped white pews throughout the sanctuary.

In the vestry to the rear of the chancel, the faithful minister of the church, Martin Luther von Ludwig, was kneeling before his desk in prayer. Up until five minutes ago he had been surrounded by the strongly supporting prayer circle of his session—the devoted men who always met with him for twenty minutes every Sunday morning in prayer preparation for his ensuing service. But, as was their invariable custom, they had all slipped out quietly in order that the pastor might have the last few moments before entering the sanctuary, alone with his God.

Never had Martin Luther von Ludwig's need of God been so consciously intense as now. From the moment of his awaking at seven thirty, after but three hours of graciously God-given sleep; all through the lengthy performance of his invariably meticulous robing for the pulpit; his unhurried private reading of the Word; and, finally, his hasty breakfast, he was in vital and vivid communion with his Lord and Master, seeking His guidance and His wisdom, His upholding and protection; resting in His comfort; drawing heavily upon His grace and strength.

And now, at last, the moment had come when he must face the foe—when he must do heavy battle for the Truth.

The organ voluntary was within but three bars of its conclusion. With conscious power in the Lord, strengthened with might by His Spirit in the inner man, Pastor von Ludwig softly turned the doorknob and stepped out into the chancel of the church, in full view of all the thousand-strong and tensely waiting congregation who stood reverently to their feet upon his entrance. As for a moment he paused, the first object upon which his eyes rested was the beautiful white dove floating down from the muraled ceiling on its golden cord—symbol of the presence of the Holy Spirit, symbol of purity and peace.

But instantly, with terrified shock—so great and so startling was the contrast—the minister of Christ became aware of the presence also, within the sacred edifice, of yet another symbol: the terrible symbol of the spirit of wickedness, the symbol of that which was altogether anti-Christ: even the emblem of Nazi totalitarian might—yeah, verily, the *swastika*.

For just as on that frightful Sunday morning, a year ago, when his pulpit had been commandeered by the National Socialist Government for the special service honoring the newly appointed Reichsbishop of the German Christian Church, even so today the sinister device was raised aloft upon a dozen banners supported by as many officers of the

Nazi SS Elite Guard. These twelve men were ranged in a semicircle before the altar, directly facing the congregation in the nave. As the pastor's quick glance swept in dismay over this desecration within the house of God, his face froze with sudden horror. For at the very center of the semicircle of swastikas, like statues of stone, were his own two sons—Bernhardt and Bruno.

Before he could recover from this most awful blow, the undershepherd of Charlottenburg noted with consternation another sinister irregularity within his Confessional Church—this an altogether unprecedented one: twelve empty pews across the front of the sanctuary, on either side of the high white pulpit, their usual occupants crowded into pews behind them. What could such a thing as this portend? He paused apprehensively.

And then, in accordance with his usual procedure, the pastor walked slowly forward to the front of the chancel. Gripping the rail with both hands, as if to steady himself before his congregation, he waited for the organist to begin playing the Doxology, with which the morning service always opened. But to his dismay and grief, the leader of the music did no such thing. Instead, he modulated swiftly from his voluntary into a blaring, high-pitched military march—on the very first note of which the large double doors of the sanctuary suddenly swung open, and there poured down the center aisle a detachment of one hundred *Schutz Staffeln*, the picked group among the regular armed Nazi soldiers comprising the core of the terror-inspiring Gestapo. All were clad in the *Schutz Staffeln* uniform: black shirt and trousers, and close-fitting black cap emblazoned with the lurid insignia of white skull and crossbones.

At their head, magnificent in full-dress military regalia, arrogantly marched their S.S. Elite Guard leader: Herr Kommandant Konstantin von Wolfmacht. Goose-stepping in precise military manner, they all turned right or left at the pulpit and filed silently into the empty pews which—upon previous order from Nazi headquarters, entirely unknown to the pastor—had been especially reserved for them by the threatened and terrified head usher.

During the long-drawn-out pompous ceremony of their

taking their seats, while the congregation also resumed their places and Pastor von Ludwig stepped to his reading desk, he had time to get the situation—and himself—under firm command. At the conclusion of the processional music he announced the opening hymn, swiftly changing the one previously selected to "Ein' Feste Burg"—the hymn always chosen for particularly important and impressive services. The congregation again rose, militantly, to their feet and began to sing it vigorously. The Nazis, however, remained stoically seated, their faces frozen to flint and ice.

Always sung with fervor, on this critical Sunday morning the stirring hymn of Martin Luther resounded through the vaulted arches with peculiarly strong challenge. The thousand voices were joined as one in impassioned declaration:

And though this world, with devils filled,
Should threaten to undo us.
We will not fear, for God hath willed
His truth to triumph through us.
The Prince of Darkness grim,
We tremble not for him;
His rage we can endure,
For lo! his doom is sure:
One little word shall fell him.

The singing of the entire hymn accomplished two definite benefits for Pastor von Ludwig. It gave him more time in which to make the necessary readjustment to the exigencies of the present disturbing occasion. But, furthermore, the ringing words of Luther's triumphant faith made his own faith yet more vigorous and daring. By God's grace and by the empowering of His Holy Spirit even through himself, Martin Luther von Ludwig—God's Truth would triumph gloriously.

"God is our refuge and strength, a very present help in trouble." Immediately following the conclusion of the hymn, the strong, vibrant voice of the intrepid minister rang through the sanctuary as he began the reading of the Scripture for the day.

With each new utterance of Holy Writ his voice became still more strong, more resounding, more and more victorious.

"Our hearts this morning," he began by way of introduction, "are united in fervent intercession to our gracious and merciful heavenly Father in behalf of our brethren in the Confessional Church—pastors and laymen alike—who, during this past week, have swollen the already vast ranks of victims of the Nazi government, arrested because of their faithful devotion to their Lord. As each name is read, let us plead with Him for His protection of these precious lives, His comfort for their broken hearts, and His speedy deliverance of each one of them from their cruel captors."

In breathless suspense the worshippers heard the names pronounced by their beloved pastor—slowly, profoundly, with undertones of anger and of deep resentment at such outrage:

"Pastor Hans Feldtmann—arrested last Monday morning. Now in the Dachau Concentration Camp.

"Pastor Heinrich Schmidt—arrested last Tuesday evening. Now in the concentration camp at Buchenwald.

"Herr *Doktor* Erling Ormundt—arrested the same evening. Also in the concentration camp at Buchenwald.

"Herr Julius Baumgarten—dragged from his bed and arrested during Friday night. At present in the Plotzensee Prison.

"Herr Bürgermeister Otto Frank Franz von Kampfen—arrested early yesterday morning. The charge: Treason against the National Socialist Government. Now in Dachau Concentration Camp under sentence of death. *Awaiting execution.*"

A low moan of horror swept through the sanctuary. A woman sobbed aloud. Strong men wept. The Nazis rudely shuffled their feet.

The pastor laid aside the roll of names, thus concluding this feature of the morning service. As he did so, the foot-shuffling of the invaders of the sanctuary ceased. But the Nazis all leaned forward in their pews, with an air of hawklike scrutiny—even as vultures ready to swoop down upon their prey. Another moment of tense silence—almost electric—pervaded the entire church. And then, again, the voice of Pastor von Ludwig rose strongly, authoritatively:

"Following our sermon this morning, and our closing hymn, Holy Communion will be celebrated. All who love our Lord Jesus Christ in sincerity and truth, and have received His gift of eternal life through faith in His atoning death upon Calvary's cross for our redemption, will be invited freely to partake of the elements upon the Communion Table.

"And now, my beloved, we shall continue our worship in the presentation of our gifts unto God. This morning's offering will be devoted to the relief of the wives and children of members of our own church who are in prisons or concentration camps. The ushers will please come forward."

From several directions eight men converged toward the chancel and received from the pastor's hands the large brass collection plates, which they then passed through the congregation. As they did so, the choir sang the lovely anthem "Jesu, Joy of All Desiring." When the task of receiving the offering was completed, the ushers brought the heaped-up and overflowing plates forward to the chancel for the prayer of dedication.

But scarcely had the organist modulated into the beautiful melody of a cherished prayer hymn, when it was rudely drowned out by another and—this time—a most vicious shuffling of the Nazis' feet. Before the horrified congregation could sing the "Amen," four of the officers rushed forward from the front pews and leaped up the chancel steps. Savagely thrusting the pastor aside, they seized the collection plates angrily, while the voice of their leader, Konstantin von Wolfmacht, rang out the stentorian command:

"Halt! *HEIL HITLER!* In his exalted name, and upon the authority of the National Socialist Government, we confiscate this money! You have collected it, sir"—this he said wrathfully in direct address to Pastor von Ludwig—"in flagrant violation of our Fuehrer's Proclamation sent to all Confessional churches throughout Germany only last week."

Keeping the saintly minister of Christ shoved into the background, the *kommandant* drew from his vest pocket an impressive-looking document, fastened with a large red-ribboned seal.

"You, sir, will see to it that this unequivocal proclamation of our noble Fuehrer is *obeyed*. As of this day forward! HEIL HITLER!"

Released from his obscurity behind the four Nazi intruders upon the sanctity of the altar, Pastor von Ludwig stepped slowly down from the chancel and majestically ascended the steps of his high white pulpit. Trembling with inward rage, yet in perfect self-command and in full command of his entire congregation, who hung tensely upon his every word, with all the dignity of his high office and all the forcefulness of his Spirit-empowered utterance, he hurled into the very faces of the blaspheming Nazis his daring ultimatum.

"In the name of the Father and of the Son and of the Holy Ghost, I defy every one of the orders which you, gentlemen, have just pronounced in the name of your Fuehrer, Adolf Hitler. Our fuehrer is our Almighty God! Him and Him alone do we recognize. Him and Him alone do we obey. Upon *His* authority and by *His* command, and in *His* all-glorious name, we shall continue our accustomed church collections.

"My people," he thundered, "in the glorious history of our beloved Church we have reached a tremendous crisis. We have come to a decisive crossroads in our destiny. Two mighty forces, in diametric opposition each to the other, are in a death grapple for supremacy. On the one side are the forces of righteousness, of holiness, of truth and virtue—the forces of God and our Lord Jesus Christ and heaven. On the other side are the forces of evil, the forces of spiritual disintegration and decay, the forces of blasphemous negation—the forces of Satan and of hell. To every one of us this morning comes the stern command of the Lord God: *Choose you this day whom ye will serve.*"

For fully fifty minutes the sermon continued, the pastor pouring forth with brilliant delivery a flood of eloquent, impassioned utterance. Argument was piled upon argument; appeal upon appeal; invective upon invective—all with unassailable authority and unanswerable logic because of the indubitable fact that every declaration the intrepid minister of Christ proclaimed was based squarely and challengingly upon the impregnable foundation of the Word of God.

At length he brought his powerful message to its conclusion: "And now, in view of all these forces which have inundated Germany as with a tidal wave, I call upon you, my beloved people, in this dark and terrible hour, to stand true to

Christ—to stand true to your convictions as loyal citizens of Germany and as loyal citizens of heaven."

The saintly minister of Christ bowed his head low over the pulpit while the organist played and the choir sang softly the concluding beautiful chorale:

The LORD bless thee, and keep thee;
The LORD make His face shine upon thee,
And be gracious unto thee:
The LORD lift up His countenance upon thee,
And give thee peace. Amen.

The elders came forward and took their places; the solemn, beautiful Communion service proceeded forthwith. Two elders lifted the snowy cloth that covered the bread and wine. Slowly the worshippers rose from their pews and filed down the aisles, the occupants of the gallery descending the curving white stairs and following after them. In turn they all knelt at the Communion rail before the altar, where the faithful servant of the Lord, assisted by another godly elder, dispensed to each successive partaker first the bread and then the cup.

Each communicant was personally known to the pastor and loved by him as his own dear child. This was no perfunctory mass rite. It was the solemn Ordinance of Holy Communion, wherein the undershepherd of the Great Shepherd of the flock fed the sheep and the lambs of his cherished fold with the sacred symbols of the body and blood of Christ.

As with the tenderness of a father he scanned each face before him, gradually his own face became troubled, sad. For several accustomed faces were missing from the Communion Table. As he completed his task of dispensing the elements to the last kneeling circle of worshippers, and they began to file down from the altar, anxiously his glance swept over the pews. Each pew and each family occupying it was inscribed upon his memory as it was indelibly inscribed upon his great loving heart.

"Remember," he declared authoritatively, "what I said before the sermon when I announced this Communion service as following thereafter: that *all* worshippers—*all* who love our Lord Jesus Christ, all who are born again through faith in

His atoning blood—are welcome at His Table, regardless of race, regardless of age, regardless of circumstance.

"Come!" he pleaded tenderly, "Jacob! Isidor! Rebekah! Sarah! David! Will you not come? Come, my dear ones, come to the Table of His blessed Son. Come, my beloved children! Come to the Memorial Table of your Lord!"

But still the individuals thus entreated remained frozen to their pews, all their faces now quite white with fear.

One brave soul only ventured forward—Old Herr Isaac Mandel. Falteringly, glancing surreptitiously to right and left, at length he reached the Communion rail and reverently knelt before it. But even as he waited in awed expectancy for the token of the body of his Lord to be placed within his upturned palm, suddenly two of the Nazi officers rushed forward from the front pew and lunged upon him savagely. One of them was the *kommandant*—Herr Konstantin von Wolfmacht. Seizing his collar, they dragged him viciously backwards with a volley of oaths.

"You cursed *Jew*! You filthy swine!" von Wolfmacht roared. "What business have *you* at a Communion Table—or even in a church at all?" Angrily jerking him upwards to his feet, the *kommandant* turned him over to his fellow officer, to be kept in custody for the present, and to be dealt with later.

And then in fury von Wolfmacht turned upon Pastor von Ludwig. "You dog!" he hissed before the whole terrified congregation. "You are worse than they are! The Jews are bad enough, but you are infinitely worse! You have dared to defy *our* command—the command of *Adolf Hitler*! Did you not hear it? We read it to you distinctly: that only *pure Aryans* could celebrate Communion—and you have deliberately invited dirty Jews!

"Martin Luther von Ludwig! You are under immediate arrest—on the most direful charge of *treason*!"

Panic instantly ensued. The congregation still groaning, and now sobbing and gesticulating wildly, rushed from their pews and choked the aisles as they attempted to surge down them to surround and protect their beloved pastor. But upon von Wolfmacht's shouted order, the whole contingent of one hundred Nazi soldiers, plus the twelve who carried the swastika banners, charged against them and held them back.

High aloft over all the awful frenzy of fear and hate, still there floated gently downwards the beautiful white dove of peace.

Above the din and wild confusion, von Wolfmacht thundered out his further orders:

"Holtzwarth! Schwartzmann! Clear the building immediately! And you—Lindstammer, Oberlinger, Helmuth! As soon as it is cleared, lock the front doors on the outside and seal them with the Nazi seal! Everybody understand! This church is closed—barred and bolted and rendered completely inoperative—until further notice. And this pulpit is permanently closed to this foul traitor, *Martin Luther von Ludwig*!"

While the Nazis were rudely shoving the despairing flock away from their beloved undershepherd, and out through the massive front doors, and while the *kommandant* and his henchmen stood silently pinning the arms of their victim behind his back, suddenly von Wolfmacht relaxed his grip upon him. Summoning another officer to take his place, in incisive tone he gave his final order:

"Grunewalt! von Barmen! Hold this prisoner tightly. Take von Ludwig into the vestry and strip him of his high-priestly robes. It will be easier for you to hold him there until I come. Be sure the door is firmly locked and bolted. Open it to me when you hear me knock and give the password. Remember, *your lives for his if you fail to deliver him to me!*"

Gloatingly the two underofficers appointed by von Wolfmacht to their fiendishly welcomed task of escorting the arrested pastor, for the last time, to his vestry—and thence to his doom—still holding his arms behind him in a viselike grip, shoved him roughly forward and marched him triumphantly across the chancel, and thence out through the rear door into the corridor.

But their triumph—their coarse gloating—was shortlived. For to their great discomfiture, to their utter consternation and dismay and terror, no sooner had they closed the door and turned toward the vestry, when suddenly *their* arms were pinned behind *them* and they were dragged backwards forcibly and separated from their prisoner, as eight strong men bore down upon them instantly within the corridor.

For the God of Deliverance—long before ever the Nazis had entered the sanctuary, even before Pastor von Ludwig himself had entered it—already had been at work.

Quietly and unobserved, each of the eight men had taken his predetermined post during the singing of the final hymn. And there, for the remainder of the service, every man had faithfully held his guard, tensely waiting for the tempest to burst—as burst it did indeed with all the fury of a tornado, even at the Memorial Table of our Lord.

Quickly above their pastor's flowing ministerial gown they wrapped a concealing long, dark cloak—pulling down over his eyes, at the same time, a heavily visored cap. And then they rushed him down a flight of narrow stairs and out through a rear door on the basement level—down a lengthy corridor and outdoors through a seldom-used basement exit—then up another flight of stairs leading to a hidden lane whence they emerged into a secluded street—then swiftly around a corner—around another corner—and thence into a handsome black limousine which stood all ready and waiting for them.

With blinds tightly drawn, the car proceeded cautiously up one street and down another, around and around a circuitous route designed to outwit all pursuers, until the city limits were reached. And then, once safely out upon the broad highway, with Charlottenburg left well behind, the driver pressed the accelerator and the car plunged full steam ahead, tearing wildly on toward its carefully and completely preplanned destination.

Thus through the mighty operation of the Holy Spirit, in answer to the swelling volume of importunate believing prayer for their beloved pastor by his faithful session and by the entire Confessional Church membership, as well—which prayer ascended ceaselessly from their anguished hearts to the throne of grace—his deliverance from the cruel enemy was miraculously wrought.

Straight to the selfsame prearranged destination the limousine bore Pastor Martin Luther von Ludwig—even to the Jewish refugee shelter within the mansion of his devoted friend, Dr. Benjamin Rothschild.

For this, too—his concealment in the stronghold so magnanimously provided by the greathearted Hebrew within his own luxurious home for his hopeless and despairing Jewish brethren—was all a part, and was indeed the climax of the whole most carefully preconceived plan for the pastor's deliverance from Nazi fury.

Fritz was at the wheel of Dr. Rothschild's limousine when Pastor von Ludwig was rushed into it for his hazardous escape from totalitarian revenge. And Fritz it was who carefully guided the car over a route that he had previously made certain would be unfrequented by Nazi soldiers at that particular Sunday morning hour. And Fritz it was also who, when at last the car reached Dr. Rothschild's gates, had himself with utmost courtesy and solicitude—yes, even with filial tenderness—led the trembling pastor most cautiously through the dense grove of spruce trees and into the mysterious cottage buried deeply within its gloom; thence through the secret underground tunnel to the secret door of entrance into Dr. Rothschild's home.

As Pastor von Ludwig waited breathlessly, Fritz pressed the tunnel alarm bell—three short, sharp rings; then two long-drawn-out ones—exactly as the master of the Hebrew house had given previous direction to his friend.

Quickly from within there came the muffled query: "Who comes here?"

The pastor himself made excited reply in two eager words only—the password and his name: *SHALOM! Von Ludwig!"*

Instantly the door was slid wide open and Martin Luther von Ludwig stepped inside—straight into the outstretched, warmly welcoming arms of his devoted Hebrew friend. For a moment they remained in close embrace; then each gazed at the other in complete silence, both men overwhelmed with strong emotion and a sense of reverent awe.

Dr. Rothschild was the first to find his voice.

"Martin! Thank God you are *safe*! Thank God you are *here*! Sooner than ever I had dared to hope!"

To all of which Pastor von Ludwig replied simply, albeit with profoundest feeling:

"Yes, Benjamin. Thank God indeed that I am here with *you*, and safe for some little time, at least. And I am here sooner than I myself, as well as you, had even dreamed. I thank my merciful heavenly Father. Great is His faithfulness. And I do thank you, my dearest friend, with all my heart!"

And then with his beautiful, silvery head bowed in deep humility, he added fervently: *"Praise God from whom all blessings flow!"*

Chapter 13

Home Foundations Crash

With Fritz in full control of all the housing arrangements within the shelter, and with Pastor von Ludwig there to lend his strong aid for any emergency that might arise among the forty hidden Jewish guests, Dr. Rothschild at last felt it safe to spend the major portion of his time at the hospital. There, he was very sure, he was more greatly needed even than at home.

Nothing escaped the visiting Nazis' cold, penetrating gaze. Public wards and private patients' rooms alike were intruded upon, frequently at moments most embarrassing to the nurses and also to the visiting physicians. The operating theatre was rudely entered, even when a patient might be upon the table at the most critical juncture of a major operation. Even the sacred solemnity of a deathbed was heartlessly desecrated.

But it was upon Dr. Rothschild himself, gradually but surely, that their most vicious hatred concentrated. And upon him, at last, their venomous arrows fell. He was a Jew. He dared to set himself up in professional authority over the whole hospital. He dared to issue orders even to Aryan physicians within its walls. He dared to admit and administer treatment to Jewish patients. The Jews were the scum of the earth. He himself was the scum of the earth. Just wait! He would see, soon enough, how long he would remain upon his self-exalted pinnacle!

The Nazis demanded that Dr. Rothschild fill out lengthy questionnaires giving all possible information concerning the hospital and concerning himself as its self-constituted head. The queries were involved and frequently they were most insulting. How long had Dr. Rothschild been practicing? How long had he been in this hospital? What qualifications and credentials could he produce to prove him capable of directing so vast an institution? How many patients had he operated upon himself? How many of them had he killed? What papers could he show to certify that he was accredited by Adolf Hitler? Was he completely loyal to him?

Hospital equipment was arrogantly confiscated. The lobby was stripped of its luxurious furnishings. The elegant upholstery, the brocaded draperies, the handsome tables and lamps, the priceless Persian rubs, the rare porcelains—all were ruthlessly removed and carted off in trucks, their places left bare and desolate. At last one art treasure only remained within the hospital—the beautiful oil portrait of Sharon Rothschild.

Necessary records were torn up with ribald jest. Patients' charts ripped asunder and their sheets of paper rolled into squills for lighting pipes or cut into squares for rolling cigarettes—the endless butts of which, together with drunken spittle, were strewn filthily all over the erstwhile spotlessly shining place. The magnificent Sharon Rothschild Memorial Hospital, in its every department and down to its minutest detail, was ruthlessly disorganized, completely devastated. It was now almost a month since Dr. Rothschild had received Pastor von Ludwig into the refuge of his home. During that month, both within his home and within his hospital, his own perils and distresses at the hands of the Nazis had steadily augmented. But the deepest of all griefs still lay ahead for Benjamin Rothschild. And at last, as the climax to the full tale of his sorrows within his cherished hospital, the awful blow came swiftly crashing down upon him.

Joseph—his and Rose's so dearly beloved elder son, their joy, their hope, their pride—Joseph, within but six weeks of completing, with highest honors, his internship within his father's great institution, and of being installed thereafter as a resident surgeon, was suddenly and without any warning whatsoever summoned before a Nazi high tribunal in the hospital lobby. And there, right below the portrait of his sister, her lovely laughing face looking eagerly down upon him; and in the presence, as well, of his utterly helpless father who also had been summoned by the Nazis—purposely and with the cruel intent that he might witness his son's disgrace and degradation—Joseph was commanded to surrender his room, his uniforms, and all his equipment, lay down his work, and leave the hospital on two hours' notice, never to return. The sole charge laid against him: he was a *Jew*.

Stunned in every fiber of his being, Joseph went home, where, by the hour, day after day, he sat around dully, wrapped in deepest gloom, listless and inert, forlorn, dejected, hopeless—the brilliant young surgeon, distinguished son of his distinguished father, just about to launch upon his high and noble professional career.

Joseph's dismissal had taken place on a Saturday afternoon early in January. All day Sunday, Dr. Rothschild had remained at home, striving earnestly, but altogether in vain—even with Pastor von Ludwig's strong assistance—to console and fortify his heartbroken mother. Both of them were utterly crushed. With but very little more success Dr. Rothschild strove to fortify himself, as well, for what he knew with perfect certainty now lay before him—before them all—inevitably and irrevocably.

But on Monday morning, notwithstanding, after a night that was completely sleepless, he arose before dawn and set his face like a flint toward his hospital. He must go to it. No matter how terrible the shrinking of his very soul, he *must*. We must strive by every possible means within his power to save his beloved enterprise from complete destruction.

It was not quite seven o'clock—the hour for the new shift to come on duty—when Dr. Rothschild reached the hospital. But already the pack of angry wolves was waiting for him, all sniffing hungrily for his blood. Even before he entered the imposing doorway—beneath the portal bearing the beloved name "Sharon Rothschild"—he knew the worst. Through the large glass panels he could see them at the far end of the lobby, drawn up into stiffest military formation—a dozen of the Nazi SS Elite Guard officers. They stood six abreast in a double line, directly under Sharon's portrait, Konstantin von Wolfmacht, as usual, at their head.

As the world-famous Hebrew surgeon, the founder and director of the great humanitarian institution walked firmly and majestically down the lobby—into their very jaws—the Nazi *kommandant* rang out the stentorian order:

"Herr *Doktor* Benjamin Rothschild! Halt!"

With his distinguished head held strongly uplifted, his voice, his eyes, his entire bearing under rigid control, quietly Dr. Rothschild made reply:

"Good morning, gentlemen. What can I do for you?"

Scorning his gracious approach, von Wolfmacht again gave authoritative dictum:

"HEIL HITLER!"

Benjamin Rothschild distained the ultimatum. It was repeated fiercely in infuriated tone:

"HEIL HITLER! Do you not hear me? Heil, you dog of a Jew! I command you, HEIL!"

The proud Hebrew drew himself up to his magnificent full height. His spirit unbroken, he looked squarely into von Wolfmacht's evil eyes. With immeasurable contempt he made ringing reply: "I refuse!"

"You *refuse*! You refuse to acknowledge our almighty Fuehrer?" Von Wolfmacht rushed upon him with ruffianly blows of his fists. "Then take *that*, you filthy Jewish swine! Take that—and that—and *that*!"

The Nazi punctuated his insulting words and blows with still more insulting and cruel blows from the butt of his revolver. Dr. Rothschild staggered under them and fell prostrate to the floor, directly in front of the picture of his lovely, laughing little daughter. Instantly at von Wolfmacht's signal, a couple of the Nazi officers dragged him the full length of the lobby and across the inner vestibule to the great bronze doors. Opening them wide, they kicked him viciously through them and down the handsome marble steps. He lay at the foot of them, the greathearted originator of Germany's foremost children's hospital. Before that same munificent house of healing—erected "to the glory of God for the alleviation of suffering of all children within the Fatherland regardless of race, creed, or circumstances, in sacred and tender and imperishable memory" of his beloved little only daughter, Sharon—Dr. Benjamin Rothschild lay on the snowy ground, bruised and bleeding and broken.

Once again and with finality, the *kommandant* thus haughtily addressed his helpless and now hopeless victim:

"Herr *Doktor* Benjamin Rothschild! You Jewish cur! So

there we have it! Do you understand me now, I wonder? Listen to me! First and foremost: never again dare to set foot within this Sharon Rothschild Hospital! You have polluted it far too long already. Its doors are now sealed against you and all your filthy race forever—by command of our glorious Fuehrer Adolf Hitler. And listen further! *This place too*—together with all its surrounding park and gardens and outbuildings, and all its contents—is, as of today, confiscated in his name and upon his authority. Still further! All other property whatsoever to which you hold title in Germany, whether real or personal, and wheresoever situated, becomes, as of this moment, forfeit to the National Socialist State.

"Listen still more carefully! For the present, you and your family will remain in your house—*our* house now, understand—under our protective custody. But for the immediate present only, remember! Merely until such time as we can conveniently get you all properly disposed of!

"Every day, at twelve noon, you will report for inspection by our SS Elite Guard.

"There! That is all for now. *Get up, you swine!* Stand on your two feet!" Von Wolfmacht punctuated this, his final word to Dr. Benjamin Rothschild, with a vicious kick. And then without waiting for his agonized victim to obey his order—to accomplish the impossible—he turned arrogantly to his Nazi underofficers and gave peremptory command:

"Close ranks, men! Forward march! HEIL HITLER!"

Gretel was kept in fairly close touch with conditions in the mansion, through occasional letters surreptitiously sent to her by Joseph. These were always typed on very ordinary paper, without date or address or signature, in a code which he and Gretel had long since devised—and thus made secure against identification through possible interception. They were mailed, always in the dead of night, either by Joseph himself or by Moische, in a mailbox on a secluded street far enough removed from their dwelling safely to conceal their source.

Gretel, in reply, whenever she had opportunity, wrote little notes to Joseph, addressed to the Berlin Post Office General Delivery—since mail no longer was delivered to Jewish homes. All the Rothschild mail was now called for by the faithful Fritz. Her missives were always in optimistic vein. Poor Joseph—and all the other loved ones—had quite enough trouble of their own without hers being added. And especially did she never mention one word concerning Konstantin von Wolfmacht.

The letters uniformly bore the impress of forced cheerfulness, of bravely attempted optimism for her sake, lest she be alarmed and saddened by them. But between the lines and underneath the so carefully veiled words she could read clearly that the defenses—the defenses within the cherished house itself and within the hearts and lives of all the dear ones dwelling there—were crumbling. This fact was completely transparent to her in the pitiful appeal that always ended every letter: "When can you come home to us? We *all* need you!"

At last Gretel could bear it no more. She would go to them! The risk of discovery by the Nazis was far less than the risk of utter heartbreak for them all in their continued separation. She would take every possible precaution, guarding all her words and movements with utmost secrecy and prudence. But go she would at her very first opportunity. For go she *must*.

Gretel crept stealthily toward the secret entrance to the Rothschilds' hideaway. As she reached the door, her heart bounded with joy. In a moment she would see her *Joseph*! She knocked softly at the second secret door and again called the secret password: "*Shalom*." And then as she recognized the beloved voice in the muffled query: "Who's there?"—she cried out in low but ringing tones: "Joseph! Oh, Joseph darling! Open quickly! It's Gretel!"

With thrilling joy on his part also, Joseph flung wide the panel door; and the next instant he and Gretel were in a transport of delight, each in blissful reunion with the other. He drew her eagerly into the library, where, at the further end, Dr. Rothschild lay feverishly upon the divan, while Moische, in listless mood, was sitting beside him in a vain attempt at reading. Upon Joseph's electrifying announcement: "Father! Moische! Here is Gretel!"—they both sprang up in glad surprise and came forward with alacrity to greet her.

But in the midst of Gretel's ecstasy over being reunited

with these three dear ones of her future family, she experienced a swift surge of pain as she looked into their so sadly altered countenances. All three of them bore unmistakably the marks of cruel suffering. Dr. Rothschild had aged ten years. It was scarcely three weeks since Gretel had last seen him at the hospital, but already his hair, then raven black, was now flecked heavily with white. His face was ashen gray and drawn, his eyes sunken with deep sorrow. His frame was thin and stooped, and his step—always before so elastic with eagerness and vigor—was now faltering and feeble. Joseph and Moische, except for wanness, both looked physically fit, but they, too, bore clearly the ravages of grief.

Mrs. Rothschild was upstairs, trying to rest. Her sleep had been so terribly broken, Joseph told Gretel sadly.

He must go up to her now to see if she were quieted. Would Gretel care to go with him? Yes, indeed, she assured him eagerly. She was longing to see his precious mother.

Together they went up to her room. They found her tossing convulsively upon her bed, with piteous moaning.

"Mother darling," Joseph called softly, approaching her with utmost gentleness. "I have a wonderful surprise for you! Guess who is here?"

Mrs. Rothschild turned startled eyes upon him. "Who?" she asked excitedly, a tone of quick fear in her voice.

"Someone, little Mother, we all love very dearly. It's *Gretel*!"

"Gretel?" she echoed incredulously.

"Yes, dear," Gretel herself replied lovingly. "I am *here*—with you! I just had to come to see you!"

Mrs. Rothschild's reaction was a sudden burst of tears, as she flung her arms wildly around Gretel's neck and drew her close.

"Oh, Gretel, Gretel, it is all so awful!" she moaned hysterically. "Those wicked, wicked men! They have taken away from us *everything*! Our money! Our cars! Our beautiful silver! And our hospital—Sharon's hospital. And they have put my husband and son out of it forever! We have nothing left—nothing! Oh, what shall we do! What *shall* we do?"

Gently Gretel tried to disengage herself from the frenzied woman's wild embrace, but she was clutched as in a vise.

"Oh, do not leave me! Do not leave me!" the heartbroken wife and mother shrieked.

Gretel glanced at Joseph significantly. He nodded gravely in assent. Then very deftly, very tenderly he administered morphine. Gradually the storm within his mother's breast subsided. The arms dropped; the tense nerves relaxed; the convulsive body quieted; the hysterical outcry ceased.

"Oh, my mother! My mother!" he moaned inconsolably. "Oh, Gretel darling, to see her suffering so terribly! I cannot bear it! I cannot bear it!"

"I know it, Joseph. I know all about it, darling." Gretel soothed him with most tender endearments. "But be comforted, beloved. Your precious little mother will be better soon."

"Oh, no, never! Never, Gretel! She is breaking! And my father is breaking! Everything has crashed! Oh, it is all too awful! I can stand what has happened to myself—I will get over it in time. But to see *them* in such agonizing grief—my beloved father and mother and my only brother—Oh, Gretel dearest, that is more than I can possibly endure!"

For reply Gretel only continued her caresses, her endearing, soothing words. Gradually they had a quieting, a strengthening effect. At last Joseph drew himself upright and brought his emotion under firm control. He led Gretel to the window seat behind the palms and drew her gently down beside him.

At length Joseph broke their sorrowful reverie. Manfully he spoke the grave, reluctant words he felt, in honor bound, that he must speak.

"Gretel"—his voice broke and he faltered. Gently she urged him to continue. "Yes, Joseph? What is it, dear? Speak to me freely of all that is upon your heart."

"Gretel," once more he addressed her—this time resolutely—"when I asked you to marry me, eight years ago, all the future seemed radiant before me. I felt I had everything to give you: our honored name and prestige in Germany; our family position and wealth; my share, as a son, in our beautiful home; every expectation of a successful career for myself.

"But now, *now*—everything is completely swept away, *everything*! Our social rank is obliterated: no longer are we rated in Aryan Germany as Rothschilds; we are scorned and ostracized as Jews.

"And so," Joseph continued bitterly but bravely, "I know that I now have no possible right to hold you to our engagement. It breaks my heart to do it; but I recognize, Gretel, that in sacred honor I must offer to release you from your promise to marry me. I *must,* for I have nothing now to give you—absolutely *nothing.*" He buried his face in his hands and again he wept.

Tenderly Gretel gathered him into her arms. For a full moment she held him with quiet strength until the storm was spent. Then she raised his head gently and compelled his gaze into her eyes. She smiled into his triumphantly.

"You have nothing to give me, Joseph? Nothing? Is your wonderful love nothing? Ah, to me it is everything! Everything in the whole world!"

"Oh, Gretel, my darling!" he answered rapturously.

And then playfully she placed her hands upon his shoulders and shook him vigorously.

"Joseph Rothschild!" she exclaimed with mock severity. "Never speak to me like that again! Never speak about releasing me from *you;* but rather"—here she pleaded with fervent entreaty—"*set me as a seal upon thine heart, as a seal upon thine arm: for love is strong as death . . . Many waters cannot quench love, neither can the floods drown it: if a man would give all the substance of his for love, it would utterly be condemned.*"

"Oh, Gretel, you are *heavenly*! Oh, my darling, how can I ever be worthy of a love like yours? With such a love supporting me, I feel strong to triumph over Adolf Hitler himself and the Nazi state and over all the hosts of hell! But only, dearest, if we are outside of Germany. For here, within Germany, there is utter chaos on every hand. And until the satanic power of Hitler is completely broken, that chaos will increase. No, Gretel, there could be no possible door of opportunity, no possible happiness, no possible safety for any Jew in Nazi Germany. Do you not agree, then, dearest, that it would be wiser for us to leave—just as soon as God shall open up the way?"

"Certainly, Joseph. I agree to anything you say."

"You would be willing to go with me, darling?"

"To the farthest star!"

"Not quite that far—for yet a little while, at least," Joseph replied happily. "Pray God we still may have many joyous years together here on earth. But where I do hope to go, dear, just as quickly as possible, is far away from Germany—far away from all our Nazi foes—far away from—"

"Where, Joseph?" Gretel interposed excitedly. "Have you any definite place in mind?"

"Yes! Oh, Gretel, darling! The most wonderful place in all the world!" He spoke ecstatically, with glowing countenance. The light of a new and joyous hope was shining in his eyes.

"Oh, Joseph! *Where?*" Gretel's question was half in eager expectation, half in fear.

"Listen! I will tell you where! Oh, Gretel, my beloved, we must go—to *Palestine*!"

Chapter 14

Battle of Wills

Upon her return to the hospital, Gretel began at once to set plans afoot for reopening her father's home, as he had requested. She called Klara Kronin and arranged for her to go to the house to get everything ready for occupancy. Gretel would spend her first free weekend there. Not only would Klara remain with her then, but she promised to stay on. She would keep the place open and in constant readiness for subsequent homecomings—both of Gretel and her father.

The faithful housekeeper was overjoyed at the prospect of returning to the manse and to her beloved "Fräulein Margarete." The good woman had grieved deeply for her gracious young mistress and her saintly father and their broken home. Yes, certainly, she assured Gretel, she would go to the house on the morrow and put everything in apple-pie order. And she would have a fine supper all prepared and waiting for her lady, just as soon as she knew what evening to expect her.

"And have the manse well lighted, won't you, Klara?" Gretel pleaded. "It has been dark so long. I could not bear to see it dark when I come home."

"Yes indeed, ma'am! I'll have it shiny bright. Trust Klara Kronin for that! And all ready and comfortable for that grand man of God, your precious father—just as soon as he can get there, too, Lord bless him!"

When Saturday evening came, the very moment Gretel was released from duty she went quickly to the nurses' residence, changed from her uniform to house wear and packed her weekend suitcase. And then she hurried to her car and started off for Charlottenburg and home. Faithful to her promise to Klara, she omitted supper at the hospital. She was hungry, but she would wait and do full justice to the delectable meal she was perfectly sure Klara would have prepared for her.

Her drive was a depressing one. She took no delight whatever in the prospect of spending the lonely weekend in the place that had been—oh, so long, long ago, it seemed!—the center of vivid life and love and joy. The very thought of entering the house with all of its sad changes was torture to Gretel.

At last the car entered Charlottenburg and finally came to the von Ludwigs' street. But before she quite reached the manse, Gretel turned the corner nearest it and drove halfway up the block to the service station where she always left her car to be checked and refueled. And then, carrying her suitcase and her nurse's hooded cape, she started walking back toward the house.

When she reached the corner, before turning it, a shudder of grief shook her from head to foot. She stood still for a moment and closed her eyes, as if she dreaded ever again to see the place that of all places on earth had been the one most dear.

But she must go on. With a quick upward prayer for courage and strength, she opened her eyes and turned the corner—and suddenly the manse stood in full view.

Shocked and astounded, Gretel beheld it. From top to bottom it was ablaze with light, every window brilliantly illuminated. It was that ridiculous Klara Kronin, of course! "I told her to be sure to have the house well lighted, but certainly never meant for her to set it on fire," Gretel said to herself.

But instanteously Gretel's amusement turned to horror. For as she started up the cement walk and approached the steps leading to the veranda, she saw, waving above it, an emblem of most sinister foreboding: the swastika-emblazoned flag of the Nazi government.

She stood rooted to the spot in sudden terror. Whatever did it portend? The *swastika* flying from her father's house! And then another wave of grief swept over her. Her beloved father! And he in exile!

Stealthily Gretel climbed to the top of the steps and peered through the doorway into the living room beyond the hall. Trembling violently from head to foot, she became aware, with hideous sickening, of heavy fumes of liquor and tobacco.

Cautiously she surveyed the wild scene her father's house presented. Within the living room her two elder brothers, Bernhardt and Bruno, were standing in the midst of perhaps a dozen other Nazi officers—all of them singing lustily. Seated at the piano, playing the horrible music, was Konstantin von Wolfmacht. A number of the men, her brothers and von Wolfmacht included, clearly were intoxicated.

Safely concealed on the veranda, Gretel stood for several moments in a panic of indecision. Whatever should she do? Should she beat a swift retreat? Or should she enter? And if she entered, would it be wiser for her to attempt to steal upstairs to her own room unobserved? Or should she march boldly in upon the boisterous scene and make the rude invaders aware of her presence immediately?

A flood of hot indignation surged up within her. This! *This!* In her saintly father's house! This desecration! This fearful profanation! Yes, certainly she would enter. And she would let them know in no uncertain terms that she was there. It was her *right*: this was her father's house, and she was her father's daughter. Nay, it was more than her right: it was her bounden duty to protest against this infamy. She was here as her father's emissary—in filial obedience to his most earnest wish. To flee would be to disobey him. To flee would be to surrender to the enemy all the sacred traditions of their honored family name. The noble name of Luther von Ludwig! And to think that this name, this family, was being thus betrayed by its two eldest sons!

She breathed a fervent prayer for help, and even as she prayed, she felt herself invested with a mysterious calm, with a miraculous, supernatural defense. Bold as a lion she entered her father's house.

She pushed the door wide open and stepped into the hallway. She set down her suitcase with a deliberate thud to make her presence known. And then with quiet dignity, she entered the living room and stood, with perfect composure, before the astounded Nazis. The music came to a crashing stop.

"Gretel!" Bernhardt and Bruno exclaimed in startled concert. "What on earth are *you* doing here?" Bernhardt demanded, marked displeasure in his tone. All the other officers stared at her in awkward confusion. But only for a moment. After the first shock of surprise, they stiffened suddenly into their accustomed haughty pride.

Her poise was superb. Quietly she made reply to her two brothers. With charming ease she said simply: "I have come home, boys, to spend the weekend." And then in a tone that was entirely courteous but, nevertheless, authoritative, she added, "I see that we have guests this evening. Will you present them to me, please?"

Bernhardt scowled darkly. It was Bruno who recovered sufficient presence of mind to perform the proper formalities of the occasion. "Gretel"—he addressed her with strained graciousness—"permit me to introduce our Nazi friends. Gentlemen, this is our sister, Fräulein Margarete von Ludwig."

Von Wolfmacht immediately rose from the piano and stood before Gretel with an air of complete self-possession. His bearing was proudly military and aggressive. His shoulders were rigidly squared. His head was held high. On his handsome, cruel face there was a cynical smile. His voice was oily, calculating, crafty.

"Ah, *guten Abend,* Fräulein Margarete! Our distinguished nurse! This is indeed a rare and unexpected pleasure. Your presence confers upon us a signal honor. We welcome you into our happy circle most heartily." He made a low, sweeping bow before her. His left arm was placed impressively across his heart. With his right hand he coolly seized Gretel's hand, and—in full view of her brothers and his fellow Nazis—raised it insolently to his lips.

Gretel burned with anger. Swiftly she tore her hand from his grasp. Her eyes blazed into his the unspoken words: *How dare you!*

But then suddenly she experienced another terrible rush of fear. Von Wolfmacht was a Nazi officer. And all these other men were Nazi officers. Should she not flee the house at once? In agony of mind and heart, again, imploringly, she cast herself upon her God. And again and instantly, she was fortified.

She flashed a triumphant smile at the still awkward, uncomfortable Nazis. "Please do not let me interrupt your music and your happy evening. Go on with it, by all means. But if you kindly will excuse me, gentlemen, I must retire. *Gute Nacht!*"

"*Gute Nacht!*" A chorus of embarrassed replies followed her through the doorway. In the hall she picked up her suitcase and her cape and, without turning her head, started toward the stairs, which, in an alcove at the rear of the hall, were concealed both from view and from hearing of the men within the living room.

Von Wolfmacht sped swiftly after her. Entirely unabashed by her recent rebuff, he caught up with her just as she reached the foot of the stairway, her suitcase in her hand.

"Permit me to assist you, *mein liebes* Fräulein Margarete!" His tone was gallant now—gallant and ingratiating. His smile was altogether charming. "Permit me, will you not, to carry your case for you?" He extended his hand toward it inquiringly.

Gretel was aghast at his effrontery. Again fierce anger burned within her. But stronger even than her anger was the sudden thrill of new terror that shot through her entire being. For with horrifying shock she realized that she was now completely at von Wolfmacht's mercy. Caution warned her sternly. She dared not let him see her fear. Rigorously, therefore, she steeled herself to an attitude of cool composure.

"No, I thank you, Herr von Wolfmacht. My suitcase is very light. I can carry it myself quite easily." Tone and bearing were perfectly controlled.

The gallant smile of the SS Elite Guard officer changed instantly to one of subtle cunning. It curled superciliously about his thin, cruel lips.

"Very good indeed, *mein* fräulein. As you prefer, of course. I only hoped I might be of some little service to you." He made a profound bow, unctuously.

As her sole reply, Gretel merely nodded her head with another, and very carefully modulated, "*Gute Nacht.*"

Swift as lightning von Wolfmacht stiffened into ice and steel. He sprang after her angrily. Not so dared any woman snub him—*Konstantin von Wolfmacht*! He would assert his Nazi authority. "Wait!" he commanded sternly, drawn up in haughty SS arrogance to his fullest height. "Wait, Fräulein Margarete von Ludwig! Before you leave I wish to have a talk with you!"

"About what?" Gretel's heart beat wildly. Without turning her head she halted dizzily upon the third step upward.

Savagely von Wolfmacht laid a detaining hand upon her shoulder. "Wait!" he repeated his command in a menacing voice. "Come back here, you proud young rebel! There are several things we have to talk about." He tightened his grip upon her shoulder and dragged her backwards down the three steps. She winced with pain and fright. Rudely he wheeled her about to face him.

"Yes, my sweet friend," he continued in a significantly lowered voice, "there are a number of things that have to be explained. You have never given me opportunity to talk with you before. Now I have the opportunity, and I intend to make the most of it. Here, you may sit if you care to. Just rest yourself quite comfortably, Fräulein Margarete, for a nice, long chat." The words *Fräulein Margarete* were spoken with a slow, sarcastic drawl. He released his hold upon her and drew from the hallway a stiff spindle chair. "Here, sit down!" he ordered harshly.

"Thank you, I prefer to stand."

"Very well, stand then!" he retorted surlily. "But you will stand right here until you have answered all my questions."

Once again, faith and fear did heavy battle within Gretel's breast. She felt herself becoming numb. Icy fingers seemed to clutch her throat. In silent agony she cried out of the depths to God. *Oh, my Father! Help me! Help me*! she implored. Swift as an arrow the desperate prayer sped upward to the Throne. And as swiftly came the Father's answer to His terrified and helpless child: *Fear thou not, for I am with thee. Lo, I am with thee always.* And once again the storm was calmed. Gretel stood before her captor with unflinching steadiness and looked straight into his cold, cruel eyes. "Yes," she said quietly, "what is it that you wish to ask me?"

He replied vindictively. "I wish to ask you"—again the steely glint within his eyes—"I wish to ask you first of all, why it is, Fräulein von Ludwig, that you so constantly avoid me?"

"Avoid you! When have I avoided you?"

"You know when, perfectly well. In the hospital. Whenever I have tried to speak with you alone."

Gretel parried the issue. "Oh, in the hospital! But you must remember, Herr von Wolfmacht, I am a nurse on duty. My time is not my own."

"But you have never allowed me to make an appointment to meet you outside the hospital."

"Certainly not. I do not make outside appointments—except for business purposes—with strangers."

"*Stranger?* There, that is it exactly! That is my entire argument. You have persisted in treating me as a stranger when you knew—when you must have known—that I want to be your friend!"

"But why should you desire to be a friend to *me*, Herr von Wolfmacht? You are a wealthy, distinguished officer of the German army. I am only a poor undergraduate nurse. *I* am nothing in the world to *you*."

"Nothing?" he repeated passionately. "You? Nothing to me? You are everything to me! Do you not know it, my beautiful Margarete? Have you been so blind, my darling? Have you not seen it? Have you not felt it? Surely you must have seen it with your woman's eyes. You must have felt it with your woman's intuition—my constantly deepening interest in you—my admiration—my undying love! Oh, tell me that you know I love you!"

Gretel struggled fiercely for release, but he held her with an unyielding, viselike grip. With amorous ardor he poured forth a flood of extravagant endearments. "Margarete! Lovely Margarete! Adored one of my heart! You are the most entrancing woman in all Germany—in all the world! I love you! I love you! I love only you! I have always loved you from the first moment that my eyes beheld you! Tell me, my beloved, my precious Margarete, that you will *marry* me!" Throwing off all restraint, he crushed her to his heart in wild embrace.

Gretel turned sick with loathing. The monster had even dared to pollute her lips! In a frenzy of horror and fear, she writhed to free herself. "Let me go! Let me go!" she gasped breathlessly. Her voice froze in her throat.

"Promise me first," von Wolfmacht pleaded. "Promise me, my darling, that you will be my wife!"

"Never! *Never!* Let me go! *Let me go!*" Half-crazed, with a force born of sheer desperation, at last she wrenched herself free from his caress and recoiled in utmost horror.

He withdrew from her a few paces and stood with his arms rigidly folded, his head thrown back, scrutinizing her intently in a stare that was now entirely cold and calculating—so swiftly did the Nazi's tempestuous nature veer from ice to fire and from fire back again to ice. Each silently took the measure of the other. Each watched the other with lynx-eyed tenseness.

Gretel was conscious of a numb paralysis creeping over her—a horrifying feeling as of suspended animation. With both hands she grasped the newel-post of the staircase lest she swoon and fall. What further questions would the fiendish brute dare to ask her?

At last the Nazi broke the lengthy silence—during which he had probed to the very depths of Gretel's soul with his cold, appraising stare. And finally the one question which above all others she had dreaded most was formulated by his cruelly curled lips.

"Aha!" he exulted. "Aha! I begin to see the light. Yes, I see! I see! I understand *now* why you refuse me. There is a reason why you reject von Wolfmacht—Konstantin von Wolfmacht, oberoffizier of the SS Elite Guard of Berlin! Ah, yes, indeed, I see!

"And that reason is . . . Do not try to evade my query, Fräulein von Ludwig. For understand, I am asking it now not personally, but in my official capacity—and because, as a faithful Nazi, it is my duty to obtain this information.

"So you will answer me without delay and without subterfuge or any equivocation whatsoever. Here, then, is my question: Is not the reason for your refusal to marry me—is not the reason Dr. Joseph Rothschild, that damnable young *Jew*?"

The hot blood surged furiously into Gretel's face, while an icy terror clutched her heart. "What do you mean?" she choked. Again her voice froze in her throat. She trembled violently.

"Aha!" von Wolfmacht gloated. "Aha! Excellent! I have my answer. You need not try to put it into words. That will not be necessary. Your countenance is quite reply enough. Your agitation, your crimson, guilty face, your frightened eyes—all confirm my worst suspicions. And they all confirm the evidence I have already received."

"Evidence!" Gretel exclaimed in a hoarse, convulsive gasp.

"Yes, evidence. From those who have been watching you at my command—your close companions in the hospital, the *Aryan* nurses. And as further witnesses, my proud young fräulein, your own two Nazi brother! They have been reporting faithfully to me for weeks. They and the nurses all confirm what I have seen for myself, more than once, in the hospital—that Jewish intern's insolent glances in your direction.

"But far worse, your brothers tell me that they have known for years of this currish Hebrew entertaining amorous intentions toward you, and of your own undeniable satisfaction in them. Why, then, you are wondering, have I not spoken of this earlier? Why did I not long ago order the discharge and disgrace of this vile Jew? Why did I allow him to stay on as long as he did? Simply for one reason: I could not believe the evidence of my own senses—nor the evidence of these trusted informers. I could not bring myself to believe that all this was true of you. I absolutely could not credit such a thing! That you, Fräulein Margarete von Ludwig, with your high birth and breeding, could so take leave of your intelligence—of your *sanity*—as to permit this degradation of your German womanhood. Surely there must be some terrible mistake. Surely, surely, you could never receive attentions from—you could never contemplate marriage with a . . . *Semite*!"

Gretel swayed dizzily—then sank limply to the floor, her face buried in her hands. A prolonged, low moan of anguish rocked her frame.

Her tormentor followed up his advantage ruthlessly. "Poor little girl," again he murmured with shrewdly calculated gentleness, "you are not yourself tonight. You have been badly shaken. All this outrage has completely overwhelmed you. You have been the victim of a cruel delusion. You have been the innocent, unsophisticated plaything of a vicious parasite upon our glorious nation—a low, vile, degraded *Jew*.

"But there, there, my dearest Margarete, do not tremble so. You need never again have fear of this outrageous wretch. I promise to protect you. Upon my sacred word of honor, I shall protect you against any further insult from him.

"If necessary, I can—and will—invoke the laws of Nürnberg against this Hebrew who would thus destroy you. These laws have been promulgated and will be executed relentlessly against any and every Semite who threatens the debasement of the womanhood of Germany, according to the Nürnberg decree, any Jew who dares to marry an Aryan woman is liable to punishment by *death*.

"Stop trembling so violently, Margarete! Come, my darling, I shall help you. Together we will get rid of this terrible scourge which threatens your whole future. Just a little patience on your part, with fortitude and high resolve, and soon you will be filling your rightful place in Germany—the place to which your beauty, your intelligence, your charm, your *Aryan birth* so abundantly entitles you. Yes, your place—as one of the First Ladies of our great Nazi Super-State. As one of the leading exemplars of pure Aryan womanhood. As one of the glorious future mothers of our glorious Nazi Supermen. The whole power of Nazi Germany is behind me, at my immediate call, for your safeguarding. So good night, my dearest Margarete. Good night! And sweetest dreams!"

With the last ounce of strength that she possessed, shaken like a reed in the wind, she lifted herself from the chair and started up the stairway, utterly weak and unutterably weary. She attempted to drag the suitcase behind her. Without a word von Wolfmacht quietly but commandingly seized it from her hand and bounded ahead of her to the top, setting the case down at the head of the stairs. Then he turned and quickly descended, meeting Gretel face-to-face on the landing midway between the two sections of the staircase.

Gretel avoided his eyes and was just about to pass him in silence and continue her way upwards, when suddenly a new horror confronted her.

High on the wall above the landing, at the turning of the stairs, there hung a long, gilded picture frame. Always from Gretel's earliest remembrance this had contained a portrait of her mother in her wedding dress. But now her mother's likeness was gone. In its place there was a life-size painting, in oils, of *Adolf Hitler*.

He was in full army uniform, the most conspicuous part of which was the red armband whereupon was blazoned the sinister black swastika. His face, under the military cap, wore an expression of arrogant taciturnity and ruthless cruelty.

As Gretel recoiled, aghast, she saw von Wolfmacht suddenly drop upon one knee before the picture. Raising his right arm high in the Nazi salute, he emitted a vociferous "HEIL HITLER!"

The effect upon her was dynamic. Instantaneously she was electrified into new vitality, steeled into new lionlike courage and ferocity. With a daring born of righteous, white-hot anger, she accosted the Nazi squarely, as he rose to his feet, and turned blazing eyes upon him. Unrestrained now by either fear or prudence, she poured out a flood of fury.

"Konstantin von Wolfmacht! What is the meaning of this infamous outrage? Wherever did this iniquitous thing come from—this portrait of Adolf Hitler? What is it doing in my *father's house*? And what are *you* doing here? I demand an answer! And who are all those ruffianly men you have brought in with you? What is the reason for all this wild disorder? Here! In the home of Pastor Martin Luther von Ludwig! My own beloved father! What is the meaning of this unwarranted invasion? I demand an answer!

"And *who* put that shameful picture in this frame? It must be removed at once! I insist! I will not have it! It is an outrage—a wicked outrage! It is a most unholy desecration!"

As an SS Elite Guard officer—as an ardent disciple of Hitler—it was not von Wolfmacht's turn to let go a torrent of rage. In the full dignity and authority of his exalted rank he towered over his accuser menacingly. The erstwhile show of tenderness was gone completely. The mask was off. The Nazi stood forth in his true colors, brazenly.

"Stop instantly! I command you! How dare you call the portrait of our glorious Fuehrer an 'outrage' or a 'desecration'? How *dare* you! Do you realize what you are saying—or to whom you are saying it? I warn you! Be very careful of your words or you will find yourself in serious difficulty with the authorities—as a traitor to our Nazi State!

"Now, if you will calm yourself, you wild hyena, I shall be happy to explain to you the meaning of everything you see tonight within this house. Doubtless it will be painful to you to hear it, but it is better that you know the entire truth. So hear me, my dear Fräulein von Ludwig, quite carefully." He stood a few paces away from Gretel, his arms folded, his head thrown back, a look of contempt and cold disdain upon his foxlike face. Gretel quailed before his steely eyes. Once again she felt herself near collapse.

"Are you ready?" he began tormentingly. "All right, then, listen to me. You want to know how it was that this portrait of our beloved Fuehrer was hung here. It was *I*. I hung it here myself, this morning."

"You? *You?*" Gretel choked convulsively. "How dared you? What right had you? What possible right to intrude within our home—to violate its most sacred privacy and honor?"

"What right? I had every right. And I assure you there was no intrusion, no violation of the 'most sacred privacy and honor' of your home. Because—you may as well know the truth at once, however distressing it may be to you—this is your home no longer! For no longer is this house the property of Pastor Martin Luther von Ludwig, your so highly honored and honorable father. By his treasonable utterances against our Fuehrer and against our Nationalist Socialist Party, he has forfeited all his possessions to the State. And so, as I have already told you, I hung this picture here myself—this morning. A hard time I had of it, too"—he chuckled reminiscently—"for an old woman tried her best to stop me."

"Klara Kronin! Our honored housekeeper! Where is she?" Gretel demanded.

Von Wolfmacht shrugged his shoulders insolently. "How should I know? All I do know is that she is no longer here. I sent her away. *You* are here tonight as my most welcome and highly honored guest."

"Then I shall leave this house at once!" Gretel cried out in horror. "Let me pass! How dare you! I tell you, *let me go!*"

"Ah, no, you do *not* go! You stay right here! But as my most welcome guest, I do assure you. And so, I bid you a fond good night."

"Wait!" he repeated, laying a detaining hand upon her arm, "Before you leave, another kiss, my sweet." He drew her, aghast and writhing, again within his arms in close embrace and pressed a passionate caress upon her lips. "Ah, my lovely Margarete," he murmured, rapidly veering once again to tender tone, "our *betrothal* kiss!"

With superhuman force she tore herself away from him in

furious anger. His reaction was one of insulted dignity coupled, at the same time, with willful determination. "Very well, then!" he addressed her harshly, "resist me if you can! For remember, my beautiful, proud queen—remember what I have just told you: I am *Master* of this house. And this is where you stay tonight. And—never forget this—behind me is the full might of Nazi Germany and of Adolf Hitler.

"And I want you to understand this—quite perfectly, without any mistake whatsoever: I have fully made up my mind. My purpose is fixed, unalterable. You are the woman I am going to marry. If I had any doubt of it before, I have become convinced tonight that no other woman in all Germany, in all the world, could so superbly grace the position of wife to Konstantin von Wolfmacht. If my mind had entertained the slightest question of that fact, just these last five minutes have settled it forever. For in your rage you are magnificent! You look like the very Goddess of Thunder! You are a true daughter of the Vikings—a perfect Aryan! You will make a glorious mother of Nazi Supermen!

"And so, my beloved one, we are betrothed." He drew her as if again he would embrace her. But suddenly she seemed to be invested with an aura of protection—an invisible wall of holy defense which even he, von Wolfmacht, realized he dare not try to penetrate. He retreated several steps, his arms folded rigidly, and stared at her in silent wonder.

But as she turned away from him, sick with loathing, and rushed stumbling up the stairs, he found his voice—his aplomb—and flung after her one parting, petrifying shot: "*Gute Nacht,* my darling Margarete! Auf Wiedersehen! But until tomorrow only. Tomorrow morning I proclaim you as my bride. At high noon, in the Domkirche of Berlin, you will become my wife."

Chapter 15

Rendezvous with Death

Paralyzed with horror, Gretel reached her room. It directly faced the stairway. Shuddering as she closed the door, her last glimpse outside of it was of von Wolfmacht still standing upon the platform beneath the portrait of Adolf Hitler, his eyes straining after her retreating figure with a sinister glint of triumph and of proud possession.

Breathless, she turned the key in the lock and silently slid the bolt above it. A dart of terror shot through her. She seized the knob and tried the door. It was rigidly tight. The lock, the bolt, were strong. The breath returned to her body. But her heart still pounded so wildly that she nearly strangled. She feared she was going to swoon.

The room was in darkness save for the bright beams of the full moon streaming through the casement window and for the reflected light from fresh snow upon the ground. Dim rays of electric light also filtered in from the hall through narrow panels of glass, curtained with heavy mesh, on either side of her door. By the combined illumination Gretel tiptoed to the center of the floor, where, for several moments, she stood transfixed with anguish. She clasped and unclasped her hands in desperation. Her whole body swayed back and forth convulsively beneath the terrific tumult of her spirit.

Then suddenly, in sheer exhaustion, she flung herself face downwards upon her bed and broke into a wild torrent of sobbing, the frenzied nerves giving away at last. She moaned in terror, in agony, in complete despair, and buried her head deeply into the pillows to smother the sound.

She tried to think consecutively. But it was impossible. Her brain was on fire. Her heart was ice and stone. The bed rocked under her heavy groaning.

She lay thus for perhaps an hour. And then, at last, utterly prostrated, mercifully she dropped asleep. It was for a few moments only, but even this brief period of unconsciousness had a beneficial effect upon her. She awoke more tranquilized. Dazed at first, gradually as she became oriented, the brain confusion cleared, and reason once again began to function. The anguish of her heart remained, but despair had given way to hope. The passionate sobbing had ceased. In its stead there was soft weeping only—interspersed with occasional low moans: "Mother . . . Father . . . Joseph . . . Oh, my beloved Joseph! *Joseph!*"

The tears effected a gentle ministry of healing to the so sorely wounded spirit. The awful tension eased. Gradually a sense of peace stole softly over her. For, penetrating even the deep agony, the consciousness of God's presence and protecting power again became vividly real. Intently she listened for the dear, familiar "still, small voice." And in the silence of the moonlit room, as she now lay perfectly relaxed in childlike trust, the Spirit breathed into her stricken heart His own sweet words of consolation.

In quietness and in confidence shall be your strength. This was the promise from the Word of God that next flashed vividly upon Gretel's mind. And joyfully she realized that His own quietness and confidence had been swiftly granted to her. Thus consciously did she realize new strength. Consciously did she feel herself endued with power stronger than all the power of the enemy. She knew that she was strengthened with might by His Spirit in her inmost being.

As Gretel continued to pray, suddenly an outburst of raucous voices sounded from the living room, directly beneath her. The Nazis evidently were taking their departure.

Noiselessly she slipped off the bed, threw her nurse's cape about her, and tiptoed to the casement window. It was slightly open. Through it, in the moonlight, she could see the officers emerging from the house, one after another, wrapping their greatcoats tightly around them, for the February night was cold. Without exception the men walked with intoxicated steps, albeit with their characteristic Nazi arrogance and pride. Gretel watched them intently, cautiously screened from view behind the casement draperies. Three of them—one of whom she recognized as von Wolfmacht—returned to the house, while the others drove off in their high-powered, shrieking racing cars. And then she heard the front door violently slammed shut.

With strained ears she heard the few remaining voices downstairs, immediately below her room, but she could not discern how many there were, nor what they were saying. There was merely an indistinct buzz of conversation, with a tone of rising asperity. The buzz increased in volume and contention, but still Gretel could not clearly hear the words.

As she listened in the tense midnight silence, suddenly a story, long forgotten, flashed vividly before her memory. How very curious, she reflected, that this particular story should return to her at such a time as this present awful hour. How entirely irrelevant it seemed. But return it did undoubtedly, strikingly, insistently.

The dramatic tale had to do with the Civil War in the United States of America. The heroine was a beautiful, brilliant Southern woman, a true daughter of the Confederacy. She was the unhappy prisoner of a Northern general, in her own colonial plantation mansion—which had been commandeered by him for the housing of a group of his Union officers.

Upstairs, ignominiously locked by him within her own private boudoir, directly above the room downstairs in which the general and his aides were holding conference, the mistress of the mansion heard distinctly through the open chimney flue—which served both the upper and the lower fireplaces—this leader of the Northern troops discussing with the staff a daring plot to seize a certain strategic stronghold of the Confederate army.

Breathlessly, in the darkness, through the early hours of the night, the proud Southern woman listened to the details of the proposed Northern raid. And then in the silent dawn, when at last the enemy were sleeping heavily in rooms upon the lower floor, she made a miraculous exit from her home—through an open window and down a thick climbing vine—and a still more miraculous entrance into the Southern army headquarters and into the very presence of the Confederate commanding officer.

And there she told her story. Her strange, impassioned words, considered pityingly, at first, as the ravings of a demented patriot, finally were recognized as a true report. Rapid action ensued, and the day was saved for the Confederacy.

As Gretel pondered this long-forgotten tale of far away and long ago, swiftly her sensitive spirit discerned that it was not at all irrelevant to the present situation. It was definitely pertinent thereto. Assuredly it was sent of God—directly recalled to Gretel by His Spirit for her immediate inspiration and instruction.

With fast-beating heart she crept to the fireplace and knelt upon the fireless hearth. She crouched low that her ear might be as close as possible to the chimney wall. The result was immediate and electrifying. With perfect clearness she could now hear every word the men were speaking.

She caught, first of all, her brother Bernhardt's voice. And he was pronouncing her own name. His tone was one of utter contempt and cruelty.

"Gretel, my sister, is an awful fool!"

"Not any longer, Bernie!" It was von Wolfmacht who made reply. His tone was jubilant, exultant.

"Not any longer? Whatever do you mean?"

"I mean"—von Wolfmacht answered him with proud satisfaction—"I mean I agree with you perfectly that your sweet sister *was* an awful fool—ever to allow herself to be duped by that damnable Jew. But she has come to her senses, and that is all over now, thank heaven!"

"All over with?" Bruno echoed in astonishment. "What do you mean by *that*?"

"I mean by that"—von Wolfmacht measured each syllable impressively"—"I mean, my dear brothers von Ludwig, that I have the honor of announcing your sister Margarete's betrothal to myself! I am marrying her, in the Domkirche, at high noon tomorrow!"

"You, marrying Gretel tomorrow!" both brothers exclaimed in astounded chorus. "This is welcome news indeed!" Bernhardt added joyously.

"Magnificent!" Bruno seconded. "We are delighted!"

"Thank you both." Von Wolfmacht smiled complacently. "I knew that we would win the day."

"But however did it happen? Yours and Gretel's engagement, I mean. And when?" In blank amazement Bernhardt pressed his question. There was a shade of doubt in his tone.

"When did it happen? An hour ago only. And how? Ah, that was a very easy matter, I assure you. On my authority as oberoffizier of the SS Elite Guard of Berlin, I simply claimed your sister for our Nazi State."

"But was she quite willing? Did she herself consent?" Bruno's question held a note of distinct uneasiness.

"Willing? Consent?" von Wolfmacht echoed contemptuously. "What does a woman's consent or willingness have to do in a matter of this kind, when the interests of our Nazi Party, of our Nazi government, are our chief concern?

"You both know me to be a man of quick action. Once I make a major decision, I put it into immediate execution. And so, when your charming sister came here tonight, and I had an unexpected and most favorable opportunity to talk with her at considerable length, I informed her promptly—and I now inform you officially—our marriage will take place at high noon tomorrow. It will immediately follow and will conclude our Nazi full-dress military parade tomorrow morning."

The reaction of both of Gretel's brothers to von Wolfmacht's amazing utterance was stunned silence. Their high commanding officer's entire purpose and program was so breathtaking, so daring, so absolutely ruthless—it defied not only all precedent, but also all possible opposition.

Timidly, therefore, almost apologetically, Bruno essayed merely one objection. Lamely he suggested one problem in the way of the successful accomplishment of von Wolfmacht's totalitarian decree. "But what about young Rothschild—our sister's accepted suitor? She has been engaged to him for years. Has she consented to give him up? Would he ever give her up without a desperate battle first? Pardon me," he added quickly, as von Wolfmacht emitted a vicious oath, "but I confess I do not understand this aspect of the question. Just how does Joseph Rothschild fit into this new picture?"

Von Wolfmacht's tone as he replied was one of rage.

"How does that accursed Jew fit into a purely Aryan picture? He does not fit into it at all! He will be completely eliminated from your sister's life. Do not think for one moment that I have neglected *this* trifling detail in plan. I have made all my arrangements very carefully.

"I have already instructed my two lieutenants, Füchs and Reinfelder. You saw me talking to them outside, perhaps, just before they drove away. They have my orders to assemble twenty carefully picked Nazis here at this house at four o'clock tomorrow—no, this morning. You, Bernhardt and Bruno, will join them. We all will then drive in army trucks to the Rothschild mansion and apprehend our prisoner—young Dr. Joseph—at five o'clock. And then we will drive back with him, manacled and blindfolded, to the Brandenburger Thor. And there, in front of the von Bismarck statue, he will be properly taken care of—by the firing squad. As an enemy of our Nazi Party; as a traitor to our Nazi State; above all, as a *Jew* who has dared to attempt union with one of our pure Aryan women: at six o'clock in the morning, on this eleventh of February, 1937, Joseph Rothschild will be . . . liquidated."

Liquidated! Joseph! "Oh, dear God, *no!*" Gretel gasped. Her senses reeled in agony, in horror. She still was kneeling on the hearth, close to the chimney flue through which she had heard the sentence of death to her beloved. She sat back upon the floor, as cold as a stone. Her heart was completely numb—frozen with this paralyzing new grief and terror.

"Oh, God, save him!" she groaned. "*Save* him!"

She must *act*. And act quickly! But, oh, in just what way, and how? Again, completely helpless, she flung herself upon Omniscience and Omnipotence. God alone could give her the desperately needed wisdom. He alone could give her strength.

She still was sitting on the floor, her hands clasped about her knees. Once more she inclined her ear tensely toward the open chimney flue. And again she heard the voices in the room below quite clearly. The words came to her with perfect distinctness.

Again it was von Wolfmacht who was speaking. "Well, come on, men," he said commandingly, "it's after one; let's get upstairs to bed. We must have a few hours' sleep, at least. We have a tremendous day ahead of us. How very happy

Herr Hitler will be when I tell him there is one less Jew in the world!

"Perhaps I shall take my lovely bride along with me to see him. That would make a charming honeymoon—a few days with our glorious Fuehrer in his majestic mountain stronghold.

"But come! We must not delay any longer. We must get off to bed for a couple of hours' sleep, anyway. Remember! We all meet here in this room at four o'clock precisely for our pleasant little sunrise party at the Brandenburger Thor at six with our dear Jewish friend—Dr. Joseph Rothschild."

The heavy footsteps began to ascend the stairway. Gretel felt as if every drop of blood was draining from her body, so ghastly was the horror of it all.

But still another horror suddenly convulsed her when, cautiously tiptoeing to her door, she peered through one of the narrow, curtained panes of glass that framed it—she herself invisible to outside view. She could see the men quite clearly as they emerged from the lower flight of stairs upon the midway platform. There were five of them—von Wolfmacht first, then Bruno and Bernhardt and two other officers whom she did not know. The five sounded like twenty-five.

There was one last awful moment of agony and suspense as the five men ascended the upper flight of stairs—then paused at the top, just outside Gretel's door. Across its upper panel, in the old-fashioned German house, there was a sliding bar of heavy wrought iron. Gretel's breath froze in her throat when she saw von Wolfmacht come close to the door and raise his arm . . . and then heard him shoot the bar forward into the opposite slot in fast-locked position . . . then try the doorknob to make sure. Her heart skipped a beat . . . and then it pounded furiously as the men, after a curt *"Gute Nacht"* to each other, passed on to their respective rooms. Von Wolfmacht was the last to go. He lingered for a full moment first, surveying the barred door with gloating. A triumphant evil light glinted in his eyes. His captive was safe inside—imprisoned securely until noon tomorrow.

Gretel remained absolutely motionless, scarcely daring to breathe until the last retreating footsteps had died away; until the last voice was hushed; until through closed doors and the long hallway she could hear, finally, the heavy snoring that betokened deep sleep.

And then with electric swiftness she became alert and a-thrill. All the paralyzed faculties aroused suddenly to new and conscious power. Instantaneously the fevered brain became calm and clear and keen. The nerves became steady and strong. Fear retreated. In its place there was cool-headed courage and determination.

Again she glanced at her watch in the moonlight. It was now twenty minutes to two. In only a little more than two hours—at four o'clock—the Nazis here in the house would be awake and meeting downstairs with their returning companions. At five they all would arrive at the Rothschild mansion. At *six*! One last shudder shook Gretel from head to foot. But she repressed it sternly. She dared not weaken now. Her will became iron. Her brain was electric. All was taking form at last, just when it was to be done. Before ever six o'clock should strike—before five o'clock—Joseph must be well upon his way toward the German border! Toward Palestine!

Gretel now was standing in the center of the room. She could always do her deepest thinking in upright position. She lifted her head heavenward in rapt and reverent awe, as if to catch the slightest whisper of the Spirit's voice. With the moonlight streaming full upon her face and transforming her lustrous hair into a halo of glory, never had she looked so beautiful. Upon her countenance there was now an expression of peace. In her eyes there glowed the light of exalted vision—the light of high and holy resolve, of self-surrendering devotion. The light of *love*.

The plan was now complete in every detail. And Gretel knew that it was perfect. She knew it was God's perfect will for her and Joseph.

Quickly she emptied the small suitcase she had brought with her, replacing it with a large one which she drew noiselessly from her clothes closet. This, she knew, was all that she could possibly take with her. Therefore she must select carefully from among all her treasures only such articles as the case would contain, above her strictly necessary clothing and her toilet accessories. The rest she must leave behind—forever. For with her keen discernment she perceived clearly that she was bidding this precious room—this whole dear, dear home—her last good-bye. It was hers no longer—nor her saintly father's. it was now the possession of their cruel enemy, Adolf Hitler, who had stolen it from them ruthlessly.

A wave of bitter sorrow surged suddenly over her with almost overwhelming force. A flood of memories welled up within her heart—all the tender associations of her childhood and her girlhood connected with this very room. But sternly she repressed them. She had no time to indulge in memories, however sweet. She dared not dwell upon the past. She must go swiftly, resolutely forward. Life and death hung in the balance by the margin of an eyelash. And the life or the death of the one, above all others, without whom her life would be nought but living death.

Rapidly, therefore, she performed the most heartbreaking task of choosing among her cherished treasures those few that she might take with her; and of rejecting the far larger number that she must relinquish. She dared not turn on any light. The moon alone must still suffice. By its illumination she searched through her desk, her closet, her dresser drawers, her bookshelves—and then packed tightly into the big suitcase the articles of final choice.

First of all, there was her Bible. And then—following the few essential articles of clothing and her toilet kit—there were the photos of her family. Her father and her mother, her two younger brothers. And then—Bernhardt and Bruno. Oh, God, Bernhardt and Bruno! She must take their pictures, surely. How greatly now would these two poor boys need her prayers! Her grief and shame for them were inexpressible.

Next, ten or a dozen only of her choicest books; a few small pictures from her wall, together with various trinkets and other articles of particularly deep association; the packages of Joseph's and of her father's and her mother's letters; her leather writing case filled with other letters and important papers; her nursing kit; her camera; her flashlight; and the large suitcase now was full to overflowing. Quickly she closed and locked and strapped it.

Gretel bathed her face and hands and brushed and rearranged her hair. Then deftly she changed from the house dress she had been wearing to a fresh white nurse's uniform.

From her dark pumps to her white, low-heeled hospital shoes, over which she drew her high galoshes, she was ready. Finally, over her dark blue nurse's cape and hood she prepared to make her move for freedom.

Her heart beat high with trepidation as she prepared to get herself and her suitcase safely out of the house. The suitcase was a major problem. But even this one important part of the entire intricate plan had been carefully thought through in advance. Noiselessly Gretel withdrew the sheets from her bed. Then seating herself upon it and taking a pair of scissors from her purse, she began—still perfectly noiselessly—to cut the linen into strips. She dared not tear them off, lest even that slight sound awaken the sleeping Nazis. She braided and knotted the strips together to form a strong rope. One end of this she tied securely to the handle of the suitcase, carried the case across the room, and then—breathlessly—she lifted it over the sill of the open casement window and slowly, laboriously, lowered it until it reached the snowy ground below.

And now, at last, for the most precarious operation, thus far, of the entire dangerous adventure—her own safe exit unobserved. But this also had been worked out previously with most painstaking care.

The door, she knew, was bolted on the outside. But in any case, even had she been able to open it, that means of exit was ruled out. For she dared not risk a possible creaking board within the hall floor or the staircase, or the opening and closing of the heavy street door downstairs. No, there was but one way out—the sturdy vine! But that way, she felt perfectly assured, had been directly revealed to her by the Holy Spirit—through the so strangely recalled story of the Southern woman's escape from her home, beleaguered by the enemy, in the selfsame manner.

And thus, with strong faith in her God—albeit with much trembling of the flesh in this entirely unprecedented and most difficult feat—Gretel gazed shudderingly downward upon the leafless ladder. She turned her head for one last moment and looked back into her room. But she dared not linger. Time was flying on too rapidly. It now was nearly three o'clock. But for still another reason she dared not stay—lest she be overwhelmed in that final moment of departure by the flood of tender memory and sorrow that, already, was welling strongly up within her heart as—forever—she bade farewell to her beloved home.

Only one last brief glance, therefore; a quickly breathed final prayer for help in this immediate desperate need; and for courage to turn her back upon the past completely and go resolutely forward all the way of God's appointment. And then, by a supreme effort of muscle and nerve and will, the brave girl climbed out over the windowsill, firmly grasped the heavy vine—and slowly, painfully, began her perilous descent. The rough tendrils pierced her hands. Twice her feet faltered and nearly slipped. All the way down there was a terrifying sense of being pursued and recaptured. But at length she triumphed! The ground was reached in safety. Her feet sank into the soft snow. The first stage of the dangerous adventure was successfully achieved. She was on her way to Joseph! On her way to warn him in time, to rescue him from the frightful fate that so soon now would be sweeping down upon him.

She untied the braided linen rope from the suitcase and left it lying in the snow—a token to von Wolfmacht. And then, with the heavy suitcase in her hand, she started forward upon her fateful purpose.

She walked up the street and around the corner to the service station where she had left her car. She was comforted with the assurance that she would find it in perfect condition and well supplied with petrol for all the long journey that would lie ahead of it. Moreover, so far away from the house there would be no danger of her being heard when she started the engine.

One possible awful peril might confront her at the service station. She might find there some Nazi officer who would, of course, detain and question her. For Nazi officers were everywhere at every hour, day or night. But, happily, when she reached the station, no one was there except the night attendant—a fine old man, intensely anti-Nazi in his convictions—well-known to Gretel for years, and always friendly and most helpful to her.

Was Fräulein von Ludwig—as he always addressed her most courteously—going out on duty? "Yes," Gretel assured quite truthfully.

"Not a serious case, I hope?" he asked with genuine concern.

"Yes, very serious," she replied gravely. "A case of life or death."

At Gretel's request the attendant put into the trunk of her car an extra five-gallon can of petrol, carefully covering it with a heavy rubber blanket, as protection to anything else within the trunk. Also at Gretel's most urgent request, he gave her a sheaf of his newest maps—a very fine map of Germany, and maps of all the other European countries.

Thus supplied, she started off upon her fateful journey. She drove as rapidly as traffic laws would allow, choosing always the less-frequented streets. For always there was the fear of the Gestapo halting and searching her car and interrogating her. And irresistibly there was still the strong sense of being pursued by the frustrated, infuriated von Wolfmacht and his Nazi henchmen.

At the intersection of the street on which she was driving and the main Berlin-Munich highway, Gretel knew there was a small quick-lunch shop, open all night for the accommodation of motoring tourists. Here she stopped and ordered for herself, first, a bowl of hot soup and a sandwich, for she had had no food whatever since the previous noon, and she was feeling weak and faint.

She ate them ravenously at a small rear table; and then she purchased a ready-prepared lunch basket, requesting the proprietor also to fill her half-gallon thermos jug with strong black coffee. Then to these provisions she added a carton of various foods selected quickly from the well-stocked tourist shelf: canned soups and meats and milk, half a dozen small packages of cheese and butter, little sacks of sugar and salt, a large bag of oranges and apples, and a dozen long bread sticks. The obliging owner of the shop carefully packed all these supplies in the trunk of her car—as far removed as possible from the can of petrol. He wondered curiously at Gretel's urgency and haste and her apparent great agitation, but politely he said nothing.

Once again Gretel started off upon the road. She was now on the last lap of her feverish trip to the Rothschild mansion—to intercept Joseph's rendezvous with death.

The way seemed interminable, for still there was that dreadful sensation of being pursued. Added to that was the fearful nervous tension in the race against time. It was now almost three thirty. In only half an hour more the Nazis would be assembling in the manse . . . And after that . . . ! Almost in a frenzy Gretel raced the car at still greater speed.

At last the mansion came in view, and soon the familiar bronze gates were reached. But instead of entering them and driving down through the long avenue of oak trees to the front entrance, Gretel turned off her headlights and followed the outside roadway bordering the high brick wall until she came to the secluded road at the rear of the house. She traversed this slowly until she reached the entrance to the spruce grove. Here she turned her car until it faced due westward, toward the Holland border. Then very cautiously she backed it into the dense grove until it was entirely concealed from all possible outward view. And then—with no light save her flashlight, and the moonbeams faintly filtering through the tall trees upon the snow—she continued moving the car backwards along the narrow path through the trees, as close as possible to the hidden cottage with its secret entrance to the underground tunnel.

And there at last, her precarious journey ended, she turned off the engine—first making perfectly sure that everything was in readiness for a quick restarting.

Getting out of the car and once more dragging the heavy suitcase behind her, she plowed her way dizzily through the snow, the remaining distance to the cottage—and thence through the tunnel, now lighted only by her flashlight. All its entire length she seemed still to hear the onrushing footsteps of the Nazis—still to feel von Wolfmacht's fingers clutching at her throat.

She remained before the secret sliding-panel door long enough to draw from her chamois safety bag the small purse of money concealed therein. And then she drew out one of her three most sacred treasures: her mother's wedding ring. This she slipped upon her finger, gazing at it for a moment with fascinated awe. For the twentieth time she glanced at her wristwatch. *A quarter to four!* Oh, she groaned, she must hurry . . . *hurry!*

She paused for only one more moment—that she might gather strength and courage. She prayed one final agonizing prayer: "O, my Father, hold me! O God, save Joseph! Save him, Lord, oh, save him! O Father, save us *both*! Shelter us beneath Thine almighty wings. And keep us in the center of Thy perfect will. In Jesus' name. Amen."

And then she grasped the door in reverential trust, her eyes shining with the light of high and holy purpose. That fateful door! Beyond it was *Joseph*—her heart's best beloved. Beyond it lay her heroic mission to rescue him from a hideous death. Yea, more! Beyond that door of destiny lay the strange new life to which she was now committing herself deliberately, irrevocably, proudly—yea, even with joy inexpressible: the life of identification with Joseph's suffering Hebrew people.

And thus, with no less glorious a spirit than that of Joan of Arc riding forth to the defense of her beloved France, did this superb young German girl—this pure Aryan born and bred, this proud direct descendant of Germany's Martin Luther—rush forward in the intensity of her ardor to the defense and rescue of *her* beloved Israel. For not only Joseph, her affianced husband, but his whole Jewish family—nay, his entire Jewish race—did Margarete Luther von Ludwig envision as ruthlessly appointed victims of Nazi violence and hate.

Chapter 16

Fearful Plot

On that same cold winter night in Berlin, within the lordly house of Rothschild, three men lay sleepless.

Dr. Rothschild—his brave courage of the daylight hours completely fled before his unnerving persistent insomnia—now moaned and tossed upon his bed in a torture of mental confusion and distress. He viewed his world as absolutely shattered and in ruins. And before the task of reconstruction he felt himself utterly helpless and hopeless. Almost his very faith in God was trembling in the balance.

Pastor von Ludwig, an exile from his home and church, in hiding from his tormentors, also was wide-eyed. But, relaxed in body and in mind, he was resting peacefully. His world was too wrecked, but his glorious faith remained undaunted. Over all the awful sorry his spirit rose triumphant. As he lay, staring into the blackness of the refugee shelter and into what seemed the immeasurably greater blackness of the future, still could he sing within his heart: *Ein' feste burg ist unser Gott.*

And Joseph! Poor, unhappy Joseph! *His* brave spirit of optimism—his glad hopes for the days ahead so joyously declared to Gretel and their fathers on that last wonderful evening they had spent together here within his home—that buoyant spirit was now, in the long, wakeful hours of darkness, totally submerged beneath an irresistible, swift wave of terrible depression.

Three splendid men. And each one battling alone, through the silent watches of the night, with his own heavy grief—when, instantaneously, upon the ears of all three there fell a startling sound: the ringing of the alarm bell from the underground:

Clang . . . clang . . . clang . . .
C-l-a-n-g
C-l-a-n-g

Breathlessly, their hearts pounding with sudden fear, all three men sprang from their beds, swiftly donned their dressing robes and noiseless slippers, seized their flashlights, and rushed from their respective places of seclusion. Then in utter silence, from their three separate directions, they converged upon the recreation room and its portentous tunnel door, whence the alarm bell still was ringing.

From his cubicle within the near-adjacent shelter, Pastor von Ludwig was the first to reach the door. For an instant he stood before it, perfectly still, keenly listening. And then in hoarse voice he called out furtively: "Who comes here?" Breathless with suspense, he heard the low, imperative reply:

"Oh, Father dearest, is that you? It's Margarete! Open quickly, *quickly*! Let me in! *SHALOM!*"

Pastor von Ludwig's heart beat violently as he recognized his daughter's voice—as he detected in her impassioned outcry unmistakable warning of impending peril. By this time Dr. Rothschild and Joseph also had reached the scene, and they, too, had recognized the voice and its alarming tone.

In a chorus of mingled amazement, joy, and fear—all, however, most cautiously suppressed—each of the three men cried out his own ardent welcome of their so strangely come nocturnal messenger:

"Margarete, my dear child!"

"My little sweetheart, Gretel!"

"Oh, my darling!"

But it was Joseph who, rushing forward, slid back the secret panel and drew his beloved from the underground tunnel into the dimly lit recreation room and into his convulsive, glad embrace. He scanned her face anxiously. It was white and drawn with anguish.

"Gretel, my precious one!" he exclaimed in sudden terror. "Tell me, sweetheart, what is it? What is wrong?" he pleaded tenderly.

"Oh, Joseph, Joseph! Oh, my beloved, hurry! Oh, hurry, *hurry!* There is not a moment to lose. Oh, save him! Save him!" she shrieked imploring to their two fathers. "The Nazis—"

"My daughter!" Pastor von Ludwig commanded almost sternly. "What brings you here . . . and in the dead of night? There must be some reason. Tell us what it is, at once!"

Gretel was powerless to speak, so awful was her fear, her grief. Dr. Rothschild quietly interposed. "Wait, Martin," he said authoritatively. "She is exhausted. She is under frightful strain." He drew her gently from Joseph's embrace and led her to a couch. He sat down beside her, placing his arm around her soothingly. "Rest here, dear child, for a few moments. Then you can tell us what it is that troubles you so deeply."

"Oh, it is all so awful!" she exclaimed in anguish. "It . . . it is *Joseph*! He is in fearful danger! He must get out of Germany at once! The Nazis are planning to kill him! They are coming here at five o'clock to arrest him and take him to the Brandenburger Thor! At six he will be *shot*! By a Nazi firing squad. Oh, save him! Save him! Oh, my Joseph!"

Again Gretel's frenzied nerves gave way. Her voice rose to a near shriek. She sprang quickly to her feet and flung her arms around her beloved—fiercely, protectingly, as if she would shield him against his cruel enemies to her own last ounce of strength, to her own last breath.

All three of her hearers stood rigid with horror. Joseph's face blanched. For an awful moment there was tense silence. Then Pastor von Ludwig burst out passionately, "Joseph? Kill him? Whoever would dare to?" Blazing anger and cold fear together nearly overmastered him. The two Rothschilds, father and son, gripped hands despairingly. The father groaned aloud.

"But why?" Pastor von Ludwig continued insistently. "Why do they want to murder Joseph? What is their charge against him?"

"Their charge?" Gretel repeated bitterly. "He is a *Jew*. And he is going to marry *me*. They have found it out. And for the crime of a Jew daring to marry an Aryan, the Nazi penalty now is *death*! That is why they are going to murder my lover, because he, a Jew, aspires to marry a German."

"But, my dearest Gretel . . ." Again Dr. Rothschild assumed

quiet, firm command of the entire tense situation. "What makes you believe this? And how did you become aware of their design to kill him?"

"Because I overheard them talking."

"You overheard them talking? You overheard whom?"

"Konstantin von Wolfmacht—their *oberoffizier*—and a number of his SS Elite Guard. I tell you, Dr. Rothschild—father . . . Joseph darling . . . it is true! They have it all planned out with diabolical precision. I tell you they are coming here at five o'clock! Joseph is to be shot at six! And it now is almost four! Oh, hurry. *Hurry!*"

"But Margarete, wait one moment," her father demanded. "Tell us, my daughter, *where* did you hear all this? Tell us exactly what has happened."

"I'll explain everything, Father, later. There isn't time now. I tell you, the Nazis are coming here at *five*! It is absolutely true! The Nazis are coming! Joseph must flee for his life! Go now quickly! Oh, Joseph, hurry, darling, hurry!"

But Joseph still stood rooted to the spot, completely stunned. In a very agony of fear, Gretel shoved him toward the stairway. "Oh, Joseph, *please*, beloved, go get dressed and packed!"

At last the frightful nightmare registered in Joseph's horrified brain. Manfully he regained his self-control, his courage. Drawing himself up strongly to full height, he turned Gretel and took her hands in both of his. He looked bravely, tenderly into her eyes. "Gretel, my darling, we are in God's hands. He will give deliverance. We must both be strong and unafraid. Yes, I shall get out of Germany at once, as God may lead. And you will follow me, beloved, as soon as possible. You all will follow me. Come, Father, I am ready."

They started up the stairway, arm in arm, the Hebrew father and his son—his beloved elder son, his firstborn, condemned to die at dawn.

Left alone with her father, Gretel buried her face upon his breast and wept piteously. He enfolded her gravely within his arms and stroked her beautiful hair with utmost gentleness. He then drew her toward the couch and seated himself beside her, holding her hand within his own with a firm, loving grasp.

"Now tell me, my daughter. I must know everything. Where was it that you heard this fearful plot?" Again he pressed the question she had before evaded.

Gretel hesitated. She looked at her father with his dear, sad, aging face. Could she add to his cup of sorrow this further bitter draught—her report of the ruination of their home?

"Tell me, Margarete," he insisted firmly. "I have to understand the entire situation. Where did you overhear this Nazi plot to murder Joseph? Where and how?"

"In our home, dear Father," Gretel answered sorrowfully. "Or . . . I mean . . ." she continued in halting tone, "in what *was* our home. We have still more trouble, darling. I . . . I cannot bear to tell you . . ."

"Go on, my daughter. Do not try to spare me."

"Oh, Father! It is our dear home no longer. Adolf Hitler has commandeered it for the Nazis. It is now a neighborhood headquarters for his SS Elite Guard officers. Konstantin von Wolfmacht is in charge."

The silvery head bowed low in silent grief. But for a moment only. Bravely the saintly pastor of the Confessional Church of Germany raised his face to his daughter's, and with a smile of heavenly radiance, he answered her: *"It is the* L*ORD: let him do what seemeth him good."* And then he added triumphantly:

Let goods and kindred go,
This mortal life also:
The body they may kill:
God's truth abideth still,
His Kingdom is forever.

Calmly her father listened as Gretel recounted to him her terrible experience in their beloved home. As she told him of her dramatic discovery of the Nazis' murderous plot against Joseph, through the strange medium of the chimney flue, he cross-examined her closely. "You are perfectly sure, my daughter, that you overheard his words correctly?"

"Yes, Father. There is no possible doubt of it. He gave his men exact orders. They were to sleep for a couple of hours, then meet there again, in the living room, with the other Nazis who were to return at four o'clock. And they they were all to come here to arrest Joseph at five—and take him to the firing squad."

"But why, my child? Why? You are keeping something back from me, Margarete! I must insist upon knowing everything! What is von Wolfmacht's reason for attempting to dispose of Joseph because Joseph is going to marry you?"

"Oh, Father, the reason is too awful! Konstantin von Wolfmacht is determined to marry me *himself*!"

"Margarete!" the saintly man of God cried out in horror. "But you sent him word . . . I sent him word . . . that we absolutely refused to entertain his proposal for one moment!"

"But he will not accept our refusal. As the SS Elite Guard *oberoffizier*, he is commandeering me to be married to him at *high noon*, this very day! Oh, Father, save me! Save me, too! I am in danger more terrible than Joseph's!"

Astounded, Pastor von Ludwig looked at his daughter in dismay. Von Wolfmacht! Marry you! At high noon today! Whatever does this mean?"

"Oh, Father, it was all so ghastly! Von Wolfmacht is a monster! He enraged me beyond endurance. He said he was master in *our* house. He made me his prisoner. He locked me in my room. He insisted he was going to marry me himself. This very day. Just as soon as he had 'liquidated' Joseph!" Gretel rehearsed the several horrors in agonized gasps. And then again she cried out imploringly, "Oh, Father, save me! *Save* me! Oh, save us both! Oh, won't you, Father darling? Won't you?" She clung to him convulsively. Her voice chocked in her throat.

"Assuredly I will. My own beloved little daughter! I will indeed—to the very utmost of my power. But how . . . *how*?"

"Father!" Gretel implored him passionately. "Listen to me, dearest Father. I know how! God has revealed it to me plainly. There is just one way!"

"Yes? Yes?" he queried eagerly. "And what is that?"

"That way—the only possible way—is this: *you must marry me to Joseph!* Father! You must marry us right now! Oh, dearest Father, quickly, *quickly*—before von Wolfmacht gets here!"

Before her astounded parent could reply, Dr. Rothschild reentered the room, fully dressed. "Joseph will be down shortly; he is all ready to go," he announced sorrowfully. "Just now he is with his mother—for their final few moments together." He looked intently at his agitated guests. "What is it?" he exclaimed in instant alarm. "Is there anything further wrong?"

Pastor von Ludwig nodded his head gravely. Gretel turned toward the father of her heart's beloved in piteous appeal. Again she cried aloud her passionate entreaty. "Oh, dear Dr. Rothschild, you will help us also, will you not? I have just been telling Father he must marry Joseph and me at once—immediately—without a moment's delay. Oh, please, *please*, both of you! Oh, it is our only hope!"

The two fathers exchanged glances of dismay. Dr. Rothschild gazed searchingly, first at Gretel's face and then at her father's. The anguished utterance of his faithful pastor and friend, in reply to his gaze, fully enlightened him with startled suddenness.

"Benjamin! This whole affair is more terrible than anything we ever dreamed of! Von Wolfmacht is murdering your son in order that he himself can marry my daughter!" Briefly he recounted what Gretel had just told him. Dr. Rothschild groaned. "This is horrible, horrible! But surely, Martin, there must be a way out for our dear children. God will help us find it."

"God *has* helped us. We have already found it," Gretel insisted fervently. "I tell you that is the only way: Joseph and I must be married before he leaves. He has got to go," she moaned. "He dare not stay another half hour. And he dare not take me with him as he flees. But although we must be parted for a little while—only until it will be safe for me to follow him—at least we shall be married."

Reverently Pastor von Ludwig made reply. "Come!" he entreated. "We shall put this whole fearful crisis into our heavenly Father's hands. He will give us wisdom. He will give us comfort and courage and strength. Let us pray."

Humbly they knelt before their Lord. The saintly pastor lifted up his voice in passionate pleading:

"O God, our help in ages past, our hope for years to come, have mercy upon us . . . !"

No sooner had the two fathers and Gretel risen from their knees when Mrs. Rothschild burst suddenly upon the scene, followed by the bewildered Moische. "My darling, darling Gretel!" she cried excitedly. Tense with emotion, she crushed the lovely girl to her heart. "My darling, my darling!" she repeated hysterically. "Joseph has told me *everything*! You have come here to save his life already! From those dreadful Nazis! But my precious Joseph . . . my firstborn son . . . he has got to go away to hide from them! He has got to leave me! He has got to leave his mother!"

She turned suddenly toward her husband. "Benjamin, my dear one, what shall we do? Whatever shall we do without our Joseph?" She wrung her hands and wept in piteous appeal. Dr. Rothschild calmed her as only he knew how to do, while Pastor von Ludwig calmed the now-terrified Moische. Gretel withdrew to a corner by herself alone, wrapped in her own profound reflections.

And then noiselessly, but with the force of an electric shock, Joseph suddenly descended the stairway and stood silent in their midst.

Chapter 17

Hastened Vows

In the dimly lit room, he looked very pale, but his bearing was one of perfect pose and calm. He was dressed inconspicuously in a dark suit with dark tie and shoes. A gray topcoat was over his left arm, with a gray fedora in his hand. In his right hand he carried a suitcase. Upon his beautiful face there was a look of quiet strength; in his eyes, the peace that passeth understanding.

He stood for a moment in profound silence, gazing upon the faces, one after another, of all his loved ones. He set his suitcase down and threw his coat and hat upon the table. And then he walked over to Gretel, and gravely, quietly, he drew her into his arms and kissed her.

"My darling!" he murmured tenderly. "I must leave you, Gretel. But only for a little while. We are in God's hands, beloved. His will be done."

And then fondly he embraced his mother. She threw her arms around his neck and clung to him in desperation. "Oh, my Joseph! My beloved Joseph!" she moaned hysterically. "Whatever shall I do? They cannot, no, *no*, they cannot get you, those wicked, wicked Nazis! They cannot take you away from your own mother! My precious, darling boy!" She drew back and gazed into his eyes adoringly. Again she wrung her hands in anguish. Dr. Rothschild drew her gently into his own strong embrace, thus leaving Joseph and Gretel for their last sacred moments together alone. What they said, each to the other, none ever knew save only they themselves and God.

At length they rejoined their fathers, who stood, together with Mrs. Rothschild and Moische, across the room. By now, Gretel also—equally with Joseph—was controlled and strong.

"Joseph dearest," she admonished him quietly, "you must

hasten now to get away. Just as quickly as possible. It is a quarter after four. They are coming for you at five.

"Now listen carefully to the directions I know that God has shown to me so very clearly. When you leave, you will go through the tunnel and through the cottage into the grove. You will take my car—no, dear, I do not need it, but you do, most emphatically. So you *must*, Joseph, take my car. It is all ready, in perfect order—the tank filled, with an extra can of petrol in the trunk; also a chest of food and a large jug of water. There are maps and a flashlight in the glove compartment. Tools and first-aid kit under the rear seat.

"And you will slip *this* over your shoulders and your head before you start: my nurse's cape and hood. Together with a Red Cross I have painted on the car door, it will disguise you as a Red Cross nurse going out on early morning duty. Crouch down as low as possible to camouflage your height.

"And here, Joseph, take this purse—no, dear, you must not refuse it. There is not much in it—only my last student-nurse allowance. But every little bit helps, and you yet have need of it. For remember, darling, a long, uncertain journey lies before you.

"The car is facing the back road—headed toward the border. You must get across it, Joseph, just as speedily as possible! Completely out of Germany! Into Holland! That is your safest place at present. Numbers of the Dutch families are opening their homes and hearts to Jewish refugees—taking their very lives into their hands for their protection. God will lead you, beloved, to one of these Christlike homes—to exactly the right one.

"Just one thing more," she murmured tenderly, "that you must take. Here, dearest, is this little Testament you gave me, with all the wonderful promise verses we have marked and memorized together. They will be your comfort and your strength. And here in the front of the Testament, beloved, this little picture. It is the snapshot—do you remember?—that Moische took of you and me together at our beautiful Friedensruhe on our engagement day. Whenever you look at it, Joseph my darling, let it assure you that what we said to each other on that glorious day we shall say eternally: *'I love you.'*"

"My beloved Gretel! Oh, you are wonderful, *wonderful*! Thank you, my darling. You have given me new courage and new hope. I know that you have spoken wisely. Yes, your plan is perfectly clear—and feasible, I am confident. I shall flee at once to Holland. But you will follow me, my beloved, just as soon as it is possible?"

"Yes, Joseph! Just as soon as God shall open up the way. My place is with our loved ones here, with your precious family and with my beloved father."

As Joseph and Gretel were conferring thus alone together, and Moische was striving valiantly to strengthen and console his mother, Dr. Rothschild and Pastor von Ludwig were by themselves, apart from the others, most earnestly discussing Gretel's astounding demand that her father marry her to Joseph immediately, before his so tragically enforced departure.

"Have you any light on the question as yet, dear Martin?" Dr. Rothschild pleaded earnestly.

"Not clearly, thus far, Benjamin. There are so many conflicting arguments, for and against this radical step—do you not believe so?"

"Yes, so it would appear to me, quite definitely. But my own feeling, Martin, is that our beloved children might better delay their marriage still further—until Joseph is safely out of Germany and sufficiently secure elsewhere to be able to take care of Gretel when she is able to go to him. Do you not agree with me that this would be the wiser plan?"

"I do, Benjamin, assuredly. Rather than have the precipitous marriage now, that my daughter is so vehemently urging, I feel it would be far wiser to wait until the whole situation clears throughout all Germany."

Upon Joseph himself the effect of the emergency was to steel him to instant action. Sternly crushing down his own turbulent emotion, he disengaged himself gently from Gretel's passionate embrace. Without one backward glance he strode heroically toward the tunnel. Already his hand was upon the secret panel door. But again Gretel detained him firmly. A terrible struggle was tearing her heart. She had hoped that her father would explain to Joseph his plea for their immediate marriage and would give them his consent.

But he had spoken not one word, either to Joseph or to herself. Surely his silence must imply refusal. A quick searching glance at his face and then at Dr. Rothschild's confirmed her fears. Both looked unconvinced. Both remained grave.

The panel door began to slide slowly open. One moment more and then . . .

"Joseph!" Gretel cried out in agony. "Wait!" Oh, she could never let him go like this! They must be married first! They *must* be! "Wait, Joseph," she repeated commandingly. "There is something else I have to tell you first . . ."

He stood hesitantly. "Yes? What is it, dearest? Tell me quickly. I must *go* . . ."

"Oh, Joseph darling, listen to me! Before you go, we *must be married*! By Father. Right now, immediately!"

Joseph gasped in amazement. "Married? Right now? But why, beloved, why?"

"For my protection! If you leave me, Joseph, unmarried to *you*, I shall have to be married at noon today to Konstantin von Wolfmacht!"

"You! Married today! To Konstantin von Wolfmacht!" Joseph exclaimed in horror. "Whatever do you mean, Gretel?"

"I *know* it, Joseph. Von Wolfmacht has served notice upon me that he intends to marry me himself. Today! At high noon! By his authority as SS Elite Guard *oberoffizier*, he has commandeered me to become his wife! I am utterly at his mercy!" Gretel looked at her father imploringly. "Oh, save me, dearest Father—Dr. Rothschild—Joseph! *Save me!*" Again the tense nerves threatened to give way. Again she became hysterical.

The three men looked at one another in alarm. Pastor von Ludwig placed his arm around his daughter protectingly. "Margarete, my dear child," he pleaded anxiously, "would it not be better to wait until we know that all is well with Joseph, until he is safely out of Germany and the way is clear for you to rejoin him? Surely God will shield you from von Wolfmacht. Should you not wait, then—just a little longer—before you marry Joseph? I believe so, and Dr. Rothschild feels so, too, dear daughter."

"Probably our fathers are right, dearest," Joseph began anxiously.

"No . . . *no!*" Gretel insisted vehemently. "I tell you we must be married before Joseph leaves! Right now . . . at once . . . immediately! We shall never have another opportunity. If you do not marry me now, Joseph, before you go, we shall be lost to each other forever. I *know* it. And I tell you, it is my only hope of safety. If I am not already married to you, I shall be completely in von Wolfmacht's power—with the entire might of the Nazi army and of Adolf Hitler behind him. It is all too hideous to contemplate. Von Wolfmacht will track me down like a hunted prey and carry me off to a life of unimaginable horror. Oh, I implore you, Father darling, please! Please marry me right now to Joseph! Oh, dearest Father, hurry . . . hurry!"

"I fear, my daughter"—he spoke to her in gentlest tone—"I fear, dear child, that you are in serious danger in either case, whatever course you take: whether you marry Joseph now or whether you do not. It is true, as you say, Margarete, that if I marry you to Joseph now, it would nullify the otherwise awful peril of an enforced marriage to this monster. But at the same time, on the other hand—you must face the fearful truth squarely—if and when von Wolfmacht finds out that you have married Joseph, his vengeance would be terrible. It would pursue you relentlessly. It would mean, eventually, no doubt, your death."

Gravely, heartbrokenly, Dr. Rothschild added a note of still further warning. "Joseph, Gretel—your love, each for the other, is exalted, very beautiful. No one longs for its consummation more than I do. I know, Martin, that you, as well as Rose and myself, with all our hearts would delight to see these two dear children of ours happily married, and our two houses thus truly united. We desire our fair Germany only delivered from its present awful reign of tyranny and cruelty. But with wide-open, disillusioned eyes we must, all of us, face the terrible truth. We have fallen upon evil days. Violence and horror stalk abroad untrammeled.

"You, Martin and Gretel, as Aryans, can in measure evade the Nazi net. But as long as Adolf Hitler lives—or, at least, until he is shorn of his nefarious power—we who are Jews cannot escape. And so, my dearest Gretel—my poor little sweetheart—that is the cruel truth which you must face squarely and unequivocally. To you, Joseph, dear boy, doubtless it would mean when your marriage is discovered, immediate death. Or else it would mean what is infinitely worse than death: life imprisonment within a Nazi concentration camp, with daily, hourly, incalculable cruelty and horror.

"For yourself, our precious Gretel—and doubtless for your dear father, as well—it would mean, in all probability, a long term of imprisonment, either in a concentration camp or jail, together with confiscation of all your property; if it would not mean even the death sentence.

"But at the very least—even if you and Joseph might both escape von Wolfmacht's vengeance—unless you both could get out of Germany, it would mean for you, Gretel, my poor, dear child, unremitting and relentless persecution."

As Dr. Rothshcild concluded his direful warning, everyone stood rigid with grief, stunned to tensest silence. And then that silence was broken by Joseph suddenly bursting into the argument. With a deep groan he tore himself away from his father's now encircling arm and stood, several paces away from Gretel, aloof and apart. He gazed upon her beautiful face—never so beautiful as now—in an agony of hopeless love.

"No, no, my darling," he cried out in a heartbroken voice, "it can never be! I see it all with perfect clarity now. My love for you has been so blind, so selfish. But I see it now. Our marriage never, never can be realized. I must give you up forever! Because my love for you, my darling, is too deep, too true, ever to allow you to accept such sacrifice, such suffering."

Joseph came over to her and took her into his arms for one last solemn, sad embrace. "Good-bye! My precious darling! My beautiful, beloved Gretel! The Nazis are coming for me soon. I shall not resist them. I shall go with them quietly for your dear sake. I have no fear. Death is a small price to pay for your wonderful love and all that it has meant to me these many years. Good-bye, my own beloved. Do not grieve for me. God guard and keep and bless you. Good-bye. No, not good-bye. Auf Wiedersehen! For we shall meet again in heaven."

With a heartbroken moan he tore himself away from her and turned abruptly toward the stairway. Not the tunnel. No, he would go upstairs and meet the Nazis bravely face-to-face when they entered the front doorway. Blinded with tears he started rushing toward the top.

But Gretel bounded after him. Laying a firm, detaining hand upon his arm, she drew him back. "Joseph! Wait!" she cried compellingly. "Wait! There is one thing more that I must say to you before you go. Listen! All of you—Joseph, Father, Dr. and Mrs. Rothschild, Moische—listen to me, every one of you! Listen carefully to what I have to tell you."

Her voice, her bearing, her tremendous intensity of purpose had an electrifying effect upon all her startled hearers. Joseph halted suddenly in his frenzied exit from her presence and stood, midway upon the staircase, one step above her, looking down upon her in rapturous wonder. Half in fear, half in joy, again he placed his arm around her, as if he must protect her. Together they turned and faced the loved ones standing in awed silence below them.

Majestically Gretel dominated the entire scene. Quietly, but with unanswerable force, she addressed the semicircle of rapt listeners.

"Wait!" Again she commanded insistently. "Hear all I have to say before anybody speaks one further word. There is something that I must explain. It is something very particular. I must try to make you all understand.

"You must not think, any of you, that my determination to marry Joseph is a hasty, unreasoning, immature, or hysterical decision. I have been weighing this whole tremendous question for years. And my choice was made long ago and irrevocably. Joseph Rothschild is the man of my heart—and the man that, by God's grace, I am going to marry.

"And so, Joseph my beloved, this is to you my final word of exhortation: '*Entreat me not to leave thee, or to return from following after thee; for whither thou goest, I will go: and where thou lodgest, I will lodge: thy people shall be my people, and thy God my God.*'"

With a quick sobbing catch of her breath and in deepest solemnity Gretel concluded the immortal words—the immortal appeal of love:

"'*Where thou diest, will I die, and there will I be buried: the* L*ORD* *do so to me, and more also, if ought but death part thee and me.*'"

Looking full into Joseph's eyes with the seraphic gaze of triumphant love, she held out her arms for his embrace. Never were marriage vows fraught with more profound intensity of meaning. Through the dim stillness of the room, Pastor von Ludwig's voice rang out, vibrant with deep feeling. They knelt before him. The beautiful silvery head bent over theirs—one of his hands placed tenderly upon Joseph's raven-black hair, the other upon Gretel's pale-gold, luxuriant tresses. In a fervor of love and compassionate entreaty, he prayed:

"God the Father, God the Son, and God the Holy Spirit, bless, preserve, and keep thee; the Lord mercifully with His favor look upon thee; and so fill thee with all spiritual benediction and grace that ye may so live together in this life that in the world to come ye may have life everlasting. In the name of Jesus Christ our Lord. Amen."

Scarcely was the "Amen" uttered, scarcely had the bride and bridegroom risen to their feet, when there came from above a sudden sound—a succession of sounds that struck terror to every heart. First there was the rumbling of heavy trucks, then heavy footsteps on the front veranda, and then furious pounding upon the outside door, as if with the butt of a revolver.

"The Nazis!" all exclaimed in horror. Breathless, they stood rooted to the spot—the bride and bridegroom and all the others. And then a still more terrifying sound: the splintering of wood, as the great front door came crashing in before battering rams. And instantly the heavy footsteps—an army of them—tramped, approaching rapidly, immediately overhead.

Gretel was the first to regain presence of mind. Seizing the nurse's cape and hood, she fastened it swiftly about Joseph and thrust his suitcase and a flashlight into his hands.

"Quick, beloved—go!"

She shoved him toward the tunnel.

The two fathers next became alert. They rushed to the secret door and slid back the panel.

"Quick, Joseph! Go!" they repeated Gretel's warning.

Only one instant of passionate embrace, first of his mother and then of his bride; an anguished grasp of his father's hand—and Joseph suddenly was gone. Suddenly swallowed up in the dark tunnel underground. Suddenly gone out into the yet deeper darkness of the terrible unknown future.

The footsteps above them came nearer and yet nearer—then receded—then grew fainter in the distance—then still more faint. Their tread muffled by the thick Persian runner, the men were now ascending the staircase to the upper floor of the mansion. It would take several moments to search through all its broad expanse, through all the numerous large rooms. That would give them time for planning, these captives in the basement. But whatever could they do? They felt themselves caught like rats in a trap.

Pastor von Ludwig collected his faculties first. "Go, Benjamin, quickly—with Rose and Moische! Follow Joseph to the car! You still have time!"

But Dr. Rothschild shook his head sadly. "No, dear Martin, it is hopeless. Our house is doomed. For us it is the end. We are Jews. But *you* go, my friend—you and your precious daughter. For you there is still a chance. You are Aryans. Hurry! Go! Either follow Joseph or, at least, hide, both of you, within the shelter! That is the safest place possible. The Nazis have never yet discovered it."

The footsteps were once more approaching overhead. The Nazis were again upon the first floor. They were searching—searching . . . searching, overturning furniture ruthlessly. Soon they would discover this lower stairway . . . and this basement room . . . and then . . .

"Quickly, Martin! Go!" Dr. Rothschild implored. "If you stay, it will mean your certain death!"

He turned to Gretel and seized her hand. She still was clinging mournfully to the panel door which had closed so swiftly, so cruelly, upon her bridegroom.

"Come, dearest Gretel! Hurry! You and your father can still escape. Go, my poor child! Go quickly!"

But again Gretel electrified them all. Standing suddenly upright, she confronted Dr. Rothschild bravely.

"No, dear Dr. Rothschild—*Father* Rothschild now, for I am married to your son. Now I am your daughter—and a daughter of your people. Therefore I stand with you to the end."

"And I stand also, Benjamin, with you and with my child. With *Israel*." Pastor von Ludwig smiled a brave, sad smile. And against every argument, every passionate entreaty of his Hebrew friend, he remained immovable.

Another crash upstairs. This time it sounded as if the ceiling was coming down on top of them. The Nazis now were in the library, directly overhead.

One breathless moment more and then the coarse shouting of a military command: "Here! This way, men! Downstairs! HEIL HITLER!" It was the voice of Konstantin von Wolfmacht.

The next instant the panel door at the top of the stairway was kicked rudely open, smashed to splinters, and the Nazis twenty strong came pouring down. At their head, directing them—in the full uniform of an SS Elite Guard officer—marched *Fritz*! Von Wolfmacht was at the end of the procession. Directly in front of him at the rear of the others officers—also in full Nazi officers' uniform—were Bruno and Bernhardt von Ludwig. Both of their faces turned completely to stone, they looked neither to the right nor left.

Above every other emotion, at the sight of his two sons—*here* and upon such an errand!—once again Pastor von Ludwig groaned with unutterable grief.

But when Dr. Rothschild's eyes fell upon Fritz, his very senses reeled with revulsion. *Fritz!* For long years his faithful and devoted servant. He whose loyalty and love his magnanimous Hebrew employer had never once doubted, whose noble integrity he had never once impugned. Dr. Rothschild was stunned with heartbreaking sorrow. Not *Fritz*? Oh, no, no, impossible! Such a thing as that could *never* be!

But it *was* possible. It was all too cruelly true. And then swiftly, in one blinding flash of comprehension, the whole inner meaning of Fritz's attitude and actions over the past several weeks became vividly clear to Dr. Rothschild. Action and explanation fitted like hand to glove. All was now quite plain: Pastor von Ludwig's miraculous escape from the Nazis at his church that last Sunday morning and his unimpeded swift motor ride with Fritz to Dr. Rothschild's mansion . . . previously cleared them from his route to the refugee shelter—where he himself would keep their quarry under his own protective custody until the time was fully ripe for the Nazis to make a dramatic capture . . .

Fritz's great sympathy with all the Jews within the shelter, and for all Jews throughout Germany . . .

Fritz's unwearied and most efficient and solicitous service

not only for the Jewish refugees within Dr. Rothschild's home, but particularly for Dr. Rothschild himself and all his family and, very particularly, for Pastor von Ludwig. And the explanation of this was the clearest and saddest of them all. This whole program of devotion had been prearranged by the Nazis—by von Wolfmacht himself conspicuously—down to the last-minute detail; and had been executed by Fritz for a high reward, to be paid to him by the National Socialist government when their foul design should be fully accomplished.

In one more lightning flash of spiritual illumination, the full understanding of Fritz's subsequent behavior was vividly revealed. The pattern and precedent of his perfidious betrayal of his master was now crystal clear: for *thirty pieces of silver*, Judas had betrayed *his* Master with a kiss.

Dr. Rothschild made one last frantic appeal:

"Martin! Gretel! Go, I tell you. *Go!*"

But the only reply of the Aryan father and daughter was to stand magnificently strong and face unflinchingly their swiftly oncoming foes.

The Nazis rushed down the stairway and into the room like a pack of hungry wolves, sniffing for blood. The whole twenty Nazi SS Elite Guard officers came crashing in. At the rear of the line, as they reached Pastor von Ludwig, his two sons cravenly tried to hide themselves from view. Stolidly they averted their eyes from their father's agonized gaze. But they cast surreptitious glances all about the recreation room—the selfsame room where they and their two younger brothers, as growing boys, had played happily together with the Rothschild boys—their closest boyhood and young manhood friends.

Von Wolfmacht plunged from the stairway into the room. He gave a snort of fiendish glee. He was tracking down his victim: that abominable *Jew*, Joseph Rothschild. Ha! At last he was bringing him to bay.

But where was he? The haughty SS *oberoffizier* looked around the room sharply. "Joseph Rothschild!" He gave shrill command: "Come forward and surrender! HEIL HITLER!"

But no Joseph appeared. Von Wolfmacht turned swiftly upon his father: "You, Benjamin Rothschild! Deliver up you son. Where is he hiding? Surrender him to us at once!"

And then suddenly he espied the sworn foe of Adolf Hitler

and the National Socialist Party: Pastor Martin Luther von Ludwig. He snarled like a vicious animal.

"*Ach!* Is it you? Von Ludwig. At last we have found you, you slippery fox! *Ach,* but you will not get away from us this time, I promise you. Forward, men! Arrest this scoundrel! This time, my good friend, you go to concentration camp. Oberholtzer, Kleinhaupt! Put on the irons. Take him over to that corner. Guard him until we find Joseph Rothschild. Your life for his, each of you, if you let him slip your grasp."

The two Nazi officers sprang forward to do von Wolfmacht's bidding. The gentle undershepherd of the Confessional flock was manacled in heavy chains and marched, unresisting, into the dark, farthest corner of the room. Like the Good Shepherd before him, led as a lamb to the slaugher, he opened not his mouth.

But out from another shadowy corner of the large basement chamber, someone hitherto unobserved—his daughter, Margarete—sprang forward to her father's defense. She confronted von Wolfmacht fearlessly, with blazing eyes.

"You may send me to the concentration camp, Herr von Wolfmacht, if you will, but you release my father!"

He wheeled upon her with a howl of mingled rage and mocking glee. "You! You here, my charming lady? I thought we had you locked up safely for the night. However in the world did you escape from *me*? Ah well, never mind! You need not bother to explain. I have you safely now, my dearest Margarete: that is all that matters. You may be perfectly sure I shall never let you get away from me again. We shall be keeping our little appointment, you and I, at high noon today. Allow me, my kind friends," he added with a sinister leer at Dr. and Mrs. Rothschild, "allow me to present to you my bride! Fräulein Margarete von Ludwig marries me in the Domkirche this day at noon!"

Once again Gretel merited von Wolfmacht's description of her: "magnificent." She was truly that as she stood before him, face-to-face, with regal dignity, with regal indignation held superbly in control. Unflinchingly she looked straight into his wicked eyes.

"That, Herr von Wolfmacht," she answered him in a quiet, steady voice, "is impossible."

"What is impossible?" he questioned with a sneer.

"For me to marry *you*."

"Why is it impossible, my lovely queen?"

"Because I am *already married to another*. Since last you saw me, Herr von Wolfmacht, I have married Dr. Joseph Rothschild."

The Nazi scowled darkly. "This is no time for jesting, fräulein!"

"I am not jesting. It is the truth. Will you confirm it, Father?"

"Yes!" Pastor von Ludwig cried out from his dark corner in ringing tones. "Yes," he repeated with dignity and fearlessness, "I do confirm it. I have just performed the marriage ceremony. Dr. Joseph Rothschild and my daughter are now man and wife."

Von Wolfmacht's fury knew no bounds. Like a lion suddenly divested of his prey, he roared and raged. He turned, first, upon Gretel with a howl of vengeance.

"Joseph Rothschild! You married *Joseph Rothschild*? You, an Aryan? You married *him*—a *Jew*? Where is your sense of decency? Your sense of Aryan honor? When did you marry him?"

"Not half an hour ago."

In reply to this astounding information, von Wolfmacht wheeled next upon the father of the bride. In a burst of nothing short of satanic hate, he poured the vials of his wrath upon him.

"You! Von Ludwig! So it was *you* who married them, was it? You married your own daughter to a filthy *Jew*! Where is *your* sense of decency and honor? Are you aware, sir, that your score is adding up very dangerously high? This last perfidious act is still another Nazi charge against you—on top of all our other charges. This is still another capital offense.

"But did any of you ever imagine"—he sneered derisively—"did you ever imagine that such a marriage would be validated by our National Socialist government? It will be declared null and void without delay, I promise you.

"But where is Joseph Rothschild now? We are here for the express purpose of arresting him and marching him before a firing squad. I demand, Rothschild, that you produce your son immediately.

"Nazis! Forward! Fritz take command! Make thorough search of this entire house and all the grounds. Ransack every nook and cranny. Do not leave one plank or stone unturned. Search every slightest corner. *Find Joseph Rothschild!"*

The SS officers climbed the stairs and again, with their heavily thumping tread, stormed through the Rothschild mansion. Von Wolfmacht seated himself luxuriously in a large wing chair and drew out his Meerschaum pipe. He lighted it, then puffed at it slowly and deliberately. "I shall stay right here"—he smiled with cunning satisfaction—"until our honorable Herr *Doktor* Joseph Rothschild is produced. Then we shall proceed with him at once—to the Brandenburger Thor. You may wait with me here, my good friends, for the pleasure of bidding him a long farewell. Be seated, ladies and gentlemen," he added derisively. "Make yourselves quite at home—as my most welcome guests."

The relentless search continued for forty minutes. But in vain. The men returned at last, insisting it was hopeless. Joseph Rothschild assuredly was not anywhere within the house or grounds.

Von Wolfmacht rose swiftly from the comfortable chair, laid down his Meerschaum, and snapped into rigid military posture. "Go, von Heinrich, quickly! To the telephone! Alert Headquarters. Have a general alarm sent out all over Germany to roadblock every highway. And have complete control established all along the borders. Send out a full description of the man we want—the man that we intend to get and *liquidate."*

Von Wolfmacht then turned to Dr. Rothschild. Sardonically he addressed him:

"And so, my fine friend, your son Joseph thinks he has eluded us. Very well, then. Very good. Very good, indeed. We shall take *this* young man, Herr Rothschild—your other son—with us and send him to the concentration camp. We shall keep him there, quite safely, under our protective custody, until Joseph is delivered to us. Herr Mannerheim . . . Herter, handcuff this boy. Hold him over there with our other prisoner until I give command to march."

As the two Nazi officers obediently snapped the chains on the terrified Moische, his mother sprang toward von Wolfmacht and fell on her knees before him with imploring outcry:

"Oh, no, no, *no*! You can never take my darling boy! Oh, sir"—she wrung her hands and moaned piteously in anguish—"you do not understand! This boy is my little Moische—my own dear baby yet. He needs his mother. I always have to take such care of him. Oh, I am telling you, sir, you cannot send Moische to a concentration camp! Never, never could he stand it."

Von Wolfmacht howled derisively, the other Nazis also joining in the mirth. "I am afraid, my good woman, your 'precious, darling Moische' will have to learn how to stand it," he said brutally. He thrust the agonized mother roughly aside with his foot. Paying no heed whatsoever to the terrified shrieks of the lad, nor to the distress of his father, nor yet to the attempted remonstrance of Pastor von Ludwig and Gretel, he made short work of the pitiful young hostage for his brother Joseph.

"Attention, men!" again he commanded. "HEIL HITLER! Forward, Mannerheim and Herter, with your prisoner! Proceed with him in your car at once—to *Dachau*!"

While the remaining Nazi officers stood stiffly at attention, alerted for their *oberoffizier*'s next command, he strode over toward Dr. and Mrs. Rothschild and Gretel, all three huddled together in a corner, a most dejected, pitiable little group. Confronting them with a supercilious smile of malicious cunning, he addressed them unctuously:

"Well, my excellent friends, two of our delightful party are being nicely taken care of. And now we purpose to complete our job of 'mopping up'—of clearing out all the Jewish vermin housed beneath this roof. Fritz, my good comrade, you have been giving us interesting reports lately about Dr. Rothschild's distinguished Jewish refugees. Now we want to have the great pleasure of meeting them. Will you be kind enough, sir, to lead my men to their shelter?

"You, Rothschild, and your lovely little wife will still continue to remain right here in this house—*our* house now, of course, remember—under our protective custody, until such time as we shall choose to dispose of you otherwise. You will still observe the same rules we laid down for you a month ago.

"One more thing. You are forbidden, expressly, to sit upon any of the benches in any park or along any boulevard. Our Aryan benches are not to be contaminated by offensive Jews. And you, of course, will not attempt to enter into conversation with any Aryans. They would properly regard it as an insult.

"Limit your time outside strictly to these allotted two hours. The remaining hours of the twenty-four you will remain inside this house, with all the shades drawn down.

"Frau Rothschild! So be it! By your acceptance of that Semitic name and of the cur that bears it—by your confessed marriage to a Jew—you realize, of course, that you have put yourself outside the pale. You have debased and degraded your exalted station. You have renounced your Aryan birthright. You have desecrated your pure Aryan womanhood. You have become a traitor to your country—an enemy of Germany. You have rendered yourself entirely unworthy of any further confidence whatever. Henceforth you are ostracized from Aryan society. You have cut yourself off forever from association with people of respectability and decency.

"You surely understand," he added arrogantly, "that my magnanimous offer is now, of course, automatically rescinded and annulled—my offer to confer upon you the exalted honor of making you my wife, and thereby elevating you to the proud position of the foremost Nazi woman in all Germany. By your baseness you yourself have forfeited this supreme opportunity which, so easily, might have been yours for life.

"And now, my dear Frau von Ludwig-Rothschild"—he drawled the new name superciliously—"what shall be the penalty of your misguided choice and act? Since you of your own free volition have elected to identify yourself with *swine*, so be it. You shall remain right here with them, in their *sty*.

"Rothschild, whenever any Nazi officer confronts you, it is your duty to honor him with the proper Nazi salute: HEIL HITLER! I command you, you Jewish vermin, to *HEIL*!"

With greatest effort Dr. Rothschild drew his stooping, shivering frame to full height and in a mood of righteous indignation he looked von Wolfmacht squarely in the face. Once again, as in the hospital, he defied him. "I refuse!" he replied majestically.

"You *refuse*!"

"Yes, Herr von Wolfmacht, I do refuse! I refuse utterly to *heil* Adolf Hitler or to yield one iota of respect to him or to his whole nefarious Nazi government. For I can feel no respect. I have to accept his indignities and outrages upon myself and upon my house and family because I am powerless to avert them. But to salute your infamous Fuehrer, to render him one atom of honor or of recognition, I tell you, I positively and disdainfully *refuse*!"

Von Wolfmacht lunged at him savagely. "Very good, then, you Jewish scum of the earth, take *that*!" He struck him viciously with his fist, almost felling him. Dr. Rothschild winced with pain and anger, but his spirit remained unbroken. Quickly he regained his equilibrium and stood facing his tormentor with a quiet, invincible power which irresistibly held von Wolfmacht at bay. By this time Mrs. Rothschild and Gretel also had appeared and had taken their places one on either side of their loved one, regarding him with mingled admiration and alarm. Bernhardt and Bruno von Ludwig stood at haughty attention behind their commanding officer. Their countenances were inscrutable. As their only sister appeared before their view, not one flicker of recognition did either one of them accord her.

And then von Wolfmacht stated his cruel errand:

"Very good, then, Rothschild, very good indeed. Since your refuse to *heil* our glorious Fuehrer, as an alternative you will be compelled henceforth to serve him. From this day forward you will obey the slogan of your boasted New Testament. There are a few decent precepts within this archaic book, we grant you, including this one: 'If any would not *work*, neither should he *eat*.'

"And what is more, your work stands fully ready at hand and waiting for you. Last night we had a heavy snowstorm. Berlin needs shovelers. It is not seven o'clock. Go and dress yourself. You had better dress warmly. It is way below freezing outdoors. And then you may eat breakfast here—as *our* guest, understand, and upon *our* bounty. Then in exactly one hour from now—at eight o'clock—we will drive you to the Stadthaus. You will report there to the street-cleaning department, and your shovel and time card will be given you. Also the yellow *J* for *Jew*, which the overseer will fasten onto your back. Any attempt to remove it—remember, my good friend—is punishable by instant shooting. I hope you quite understand!

"And this indolent, insolent new daughter-in-law of yours, Frau Joseph von Ludwig–Rothschild"—he sneered at the new name mockingly—"she, too, is under the same command. If *she* will not work, neither shall *she* eat. Do you get that, my charming Margarete? You will report for nursing duty again where you temporarily abandoned your post.

"As for Frau Rothschild, she is much too weak and too ignorant to be of any use whatsoever to our Nazi State. Therefore—until we decide otherwise, understand—she may continue to remain here in idleness. She may eat the bread that you, Rothschild, from now on, will have to earn for her."

With diabolical refinement of cruelty, the officer thus plotted his further wicked revenge upon the woman who had dared to flout him. She was a prisoner of the National Socialist Government. And all because of her unpardonable crime of marrying a Semite.

On one of the later-winter evenings—now becoming more and more frequent—when the Nazi guard, after bringing Dr. Rothschild and Gretel home, remained for an hour of revelry, this time von Wolfmacht was among them. As they were finally preparing to leave the house, following their wild carousing and their usual demand of Gretel for hot coffee, Rose suddenly flung herself at the *kommandant*'s feet. Seizing his hand and looking up into his face imploringly, she besought him with piteous tears:

"Oh, Herr von Wolfmacht! When can I have my Moische? When will you bring him home to me again? Oh, I shall die if I cannot have my precious son!"

Rudely he shoved her aside. "I will bring you your Moische," he answered her sternly, "when you deliver up your *Joseph*."

She wrung her hands despairingly. "But we have told you, over and over again, we do not know where Joseph is!"

"Very well, then, find him. Until you do find him, and hand him over to us, you will never see your Moische." Without another word he strode arrogantly toward the doorway.

But Rose Rothschild was not thus to be denied. She now was thoroughly aroused. "Oh, Herr von Wolfmacht! Dear Herr von Wolfmacht! Oh, I beg of you, do bring to me my little Moische! Oh, dear, kind Herr von Wolfmacht, *please*! Oh, do bring him home to me, I beg of you—my precious little Moische, my baby boy, my darling! Oh, dear, *dear* Herr von Wolfmacht, do, please, bring Moische *home*!"

Von Wolfmacht halted his departure. In reaction to Mrs. Rothschild's importunity, a new and altogether self-pleasing idea took root in his mind. He smiled cunningly, first at Gretel and then at Moische's sorrowing parents. "All right, my good friends," he said sardonically, "if you want to see this precious boy of yours before you die, you may do so—for thirty thousand *marks*. The very day you give me thirty thousand marks, I shall bring him home to you again."

"Thirty thousand marks!" Dr. Rothschild groaned. "Wherever could we get thirty thousand marks? You have not left us thirty marks in all the world."

Wolfmacht shrugged his shoulders and turned to leave. But Gretel intercepted von Wolfmacht at the doorway. For during her mother-in-law's heartbreaking appeal to him, and still more firmly during his heartless rebuff, a new idea had taken root in her mind. In a flash she perceived a solution to the fearful problem.

"Herr von Wolfmacht," she said quietly. "Do I understand correctly that for thirty thousand marks you will restore Moische Rothschild to his parents?"

"Thirty thousand marks is what I said. What I demand. In cash."

"You promise?"

"I promise."

"Very well, sir. I thank you. You may bring the lad at nine o'clock tomorrow evening. The ransom money will be here for you in full—thirty thousand marks."

Chapter 18

Ben-Oni, Son of Sorrow

When the noon hour came the next day, after her long, hard morning's work, Gretel did not withdraw, as frequently she must, to a secluded corner for the needed rest. Instead, she threw her cape about her and sped as upon wings of wind to the nearby Wilhelmstrasse and to the proud firm of Hoffmeister and Son, Jewelers.

At once she sought and was admitted to the private office of Herr Heinrich Hoffmeister, senior proprietor of the wealthy establishment.

He greeted her courteously. And then he regarded her quizzically. There was something vaguely familiar about this handsome, exhausted-looking young woman. Clearly she was perturbed. Who was she? And what was her errand?

Gretel went straight to the point. She had no time for circumlocution. Nor did she dare temporize with the danger of wavering purpose at the crucial moment. "Herr Hoffmeister, do you remember this ring?" She held it temptingly before the diamond merchant's gloating eyes.

"*Ach, ja, ja!* I remember it well! The Gerber diamonds and the Ehrenburgher ruby! The finest jewels I have ever sold. And you . . . you? I know your face, but, pardon me, I cannot recall—*Ach, ja, ja*! I remember you now so very well. It was you who came here that day with young Herr *Doktor* Rothschild. He had bought this ring the week before, and he brought you here with him to have it more properly fitted. *Ach, ja, ja!* I remember perfectly. You were a very fortunate young fräulein to be given such a ring as *this*!"

"Yes, I was indeed. This was my engagement ring. And this one is my wedding ring. I now am Dr. Rothschild's wife."

"*Ach* so! I congratulate you, Frau Rothschild, with all my heart. And your husband? He is . . ."

"My husband is . . . missing, Herr Hoffmeister. You know, sir, he is a Jew—the son of Dr. Benjamin Rothschild."

Good Herr Hoffmeister's eyes filled suddenly with tears. He was fatherly and kind, and at once he understood. For he was a true German of the old and truly noble school, utterly abhorring Naziism and everything that Naziism stood for.

"Herr Hoffmeister"—Gretel plunged swiftly into her difficult mission, lest her high resolve should fail—"Herr Hoffmeister, I happen to know how much Dr. Rothschild paid for my ring. Never mind how I found out. But the price was thirty thousand marks. That is correct, is it not?"

"*Ach, ja, ja!* That is correct. I remember well. So many times have I regretted that I ever parted with it—the very finest jewels I have ever acquired or ever knew."

"Would you care to buy this ring back, sir, for the same price—thirty thousand marks?" Gretel tried hard to make her voice sound strictly businesslike, impersonal, detached. But the inevitable quaver in it did not escape the sensitive, sympathetic German ear.

"Buy it back. . ." he answered in amazement. "Very gladly would I do so. But are you sure, Frau Rothschild, that you would be willing to part with it yourself?"

"I . . . I *have* to, Herr Hoffmeister. It is a case of most urgent, immediate necessity. Excuse me, please, that I cannot make explanation."

"*Ach, ja, ja!* I understand, I understand," he replied in tender tone. "*Jawohl*, Frau Rothschild! I will very gladly let you have the money for the ring. But we shall regard it merely as a loan without interest, not as a final sale. I shall pray the dear God to give you back your husband soon—and then your ring, as well."

Quietly Gretel slipped the little velvet case containing her treasure into Herr Hoffmeister's extended hand. The light from his desk lamp played upon the dazzling jewels, drawing out their wonderful beauty as never before. Within less than ten minutes the transfer was complete. The papers of exchange were signed and sealed. The ring was fast locked within Herr Hoffmeister's strongest vault. From the same vault there was brought out a chest filled to overflowing with German banknotes. Carefully Herr Hoffmeister counted out the full amount of von Wolfmacht's extortionate demand—thirty thousand marks. The full amount of the ransom money.

All through the long afternoon—still a prisoner of the Nazi State—she performed her menial drudgery within the hospital, amazedly conscious of a sense of buoyancy, of a strange exaltation of spirit. Not since the tragic departure of Joseph and Moische and her father, had she known such inner peace.

When at last, at half past seven, the Nazi prison car as usual deposited her and her father-in-law at the great bronze gates, Gretel rushed into the house and poured out upon the table the flood of banknotes before Dr. and Mrs. Rothschild's astounded eyes.

"Look! Look! Dearest Father and Mother, look! The *ransom* money!"

For a terrifying moment Gretel feared the sudden shock of joy would prove too great for Moische's parents. Both of them almost swooned. But under the solicitous and tender ministrations of their daughter-nurse, gradually they recovered strength. And soon all three of them were laughing and crying and embracing one another in a very delirium of ecstasy.

While Mrs. Rothschild and Gretel together assembled the now precariously meager food for their evening meal, Dr. Rothschild feverishly was counting out the banknotes. One thousand . . . two thousand . . . three thousand . . . four . . . five . . . six . . . ten . . . twenty . . . twenty-five—yes, it was wonderfully true, there they all were: *the entire thirty thousand marks*!

"But, my darling daughter, wherever did this money come from?" he asked her apprehensively.

"God sent it to us, dearest Father. Never mind now. *He* sent it. It is here, and that is all that matters. Our precious Moische will be home soon!"

"Oh! When will he be home?" his mother asked imploringly. "My darling little Moische! Oh, dearest Gretel, tell me *when*?"

"Soon, dear. Very, very soon. For von Wolfmacht promised."

"He promised . . . ?"

Very gently, adroitly, she broke to them the thrilling news.

Moische was coming home that very evening! Within that very hour! Yes, praise God, it was really true! Moische was coming *home*! Von Wolfmacht himself was bringing him at nine o'clock. For he had *promised*!

As the hour drew near, a hush of keen expectancy fell upon the house of Rothschild. And then—even before the chiming had died away and the hour of nine was struck in deep, bell-like tones—they heard the long-accustomed and long-dreaded sound: the tramping of heavy Nazi footsteps on the front veranda. But tonight they heard the footsteps—for the very first time—without dismay or fear. Tonight they heard them with thanksgiving and with joy. For tonight—this very moment—*now*—the Nazis were bringing Moische home!

Eagerly they all rushed forward to the door to greet him. Dr. Rothschild flung it wide. Breathlessly they all peered through the opened entrance—up and down the great veranda they strained anxious eyes—and then . . . then . . . they all drew back and looked at one another in dismay.

Where *was* he? Oh, where? *Where?* Where was Moische?

Only Konstantin von Wolfmacht stood at the doorway. The SS Elite Guard *oberoffizier*, the Herr *Kommandant*, stood haughtily before them—and he alone. Over his arm he carried his military greatcoat. Something bulged beneath it.

He entered the doorway arrogantly. Importantly. Impressively.

"Have you got my money?" he questioned Gretel directly with a snarl. His tone was wolfish, cold as icy steel. His whole bearing was threatening, alarming.

Mrs. Rothschild sprang toward him intrepidly. "Yes!" she responded eagerly. "We do have it—every *pfennig*! Look! Just look at *this*, sir! Here it is!" Excitedly she led him to the table where the banknotes had been placed and where they were all spread out awaiting him. But suddenly a cold fear seized her. The lovely smile—entirely wasted on the Nazi high commander—vanished swiftly from her face. She began to tremble violently.

"But, Herr von Wolfmacht!" she addressed him in an imploring tone, "I do not understand. Oh, oh, please explain it to me! What *is* it? There is something *wrong*! Here is your money, the full amount—every *pfennig* of it—right here, all ready for you. But where is my Moische? You promised you would bring him home to us this evening."

"Yes, Herr von Wolfmacht," Dr. Rothschild interposed, "it is true we do not quite comprehend the situation. Where is our son? I thought you were going to return him to us tonight, in exchange for these thirty thousand marks."

"That is perfectly true, Father," Gretel assured him. "Herr von Wolfmacht did thus promise." She looked squarely into the cold, merciless eyes of their Nazi captor and added accusingly, "Perhaps, Konstantin von Wolfmacht, you may recall your exact words to me last evening: 'I *promise*. I promise *faithfully*. I will bring Moische Rothschild."

The haughty SS Elite Guard kommandant disdained to reply to any one of his three interrogators. Gloatingly he started counting out the money and stuffing the huge stack of it into his pockets. "One hundred . . . five hundred . . . one thousand . . . fifteen hundred . . . two thousand . . ."

"But *Moische*! Where is Moische?" Rose Rothschild was now weeping piteously. Dr. Rothschild and Gretel were both grim.

"Twenty thousand . . . twenty-five thousand . . . twenty-eight thousand . . . and thirty thousand marks! Correct. Very good. Very good indeed." The monster leered at his tortured victims with cunning satisfaction. In his eyes there was a glint that was completely ghoulish. He turned toward the door as if to make his exit. He gathered up his military greatcoat from another table.

Paralyzed with a sense of frustration and of utter helplessness, Dr. Rothschild and Gretel both let him sweep arrogantly past them without a flicker of resistance. But the mother in Israel rushed after him wildly. Frantic with disappointment and grief, she seized his arm in a vise-like grip and shook him with all the violence her diminutive, frail body could command.

"Herr von Wolfmacht!" she screamed at him in shrill crescendo. "You wicked, wicked man! How dare you do what you are doing? You are carrying off our money! Thirty thousand marks! But you have not brought us our boy! Where *is* he?"

Von Wolfmacht looked down upon her with supreme contempt. "I did bring your precious Moische," he replied. His voice, his face, were ice.

"You . . . brought . . . my . . . Moische? I do not understand!"

The Nazi's lips curled superciliously. With a sinister leer he drew from underneath his greatcoat an oblong parcel. It was carelessly wrapped in coarse brown paper. It was about ten inches in length, and half as wide and high. With elaborate mock ceremony he deposited it upon Moische's own beloved piano.

"Moische! Moische! I want . . . my . . . Moische! Where is he? Where *is* he?" Rose Rothschild by now was entirely distraught—convulsed with an uncontrollable flood of weeping.

Rigid with horror, Dr. Rothschild and Gretel heard von Wolfmacht make derisive, nonchalant, marble-cold reply: "Here, woman! Here is your sweet Moische! Right here on his piano. Within this box. His ashes."

The final appalling chapter in the annals of the Hebrew house of Rothschild sped to its swift conclusion. Even before sunset of the following day, the last grim record was written—the last awful tragedy was enacted.

Upon Dr. Rothschild's ineffaceable memory, in horrifying outline, there would be indelibly imprinted for the remainder of his life, the very last scene of all, as he and his loved ones passed forever from their beautiful, beloved home. . .

A black, heavily armored prison van, driven by a Nazi soldier. In the interior of this van, sidelong seats running vis-à-vis. On the one side, a stiff row of Nazi storm troopers, in the black storm troop uniform, even to the black cap with insignia of white skull and crossbones. At their head, magnificent in his full-dress regalia as *oberoffizier* of the SS Elite Guard—Konstantin von Wolfmacht.

On the opposite sidelong seat, directly facing the Nazis, Dr. Rothschild himself and his Aryan daughter-in-law, Margarete von Ludwig–Rothschild, both turned to stone. Between them, babbling foolishly and whimpering, Dr. Rothschild's once so brilliant, lovely wife—his fascinating Rose. All three of them manacled together with heavy chains.

As the van sped down the imposing driveway under the magnificent arched trees and on through the lordly bronze gates—in the direction of Dachau—Dr. Rothschild turned his agonized gaze backwards for one last glimpse, if possible, of his dear abode.

In place of the palatial mansion—built upon Dr. Rothschild's secure foundation—the mansion which for so many blessed years had stood in majestic grandeur and in warm-hearted, inviting welcome to its multitude of happy guests, Hebrew or Aryan alike—there was now, instead, only a blazing inferno, a furnace of belching black smoke and upward roaring flames.

With one long, low moan of anguish and of horror, Dr. Rothschild stared upon it fixedly. Suddenly a bitter cry escaped his lips, shrilling, piercing the frosty, early-evening air.

"O my God!" he shrieked. "Am I Benjamin Rothschild? Am I *Benjamin*—'son of the right hand'—the 'fortunate one'? Nay! Call me no longer 'Benjamin'! Call me now, rather—only and forever—'Ben-Oni'! Ben-Oni, Son of Sorrow! Ben-Oni, Son of ISRAEL!"

Chapter 19

Friends from Afar

In the fair city of Baltimore, Maryland, USA, on a quiet and beautiful residential avenue and set well back amid magnificent trees and flowers on a velvety lawn, there stands a charming white dwelling of Southern colonial design. With its broad veranda and high Grecian columns, flanked at either side by curving, wrought-iron stairways leading up to a graceful balcony above, it has an air of dignity and elegance, albeit of solid homelike comfort.

Even more charming than the outward aspect of the house is its interior. Of the same Southern colonial style, it is furnished throughout with rich mahogany antiques, gleaming crystal mirrors, chandeliers and polished brasses, and with tasteful rugs, drapes and wide-ruffled colonial window curtains of sheerest white organdie. The residence bespeaks, in every nook and cranny, the highest refinement of its beauty-loving occupants: Dr. G. Hollister Steele of Southeastern Hospital; his delightful wife, Clare; and their lovely, nineteen-year-old daughter, Elinor.

Following their attendance upon the deeply devotional service of evensong in their nearby church, all three of the members of this happy little family were gathered the last Sunday evening in June around their cozy supper table in their attractive cream and blue dining room. The table, of highly polished mahogany, reflecting in its satin surface the tall, lighted blue candles in the silver candlesticks and the exquisite pale pink camellias, was tastefully appointed with other gleaming silver and the daintiest of china and crystal. Mrs. Steele was presiding charmingly at the handsome silver coffee urn, a priceless heirloom handed down to her, through successive generations, from her great-grandfather's antebellum cotton plantation in Louisiana.

For Clare Steele was a daughter, a direct descendant, of the old Deep South. This proud fact was unmistakably attested in the essentially Southern character of every room within her lovely home, in her distinctively Southern gown, full-skirted and copiously ruffled, and particularly in her delightful Southern drawl as she smiled her enchanting smile and invitingly questioned each one at the table, in turn: "Will you-all have cream and sugah in youah coffee?" Both her husband and her daughter possessed, in high degree, the same native Southern charm.

On this beautiful June evening, together with the Steeles, another person was present at their hospital's board—a most important and most welcome guest. He was, indeed, one who soon was to become the fourth member of their aristocratic family—none other gentleman than the fiancé of Elinor Steele. *His* native heath and pedigree was proclaimed immediately in his euphonious name: Reginald Harcourt Trevelyan.

An Englishman he was truly, and a very captivating one. A Londoner born and bred, he had come to America the previous September, just shortly following his graduation from Oxford. With his hard-won MD degree, purposely he had traveled all the way to Baltimore, Maryland, and to Southeastern University and Hospital for the so eagerly coveted opportunity of acquiring specialized training under the instruction of the brilliant young American surgeon, Dr. G. Hollister Steele. The surgeon's fame, by reason of his remarkable achievement in cerebral operations, already had reached even the classic halls of Oxford.

And now this month of June, in the long-to-be-remembered year 1937, had witnessed the Englishman's successful completion, with highest honors, of his chosen postgraduate surgical course.

And it had witnessed something else! Something which young Dr. Trevelyan prized even more highly than his scholastic distinction and his advanced degree in his profession. This lovely month of roses had witnessed—just one week ago today—the still more successful completion of his ardent quest for the heart of Miss Elinor Steele, the idolized only child of his eminent colleague and exemplar, and his fascinating wife.

The sweet little romance had begun on Christmas Day when Dr. and Mrs. Steele, with their characteristic Southern hospitality, had invited a few of the lonely foreign students to their genial home for Christmas dinner. Dr. Reginald Harcourt had been seated next to the vivacious Elinor; and before the joyous feast with the ensuing delightful Christmas evening was concluded, Cupid's arrow already had pierced deeply into the heart of the impressionable young Britisher.

Thereupon followed a whirlwind courtship, rendered all the more tempestuous for the ardent lover by reason of heavy competition with rival suitors. For Elinor was truly a Southern belle—and a very lovely one. But at last the shining goal was reached. Just exactly one week earlier, Reginald Harcourt Trevelyan had won from Elinor Caroline Steele the so valiantly fought-for "Yes."

And already their happy plans were eagerly afoot. They would be married in September. The intervening months of July and August would be spent by Elinor at home in busy preparation; while Dr. Trevelyan would spend them with his father and mother and brother and sister in their home in London. The whole Trevelyan family would come to Baltimore for the wedding, which would take place—so the enraptured young couple confidently and jubilantly announced—in the University Chapel, the ceremony to be followed by the wedding reception and breakfast in the bride's beautiful residence and garden.

And then following their honeymoon—also already enthusiastically planned to include a trip to the wonderful Canadian Rockies—they would return to Baltimore, where the young surgeon would complete his internship in Southeastern Hospital, again under the presiding genius of Dr. G. Hollister Steele. Beyond that, the way was as yet unknown.

The supper hour was a very merry one as the little group of four congenial spirits talked over all these hopes for the joyful days ahead. And now another and most exciting topic was up for family discussion.

Only yesterday it was that Reginald had received a cable

from his parents in London, in reply to the glad news of his engagement to Elinor. The return message had been one of love and congratulations, and of warm welcome into their family of the promised bride. Closely following the cable to Reginald there had come another personal one to Mrs. Steele from Mrs. Trevelyan containing a breathtaking invitation. Could not Mrs. Steele and her daughter come overseas with Reginald in July for a fortnight's visit in their London home? Dr. Steele also would be most welcome if it were possible for him to get away. The Trevelyans would all be so happy for this opportunity to have their two families become acquainted with one another. And now, very earnestly, the Steeles and the prospective bridegroom were resolving the whole stupendous question.

"Oh, Daddy, Daddy!" Elinor coaxed her father rapturously, "Oh, please, *please* do let us accept! To think of going to London! And meeting all of Reggie's people! Oh, it would be wonderful! Wouldn't it, Mother?"

"Yes, dear, it would be very wonderful indeed," Mrs. Steele replied gently. And then with a mischievous twinkle in her eye, she added, "That is, if it would be quite agreeable to *you*, Reginald.

"Oh, I s'ay! Ra-*ther*!" Dr. Reginald Harcourt Trevelyan fairly exploded.

"And what do *you* say to the idea, Hollister?" his wife asked cautiously. "For, after all, you are the one who must cast the deciding vote."

Dr. Steele ruminated—slowly, judiciously . . .

But quite violently the excited Elinor cut short his deliberations. Jumping up from the table and running over to him she threw her arms around his neck and hugged him until he was nearly breathless. "Oh, please, Daddy darling, *please*! Please do say yes!" again she wheedled.

Hollister Steele could hold his own against any odds in his profession. But before his captivating daughter's blandishments he went down nearly every time. Hopelessly. And this time he capitulated utterly.

"Very well, if your mother says so . . ."

"I do say so emphatically."

"All right then, you little minx! Have it your own way. You always do."

And so the momentous question was settled. They all would go to London—in fewer than two weeks. Elinor was ecstatically, deliriously happy. All the others, though less explosive in their expression of it, nevertheless experienced a fulfilling joy.

"Oh, Daddy!" Elinor argued eagerly, "can you stay the full two weeks in London and then take Mother and me with you to Berlin—and then on to Paris? Oh, I do want to see Paris!"

"Not this time, darling. Next summer, perhaps, if all is well, we might arrange for an extended European tour, Reggie going along. But this year I could not possibly remain abroad any more than just these two weeks. And I must devote a large part of them to professional interests. Particularly, I must spend as much time as possible with Dr. Rothschild."

Elinor pouted very prettily for a moment, but at the word *professional* she did not press the question further. For she knew the bounds of her father's indulgence. She knew full well his devotion to professional duty.

Reginald Trevelyan's interest had been stirred. "Who is this Dr. Rothschild of whom you speak, Dr. Steele? You do not mean Dr. Benjamin Rothschild, the famous German surgeon?"

"Yes, Reg, I surely do. He is famous indeed. Undoubtedly he is the foremost brain specialist in all the world. In my humble opinion he is without peer. Have you ever met him?"

"No, I am sorry, I have not. But I have, of course, followed his work through the journals. For some reason, though, his writings seem to have been missing lately . . . I have always admired him tremendously. And you say you know him personally, sir?"

"Yes, I am happy to own him as a very close and cherished friend. Though I regret deeply, I have been out of touch with him for some years now. We have both been too busy to keep up personal correspondence with each other as we would like to and as we should. That is why I am so eager to contact him when I go to Europe now—that we may repair and renew our so sadly neglected fellowship.

"How long have you known him, Dr. Steele?"

"I first met Dr. Rothschild when I was in Berlin eight years ago. Through a combination of strange but very wonderful circumstances I had the priceless opportunity, for a few days, of studying under him in his own marvelous hospital—attending his surgical clinics and observing his magical technique. What is more, I had the exceptional privilege and honor of being entertained by him and his delightful family in their magnificent home—in both of their magnificent homes, I should say, for they own two: their palatial city home in Berlin and their summer home, a most fascinating medieval castle on the Rhine—with their own private airplane and pilot to convey them back and forth between them!"

"What an enviable experience!"

"It was indeed. It was one of the most memorable experiences of my life—an experience I shall never forget. I do want you all to know the Rothschilds just as soon as possible. They truly are one of the most superior families I have ever met. Distinguished to the highest degree and absolutely charming."

Reginald's interest deepened visibly. "I should love to know them!" he exclaimed eagerly. "How many are there, Dr. Steele, in this wonderful family?"

"Four. Dr. Rothschild himself and his very lovely wife—a radiantly brilliant woman—and their two fine sons. The older one, Joseph, is just about your age, Reg, and he also is a surgeon, following in his father's footsteps. I do hope that you and he can get together sometime; I am sure you would take to each other admirably.

"Moische, the younger son, will be twenty by now; he was twelve when I was there. He is exceptionally attractive—really a beautiful boy. He is a musical genius. As a pianist he has extraordinary talent. During my visit in their home, my chief delight, I remember, was in hearing Moische at his beloved keyboard. His playing, even then, when he was only twelve, was magnificent. I know I told his father and mother that I felt confident there was a great future ahead for him in the world of music. By this time he must be one of Germany's most brilliant young artists. His country can well be proud of him."

"Hollister"—Clara Steele questioned her husband thoughtfully—"when did you last hear from Dr. Rothschild?"

Dr. Steele replied in a voice that sounded troubled. "Not for a long time, Clare. It must be nearly two years now. I am becoming really quite disturbed. For the first few years after my visit in his home, we used to exchange letters, you may remember, fairly regularly. But gradually his became less and less frequent; and the last three or four, at wide intervals, seemed very strained, I thought. I may be entirely mistaken—I hope I am indeed—but I felt that his replies to my inquiries concerning his welfare were definitely evasive; or certainly not anything like as frank and confiding as his former ones had always been. And now his letters have fallen off completely. My last one to him, a few weeks ago, was returned as 'Unclaimed.' I am anxious."

"Do you believe, Hollister, that he is ill?" Clare's voice also registered grave solicitude.

"No, I do not think the reason for Dr. Rothschild's silence is illness. I wish it were only that. But I cannot so believe. If he were ill, I am very sure his wife or one of his boys would have informed me. No, I fear"—Dr. Steele's tone as he proceeded was now full of distress—"I fear," he continued slowly, as the eyes of all his hearers were fixed upon him intently, "I greatly fear some evil may have befallen him and his family."

"Oh, I trust not, sir, indeed!" Dr. Trevelyan exclaimed sympathetically.

"Evil? Oh, Daddy, what do you mean?" echoed Elinor, alarmed.

"*Evil?* Whatever evil could possibly befall any Rothschild?" Clare asked incredulously.

As Dr. Steele replied, the distress in his voice—and in his face, as well—deepened perceptibly. "You forget," he said sorrowfully, "the Rothschilds are *Jews*. The reports of Nazi atrocities against the Jews are becoming more and more outrageous. Is that not true, Reginald, in your observation?"

"Yes, Dr. Steele, so I would gather also. Though I have not personally followed the situation at all closely. I must confess I have always had an innate, indefinable aversion toward the Jews myself. That is the one racial prejudice I have definitely felt—the only one, I trust. But you are interested in them, sir? In Jews?"

"Intensely interested, Reg. But I, too, must confess it was

not until after I had met the Rothschilds and learned that they are Christians. Before that—although I had never entertained any antagonism toward them—the Jews, as such, had not particularly registered in my consciousness. And certainly it was an entirely new revelation to me that Jews of today could ever become Christians. But now, since having had sweetest Christian fellowship with the whole Rothschild family, and growing to love them as I did when I was with them in their beautiful home; and since meeting a number of other Hebrew Christians to whom Dr. Rothschild presented me, I can in all truthfulness affirm that I do love the Jews."

"What you say stirs me profoundly, Dr. Steele. And, upon my honor, I shall earnestly try to overcome my unreasoning antipathy.

"But please do not misunderstand me! While it is true, as I said, that I have always felt a natural aversion toward Jews, I, of course, could never for one moment condone Hitler's persecution of them in Germany. I deplore that utterly, as do all decent-thinking people everywhere—or in my own country, certainly. Before I left England last September, there was deepest resentment and gravest apprehension throughout all Britain—throughout all Europe indeed—because of Hitler and his relentless cruelties not alone against the Jews, but against any and all people who dare to oppose his totalitarian iron rule. During this past year since I have been away, so I am informed, the situation in Germany has deteriorated so very dangerously, and the opposition in Britain has grown so alarmingly in consequence, that relations between Britain and Germany have become more and more strained—to the point where there is now definite threat of war. The *London Times* and the *Manchester Guardian*, which my folks send me, contain stories of Nazi violence involving enormous destruction both of property and life, that are completely horrifying."

"And so," Dr. Steele observed sadly, "it is not unreasonable to fear that even the Rothschilds, despite their very great wealth and prestige, may themselves have become engulfed in the flood of anti-Semitic fury which Adolf Hitler has unleashed. The very fact that I have not heard anything whatsoever from them for so long a time now, confirms my anxiety that disaster of some sort may really have overtaken them."

"Oh, I fervently pray not!" Clare cried sorrowfully, Elinor and Reginald joining her in their exclamations of dismay.

After Dr. Trevelyan had bidden his fond good-nights and had departed and after Clare and Elinor had both retired, Dr. Steele remained alone within his beautiful moonlit garden in quiet meditation. How lovely it all was with the silvery, soft light and the fragrance of its myriad roses! Reverently he lifted his heart to God in adoration and thanksgiving. How richly He had blessed their little family since He had restored to them their precious home, their wonderful love! Great indeed had been His faithfulness!

Again, Dr. Steele's thoughts turned toward Germany and Dr. Rothschild, and again they became troubled. Where was he tonight, he wondered, at this very hour? Was he in *his* lovely home, surrounded by *his* dear ones?

Chapter 20

Mission of Mercy

Monday morning dawned warm and clear.

While the three Steeles—father, mother, and beloved daughter—were seated happily at their breakfast table, the front door bell rang. It was the postman with a Special Delivery letter for Dr. Steele. Ivy, the maid, received it and brought it to him. He looked at it curiously with mingled feelings of wonder and aversion. Wherever did a thing like that come from?

The appearance of the letter was certainly repellent. It was crumpled and ragged and dirty, smeared over with a sticky-looking substance resembling dark red paint. It comprised three or four sheets of coarse brown wrapping paper folded into a packet and tied together with a frayed black leather shoelace. Pasted across the face of the packet was a crooked row of cancelled foreign postage stamps.

The remaining space below the stamps was completely filled with the address. Thickly and very unevenly written with the same sticky red substance, as by a trembling hand, it was scarcely legible. It read merely:

G. H. Steele, M.D.
Baltimore, U.S.A.

Opening the packet, it was only with utmost difficulty that Dr. Steele finally managed to decipher its contents—written in large, sprawling characters with the same sticky substitute for red ink. As he gradually grasped the full important of the letter, his face turned pale and he emitted a deep groan. His wife and daughter looked at him, alarmed. So did Reginald Trevelyan—who had arrived just before Dr. Steele received the missive. And then, as they all gazed intently with frightened eyes, he read aloud to them the fearful tidings:

Dachau Concentration Camp, Germany, June 10, 1937.

Dear Dr. Steele:

If this letter reaches you, it will be only by a miracle of God's mercy. One of my cellmates who is being transferred tomorrow to a Nazi prison-camp in Holland promises me he will try to conceal it on his person and mail it from there.

I am writing this from Dachau, the place of unutterable horror, the abode of DESPAIR and of DEATH! I have been here for the past six weeks as a prisoner of the Nazi Government. Their sole charge against me: I am a Jew.

My precious wife is in this same camp, in the women's block. Also here in Dachau are Pastor Martin Luther von Ludwig and his daughter, Margarete (the beautiful little sweetheart Gretel, you may remember, now the wife of my son Joseph).

I do pray fervently that God will send this letter to you safely; and then that He will enable you to read it. It is so very hard for me to write it here in my cell, as I can do it only in secret snatches, between inspection rounds by my Nazi guards. It will take all day for me to finish it. My only light is the pale daylight that filters in from the courtyard through the bars of the one small window of my cell, high up above my head. All the paper that I could find was these torn and dirty sheets from a trash can. My only pen is the coarse metal tip of my shoelace. My only ink, drops of my own blood pricked from my fingers.

You may be wondering, then, why I am trying to write at all under such difficulties. And why I am writing all this to *you*. Dear friend, please bear with me patiently and forgivingly as I tell you exactly why.

Do you recall that October morning, eight years ago it was, when our whole family saw you off on the plane for America? You were going home. Home, to your beloved wife and daughter. You made me promise you then that if ever the time came when I might have need of any help you could give me, I would not fail to call upon you for it.

Beloved friend, *that time has come*! I need your help right now. Desperately do I need it! I implore you for it. Please, *please* do give it to me now! Immediately! *Before it is too late!* Oh, dear Dr. Steele, in God's name, help me and help my loved ones! Oh, help us! Save us from destruction! You are our last, our only hope.

All God's waves and billows are gone over me. I am completely broken. I am shorn of absolutely everything that life held dear. My darling, lovely Rose has lost her reason and is slowly dying. Moische, our beloved younger son, is already dead, wickedly done to death by those fiendish Nazis. Joseph, our elder son, since his flight from execution by them four months ago, has never been heard from since. Our beautiful home is gone forever. My wonderful hospital was stolen from me, and I was hurled out bodily upon the street. Our entire fortune is swept away: I now am literally penniless. Our future is hopeless. Our life is utterly wrecked.

Tell me, dear Dr. Steele, do you believe there really is a God? And does He really care? If He does care, then why, *why* all this? Is it because we are Jews? But His Son was a Jew! And I have tried so hard to follow and to serve His Son. Truly I have tried my best to love and honor Jesus Christ. But this is what I get for it. Oh, dear friend, do help me! Help me to hold my faith unbroken! Help me to keep sane! Oh, please help me to find light amid this fearful darkness! Everything is so completely black. Black with despair and fear. Please forgive me. I feel so terribly confused. Everything is all horribly mixed-up.

But, oh, dear Dr. Steele, I know that there must be a God! I *will* believe. I do believe. 'Though he slay me, yet will I trust in him.' O God in heaven, in Jesus' name, deliver us all, all Jews everywhere, from this awful Death!

Dear faithful friend, good-bye! I cannot write more: I feel so very weak. Forgive me that I have written so much. I am sorry. But I could not help it. I just had to pour my heart out: otherwise it might have burst. But at last I close. It is now almost night. Soon my cell will be completely dark.

So good-bye . . . 'God be with you' . . . my beloved Dr. Steele. Writing this letter to you brings you very close. And I do want you close. I need you desperately. I feel so terribly alone!

Good-bye! Good-bye! God bless and prosper you and all

your dear ones, and reward you very richly for all the lovingkindness you have so graciously shown to me and mine.

And now I must sign my name. But no longer is it Benjamin Rothschild, the name by which you knew me in the happier days. For no longer, surely am I a Rothschild, not by any possible claim! Instead, I am nothing but a beggar!

And certainly I am no longer Benjamin, the 'fortunate one,' as that name means. No, never again can I be Benjamin! Never again in all the world! I have a new name now. From this time henceforth I am, always and only:

In agony,

"Your soul-stricken friend,

"Ben-Oni, Son of Sorrow."

Rising suddenly from the table and clutching the blood-stained sheets tensely between his hands, Dr. Steele cried aloud in deep despair, "Benjamin Rothschild! In a Nazi concentration camp! Horrible, horrible! I must go to Germany at once! No . . . no," he protested as his wife and daughter both voiced their consternation, "no, do not try to detain me. I must start for Berlin immediately. And then on to Dachau! I must find Dr. Rothschild and my other friends."

"But, Dr. Steele," Reginald interposed gravely, "you could never get into Dachau or any other Nazi concentration camp."

"I *must* get in! I must fulfill what I know is, for me, a sacred obligation. I must find my friends and strive for their release."

"Oh, Hollister darling!" his wife pleaded. "It would be utter folly for you even to attempt such a thing—with all the might of Adolf Hitler against you. How in the world could you do it?"

"I have no idea how I can do it. I shall have to wait until I get there to find out. All I know now is that I *have* to go! I have got to do everything within my power to save my friends! Could I stand idly by while they are facing what must be their certain terrible death—their absolute destruction—in Dachau? God helping me, *never*!"

The giant airship soared above the broad Atlantic and then, at length, floated over the North Sea as it skirted the coast of

Germany, heading for the Tempelhof Airdrome in Berlin. Hollister Steele's emotions were profoundly stirred. He could not but recall his previous arrival in the great German capital eight years ago. The contrast between then and now was striking in the extreme. Then, he remembered poignantly, he had been a sick man—sick in body and desperately sick in soul. His home was broken, his loved ones estranged, all his fond hopes withered and blasted. He had been alone within a foreign land, an alien and an exile. But more than all that, he had been adrift from God—a ship without a rudder, a vessel without mooring on the stormy sea of life.

But now, how glorious the difference! His home and loved ones were restored, and a thousand times more dear than ever they had been before. His health was completely rehabilitated. His professional skies were bright. He had attained to a position of prominence and affluence and high distinction in his chosen field of surgery. Life now lay radiant before him. Above all, he had found his spiritual anchor. He now was linked consciously with Omnipotence. He was a new man in Christ. His soul had found peace—the peace of God that passeth understanding. As he contemplated the great transformation in his entire life, his heart was filled with praise. It was the Lord's doing, and it was marvelous in his eyes.

And the instrument that God had used, chiefly, in his recreation was this same wonderful Hebrew he now was come to seek amid *his* transformed circumstances. But how tragic, how terrible was the transformation in Dr. Rothschild's life! No longer would Dr. Steele meet him as he had done on that memorable first visit, when he was so highly privileged a guest in Dr. Rothschild's palatial home. Then his distinguished host had been in the full strength of his magnificent manhood, surrounded by all the devotion of his delightful family and of his host of friends, and at the very zenith of his eminent professional career: possessing an enviable share of all the good things of life. But *now,* alas! In a Nazi concentration camp, and completely broken and despairing.

It was now past sundown—too late to start upon his quest today. He would just go directly to his hotel—the Kaiserhof, assuredly. He would feel more at home there than in any other hostelry, for the Kaiserhof had been the scene of that never-to-be-forgotten professional farewell banquet Dr. Rothschild had so magnanimously given him prior to his sudden departure from Berlin.

On his way thither, his taxi driver was highly informative. Dr. Steele's knowledge of the German language, though considerably larger than at the time of his first visit, still was limited. He was sufficiently well versed, however, to follow the general import of the man's loquacious outflow. In reply to his passenger's inquiry, "Well, how are things going in Germany these days?"—the driver at once became volubly confidential.

"How are things going" he replied. "Bad, sir—bad!"

"In what way?"

"In every way, sir. Not enough jobs. Families destitute. The government topsy-turvy. Everything running completely wild. It's the Jews, sir, that's what it is—those accursed Jews. But our Fuehrer is very soon going to make a finish of them."

Dr. Steele was stunned by this venomous outburst of anti-Semitism, just upon his entrance to Adolf Hitler's stronghold. What possible hope could he have of ever rescuing Dr. Benjamin Rothschild—a *Jew*?

He went swiftly to his room and, except that he ordered dinner sent up to him, he remained in quiet seclusion all evening. He was in no mood for conversation with strangers.

After a night of fitful, troubled sleep and an early breakfast in the Kaiserhof Coffee Shop, he started off at once upon his precarious mission of mercy.

As the taxi progressed from the Kaiserhof through the streets of downtown Berlin, Dr. Steele was conscious of a number of startling changes in the general aspect of the city from what he remembered it to have been eight years before. The most conspicuous change lay in the fact that an ominous emblem now met his troubled gaze constantly: the swastika. This symbol—alike of Nazi power and of Nazi anti-Semitism—was flown on flags from every public and many private buildings in every direction.

The sinister hooked cross was further prominent upon the armbands of Nazi soldiers, many of whom were pouring through the streets, singly or in groups numbering from three or four to a dozen or twenty.

Another object that forced itself upon Dr. Steele's distressed attention was a large placard reading: Closed—By Order of Adolf Hitler. This was attached to a number of shops. Again the eager taxi driver offered further explanation: "Jewish shops, sir. The Fuehrer is running them all out of business."

As the taxi finally approached the familiar high brick wall bordering the Rothschild estate, and then passed through the great bronze gates, Hollister Steele's emotion was intense. Vivid recollections of his previous wonderful visit in this same happy abode mingled with a strange sense of loneliness in the sad realization that his then so gracious Hebrew host and his delightful family would not be here to greet him now. A strong wave of apprehension and of grief swept suddenly over him. Where were the Rothschilds at this very moment? What agonies were they suffering in that fearful concentration camp? How?—however in all the world could he, an alien in Germany, ever reach them and rescue them from their awful fate?

Eager to inspect every feature of the lordly domain as he so fondly remembered it: the magnificent trees, the lovely gardens, the palatial mansion—Dr. Steele leaned forward from the rear seat and peered eagerly through the taxi windshield.

But whatever was *this*? Startled, amazed, distressed, the emissary from America noted, first, the gardens inside of the surrounding brick wall. Where on his former visit there had been beautifully ordered groups of stately flowering shrubbery and a wealth of vivid color, there was now an unsightly mass of dead blooms amid high-grown tangled weeds, rusty and drab.

And next, to his unutterable dismay, he saw the trees! Once so luxuriant, so majestic, so completely restful with their lofty green branches, widespreading and interlacing, they now presented only shuddering blackened trunks, almost completely denuded of all their former glorious foliage.

With sickening apprehension Dr. Steele peered through and beyond them for his first glimpse of the high turreted roof of the Rothschild mansion. But not one turret, not one gleaming window, not one graceful column met his anguished view. To his horror, Hollister Steele beheld now, in its place, only broken-down, blackened stones of the former firm foundation—enclosing, and surrounded by, heaps of charred debris of what had been, beforetime, the magnificent abode. The noble house of Rothschild was indeed completely gone—"gone forever"—even as Dr. Rothschild's letter had so woefully declared. Nothing remained of it but a total ruin—a hideous, burned-out desolation.

In stunned silence, Dr. Steele gazed upon the awful scene. But his anguished reverie was suddenly cut short by a further outburst from his voluble driver:

"Do you know, sir, what this place was you had me bring you to? This here is all that's left of what was supposed to be the handsomest house in the whole of Germany. It was the home of Dr. Benjamin Rothschild, head of the Rothschild Hospital for Sick Children. Ever hear of him, sir? At one time he was the topmost surgeon in all Europe, so everybody said. In all the world, some people thought. But unfortunately, sir, he was a Jew. And so, of course, Hitler had to wipe them out. Some people think he's been deported out of Germany, God only knows where. And nobody knows anything about his family. Some folks say—"

"Drive me back to the hotel," Dr. Steele ordered gloomily.

But as the taxi emerged from the estate and began to traverse the highway leading to downtown Berlin, a new plan gradually registered within the passenger's troubled mind. "No, drive first to Charlottenburg," he reversed his direction. Assuredly he must go to Pastor von Ludwig's home. It was now ten thirty.

He rang the doorbell. But the noise within quite smothered it. He stood for a moment of awkward suspense. Then he rang the bell again—this time loudly and insistently and long. It had the desired effect. The raucous music stopped abruptly, and one of the Nazis—a man of utterly repellent aspect—strode toward the door, all the others watching him intently with curious glances.

The two men met face-to-face, the Aryan and the American, the SS Elite Guard officer and, to him, the unwelcome stranger. The officer stared at the intruder coldly. And then he spoke—in harsh, guttural tones:

"Well? And who are *you*, sir? And what brings you *here*?"

In the course of his distinguished professional career, Hollister Steele had met many difficult people and had handled many difficult situations. But never before had he encountered a personality or a situation as formidable as the personality and the situation looming suddenly before him now. Instinctively he shrank in every fiber of his being. Entirely at variance with his long-accustomed self-possession and command, all at once he felt himself ill at ease, embarrassed, at a loss for words.

Quietly, without a word, he drew from his pocket a leather case, out of which he lifted one of his professional cards. Slowly he handed it to the discourteous Nazi. The man took it with critical eyes and read it silently.

At once his whole attitude changed. His cold features relaxed. Even his harsh voice became softened, almost gracious.

Aloud he pronounced the name and address inscribed upon the card: "G. Hollister Steele, MD, Southeastern Hospital, Baltimore, Maryland." And then in astonishment and with unconcealed delight he asked the stranger, "Are *you* Dr. Steele, the famous brain specialist of America?"

The reply was given with characteristic modesty. "I am Hollister Steele; I do not know about the 'famous' part of it."

"Dr. Steele!" The Nazi extended his hand in a genuine warmth of welcome. His voice was unctuous, almost fawning. "I am most highly honored in meeting you, sir! You are famous indeed—here in Germany, anyway!"

"I thank you."

"This way, please. We shall find a quiet corner where we can talk without disturbance."

Dr. Steele followed the officer to the secluded alcove at the rear of the hallway behind the stairs and seated himself in the proffered chair. Neither he nor the Nazi had the faintest inkling of the fact that this was the identical alcove and the identical chair which, less than six months ago, Gretel had occupied during her frightful encounter with von Wolfmacht on that last horrifying night before she left—forever—her father's house. Her saintly father's house! This very house now so dastardly stolen from him and from her by their ruthless enemy!

"And now, my good friend, what can we do for you? I am interested, naturally, to know what brings you here," said the officer in his most ingratiating manner, as he drew up another chair beside his caller.

Vividly aware of divine empowering and guidance, his spirit glowingly elated by this sudden radical alteration in the Nazi's attitude and demeanor, the friend and would-be rescuer of Pastor von Ludwig and the Rothschilds again breathed a prayer, swift and importunate, for wisdom: for exactly the right word to speak, for exactly the right approach to this representative of the might of Nazi Germany—this personal representative of the all-powerful Adolf Hitler. And again clear discernment was supernaturally vouchsafed to him. At once he knew decisively: his wisest course was to come straight to the point without equivocation or delay.

"I have come on a strictly personal errand: to get information, if possible, about a cherished friend of mine who is . . . missing," Dr. Steele replied.

"Yes? And that friend is—?"

"That friend is the man who formerly owned and occupied this house which you Nazi gentlemen are now occupying: Pastor Martin Luther von Ludwig of the Confessional Church of Charlottenburg. Do you know him, sir? And can you tell me where I might be able to locate him?"

At the mention of the name "von Ludwig" the officer was suddenly startled. Again his entire demeanor changed instantly. He stiffened completely. He reverted to his former churlishness. His visage hardened. His voice became harsh. The very atmosphere turned ice-cold.

"Von Ludwig!" he repeated. "*Martin Luther von Ludwig!* What possible interest can you have in *him*? He is one of our most dangerous political prisoners!"

"Yes," Dr. Steele replied quietly, "I understand that Pastor von Ludwig is a prisoner of your Nationalist Socialist Government, in your Dachau Concentration Camp; and that is exactly the reason—one of the reasons—why I am here in Germany. I have come purposely all the way from America to ascertain if it would be possible, by any means whatsoever, to effect his release. As I have already intimated," he continued intrepidly as the Nazi scowled his fiercest scowl, "he is a most revered friend. And I want to be that friend. Can you not help me, *Herr Offizier*, to obtain entrance to him? Oh, I beg of you! I appeal to your compassion! Oh, sir, if it is at all within the realm of possibility, will you not graciously undertake for me to visit my friend?"

The Nazi folded his arms and stared at his suppliant coldly. And then critically. And then with calculating shrewdness. He was thinking, thinking deeply. This distinguished gentleman from America represented the profession he himself had so ardently coveted. He had wide influence. He had important connection. Against some future day and opportunity, perhaps, might it not be the part of wisdom—might it not prove valuable—to cultivate him now?

"Well, Dr. Steele," he began, almost apologetically, "I shall be glad to see what I can do for you. Unfortunately, however, I myself have no authority in such a matter. Sanction for you to contact von Ludwig would have to come through the director-general, Herr Heinrich Starkmann, who is in supreme command of all our concentration camps and prisons. And I must tell you frankly, sir—though I regret I have to do so—I fear that permission even to see this erstwhile friend of yours would, automatically, be denied. For in the nature of the case, a prisoner as dangerous as is Martin Luther von Ludwig could not be accorded any favors whatsoever. But on the other hand"—he added quickly as he saw a cloud of bitter disappointment pass over Dr. Steele's face—"Herr Starkmann is a personal friend of mine, and I may be able to induce him to grant you an interview and allow you to present your argument. If you will excuse me, please, I believe I can get him on the phone right now." He promptly entered a phone booth across the hallway, leaving his caller tense with emotion and expectancy.

In short time—which seemed incredibly long, however, to the anxious man awaiting him—the Nazi reappeared, his countenance wreathed in a smile of distinct satisfaction and friendliness. "Well, Dr. Steele," he said affably, "I have welcome news for you! Our Herr Gauleiter Starkmann will see you in his office in the Reichstag at ten o'clock on Tuesday morning." He extended his hand with utmost cordiality. "And now, sir," he continued, "I am sorry that I must take my leave. I have an urgent military engagement at noon. And so, my good friend, auf Wiedersehen! HEIL HITLER!"

Chapter 21

An Ally

Ten o'clock on Tuesday morning! Not until then could he have his audience with Herr Starkmann. In his appeal to the Nazi officer for entrance into Dachau on behalf of Pastor von Ludwig, he had felt definitely restrained from even mentioning his other beloved Hebrew friends, such as he had longed to include them also in his plea.

Back in the Kaiserhof, after his merciful release from his more-than-ever loquacious taximan whom he had retained to convey him thither, he gave himself up to complete solitude and relaxation for the remainder of the day, even ordering both the noon and evening meals served in his room, rather than endure the added strain of eating in the public dining room with curious eyes fastened upon him.

Not until he was alone and quiet did he realize how very acute had been his tension, alike of body, mind, and heart, ever since the arrival of Dr. Rothschild's tragic letter, nor how imperative now was his need for physical and nervous and spiritual reinvigoration. He realized insistently that he must get himself strongly in hand to meet the stern exigencies of tomorrow and of all the days that lay ahead.

Inevitably, Monday morning dawned. After a long night of graciously God-given untroubled sleep, Dr. Steele awoke refreshed and strong. Following a leisurely breakfast in the coffee shop, he set forth courageously upon his noble quest.

His first objective was the Sharon Rothschild Memorial Hospital. Here, surely, was the place where best he could obtain information about his beloved Hebrew friend, the founder and former head of this great humanitarian institution.

Entering the reception room, Dr. Steele seated himself in

the sole remaining vacant chair to await his turn for interview by the receptionist. Surreptitiously he glanced around the room. It was fully occupied, to the point of overcrowding, by about twenty patients. Dr. Steele studied their faces cautiously. They were all, old and young alike, undoubtedly German. There was not one Jew among them.

At length the receptionist approached him self-importantly. A large metal writing tablet holding a printed questionnaire was held across her left arm; a ball-point pen was poised commandingly in her right hand. Her features were typically Aryan; her expression was hard; her voice, as she addressed the distinguished gentleman before her, was ice-cold: "Your name and age."

Dr. Steele hesitated for the fraction of an instant. He was carefully deliberating—

"Your name and *age*," the receptionist demanded sternly.

"I am not a patient. I have come to see Dr. Hoffenstetter on a purely personal errand. Would you kindly give him my card and ask if it would be possible for him to grant me just fifteen minutes? I would not detain him longer. Perhaps within even only five minutes he might be able to give me certain information which I urgently require."

The receptionist eyed the card and then eyed Dr. Steele himself, frigidly. "Very well," she retorted in none too courteous a manner, "I shall give this to Herr *Doktor* Hoffenstetter and tell him what it is you want, and ask if he will see you. But of course," she added haughtily, "you would have to wait your turn."

But almost immediately the receptionist returned to him from the inner sanctum of her chief. "Herr *Doktor* Steele," she said, with decided chagrin, "Herr *Doktor* Hoffenstetter says he will see you just as soon as he is finished with his present patient. If you care to wait, sir, I shall call you."

Yes, he would wait, he assured the lady. But it so happened that the "present patient" was an emergency casualty, just brought in from a car wreck and requiring immediate surgery in the hospital, whither the physician himself took her. The waiting, therefore, would be long. Twenty minutes. Half an hour. One whole hour. An hour and a quarter. One by one the patients in the waiting room, grown weary of waiting, had left, until nearly all were gone. Happily it was now for only fifteen minutes more. At twelve o'clock exactly the receptionist reappeared and summoned him to follow her into Dr. Hoffenstetter's office.

Once again a vivid contrast! A contrast it was indeed between the man who had received him in that selfsame office eight years before, and the present incumbent. Dr. Rothschild: impressive in manner and appearance, distinguished, gracious, genial, and warmhearted in his hospitable welcome of the stranger from overseas. This supplanting new occupant—Dr. Friederich Hoffenstetter—most unimposing in his appearance and uncouth in his demeanor; harsh, abrupt, rude—altogether a completely unattractive personality.

"Dr. Hollister Steele!" Dr. Friederich Hoffenstetter greeted his visitor warmly. "This is indeed an honor to welcome you, sir. I am extremely sorry that I had to keep you waiting so long; but there was a critical operation I wanted to stay through with one of my most distinguished patients—the wife of an important Nazi official. Her case was a highway near fatality involving the spine. Very precarious. But I believe we have saved the woman's life."

"Oh, I am so glad for that. I would quite willingly wait."

"Thank you, sir. I appreciate your consideration . . . But now, please tell me what brings you here to Germany? And to me?"

Once again Dr. Steele was impressed with the wisdom—the necessity, in this instance—of coming straight to the point. "Dr. Hoffenstetter," he replied in a deliberate, firm voice, "I have come to Germany purposely to search for an old and cherished friend of mine who is . . . missing. I have come here to your office, sir, because this same friend was its former occupant, and I have entertained the hope that you, as his successor, might be able, perhaps, to give me some word concerning him. I refer to the internationally famous surgeon Dr. Benjamin Rothschild. Are you acquainted with him personally, sir? And can you tell me anything about his present circumstances?"

Even as Dr. Steele pronounced the name "Dr. Benjamin Rothschild"—in tender tones, be it noted—the Aryan Nazi confronting him stiffened visibly, a dark frown quickly overshadowing his austere face.

"Dr. Benjamin Rothschild!" he repeated in cold contempt. "No sir! I know nothing of him whatsoever. And what is more, I do not care to know. All I do know—and delight in—is that he is no longer here. He *was* here, I admit—just before I came a year ago—but he was completely purged from our profession. Fortunately so, for everyone concerned. You say he is your friend! Are you aware, sir, that he is a Jew? As such, there is certainly no place for him in this establishment . . . But I beg your pardon, Dr. Steele, I must ask you to excuse me. I have patients waiting." Whereupon he flung his office door wide open and waved his caller abruptly in the direction of the street. Thus swiftly was Dr. Steele's so long-awaited interview with Herr *Doktor* Friederich Hoffenstetter concluded.

Mortified and baffled, he stood for a moment on the outside of the handsome professional building, in the strong grip of depression and frustration.

He looked at his watch. Ten minutes past twelve, and he was hungry. He would get a bite to eat and then decide. Where could he find a tearoom? Suddenly he bethought himself of the Physicians' and Surgeons' Club where he and Dr. Rothschild had enjoyed a number of happy lunches together. It was just on the next block from the office, he recalled.

He selected a distant table and ordered lunch. It was quickly and attractively served by a polite young German *kellner*, and Dr. Steele partook of it with considerable relish. Just as he was about to begin his dessert and coffee, a most distinguished-looking German gentleman entered the dining room and seated himself directly across the aisle from him, at the very next table.

Dr. Steele eyed him intently. However, he could not see his face, for the man's back was turned toward him. But something in the imposing height, the squarely set strong shoulders, and the finely shaped head impressively crowned with a wealth of lustrous gray hair, had a distinctly familiar look. Dr. Steele kept watching him closely as, with eager curiosity, he ransacked his memory for a clue to the gentleman's identity. Could it possibly be Dr. . . . ? he wondered excitedly. Certainly it did look like him from the rear view. But Dr. Steele could not be sure. He would have to see the man's face. He would have to wait till he rose from his table and turned around. But the waiting would not be too long; already the newcomer's order had been brought to him and he was eating hurriedly, evidently deeply absorbed in thought.

And so Dr. Steele waited patiently, timing the completion of his *äpfeltorte* and coffee to fix exactly his neighbor's completion of his entire lunch. And then the gentleman rose quickly from his table and turned, directly facing his investigator. Instantly Dr. Steele hailed him with a glad cry of recognition: "Dr. Eisenleben!"

"Dr. Steele! Can this possibly be you? I am more than delighted to meet you again!"

"And I to meet you, Dr. Eisenleben!"

"But what brings you to Germany? Ah, my friend, it is a sadly altered Germany to which you have come this time!" Dr. Eisenleben's voice dropped almost to a whisper. "You, of course, know of all that has been going on . . . ?"

"Yes, yes! Unutterably deplorable!" Before Dr. Steele could say more, Dr. Eisenleben suddenly placed a restraining hand upon his arm.

"Dr. Steele, we have to be extremely careful. German walls have ears; Nazi spies are everywhere. I want you to understand, first of all, that *I* am not a Nazi. I am a German—even a 'pure Aryan,' if you will—but I am definitely not a Nazi. Their philosophy and practice I loathe with all my soul!"

"As I do also, Dr. Eisenleben! As does everyone right-minded when we realize the awful suffering and havoc they have wrought upon millions!"

"And especially their hellish atrocities against the Jews! Oh, it is ghastly—horrible! Horrible beyond all possible believing! Have you heard, Dr. Steele, what those Nazi fiends have done even to our beloved Dr. Rothschild?" Dr. Eisenleben fairly trembled with mingled rage and grief.

Profoundest sorrow choked Dr. Steele's voice as he replied, "Yes! I know it all! I have heard everything: how they destroyed his home, his hospital, his health, his fortune, his family—how they have completely wrecked his very life! Yes, Dr. Eisenleben, I have heard it all—from Dr. Rothschild himself.

"And now here I am!—to find out everything I can about the whole dreadful situation. To do everything in my power to contact Dr. Rothschild and give him aid and comfort. I wonder, Dr. Eisenleben, is it too presuming for me to ask if I might enlist *your* help, your influence?"

Dr. Eisenleben groaned—audibly, deeply. "My influence! My honored position in the Rothschild Hospital!" he repeated bitterly. "Dr. Steele, my influence is nil. I am no longer in the Rothschild Hospital. The very next day after Dr. Rothschild was thrown out, I resigned and left immediately—in protest. But also, I left because I knew I could not possibly remain there without *him*. I knew I could not by any possibility whatever work under the new regime—work under those totalitarian beasts!"

"And you are now—?"

"In private medical practice only—with my office in the professional building, the same center in which Dr. Rothschild's private office was located. And *I*, Dr. Steele—I am on the Nazi black list!"

"*You*, Dr. Eisenleben?—and you yourself a German! But why? Why, Dr. Eisenleben, *why*?"

"Because I dared openly to champion a Jew! Because I dared—defiantly—to challenge their treatment of Dr. Benjamin Rothschild! I was incensed by the outrage, the base injustice of it all, that I could not—apart from losing my self-respect—keep silent.

"In every way. I am cold-shouldered, ostracized, boycotted by the entire Hitler hierarchy, including Adolf Hitler himself. For I befriended—and defended—not alone the Rothschilds but all Jews in general, and a not inconsiderable number of Jews in particular and personally—Jews who are among my own patients. Before too long—I realize it perfectly, Dr. Steele—I well may find myself in the same place with Dr. Rothschild—in *Dachau*!"

"Oh, no, no! Never, my dear friend, never such a thing as that for *you*!"

Dr. Eisenleben shook his head sadly. "Why not? Far better men that I are in Nazi concentration camps and prisons—thousands of them. It is not at all improbable that I should follow them. I am prepared for any eventuality if only—"

Dr. Steele interrupted violently. "Dr. Eisenleben, why do you remain here? Why do you not leave Germany while there yet is time? Come back with me to America! There you could begin a new life and have a great future before you. We will gladly make a place for you in Southeastern and—"

"Dr. Steele, I deliberately identified myself with Israel in my sympathies and my endeavors, realizing fully the probable consequences of so doing."

"And those consequences are?"

"Identification with Israel in her suffering! But we know that 'the sufferings of this present time are not worthy to be compared with the glory which shall be revealed in us.' According to God's prophetic Word a glorious future is promised to His beloved chosen people, and I truly believe, dear friend, that we who stand with them in their present sorrows shall assuredly share with them in their future joy."

"May God give to me, Dr. Eisenleben, a faith as steadfast and as glorious as yours!"

"He has already given it, Dr. Steele. He has given you also a true love for the Jews—abundant proof of which is your present merciful quest. I am sadly confident that the only possible hope of your ever getting into Dachau and seeing Dr. Rothschild would be upon direct order from Herr Heinrich Starkmann, who controls all the camps and prisons throughout Germany. And for you ever to be allowed opportunity for an audience with *him*, in order to present your plea—especially if he knew the purpose of your desired interview—is, I greatly fear, extremely unlikely."

"Not only 'extremely unlikely' but, on the human level, impossible! Yes, I grant it. But with God all things are possible—even this, as I have already proven. Dr. Eisenleben, it is the amazing fact that I have an appointment to meet Herr Starkmann at ten o'clock tomorrow morning!"

"To meet *Heinrich Starkmann*! Himself! You have an *appointment*? Already? Astounding! Absolutely astounding! But however did you accomplish it? And when?"

"I did not accomplish it at all. 'This is the LORD's doing; it is marvelous in our eyes.' From the very moment that I received Dr. Rothschild's letter—just a week ago this morning—God has guided me step-by-step and opened up the way before me."

"Dr. Steele! This is the most tremendous testimony to the

power and grace of God that I have ever heard! Undoubtedly His hand is upon the whole marvelous undertaking. May His hand continue to be strongly upon yourself in all your going forward as His appointed messenger of deliverance and hope! Dr. Steele, after you have had your interview with Starkmann, I shall be most anxious to hear all about it."

"Thank you, Dr. Eisenleben. I shall be happy indeed to see you tomorrow. There are several things I would like to talk over with you fully. I want to find out all I can about the whole Rothschild family. And all about the von Ludwigs. They are in Dachau also, I understand—Pastor von Ludwig and his daughter."

"Yes, yes, it is all too true! And all too horrible! Pastor von Ludwig was . . . But I must not detain you any longer now. We will talk tomorrow."

"I really must be at my office early this afternoon. I am so very sorry, Dr. Steele. You will kindly excuse me?"

A warmhearted handshake, and then the two reunited friends parted for a little time again.

Chapter 22

The Ransom

Ominously did it approach: ten o'clock of Tuesday morning, the hour when Dr. Steele must beard the lion in his ominous den: Herr Heinrich Starkmann, the "hangman of the Gestapo."

During the last quarter hour before the deadline, that formidable personage himself sat at his desk in his private office in the Gestapo headquarters in Berlin. Half a dozen subordinate Nazis also were present within the large room, each one occupied with his particular assignment for the morning. But Herr Starkmann was entirely oblivious of them. His attention was riveted exclusively upon a letter spread open before him.

As he read it through for the second time he scowled darkly. Whatever in the world did Wertheimer mean by sending him such a letter as *that*?

But before Herr Starkmann gave way completely to his mounting fury, he reread the letter once again, this time with carefully steadied, critical appraisal of each detail it contained. As he did so his wrath subsided, his mood gradually softened, and, finally, his interest in Wertheimer's plea became definitely enlisted. Perhaps his friend had a good case after all. Certainly his letter presented his argument very adroitly. It read:

My dear Heinrich:

This letter is a follow-up to our telephone conversation this morning regarding our notorious prisoner, von Ludwig, and the man who came to me seeking his release: a Dr. Steele from America.

I believe I explained the situation fully in our talk together on the phone. As I told you in confidence, I, of course, referred

Steele to you. I surely thank you very much for arranging the appointment to interview him Tuesday morning.

To my personal and certain knowledge, this Steele is a man we might have to reckon with. He is an American surgeon of very high prestige and, as such, he undoubtedly wields large influence. You agree with me, I am sure, that it is important for us to enlist all the influence possible, particularly American influence, at this very critical stage of our foreign relationships.

Dr. Steele, for some strange, sentimental reason which is incomprehensible to me, as I have no doubt it will be to you also, appears to be deeply devoted to von Ludwig and is insistent in his pleading for the man's freedom. He has, indeed, come to Germany specifically for this purpose. May I, therefore, respectfully suggest that if you can see your way clear to favor him in his bizarre undertaking, I feel confident that this concession would yield us valuable future dividends, as well as large present advantage. Remember, this man Steele is one of those disgusting "rich Americans," and we could demand, and no doubt obtain from him, a fantastic price for von Ludwig's release. We could fully safeguard our own security by ordering von Ludwig's, and also Dr. Steele's, immediate deportation from Germany.

So, my dear Heinrich, please think the whole situation through very carefully and do the best for all concerned.

Faithfully yours,

Otto

HEIL HITLER!

The recipient of this amazing letter looked at his wristwatch. Five minutes to ten! And this Dr. Steele was coming to interview him at ten exactly. He must do some rapid thinking. Well, one thing, anyway, was clear and certain. Martin Luther von Ludwig could not be freed—absolutely *not*! He was their most dangerous political prisoner—their Enemy Number One. He must be made to pay in full measure for his perfidy.

But how could he reconcile the two diametrically opposite values? Herr Starkmann scowled yet more darkly in his increasingly puzzled thought. Well, he would wait and see how things developed in his talk with Steele. He should be coming at any moment now. It was just ten o'clock.

As the clock on the wall struck the hour, there was a loud rap on the door. In response to Herr Starkmann's stentorian *"Herein!"* a Nazi guard entered and called out the name of the man following behind him: "Herr *Doktor* G. Hollister Steele!"

Starkmann, retaining his seat at the desk, greeted his caller with the Nazi salute and a gruff *"Guten Morgen."* And then he added, "You are the man, I believe, who was sent here by Herr Wertheimer?"

"Yes sir, I am."

The director-general of Nazi concentration camps and prisons looked at the stranger hard and searchingly. "Very well," he said at length, "sit down. Now, what is it that you want?" His voice held a note of attempted graciousness.

Dr. Steele's tone, in reply, registered attempted rigid control of his inward agitation. "I believe, Herr Starkmann," he began bravely, "that Herr Wertheimer explained to you my errand—my mission to Germany—over the telephone on Sunday morning. I can only repeat and emphasize it, sir. My strong desire and my fervent position is that I might be permitted to enter your Dachau Concentration Camp and contact my friend, Pastor von Ludwig, and eventually secure his release."

"Are you aware, my dear sir," murmured the director-general, "of the character of this man you are so boldly undertaking to befriend? He has been guilty of the most heinous crimes: TREASON. The just penalty for his unpardonable sin must be exacted to the last degree. His sentence must be carried out to its extreme and final limit."

"And that sentence is . . . ?" Breathlessly Dr. Steele awaited the reply from the Hangman of Berlin. He gave it in ice-cold tone:

"Von Ludwig's sentence is one year at hard labor under severest camp discipline—to be followed, at the conclusion of the year, by a sort of terminal situation."

Dr. Steele almost swooned from the sudden awful shock. "Is there no possible appeal?" he asked in anguish of soul.

The Hangman softened visibly. "I am sorry, my friend," he

murmured mellifluously, "sorry indeed to have to disappoint your hopes, misguided though they are."

"Could you, at least, then grant me permission to enter Dachau and visit with my friend?" Dr. Steele's voice was agonized.

"Yes indeed, sir. I am glad to authorize this privilege. I shall give you a written order for admittance to our camp, which will include permission for occasional contacts with von Ludwig—but always, of course, under strict surveillance. This concession is contrary to our rule ordinarily. But I shall be happy to make this exception in your case."

"I thank you most gratefully, Herr Starkmann!"

"You are quite welcome. Is there anything further I could do for you, my friend?" Still more urgently did the "valuable future dividends" engage the Nazi's crafty calculation.

Here at last was Dr. Steele's opportunity to attempt the rescue of, at least, the Rothschilds. "Yes!" he replied eagerly. "There is indeed another and a very urgent request that I would like to make, if I may venture—"

"So? And what is that, my dear Dr. Steele?" Herr Starkmann's voice by now was soft and gracious—almost gentle. For the "dividends" were now clamoring insistently with most alluring appeal.

The messenger of mercy trembled inwardly before this symbol of the awful might of Adolf Hitler's government. But sternly controlling his agitation, he plunged forward boldly in his desperate venture to save the beloved Rothschilds.

"Herr Starkmann!"—Dr. Steele looked straight into the cold, cruel eyes of this authorized powerful deputy of the Gestapo—"I have other friends also in your Dachau Concentration Camp whom I long to visit—whom I most ardently long to see released—"

"Yes? And who are *they*?"

"They are Jewish friends: Dr. Benjamin Rothschild and his wife and daughter-in-law. If my understanding is correct, they, too, are your prisoners."

It was now Heinrich Starkmann's turn to become inwardly agitated—violently so. But his agitation, as well as Dr. Steele's, was astutely concealed. Partly to stall for time, he gave command to one of his Nazi guards: "Bring me the Rothschild dossier."

While he waited for the order to be carried out, the *Gauleiter* maintained a deeply thoughtful silence—during which Dr. Steele prayed fervently: "O God of Abraham, Isaac, and Jacob! Deliver Thy beloved Hebrew children! O God, liberate the precious Rothschilds!"

The attendant brought the desired folder and placed it on the desk in front of his superior. Herr Starkmann scrutinized it closely. Then slowly he read it aloud. "Ah, yes, Rothschild! Here it is:

"'ROTHSCHILD, Dr. Benjamin. Surgeon. JEW.

"'Conviction—Defiance against the Nationalist Socialist Government. Disloyalty toward Fuehrer Adolf Hitler. Unlawful operation of a hospital. Employment of Jews upon his staff and admission of Jewish patients. Secret harboring of upwards of 100 Jewish refugees in basement shelter within his own home.

"'Sentence—Twenty years' hard labor in Dachau, under severe discipline.

"'ROTHSCHILD—von Arnim, Rose. Wife of Benjamin. JEWESS.

"'Conviction—Aiding and abetting her husband in his subversive activities.

"'Sentence—'"

Herr Starkmann stopped abruptly in his reading of Rose Rothschild's Dachau record—then hurried on to the third and last name in the dossier:

"'ROTHSCHILD—von Ludwig, Margarete. JEWESS. Formerly an Aryan. Daughter of Pastor Martin Luther von Ludwig.

"'Conviction—Marriage to a Jew: Joseph Rothschild, son of Dr. Benjamin Rothschild.

"'Sentence—Original sentence: Hard labor for life in Dachau. Sentence commuted to fifteen years' hard labor as camp nurse in the Women's Division.'"

The chief *kommandant* of all the concentration camps and prisons of Germany closed the portfolio. His reading was concluded. But Dr. Steele imposed a question:

"Frau Benjamin Rothschild, Herr Starkmann. You did not finish reading her file. You did not read her sentence. What was that?"

Curtly the Hangman of Berlin made ice-cold reply, not one faintest trace of compassion in his tone:

"Frau Rothschild is dead. She died of a heart attack. Just one week after she entered Dachau. Too sickly and weak, evidently, to stand up to camp routine and discipline. At time of entrance, apparent mental derangement," he added heartlessly.

Once again Dr. Steele nearly fainted from sickening shock, to which was added intensified grief. Brilliant, beautiful Rose Rothschild! To come to such a frightful end! It was ghastly, horrible beyond all believing! Dr. Steele could scarcely contain himself, so profound was his sorrow and his dismay.

"Yes, Herr *Doktor* Steele," he replied in answer to the visitor's request, "you may *visit* Dr. Rothschild—and his daughter-in-law likewise—if you so desire. But as to their release, that is quite another matter. You must remember: they are Jews. And the only proper place for any Jew yet alive is within a concentration camp or prison. But we do occasionally—if there are sufficient and sufficiently justifiable reasons—make a rare exception, provided, of course, that it is made worthwhile for us to do so. But it could only be upon fixed and stern conditions."

"Yes, yes?" Dr. Steele exclaimed eagerly, joyfully. "And these conditions are?"

"The consideration for the release of these two Semites would be twofold. The first condition, the guarantee, under one thousand dollars bond, that they would be out of Germany within forty-eight hours of their leaving Dachau. The second condition, the cash payment, for each of the two prisoners before their release, of the sum, in American currency, of ten thousand dollars. Ten thousand apiece, you understand—a total of twenty thousand dollars. That together with the bond equals twenty-one thousand dollars, American. And you are prepared to accept them?"

The ultimatum had an electrifying effect upon Hollister Steele. Whereas the sudden news of Rose Rothschild's death had almost prostrated him, this pronouncement of the terms of freedom for Dr. Rothshild and Gretel stirred all his faculties to swift and vigorous acumen. It would take nearly all the savings of his entire professional career; it would cost him his intended dowry for Elinor, the new equipment he had hoped to purchase for his private office, next summer's promised trip to the Continent for all the family: all these would have to be relinquished now. But in the scale of eternal values, not one ounce did these desired benefits weigh in comparison with the saving of the Rothschilds.

Herr Starkmann repeated his interrogation: "Twenty thousand dollars cash, in American currency, is our demand for the release of these two notorious Jewish prisoners from Dachau. Do you or do you not accept these terms?"

Unequivocally—triumphantly—in ringing voice Dr. Steele made answer:

"Yes sir! I do accept them! I shall pay you the full twenty thousand dollars within a few days—just as soon as I can arrange by cable to have this amount realized from my securities and sent to me from my bank in Baltimore, America."

"Very good. Very good indeed. But you understand further, do you not?—that you must deposit a bona fide bond of one thousand dollars as pledge for the departure from Germany of these two undesirable Semites within forty-eight hours of their leaving our concentration camp."

"Yes, Herr Starkmann, I fully understand that also. The bond for one thousand, as well as the twenty thousand dollars' ransom, will be given you promptly upon receipt of my funds from America."

"But you must comprehend this, too, sir, completely: if these two Jews remain in Germany one hour beyond the forty-eight-hour deadline, this whole thousand dollars will be forfeit."

"I do comprehend it completely. I personally will engage to escort Dr. Rothschild and his daughter-in-law across the border within the appointed time."

The director-general rose abruptly from his chair and crossed over to his filing cabinet. He drew from it a printed form. Returning to his desk and taking up his pen, he filled it in with large, flourishing handwriting—in complete silence. And then he handed it to Dr. Steele.

"There," he said, "take this! It is my order for your admittance to Dachau, with permission to visit your three friends as you may desire. You will present this document to the guard at the entrance gate. He will have it conveyed promptly to the camp *kommandant*, who, in turn, will receive you and make all the necessary arrangements.

"You may go down tomorrow morning, and each morning thereafter that you may care to do so until your money arrives from America. Our Nazi plane leaves for Dachau daily, from the Tempelhof Airdrome, at nine o'clock, returning at three in the afternoon.

"You will taken an *Entlassungsschein* certificate in exchange for your cash payment with you to Dachau on the first available plane. A Gestapo officer will accompany you. Upon your arrival, you will present this document to the concentration camp *kommandant*, and he will make all the arrangements required for the prisoners' departure. You will then proceed with them immediately to the border—by the first conveyance possible—at whatever point you will by that time have decided upon.

"Remember: from the moment they leave Dachau until they are positively out of Germany, these two notorious, subversive Jews—Benjamin Rothschild and Margarete von Ludwig–Rothschild—are in your protective custody and under strict accountability. Is *that* entirely clear to you?"

"Entirely clear. And I thank you, sir!"

Again the director-general rose abruptly from his chair—a signal, this time, that the interview was concluded. With a gruff "*Guten Morgen!* HEIL HITLER!" he waved his caller—none too graciously—toward the door.

Out, once again, upon the street, Dr. Steele turned his footsteps in the direction of Dr. Eisenleben's office for the promised visit. But on the way thither he stopped, first, at the telegraph office and cabled his bank in Baltimore for the money so avidly demanded of him by Adolf Hitler's hangman.

His rejoicing in the prospect of seeing these dear friends again and very soon also was unbounded. But overclouding his joy was his deep sorrow in dear Rose's tragic death and in all the other tragedies that had befallen the noble house of Rothschild. And very, very deep was his grief that the beloved

Pastor von Ludwig must yet remain within that hideous abode of death, with death for himself—and by the most hideous means—hanging over him. But Dr. Steele's faith was strong that the saintly servant of the Lord would even yet find release from Dachau. How or when he could not venture even the faintest surmise. But—*being confident of this very thing, that he which hath begun a good work . . . will perform it until the day of Jesus Christ*—he dared to believe that as the Lord had wrought so marvelously for the rescue of the Rothschilds, even so would He intervene in behalf of Martin Luther von Ludwig. As already the God of the impossible had begun His good work of mercy in the freeing of Dr. Rothschild and Gretel, just so assuredly would He complete that work in the deliverance of His faithful minister of the gospel from the fury of the destroyer.

"Absolutely astounding! Unbelievable! Impossible!" Such was Dr. Eisenleben's amazed rejoinder when Dr. Steele, according to his agreement, gave him an account of his interview with the Nazi *Gauleiter* and its rewarding result.

In entire unity of spirit the two men exulted together in the victory Dr. Steele had won: Herr Starkmann's concession for him to enter Dachau and visit their friends imprisoned therein, and his agreement to the Rothschilds' release.

"But, Dr. Eisenleben"—he concluded his review with strongest admonition—"we shall include Pastor von Ludwig in our plans for deliverance. God assuredly will intervene. I have faith to believe that Pastor von Ludwig will yet be rescued from the lions' den."

"We shall indeed, my friend!" Dr. Eisenleben assented eagerly. The two men shook hands in solemn, fervent hope, promising to implore God night and day for deliverance.

And then Dr. Steele took his departure for his hotel, after promising Dr. Eisenleben that he would come to see him again, immediately following his first visit to Dachau.

"Perhaps you may have another friend in Dachau, Dr. Steele, before the week runs out," his German colleague answered sadly.

"Dr. Eisenleben! Whatever do you *mean*?" Dr. Steele's voice registered distinct alarm.

"I mean exactly that, my friend. The Nazi net is tightening

about me—swiftly and inevitably. For I have dared to befriend the Jews. At any hour now, day or night, the Gestapo will apprehend me. Dear Dr. Steele, I *know* it. I am fully expecting it. But I do indeed praise God! By his wonderful sustaining grace, I am also fully prepared for it."

Chapter 23

Dachau Encounter

"Abandon hope all ye who enter here." Well indeed might this have been the motto inscribed above the portal of Dachau Concentration Camp—for it would be impossible anywhere on earth to find a human habitation more utterly hopeless and despairing than this abode of desolation and death.

As Hollister Steele, on Wednesday morning, descended the plane that had brought him from Berlin and stood confronting the grim establishment, his heart grew sick with foreboding. The very aspect of even the exterior of the camp was sinister.

Through the apertures of two high barbed-wire fences, the inner fence electrically charged, he could see the gruesome pile of low, red-brick buildings of barracks design covering an extensive area. Broad dirt paths separating the several units and a broad surrounding yardwere entirely without shrubbery of any kind, except for a thick and high privet hedge behind the last row of barracks, half a dozen scrubby trees and a few patches of straggling flowers.

Stationed along the outside of the double fence were heavily armed Gestapo guards, standing in stiff formation only about twenty feet apart. At longer successive intervals—two to three hundred yards, perhaps—were high watchtowers with powerful searchlights and mounted machine guns.

Closely adjacent to the gate of the camp, on the outside, was a railroad track upon which stood ten or twelve large boxcars with broad, heavily sealed sliding doors. At the mere sight of these, Dr. Steele turned faint with sickening dismay. For he recognized them at once—by reason of reports he had heard or read from various sources—as the type of freight car that was being used to convey to concentration camps and prisons, from all over Germany and from many Nazi-invaded countries beyond, thousands of Jews slated for extermination.

But if his reflection upon the horrors on the outside of the camp enclosure agitated the American visitor, still greater would be his distress of soul at the horrors awaiting him within—when he should see at close range, and in many instances face-to-face, the appallingly wretched prisoners, Jew and Gentile alike, all of whom were there by direct order of Adolf Hitler and his nefarious National Socialist Government.

Without lingering for further unhappy ruminations, Dr. Steele swiftly presented himself at the entrance gate and handed Starkmann's order for his admittance to the Nazi guard stationed there in rigid and forbidding military posture. As he did so he said merely, "From Herr Starkmann to your camp *kommandant*, sir. Will you kindly have it conveyed to him? And may I wait here, please, for his reply?"

With never a word to the suppliant, the guard read the address on the sealed document and ordered an attendant of inferior rank to deliver it to the head of the entire concentration camp. And then, still in haughty silence, he motioned Dr. Steele to sit on a nearby bench.

As he sat waiting, suddenly a great gong clanged, and a strident voice shouted, "Roll call! Fall in!" And then from every direction—so it seemed to Dr. Steele's fevered vision—there began to pour long lines of prisoners, all converging toward a large, open courtyard located between the first and the second rows of barracks. One line filed closely in front of him, near enough for him to see their faces. He was aghast at the sight. Were these wretched creatures human beings? Or were they dumb animals cowed and overmastered in the chase?

There were men of every age, from mere boys to white-haired grandfathers. But almost without exception they all were decrepit, shriveled, lean, and old. Their forms were contorted, their steps tottering, their faces ashen gray and gaunt.

Following the roll call, the men had been assigned to their various work gangs—some to shoveling sand, some to quarrying stone, some to hauling on their backs great bundles of wood, some to laying water pipes, some to building roads.

And there they had toiled for almost seven hours, entirely unprotected from the blazing summer sun, until the gong, now clanging, demanded their immediate attendance upon this still more dreaded roll call at noon.

And now they were streaming toward it by hundreds. Dr. Steele followed them with horrified gaze. But suddenly his attention was diverted elsewhere. The camp *kommandant* stood before him in striking uniform, heavily bemedaled—a large, stockily build man with a vicious face. In his hand he held, unfolded, the document from Herr Starkmann—his order for Dr. Steele's admittance to the camp.

He gazed at the intruder with searching scrutiny. Dr. Steele rose and stood at respectful attention before him. He held himself in rigid control as the *kommandant* began to interrogate him.

"You are the bearer of this paper—Dr. G. Hollister Steele from America?"

"Yes sir, I am."

"And you desire to visit our three most notorious prisoners: Pastor Martin Luther von Ludwig and Dr. Benjamin Rothschild and his daughter-in-law, Frau von Ludwig–Rothschild." He pronounced the names derisively. And then he added with utter contempt: "And you want to have them set free!" Then he stared at Dr. Steele again—hard and quizzically. And then the mighty head of Dachau Concentration Camp did an astonishing thing—astonishing, certainly, to Dr. Steele. He extended his hand in courteous, almost cordial greeting and began to speak in vastly altered, softened tones. Breathlessly the visitor awaited his ultimatum.

"You, of course, understand, though," the *kommandant* still continued, "and Herr Starkmann told me he had made it perfectly clear to you—that upon no condition and under no circumstance whatsoever could he grant the release of Pastor von Ludwig. He, as you must know, is charged with the supreme crime of treason and is under sentence of death. But your two other friends—the two Jews—he has ordered me to discharge under the conditions you and he agreed upon."

"I thank you, sir, with all my heart!" Dr. Steele responded fervently.

But the *kommandant* had not yet completed his explanation

of the Gestapo chief's amazing indulgence. He proceeded to do this forthrightly.

"In our telephone conversation last night, Dr. Steele," he continued, "Herr Starkmann requested that I show you certain areas of our camp and explain to you its principles of operation. This is in order that you may take back to your fellow countrymen in American authentic information concerning them. For we greatly fear, sir, there has been a grave misunderstanding as to the purpose and methods of our concentration camps and prisons. I can sense, Dr. Steele, that even you yourself at this moment are entertaining the feeling that our methods are harsh. But please let me say just this: they have to be harsh for the achievement of our ultimate objective.

"Well then, my friend"—the Butcher of Dachau proceeded mellifluously—"you, personally, I am quite persuaded, will have no difficulty in understanding and appreciating our position. Because you are a surgeon. And as a surgeon you no doubt have had to deal with cancer. And you agree with me perfectly, I am sure, that cancer *has* to be dealt with harshly. If it is infesting the human body and will not yield to more benign treatment, there is only one thing to do with it: *cut it out*!

"And when you do cut it out, you cannot allow any of the softer qualities—sympathy and tenderness and all that sort of thing—to unnerve you for one instant in the performance of your operation. When you wield your knife, your mind must be absolutely clear, your will determined, your hand steady and strong. The cancer has got to be extirpated entirely—root, branch, stem, and tendril—if your patient is to live.

"And that is exactly what we are doing here in Dachau and in other centers of liquidation throughout the land. Already we have dispatched tens of thousands of Semites; but we must not stop short of our goal, which is a completely Jewless Germany. As to our methods, it is sufficient endorsement to know that every one of them has been personally devised and commanded by our glorious Fuehrer, Adolf Hitler. We who are engaged in the firsthand, actual work of extirpation operate solely upon his orders. He absolves us wholly from any personal responsibility in the matter. But we will not cease from our labors—and he will not cease from his—until our fixed purpose is altogether achieved."

"And that purpose is—?"

"That *purpose* is to make our beloved country absolutely *Judenrein*. In short: to render Germany fully worthy of taking its rightful place as the foremost nation upon earth."

Still did Dr. Steele hold his turbulent emotions—his sense of outrage, his unutterable horror—in rigid concealment. Not the slightest semblance of antagonism did he dare to show, lest he imperil the fulfillment of his mission to Germany, of his visits to Dachau: the release of Pastor von Ludwig and the Rothschilds from this iniquitous abode of Satan. He could not, however, refrain from asking this one question:

"But your *conscience*, Herr *Kommandant*, what of that? Do you not have difficulty in reconciling it with all the suffering that is inflicted?"

"Not in the remotest degree! Not any more than you as a surgeon would have qualms of conscience for the suffering you necessarily inflict upon your patient. You keep constantly in view before you, your beneficent goal: the restoration of that patient to perfect health. Therefore you are completely unmoved by his anguish and his screams."

The *kommandant* brought his diatribe to an abrupt halt. He looked at his wristwatch. "Twelve fifteen!" he announced in a startled tone. "I am sorry, Dr. Steele, but I shall have to be leaving you. The men are having their roll call now—over there in the courtyard, as you see. That should last about forty-five minutes. Every single one of our prisoners must be accounted for. Then they have their lunch. And then we allow them to remain in the yard for an hour of recreation before they return to their various work squads for the rest of the afternoon.

"You may have your visit with Rothschild during this recreation hour—for twenty minutes. And I will grant you the special privilege of having your conversation with him unattended by a guard.

"You see that tree on the opposite end of the courtyard? Behind it is a stone bench where you may have your visit with this Semite in a certain measure of seclusion and privacy.

"I am sorry that you cannot see von Ludwig today. But it will not be possible. He is in his bunk—sick. Or pretending to be! The old man fainted at his work this morning—so it was reported to me—and our head physician recommended a day's reprieve. However, he will be on his job tomorrow—unless they discover something definitely wrong with him and it is a physical impossibility for him to stand up. For we never encourage or allow any mere self-indulgence. It would make for laziness and shirking of duty, and thus demoralize our entire camp. Therefore and of necessity, it is one of our most stringent rules that the prisoners must work whether they think themselves sick or not. They either work or die."

The *kommandant* departed, Dr. Steele sank down upon the bench, completely stunned. He was altogether unnerved—numb and inert both in body and in mind. He sat thus for a full ten minutes, his very soul torn with anguish and revulsion.

Resolutely he pulled himself upward to his feet and started walking in the direction of the courtyard. He would go there at once and compel himself to gaze upon the misery that it contained, lest he falter in his resolution. But he had not gone a dozen paces before he was intercepted by a Nazi guard with a surly "Halt! Who goes there?" Quietly Dr. Steele showed the green card the *kommandant* had given him. The guard glanced at it quickly and again glanced at the intruder with a searching eye and then, returning the card, passed on without a word.

Through the interlacing branches of a tree—himself screened from observation—he peered into the courtyard where, ranged in long lines of about fifty to each line, surrounded by guards, fully a thousand prisoners were now congregated. They presented a lamentable spectacle.

Almost without exception the men were pitifully emaciated—their forms bent and shrunken; their faces, deathly pale, contorted with pain and fear; their eyes sunken, hollow, haunted. Unwashed and unshaven, clad in tattered, dirty garments, their aspect was abhorrent to an extreme degree. The majority of the prisoners wore—fastened inescapably upon their backs—the identifying ignominious yellow *J*. A number of them also wore grotesque, high-pointed foolscaps, proclaiming to all who beheld them that they were camp insubordinates, Jews under discipline. Viewed in their totality, the prisoners—Jews and Gentiles alike—formed a graphic cross-section of agonized humanity.

The Nazi had just called out the name Rosenfeldt. There was no response. "Rosenfeldt!" he called again in louder voice. Still no reply. For the third time he pronounced the name, this time with angry outcry: *"Rosenfeldt!"* A complete silence followed, tense with deadly fear on the part of all the other prisoners.

And then a sudden piercing whistle rent the air, immediately followed by the *aufseher*'s shrill command: "The dogs! Quick! Bring in the dogs!"

Instantaneously a Gestapo guard emerged from a nearby barrack, driving out before him two fierce bloodhounds. They stood for a moment irresolute before the commanding officer, awaiting his directive. He gave it in direful wrath:

"Go! Faster! *Find the bird!*"

Followed by half a dozen more guards, the dogs made a rush for the hedge behind the barracks. Yelping and growling they tore their way through it and into a ditch intervening between the hedge and the double barbed-wire fence enclosing the entire camp. And there, in the ditch, half filled with water, they found their "bird"—an unutterably wretched Jewish lad, scarcely twenty-one years old, who had deliberately and daringly absented himself from roll call in one last desperate attempt to find release from his misery—by means either of a shot from guards concealed within the hedge or, failing of that hope, by throwing himself despairingly against the electrically charged barbed wire.

Routed out of the ditch by the dogs, he was dragged along the ground by four of the guards, and into the awful presence of the *aufseher*. And there, in cringing terror, he received his sentence: forty lashes, to be followed by three days and nights incarceration, without food, in solitary confinement in a dark and wet underground cell. The hopeless victim's shrieks as he was led off to his doom cut Hollister Steele to the very heart.

He looked at his watch. Twenty-five minutes after one. And the *kommandant* was due to return to him at one thirty!

Apprehensively Dr. Steele awaited his coming. Precisely on the dot of the half hour, he appeared in view, walking straight toward the bench. He greeted his guest with studied affability.

"Well, my friend, I see that you are still here. And how have you enjoyed your visit in our concentration camp?"

Again discretion warned the alien sternly that he must keep silent. Therefore, except that he replied with the merest "Thank you, sir, I have found it very absorbing"—he spoke never a word.

"Have you discovered among the prisoners the man you want to contact—Dr. Rothschild?"

"No sir. I have not been able to locate him as yet."

Abruptly the *kommandant* turned about and walked directly toward the *aufseher*. Dr. Steele, peering from behind his protecting tree, watched eagerly as the two men became engaged in what appeared to be a most earnest conversation. And then, as the *kommandant* moved away from him, the *aufseher* again blew a blast with his whistle and called out in a shrill voice, which Dr. Steele could hear distinctly, "Rothschild! Come forward!"

His heart beating violently by reason of his deep emotion, the visitor gazed intently as a decrepit, withered prisoner emerged from the inner exercising circle and staggered toward the commanding officer.

But this could never be Dr. Rothschild—this feeble, trembling old man! For Dr. Rothschild was only middle-aged, and strong! Dr. Steele continued watching sharply as the *aufseher* talked with him and then pointed in the direction of the stone bench, evidently ordering him to go to it. And then God's messenger of mercy beheld the victim of Nazi outrage, stunned and bewildered, approaching him.

But never could this wretched creature be *Benjamin Rothschild*! Never in all the world the vigorous, vibrant, radiant personality he had known just eight years before! Dr. Steele was agonized, aghast! This pitiful offscouring of humanity, tottering unsteadily within his nearer view, was shrunken and wasted and frightfully emaciated. Dr. Rothschild had weight a good 165 pounds, at least. *This* man could not weigh more than ninety. A veritable skeleton! And Dr. Rothschild was not yet fifty-five years old. *This* poor wretch was easily seventy-five.

Clad in filthy, ragged garments, he presented a most deplorable appearance. The sparse fringe of hair that protruded from under a high-pointed yellow foolscap was snow-white. His face was ashen gray and shriveled. In his lusterless, dark eyes there was a look of haunting fear, of cringing, abject terror. Oh, no! *No!* Certainly this could not be Dr. Rothschild! Never! *Never!*

But when the forlorn figure came near enough for Dr. Steele to see his features distinctly, with shuddering dismay he recognized him. It was Benjamin Rothschild indeed, and none other.

As he approached the tree, he swayed dizzily and grasped a low-hanging limb for support. Still standing out of view behind the tree, Dr. Steele called his name softly lest he frighten him by too sudden an appearance.

"Dr. Rothschild! Dr. Rothschild! My dear, dear friend!"

Startled, the prisoner grasped the limb more firmly with both hands and peered stealthily beyond the tree. And then it was that he beheld Dr. Steele face-to-face. Swaying yet more dizzily, then violently trembling, with a heart-piercing cry of strangely intermingled terror, incredulity, and ecstasy, he fell prone at the feet of his compassionate deliverer. In full view, lugubriously fastened to the back of his tattered coat, was the ignominious, revolting yellow *J*.

Swiftly Dr. Steele knelt down on the ground close beside him, lifted him up to the bench, and gathered him tenderly within his arms—pouring out upon him a flood of endearing words, soothing him even as a mother would soothe a frightened little child.

Gradually he became more quieted. The writhing of his body and his wild sobbing ceased. Slowly the anguish assuaged. But still he wept—softly, piteously.

And then he lifted up his head and looked intently into Dr. Steele's face with growing wonderment and awe—scarcely daring to believe his eyes, to trust the evidence of his very senses!

"Dr. Steele!" he gasped hysterically, "*dear* Dr. Steele! Is it you? Is it *you*? Oh, have you really come to me? Is it true? Oh, oh, tell me! Is it *true*?" He wept again. And again Dr. Steele soothed him tenderly.

"Yes, dear friend, I am right here, close beside you."

"Oh—oh—oh!" Suddenly like a ray of sunshine bursting through a cloud, an ecstatic smile overspread the wan, tearstained face. And then still more tears. But now they were tears of joy. He hugged Dr. Steele deliriously.

"Oh, you *did* come to me! I knew you would come! I *knew* you would come! You got my letter, then?"

"Yes, I got your letter, just a week ago. And I started for Germany within three days to find you."

"And you *did* find me! Praise God! Praise God! Oh, now I know that there *is* a God!"

"Ah, yes! He truly cares. That is why He has brought me to you—to comfort you, to try to help you."

"But how did you ever get *here*? How did you ever get into Dachau?"

"God went before me all the way and opened every door miraculously—yes, even *this* door: Dachau! And so I am right here with you. And now, dear Dr. Rothschild—" But the remainder of Dr. Steele's attempted encouragement was cut off shortly by an anguished wail:

"No, *no*! Not 'Dr. Rothschild'! Never again can anyone call me by *that* name! Dr. Rothschild is gone! Benjamin Rothschild is gone forever! No longer am I Benjamin—'the Fortunate One.' I am now only Ben-Oni—'Son of Sorrow.' Call me, now and always, nothing but *Ben-Oni*!"

Not quite ten minutes more remained of their allotted precious time together. For in less than ten minutes the *kommandant* was due to return and take his prisoner away. Away to *what*? How could Dr. Steele ever tell this man, so intensely suffering before him that thus soon he would have to leave him? But he must prepare his friend for their inevitable parting.

"Listen to me," he commanded quietly. "Listen to me, Dr. Rothschild!"

"*No!*" he protested vehemently. "*Not* 'Dr. Rothschild,' I told you! Ben-Oni—only Ben-Oni is what you must call me now."

"Very well, then, dear Ben-Oni." Dr. Steele pronounced the new name of this undoubted son of sorrow with deepest sadness in his own heart for his so sorely stricken companion. "Listen," he persisted. "I must return this afternoon to Berlin—in just a few moments more—" But at this point Ben-Oni interrupted with a despairing shriek:

"Oh, no, no! *No!* Do not leave me! Do not *leave* me! Oh, dear Dr. Steele, please, *please* take me with you! Oh, take me from this awful place! I cannot *stand* it any longer! Oh, take me! Take me! *Take* me!" He clung convulsively to his one last hope.

Gently Dr. Steele tried to disengage his frenzied grasp. Again he tried to quiet him.

"Wait, my dear man," he urged him reassuringly, "wait! You must listen to me! Yes, I have to go now—in a very few moments, but I am coming back again tomorrow!"

"Tomorrow?" the prisoner asked dully, uncomprehendingly.

"Yes, tomorrow morning—and the next day—and perhaps the next. To visit with you and also with Pastor von Ludwig and his daughter. They are here, too, I understand."

"Yes, both of them are here. Both of them were arrested also by the Nazis and imprisoned here."

"Well, I want to visit with you all. And then—"

"And then—*what?*" Dr. Rothschild queried breathlessly. The light of dawning new hope was breaking through the gloom.

"And then you are going to have a wonderful surprise! Soon, Ben-Oni—no, *not* Ben-Oni, but *Dr. Rothschild*. Soon, Dr. Rothschild, you are going to be *free*!"

"*Free?* From *here*? From this horrible concentration camp? From Dachau? *Free?*" The captive's excitement—his ecstasy—was at highest pitch.

"Yes! Absolutely *free*! Within just a few days more you are going to be released! Released forever from this dreadful place—you and your dear daughter-in-law."

"And Gretel's father—Pastor von Ludwig?" Dr. Rothschild quickly interposed.

Dr. Steele groaned inwardly. How could he ever tell Dr. Rothschild the awful truth—that Pastor von Ludwig was condemned to death! Resolutely he invoked his faith. "You and Gretel will go first. Her beloved father will follow you a little later—out of Dachau."

Only one moment more! Already Dr. Steele saw the *kommandant* approaching in the distance, accompanied by a Nazi guard. What final word could he leave with his so desperately needy friend?

"Listen quickly, my dearest Dr. Rothschild! Are you listening? *'Be strong in the Lord, and in the power of his might. Being confident of this very thing, that he which hath begun a good work in you will perform it'*—to its full completion: even your deliverance. And also the deliverance of our two cherished friends: Pastor Martin Luther von Ludwig and his precious daughter, Margarete. Therefore be comforted! Be strong! Yea, be *strong*!"

The *kommandant* and the guard were already there, close beside them. Rudely, without one faintest trace of compassion or even of decent courtesy, the high commanding officer broke in upon their confidential conversation.

"Well, Dr. Steele," he said abruptly, "your time is up. This *Jew* must get back to his work. Take him at once, Kleinhaupt, to the road-building gang. The *aufseher* has assigned him there for the afternoon.

Without an instant allowed them for a farewell word, the two friends—the prisoner and his deliverer—were swiftly torn apart. Mercilessly Dr. Rothschild was marched by the guard in the direction of the present road construction, his lagging, tottering footsteps spurred to quickened pace by the cracking of the Nazi's cruel whip across his quivering shoulders.

Torn with commingled anger and fierce resentment at the outrage, but still not daring to display them openly before the *kommandant* —lest his entrée into Dachau be swiftly and irrevocably terminated—Dr. Steele, in dumb agony, gazed after his departing protégé. His dismay was unutterable.

But his anguished reflections were suddenly cut short by the *kommandant*'s sharp order: "Come! We must be going. We shall have to hurry. We shall not have time for you to see much today. But you can see more when you come tomorrow." Meekly Dr. Steele followed to the exit the brutal monster who already his soul utterly loathed.

Immeasurably relieved of the *kommandant*'s most unwelcome presence, Dr. Steele proceeded upon his way to the airplane soon to depart for Berlin. Profoundly glad to be alone at last, he tried sternly to get himself in hand. He was thoroughly unnerved. How could he ever come back again upon the morrow to such a hideous place? But come he must. He dared not fail Dr. Rothschild now. And he could not possibly leave Germany without seeing and attempting to succor the von Ludwigs.

One final distressing sight yet remained to Dr. Steele's anguished view within the Dachau enclosure. And this sight it was that proved to be the most lacerating of them all to his now near-breaking heart. For this one touched closest home! It was his last glimpse, before his departure from the camp, of his beloved Hebrew friend.

Just before he reached the exit, on the roadway leading thereto, Dr. Steele came within but a few feet of the road-construction gang—some twenty to thirty prisoners—who were feverishly engaged, beneath menacing whips of their Nazi guards, in making certain repairs. At the forefront of the gang was Dr. Rothschild, bending over a pile of rocks. Instantly Dr. Steele recognized the shrunken, withered form with the huge yellow *J* upon his back and the rakish yellow foolscap on his head.

Himself concealed behind a corner of one of the barracks, Dr. Steele watched him intently with profoundest sorrow. In his hands he held a large sledgehammer. Dr. Steele's gaze became riveted with compelling fascination upon those hands.

Those wonderful hands! How vividly did Dr. Steele remember them as they had looked on Dr. Rothschild's own magnificent operating table. Those *hands*! So beautiful then—so steady, so sensitive, so strong, so finely shapen, so white—as they had held within them the most delicate of surgical instruments: controlling and guiding and utilizing them to the saving and healing of untold hundreds of lives of little children, with a skill and an adroitness that had won for Dr. Benjamin Rothschild worldwide fame and praise and gratitude.

But now—*now*! Those very same hands—red, calloused, cruelly misshapen, ugly, nervous, trembling—those selfsame wonderful hands were now in Dachau Concentration Camp, wielding a heavy sledgehammer, *cracking stone*! He was Ben-Oni, Son of Sorrow indeed!

Chapter 24

Victorious Prisoner

The thought of returning to his hotel and spending an evening of desolate solitude, with no companionship other than his own agonizing thoughts, filled him with dismay. When, therefore, his plane landed at the Tempelhof Airdrome and he saw the friendly face of Dr. Eisenleben and realized that he was purposely there awaiting him, he experienced a sudden rebound of vast relief and a surge of immeasurable gratitude.

"Dr. Eisenleben! This is too good of you to come to meet me!" The two men grasped hands warmly.

"I was glad to come, Dr. Steele. Fortunately, I was able to leave my office earlier today; and I felt I might be of some little help to you, perhaps, after what I can well imagine you have been through in the Dachau camp."

"Oh, how very good of you! I confess I am badly shaken, and I dreaded unspeakably a lonely evening in my hotel."

"Well, we certainly can't let you have that! I am wondering, would you not come home with me for a bite of supper? I am anxious to hear about your contacts with our friends. And I do want you to meet my wife and my parents. They are all eager to meet you. So won't you come, then, Dr. Steele?"

"Thank you! I shall be most happy to, I assure you."

"Good! That's fine! Well, let us get right off. My car is just around this corner. I am sorry, my friend," Dr. Eisenleben continued as they entered the car and started toward his home, "I am sorry that I cannot offer you any but the most informal entertainment. But I am sure you will understand. My wife, as I believe I told you, is an invalid, confined almost constantly to her wheelchair. My aged mother is also very frail. And at present we have no servant. So I must warn you that you will be at the tender mercies of my father and myself for your evening meal."

"It will be delightful, Dr. Eisenleben, I am sure!"

And delightful it proved to be indeed. The simple repast prepared and served by father and son in their hospitable, warmhearted home, was an experience that Hollister Steele would never forget.

He was deeply impressed by Dr. Eisenleben's devotion to his loved ones, and particularly touched by their complete dependence upon him. Quite pathetically, they all three leaned hard upon his strength and tenderness. Both his wife and his mother were almost helpless. As his wife sat at the table in her wheelchair, he had to wait upon her for nearly every detail of the meal, even to the cutting of her food upon her plate. But despite her weakness of body, she was a woman of singular strength of character and charm, as was his mother also. Dr. Eisenleben, Sr., his father, had been, in his day, a brilliant physician—even as was now his son.

Following supper, Mrs. Eisenleben and the elderly patients excused themselves for their necessary early retiring, and Dr. Eisenleben and Dr. Steele thus were left alone for the fellowship and the exchange of confidences which they both so earnestly desired.

Dr. Steele unburdened his soul to Dr. Eisenleben of all the fearful horrors in which he had so intimately participated in Dachau; and particularly did he relate to him, to their mutual, deep distress, his experience with Dr. Rothschild.

"He is a completely broken man," he exclaimed bitterly. "I would never have known him, so altogether changed has he become. And all because of the diabolical treatment he has received at the hands of those wicked anti-Semites!"

"But you say that he and his daughter-in-law are to be released?"

"Yes, Starkmann himself has actually ordered it. It is astounding! A miracle of God's mercy!"

"A miracle indeed! Nothing short of it! But when will it be achieved?"

"By the end of the week, I fervently trust. I am to have the privilege personally—indeed, I may say I have been given the responsibility—of escorting both Dr. Rothschild and his daughter-in-law out of Dachau and out of Germany just as soon as certain papers can be cleared." Again Dr. Steele very carefully refrained from telling Dr. Eisenleben that the "certain papers" included the one wherein he would sign away to the National Socialist Government of Germany, as purloined ransom price, nearly the entire savings of his lifetime. *Greater love hath no man than this, that a man lay down his life for his friends.*

"But Pastor von Ludwig is not included in the release?" Dr. Eisenleben asked anxiously.

"No," came the sorrowful reply. "On *that* point Starkmann and his Dachua hangman both are adamant. They insist that he is their most dangerous prisoner. Therefore he is under sentence of *death.*"

"That sentence never, never can be carried out!" Dr. Eisenleben protested vehemently. "They will never dare to carry it out! It would mean an uprising of the entire Confessional Church of Germany against the government. And the Nazis know it!

"But what they are trying to do now—so I understand from certain influential members of our church who have access to the authorities and who are keeping in close touch with the whole situation—what they are trying hard to do is to make him commit suicide. They are deliberately staging a 'cold war' against him—a war of attrition of morale. They are starving him, exhausting him, insulting and degrading him in every possible way—in their vicious attempt to break down his fortitude. They are fiendishly bent upon *brainwashing* him! They have gone so far as to offer him 'sleeping pills' or a loaded gun or even a noose—for him to end his misery himself. But he scorns them, every one! God has given him the most amazing faith and strength of will. He is magnificent!

"And that same believing faith is shared by thousands, Dr. Steele. Not only is his church praying for him day and night, but all over Germany, all over Europe—all over the world, indeed—Christian intercessors are imploring God for his release."

"God grant it!"

"You say you did not see him yourself today?"

"No. They told me he was sick in his bunk—that he had collapsed at his work."

"Another of their 'cold war' tactics! They contrive collapses for him frequently. But you will see him tomorrow?"

"So the *kommandant* assured me. Do uphold me with your prayers, Dr. Eisenleben, as I strive to undertake this most formidable task."

"I give you my solemn promise that I shall indeed, Dr. Steele. But if I know Pastor von Ludwig—and no one has more grateful reason to know him well than I have had—he will accept this trial with the same fortitude, with the same gloriously triumphant faith, that he has accepted every other trial, believing as he does that all of them are within the will of God for his life."

"Just one word more, please, Dr. Eisenleben! Before I go, is there anything further you can tell me about Joseph Rothschild? Have you even one faint gleam of hope concerning him that I might take to his father and his wife tomorrow?"

Dr. Eisenleben shook his head sadly. "No, I fear not, Dr. Steele. There still is not the slightest glimmer of light amid the darkness. His disappearance has been a complete blackout. Every avenue of exploration—and many have been pursued vigorously—every one of them has proved to be a dead-end street."

"But you personally have not given up hope?"

"No. And I never shall until I have authentic official proof of his demise. I share firmly his wife's conviction that Joseph Rothschild—somewhere—is yet alive. In God's own good time he will be found."

"God grant it speedily!"

When, at noon the next day, Thursday, the plane from Berlin again brought Dr. Steele to Dachau, to his surprise the *kommandant* himself was at the entrance gate to meet him.

"*Guten Tag*, Herr *Doktor* Steele. I see you have returned to us."

"Yes, and I want you to know, Herr *Kommandant*, how greatly I appreciate your permission for me to come. I trust I may again today be allowed to visit with Dr. Rothschild—and with Pastor von Ludwig and his daughter also?"

"You cannot see Rothschild!" the *kommandant* gave gruff reply. "He is in his bunk today, as von Ludwig was in his yesterday—both of them after collapsing at their work. It is disgusting the way our prisoners cave in. No backbone. Completely lacking in morale and stamina. We do not put up with their nonsense for long, however. No, you can't see Rothschild again today. But you may visit with von Ludwig—he is back on his job again—and, possibly, before you leave for your plane at three o'clock, with his daughter also. That is, of course, if she can be released from her duties at the hospital.

"You will visit with von Ludwig at the same stone bench where you met Rothschild yesterday. It is now almost time for noon roll call. And then lunch. During these two periods you may feel free to walk about the camp as you wish—except, of course, as I made clear to you yesterday, you are not to speak to anyone or enter any building. Here, again, is your green card to ward off any interference by the guards."

Left to himself and to his reenergized most unhappy thoughts and fierce resentment, Dr. Steele spent the next hour wandering aimlessly about the camp, seeing and hearing afresh the same dreadful sights and sounds he had witnessed yesterday. Amid the several hundreds of men massed in their rigid formations and, through the whole long routine, standing wearily to the point of sheer exhaustion, he searched assiduously for the face of the pastor. And at last, to his great relief and joy, he found him!

He was the end man in the line nearest to Dr. Steele. As the line was at right angles to the bench, Dr. Steele could see his profile clearly.

He was arrayed in coarse, black, tattered garments; and he, too, had the insulting rakish foolscap on his head. But despite his degrading attire, his figure presented an impression of high dignity. He was standing erect and firm. His shoulders were squared and there was composure of muscles and nerves. His head was held high. On his face, albeit there were deep marks of pain, there was a calm serenity, an effulgence as of inner light.

He was giving diligent attention to the roll call and to the frequently interpolated snarling orders of the *aufseher*; and in every way comporting himself in a manner above all possible reproach—above even the gloating censure of the malevolent guards. Dr. Steele concentrated his gaze upon him to the conclusion of the roll call and through the scarcely less distressing operations of the lunch period, his heart torn afresh at the sight of his friend—together with a thousand other prisoners—having grudgingly doled out to him his starvation noon-hour meal. All the time Dr. Steele kept himself carefully concealed from view behind his sheltering tree.

At length lunch was completed and the men were lined up in their double circle for their "exercise"—their "recreation." Then it was that the *aufseher* summoned Pastor von Ludwig from his position and gave him instructions to proceed to the stone bench.

In dramatic contrast, Pastor von Ludwig walked toward Dr. Steele with the tread of a victor. Undeniably frail in body—emaciated, starved, almost ethereal in countenance of deathlike pallor—there was yet strikingly manifested an inward spiritual strength, a heavenly radiance that transcended everything of earth.

He approached his visitor with both arms widely extended and with a triumphant smile. In calm, albeit ringing tone, he greeted him:

"Ah, Dr. Steele! This is a joy beyond my power to express! To think that *you* have come to us—even here in Dachau! Praise God! Praise God!"

"Dear Pastor Ludwig! Praise God indeed that I have found you!" The two men held each other in a long, close embrace. Then quietly they sat down together, side by side, upon the bench.

"We must talk fast," the pastor cautioned. "There is so much I want to know concerning you—how the Lord has led you during these several years since you blessed us with your first visit to Germany. What all have you been doing, Dr. Steele?"

"Never mind about me! What *I* have been doing is quite unimportant—just the day-by-day uneventful routine tasks that pertain to the life of any busy surgeon in the United States. But the important thing—the really essential thing and the thing *I* want to know all about—is what *you* have been doing and what the Rothschilds have been doing. In fact, what everyone has been doing here in Germany!"

"Ah, our poor stricken Germany!"

"No, no! Do not try to talk about it, my dear friend. I withdraw my question; it is too painful for you. I know, everybody knows—the whole world knows—all we need to know of the atrocities, the horrors of the Hitler rule."

"Ah, yes, yes, the horrors have been monstrous! They have shrieked to high heaven! Germany has been—and still is today—a madhouse!" Although the two men were well out of earshot of all the others in the courtyard, they, nevertheless, conversed in bated breath.

"Yes," Dr. Steele responded solemnly, "so I would infer from all that I have read and heard—from all that I have seen for myself during even these few days that I have been in Germany, and during yesterday especially. Adolf Hitler has assuredly ravaged your beautiful Fatherland."

"Adolf Hitler is the adumbration of the Antichrist! He is a living incarnation of the evil one himself! I consider him the most dangerous man in all the world today—in all the history of the world. He has deluged the whole earth with agony.

"He believes that he has redeemed Germany. He believes, indeed, that he *is* Germany. He has declared, 'My aim is to make our nation the only power in the world.' He promises Germany a thousand years of peace. But I fear they will only be a thousand years of anguish."

"If such a philosophy as his prevails, that will be inevitable."

"And so you can quite readily understand, then, I am sure, Dr. Steele, why Hitler is so bitterly opposed to Christianity and the Church. His determined purpose, as I have stated, is world conquest; and in order to achieve this goal he declares that all religion must be destroyed. He has said, 'I consider all this sentimental feeling for Christianity as a kind of mental sickness.'"

"That is true of many other Nazi leaders also, is it not?—Himmler, Goebbels, Goering, Streicher, Hess, von Ribbentrop, and all the rest of the nefarious gang?"

"Absolutely so. Their ideologies are identical. Their anti-

Semitism is identical. Their cruelty is identical. The entire Nazi Party is infested with deceit and treachery and hate.

"What is most terrible of all, they are deliberately and systematically inculcating their poison into the minds and hearts of the oncoming generation. The Hitler Youth Movement is the most pernicious feature in their entire totalitarian strategy. Theirs is the most calculated and the most vicious soul poisoning of all the children of the land."

"Pastor von Ludwig, I have remembered all these years since I first met you during my previous visit to Germany, what you said to me in your tower study on that memorable Sunday afternoon when I had the privilege and joy of visiting in your home. You said to me at that time—even yet I can remember it vividly, 'The confusion in your country and in my country—the political and economic crises, the increasing lawlessness and crime, the breakdown in social standards and in family life, the deepening strife even within the Church—all these maladies spring from one common source: departure from the Word of God.'"

"Indeed I do remember that Lord's Day afternoon, my dear friend, with profoundest gratitude and praise to God. My joy in your acceptance of Christ as your Savior was inexpressible. And I, too, recall vividly our discussion of the widespread departure from God's holy Word. It was alarming at that time, but far more alarming today. The apostasy has indeed swept forward like a tidal wave, which today threatens to inundate the entire earth. Certainly it has inundated Germany violently. And Adolf Hitler is the one man above every other who has promoted it.

"This newly created State Church—the National Socialist Christian Church, they call it—then proceeded to set up the 'new order.' This included, among other demands, the complete overthrow of the Bible as 'Jewish propaganda'—substituting therefore the Nordic sagas, and replacing the patriarchs of Scripture with Nordic heroes. And, of course, they demanded unequivocally the rejection of Christ as leader. 'Jesus Christ is only a man—and a Jew to boot,' Hitler declared. And he added, 'Why should I who am able to be much more helpful than He—why shouldn't I have the right to establish a new dogma for the church?'

"Under this 'new dogma' Christian principles of brotherly love and forgiveness and of helpful service to others were treated with utter contempt. In their place the Church must exalt the Nazi virtue of militant strength and ruthless hate.

"As a result, hundreds of evangelicals, completely loyal to Christ and true to God's Word: these faithful men, when they took a militant stand for the defense of the gospel, were relentlessly torn from their pulpits and thrown into concentration camps and prisons. The pastors who were fortunate enough to escape formed what we called 'the Pastors' Emergency League'—out of which developed the present Confessional Church, in diametric and belligerent opposition to this apostate church set up by the National Socialist Government. And it is of the Confessional Church, as you know, that I am an imprisoned representative. That is why I am imprisoned—here in Dachau. Because I refused determinedly to capitulate to Adolf Hitler.

"And here in Dachau, dear Pastor von Ludwig, you have deeply suffered. I can see that plainly."

"Yes, I have suffered, it is true. But as the sufferings of Christ have abounded in me, so also have my consolations abounded in Christ. He has not permitted me to be tested above that I have been able, but has with each new testing also made a way to escape that I might be able to bear it. And constantly He is giving me the joyful assurance that 'the sufferings of this present time are not worthy to be compared with the glory which shall be revealed in us. If we suffer, we shall also reign with him. Our light affliction, which is but for a moment, worketh for us a far more exceeding and eternal weight of glory; while we look not at the things which are seen, but at the things which are not seen: for the things which are seen are temporal; but the things which are not seen are eternal.'

"So do not feel sorry for me, Dr. Steele," he continued radiantly, "but rather rejoice with me for the truly wonderful new opportunity of service with which God has been pleased to entrust me. Here, yes, *here,* in this Dachau Concentration Camp, he has given me an entirely new ministry and an entirely new and wonderful congregation: my fellow prisoners! Here, as never before, I am truly a *pastor*! I myself have seen with my own eyes prisoners beaten to death. One day I saw a young boy, not more than seventeen—such a beautiful lad he was—I saw him hammered on the head with brass knuckles until he expired in agony. I have seen the terrible transports coming by night and day, carrying sometimes as many as fifteen hundred Jewish prisoners—raided from homes for the aged, in many cases—carrying them to their doom. This place is truly the abode of death. The very atmosphere reeks of blasphemy and wickedness. One is acutely conscious here of the presence and awful power of Satan.

"But our God is the God of the most astounding, of the incredible, of the impossible. To my own amazement He has bestowed upon me what I clearly recognize as nothing less than supernatural power. He has given me in large measure what I always pray for most earnestly—'that utterance may be given unto me, that I may open my mouth boldly . . . that I may speak boldly, as I ought to speak.'"

Dr. Steele gazed at the saintly minister with amazement akin to awe. There was about him a radiance that was not of earth. His fortitude, his entire selflessness, his utter devotion to his Lord: all these gave to his countenance a light that could emanate only from heaven. There was complete composure in his bearing, perfect quietness of manner, a quality of superb inner power. Dr. Steele understood how he well might exercise holy boldness over his captors. Before his spiritual ascendancy their mere brute strength cowered.

"And what of your dear daughter, Pastor von Ludwig?" Dr. Steele asked anxiously. "I understand that she also is here within the camp. How are things going with her?"

"Ah, my beloved Margarete! My sorrow for this most precious child is deep! It is so very terrible to me to realize her anguish of soul. For a nature as sensitive as hers, the sights and sounds she has to experience every hour of every day are well-nigh overwhelming. And there is, of course, her constant grief for her husband."

"There is still no word of him?"

"Not the slightest whisper. Absolutely nothing but complete, mysterious, most awful silence. It has been so ever since my poor child was so cruelly widowed at the very marriage altar."

"Dear Pastor von Ludwig—how can I bear to tell you?"

"To tell me what?"

"It breaks my heart!"

"What breaks your heart?"

"*This*, my dear friend. The orders for Dr. Rothschild's release includes your daughter also, as the wife of his son. But it does not include *you*. I pleaded most earnestly for your discharge as well as theirs, but both Starkmann in Berlin and the *kommandant* here refuse to allow you to go. *That* is what is utterly heartbreaking to me, I do assure you!"

Amazing beyond Dr. Steele's belief was Pastor von Ludwig's reaction to his direful announcement. Dr. Steele had pronounced the verdict with the solemnity of a death knell. Pastor von Ludwig received it with a radiant smile, his whole countenance illuminated with the effulgent inner light.

"Have no sorrow and no concern for me, dear Dr. Steele. I have told you, this is my place. My God-given task is here—in Dachau. I could not accept release until that task is done. In His own good time God will lead me forth—either by way of still-continued life, or by the gate of death. It matters not which. My times are in His hand. So think not for one moment of me. Rather, rejoice with me—let us rejoice together—and praise the Lord for the deliverance of these two loved ones from this appalling abode. You say it will be accomplished soon?"

"By the end of this week, I trust. Since I was first granted interview with Herr Starkmann himself on Tuesday afternoon, he has been working on the necessary arrangements."

"And where will you send them, Dr. Steele?"

"That is not yet clear to me. Have you any suggestion, Pastor von Ludwig?"

"Yes! Emphatically so! They must go, with all possible speed, to Palestine!"

"Palestine?"

"Palestine, undoubtedly. It is their *homeland*!"

"It is Dr. Rothschild's homeland, it is true, for he is a son of Abraham. But your daughter, Pastor von Ludwig? She is not a Jewess."

"She *is* a Jewess. By her marriage to Dr. Rothschild's son, Margarete has identified herself completely with Israel. Therefore Palestine is now her homeland also. It is, therefore, the logical, the proper, the only place for her and her new Hebrew father to live. Yes, assuredly—unquestionably—they both must go to Palestine! And, please, God, may they there find Joseph!"

Chapter 25

The Fugitive Safe

All the way back to Berlin, Hollister Steele meditated upon the prospect of Palestine. And the more he meditated, the more convinced he became that Pastor von Ludwig's suggestion was a sound one. Palestine was indeed the logical, the right place for the Rothschilds to go. "And, please, God, may they there find Joseph!" So Gretel's father had fervently prayed. So, with equal fervor, did Dr. Steele echo that selfsame prayer.

When, finally, the plane reached Berlin, Dr. Steele half expected that Dr. Eisenleben would be there again to meet him as he had the day before. But he was nowhere in sight. *Detained at his office, no doubt*, was Dr. Steele's inward reasoning. But he was just as glad. He was in the mood today for solitude. He wanted to be alone to think things through—to find the solution to the several new problems now immediately confronting him. He would take the Rothschilds with him to London. There he could entrust them to the safe protection and to the wise counsel of the Jewish Christian Fellowship, that fine international organization of Hebrew men and women who openly and unitedly acknowledge the Lord Jesus Christ as Israel's Messiah and Redeemer, and strive diligently to proclaim Him as such among their brethren in every land. So with all possible speed they would go to England—to be there, Dr. Steele hoped, in time to meet Clare and Elinor and Reginald on their arrival. The *Majestic* was due in Southampton the fourteenth of July. That would be next Wednesday. This was now Thursday, July 8. All arrangements with Starkmann and the *Reichsbank* in Berlin could probably be completed tomorrow, Friday. And then on Saturday the glorious deliverance of Dr. Rothschild and Gretel from the hideous abode of death would, by God's mercy and grace, be successfully accomplished. If everything went well, they could leave Holland next Tuesday and be in good time to meet the loved ones from America, either in Southampton or London, next Wednesday. The delivering angel thrilled at the very thought.

But before he had quite finished his attractive meal served on a tray by the respectful *kellner*, he was phoned from the office. "Dr. Steele? A gentleman in the lobby to see you, sir—Dr. Eisenleben."

"Send him up to my room at once," he responded eagerly.

Quickly drinking his remaining coffee, he hurried to the elevator to greet his friend. "Dr. Eisenleben! This is indeed good of you to come here!"

"Thank you, Dr. Steele! I am so very happy to come. I tried to meet you at the airport and take you home again with me for dinner," he continued as they walked arm in arm down the corridor and entered Dr. Steele's room. "But I am sorry I could not make it. I could not get away from my office today till after five thirty, and your plane was due at five. But I had to see you as quickly as possible! I have come on a most important errand! My friend, I have tremendous news for you!" Dr. Eisenleben's face, his voice, his entire manner, all registered intense and joyful excitement.

"What is it? Here, sit down and tell me all about it!" Dr. Steele placed a chair for his visitor. But without waiting to be seated, Dr. Eisenleben cried out, triumphantly, the thrilling tidings:

"Dr. Steele! Joseph Rothschild has been found! His is alive and safe! At this very moment he is on the high seas, on his way to Palestine!"

"Praise God! Praise God, from whom all blessings flow!" Dr. Steele's excitement—and delight—equaled, if it did not exceed, Dr. Eisenleben's. "Who found him? Where? When? How did you get the word? Come, sit down and tell me everything!"

Dr Eisenleben took the proffered chair and immediately plunged into the amazing tale.

"Here is the whole wonderful story as I got it from Herr Neufeldt. He got his information from the Dutch Red Cross in Rotterdam. They passed on to him at once news they had received from civic authorities. It was startling indeed!

"It seems there was a raid, a week or ten days ago, by Holland Nazis, together with Gestapo agents from Germany, upon the home in Nijmegen of a Dutch family by the name of Van Devanter, suspected of harboring Jewish refugees. The vandals broke into the house in the dead of night, upon information supplied them, presumably, by an anti-Semitic tradesman who, for a large reward, betrayed the confidence he possessed of a secret stairway leading up to a hidden garret."

"How dastardly."

"It was dastardly indeed! Unutterably monstrous! Well, the raid was made suddenly, without one instant of warning, and not only all the Jews sheltered in the garret, but Herr Van Devanter and his entire family, as well, were herded into trucks and rushed off to a Nazi detention center. And from there, the very next day, ignominiously packed into cattle cars, they were swiftly dispatched to Westerbork, the chief Nazi concentration camp in Holland. What horrible fate awaits them there, God alone knows."

"And Joseph was with them!" Dr. Steele exclaimed in anguished outcry.

"*No!* He was not! That is the marvel of it all. Miraculously—by divine intervention, nothing less—Joseph was mercifully spared that horror. At the time of the raid, very fortunately he was asleep in a loft above the garret. And so he escaped the raid! And escaped detection! Again I say, 'Praise God!'"

"And then?"

"And then, after the raid—according to the Red Cross story as Joseph had supplied them with the details—he waited, still up in the loft, all through the remainder of the night and all through the next day, in an agony of horror and fear. And then at last, when all within the house was as quiet as a tomb, he ventured forth into the darkness of the following night and into the greater darkness of the precarious unknown future."

At this point in the earnest conversation, the *kellner* came to the door to take away Dr. Steele's tray. The gracious host suddenly bethought himself. "Dr. Eisenleben!" he exclaimed contritely. "I owe you an apology! Do pardon me, please, for being so inconsiderate. You have not had dinner. Do let me order a tray for you now, to be brought up here. Or would you prefer going down to the dining room?"

"Neither one, thank you, Dr. Steele. I deeply appreciate your kind invitation, but I must be hurrying back to my wife and my mother and father. They always worry about me until I get home."

Dr. Eisenleben quickly sketched the travels of Joseph Rothschild which took him to the high seas bound for the land of Palestine with fellow Jewish immigrants.

Dr. Steele accompanied his friend down the elevator and out upon the street, where they remained together for a few moments more in further very thoughtful conversation about Joseph and the friends in Dachau—their hearts knit together in sweetest accord of mutual sympathy and understanding. When Dr. Eisenleben finally left, Dr. Steele gazed after his retreating figure with admiration and deep emotion. "What a magnificent man he is," he reflected seriously, "so considerate of others, so completely unselfish. But how terribly he has suffered and is still suffering! His whole professional career, formerly so eminent, now almost completely blasted! And all because of his loyal devotion to Dr. Rothschild and his love for Dr. Rothschild's Hebrew people."

Dr. Steele's reflections were suddenly cut short by a sight that startled him. Just as Dr. Eisenleben disappeared from view around the corner, a man emerged from a previously concealing doorway and followed stealthily after the German physician. Instant, with utmost consternation, Dr. Steele recognized him. It was the Gestapo officer—the identical one who had stood in the shadow of Dr. Eisenleben's apartment house the night before. Had the man been shadowing him? And *why*? And what was he doing here now at Dr. Steele's hotel? Was he himself—Hollister Steele—also under Nazi surveillance? And if so, why was that? Did the Gestapo officer in any way connect him with Dr. Eisenleben? In what possible way? he wondered. Was he himself a victim of Nazi espionage? And if so, moreover, was the entire Gestapo officially behind this spying upon him? For what sinister purpose?

The whole question shook him violently. He returned to his room and tried to get his emotions under firm control, his nerves steady, his thinking calm and collected. But in vain. His brain was on fire. At last he went to bed. But it was to an entirely sleepless night.

Chapter 26

A True Daughter of Israel

Haggard and worn, Dr. Steele faced the new day—Friday. He arose at dawn with a strange sense of uneasiness and apprehension, almost of fear. What did the appearance, last night, of the Gestapo officer portend to Dr. Eisenleben? What did the day hold for himself?

Nine o'clock found him already before the door of Herr Starkmann's private office in the Gestapo Headquarters. In response to his knock, a gruff voice cried out, "*Herein!*" Dr. Steele recognized it as the voice of the director-general of the concentration camps. As the caller entered the room, that gentleman was, as usual, seated at his desk. Before him was a pile of important-looking documents through which he was thumbing with evident displeasure. He scowled at the visitor darkly.

"So it is you again!" he said none too graciously. "What are you here for this time?"

"I am here, Herr Starkmann," Dr. Steele responded eagerly, "with good news for you. I have received word that the funds for which I cabled are awaiting me at your Berlin *Reichsbank*. If you can give me the necessary identification, I can pay you the money for Dr. Rothschild and his daughter-in-law's release from Dachau immediately."

Herr Starkmann's frown turned instantly to a broad smile of satisfaction, his growl to dulcet sweetness.

"This is good news indeed! Excellent! Come, we shall go over to the *Reichsbank* at once. It opens at nine."

The two men left the Gestapo headquarters promptly and within ten minutes were inside the private office of the *Reichsbank* president, with whom, very evidently, the Gestapo authority was on intimate terms. It was a matter of only a few moments before the identification of the American stranger was successfully accomplished, the necessary papers signed and countersigned, and the full twenty-five thousand dollars in one-hundred-dollar bills, American currency, counted out and deposited carefully in Dr. Steele's receptacle.

And then immediately, while Herr Starkmann watched avidly with gloating, hawklike eyes, Dr. Steele meticulously drew off from the huge stack of greenbacks, the twenty-one thousand dollars' extortion money and handed it over to him, retaining for himself only four thousand. Five hundred of this the obliging *Reichsbank* president quickly converted into German legal tender. Herr Starkmann gave Dr. Steele the official Nazi receipt, and thus was concluded the high-handed Nazi piracy. With a few strokes of the pen, he had been denuded of nearly all his resources.

The two men left the bank at once and hailed a taxi. With parting instructions from the director-general to see him again at his office at nine o'clock the next morning, Dr. Steele drove off for the airport—where he made his plane by a mere hairbreadth's margin.

Midway of the flight to Dachau, the airplane developed engine trouble and had to be grounded for more than an hour for necessary repairs. It was well past noon, therefore, when it arrived at the entrance to the grim enclosure. Both the roll call and lunch were over, and the prisoners were hopelessly enduring another of their detested "recreation" periods. Around and around they were marching listlessly, their two circles passing each other in opposite directions.

According to instructions given him by the *kommandant* the day before, Dr. Steele, upon his admission at the gate, had gone at once to his now-familiar stone bench. From there, as previously, he watched the unhappy throng within the courtyard, himself concealed from view by the sheltering tree.

It was several moments before his searching gaze finally rested upon both Dr. Rothschild and Pastor von Ludwig—just as they, together with the *aufseher*, were about to become the chief actors in a most amazing drama.

It so happened that day, by rarest good fortune, that the pastor was marching immediately behind Dr. Rothschild. The appearances of the two men were in striking contrast. Pastor von Ludwig was walking with firm step, his body erect, his head held high, his whole attitude one of strong self-command. But the walk of his Hebrew friend, on the other hand, was feeble and tottering. His frame was drooping, his face contorted as if in great pain.

Suddenly he swayed dizzily and fell to the ground outside the double circle, directly in front of the *aufseher*. Without one shred of compassion, that worthy henchman of Adolf Hitler lunged at him with his whip, bringing it down on the quivering shoulders with snarling ferocity.

"Get up, you dog of a Jew! Get up at once and forward march!"

Instantly Pastor von Ludwig stepped out of the marching line and confronted the *aufseher* with blazing eyes.

"Put down that whip at once!" he commanded sternly. "Do not dare to strike this man again! If you do, I shall report you to the highest authorities." His bearing was quiet and dignified, his voice low and firmly controlled. But it held such a tone of powerful command that the startled *aufseher* withered before it, completely cowed by the sheer weight of the pastor's spiritual strength. His whip slipped limply out of his hand to the ground, and he himself slunk back to his place in sullen silence.

The prisoners came suddenly to a dead stop in their marching, viewing the scene with awed and terrified amazement. Holding them all—and the *aufseher*, as well—completely at bay by his manifest inward power, Pastor von Ludwig then knelt down beside his stricken friend and gathered him tenderly within his arms, pouring out words of fortifying comfort.

And then, in full view of the abashed *aufseher* and the badly disorganized prisoners, he gently lifted Dr. Rothschild to his feet. Placing a protecting and supporting arm around him, and completely disdaining the *aufseher* and the guards and their frantic, futile efforts to restore order, he deliberately led him out of the courtyard and toward his own cell and bunk within the barracks, none daring to restrain him.

Dr. Steele, silently viewing the whole astounding performance from his secluded bench, suddenly was conscious of a flood of inspiration thrilling through his entire being. "There is the answer!" he exclaimed exultantly to himself. "Right there is the key to Pastor von Ludwig's deliverance from Dachau. For their own protection they dare not keep him. They will get rid of him as soon as possible. They know he is too strong for them. Too strong for the *aufseher* and the *kommandant*. Too strong even for Adolf Hitler himself! He has upset the entire camp this afternoon. He has the power to demoralize and wreck it completely within a week, and they know it!

"But what they do not know is the reason for his ascendancy over them: that he is panoplied with the whole armor of God and is, therefore, empowered to resist all the wiles of the devil. For it is the devil—Satan himself—who is working through these cohorts of hell in a most desperate attempt to overthrow this saintly minister of Christ. But they never can succeed. They dare not kill him. They cannot make him kill himself. He is invincible. Martin Luther von Ludwig is the Nazis' toughest problem.

"Therefore, there is only one solution—only one way out of their dilemma: they have to disgorge him. They have to expunge him utterly from their hellish concentration camp."

Dr. Steele was still rejoicing inwardly over his now firm assurance of Pastor von Ludwig's eventual deliverance from Dachau, when, after a few moments, he looked up from his reverie and saw the *kommandant* approaching him.

No doubt he had witnessed the courtyard incident or, at least, had been informed of it. Clearly he was in an agitated mood. But he held his turbulent spirit well in hand as he addressed the visitor. His attitude toward him was even astonishingly cordial.

"*Guten Tag,* Herr *Doktor*! I am glad to see you again, sir—very glad, indeed. I am sorry I cannot stay now and visit with you for a few moments, but there has been a slight disturbance among our prisoners and I must go at once and quell it. Just one word, however, first.

"I want you to know that Herr Starkmann called me up from Berlin this morning to tell me you were on your way down here. He told me also what I was most happy to hear: that you had settled your obligation in full for the discharge of your two Semitic friends. He likewise instructed me to get them ready to leave with you tomorrow. Have you their *entlassungsschein* with you? Herr Starkmann said he had entrusted it to you."

"Yes sir, I have. Here it is."

The *kommandant* seized the document avidly and placed it carefully within the inner pocket of his coat. "Ah, very good!" he exclaimed with suave satisfaction. "Very good indeed! Excellent! Now we can go right ahead. Come to my office at two o'clock on the way to your plane. We can discuss all the necessary arrangements then.

In the meantime, if you care to do so, you may talk today with Frau Rothschild. I have just seen her and given her orders to meet you in the reception room of the Women's Hospital within the next fifteen minutes. The reception room is on the ground floor, just to the left of the front entrance. You can find it easily. There is a small alcove at the rear of this main room; you and Frau Rothschild may use this for a private interview. You must terminate it at two o'clock sharp. Come then to my office. But I must be hurrying off now. Auf Wiedersehen! HEIL HITLER!"

Dr. Steele quickly found the appointed rendezvous. Gretel was already there, tensely awaiting him. As he entered the room, she sprang toward him, both hands outstretched in rapturous welcome. Then suddenly she burst into a flood of tears. "Oh, Dr. Steele," she cried with uncontrolled emotion, "I was so afraid that I might miss you! That they would not let me see you after all! Oh, I could not have borne it! I could not have *borne* it! Oh, it all has been so terrible, so *terrible*!"

He drew her gently down beside him on a divan; and soon, under the influence of his soothing words, she regained her accustomed poise and calm and was able to talk with him coherently. "You knew, then, that I was here?" he asked her quietly.

"Yes, my father told me."

"Your father? When were you able to see him?"

"Yesterday. Just shortly after you had left. Father and I met each other in the courtyard as we both were on our way to our cells at the end of the afternoon work assignments; and by rare good fortune the *aufseher* allowed us to talk together. It was only for five minutes, but that was time enough for Father to tell me the wonderful news. That you were here! That you had come all the way from America purposely to find *us*! Oh, it was so good of you! So *good* of you, Dr. Steele, to come!" Her tears poured forth afresh, but now they were tears of gratitude and joy.

With keen professional scrutiny, he studied her face closely. It was very thin and tense and white. But it clearly revealed her strength of character, her nobility of soul. Through the tears she smiled at him—a radiant, brave smile. He gazed at her with frank admiration. And also with earnest questioning. Did she yet know, he wondered, that she was to be released on the morrow? She must be informed at once, for time was now running out rapidly. Certainly he himself must tell her before he left. It would be so much wiser for her to be made aware of the whole situation before the *kommandant* harshly gave her orders to prepare for her departure.

But just how should he inform her? How best could he break to her the wonderful news that her liberty was so near at hand? The sudden shock of joy might prove too overwhelming in her present depleted condition.

And what of the news that her husband had been found? That they would soon be reunited? And even in *Palestine*! What of all that? The shock of these tremendous tidings held within it an element of possible danger to her equilibrium, by reason of its sudden and violent contrast with her present awful circumstances.

Silently Dr. Steele pondered the whole weighty question. To his swift prayer for wisdom God's clear answer was as swiftly returned. The fervent suppliant knew unmistakably that his directive was divinely imparted.

He himself must disclose to Gretel right now the plan of exit from Dachau on the morrow, both for herself and for Dr. Rothschild, though not for her father. But concerning Joseph, he saw that assuredly he was not the proper person to enlighten her. That duty—that high privilege—undoubtedly would belong to one or the other of the two fathers as soon as they themselves received the information. How and when could *they* be told the wonderful news? Was he, perhaps, the one appointed of God to tell them?

It was Dr. Rothschild, preferably, who should divulge the happy truth to Gretel—but not until they were well away from Dachau. Her emotional reaction, were she able to hear it just on the eve of her departure, might prove too violent, too dangerous. Assuredly it would be too violent for her dear father. Gretel's joy would highlight his own great loneliness in being left without her.

But at least she must be prepared for her discharge tomorrow. Thus, very carefully, Dr. Steele watched for the opportune opening in their conversation to tell her of it. He perceived clearly that, first of all, he must listen patently to her confidences regarding her Dachau experiences, which, eagerly, she began pouring into his sympathetic ear.

"Oh, Dr. Steele," she repeated, "it has been so terrible, so *terrible*! I marvel that I ever could have lived through it all!"

"Yes," he replied compassionately, "it has been terrible indeed. I know it. You have suffered, my dear friend; that is very evident."

"Yes, I have suffered. I have suffered intensely, it is true. But," she added bravely, "by no means as intensely as my father and Dr. Rothschild have suffered. For dear Dr. Rothschild, especially, the whole Dachau experience has been an agonizing one. And for the one reason supremely: he is a Jew. For here in Dachau—throughout all Germany indeed—Jews are regarded merely as vermin to be trampled under Aryan feet."

"How *monstrous*!"

"Yes, it is dreadful indeed—unutterably so. But as I said, God opened up for me a marvelous means of escape. Do you care to hear about that?"

"I surely do! Absolutely so! Please tell me everything!"

"When the authorities found out that I am a registered nurse, they swiftly transferred me to work here in the Women's Hospital. And this, in comparison with the barracks, is palatial. I now have my own private cell, with a fairly comfortable cot. And—most luxurious—a hot, substantial meal at noon. They know they have to keep up the strength of their nurses. Best of all, I am released from those revolting roll calls and from the murderous outdoor labor.

"Of course, I have to work very hard in the hospital, with

long hours on duty—often from 6 in the morning until 5 in the afternoon—seven days a week. And quite frequently they transfer me to night duty, from 5 p.m. to 5 a.m. But it is the kind of work for which I have been trained and which I love: *nursing*. And the officials really treat me like a human being—which they certainly did not do in the barracks.

"Conditions in the hospital, however, are deplorable. The wards are overcrowded, and the patients' meals are atrocious. Entirely lacking in adequate nutrition. And the sanitation is positively criminal. Typhus and tuberculosis are rampant. The mortality is frightful, particularly among the aged women. Old age and weakness of any sort are held in utter contempt in Dachau.

"Often these dear old women die in the night. Sometimes as many as six or seven bodies will be laid out in the corridors the next morning, waiting for the truck to haul them off to a common grave or to the crematorium."

Dr. Steele, aghast, listened silently but most intently as Gretel completed the recital of her gruesome experiences.

"So many of the women," she continued, "in fact, all of them, are so greatly in need of comforting and strengthening. A number of them have come from homes of wealth and refinement, and Dachau has completely crushed their spirits. But I do rejoice that I have been enabled, by God's grace and empowering, to help them in some little measure.

"Not infrequently these poor, dear creatures are in terrible anguish of heart and mind as they hear of their own husbands or fathers being sentenced to extermination. Some of them are literally crazed with grief.

"One sweet little woman came into my cell last week in utter terror and despair. She herself had been sentenced to die in the gas chamber and was given just one hour to get ready. She was absolutely frenzied. But praise God! I was able to quiet her. Within a few moments I led her to the Lord, and He himself comforted her and gave her strength and courage to go forward to the frightful ordeal . . . When, a little later, the *wachmeisterin* came for her, she went out from my cell with a steady walk and—most amazingly—even with a smile upon her face, firm in her newly found confidence that this horrible death would be but the doorway to heaven."

"How very wonderful!"

"Yes, to me it was a most striking proof of the power of the Word of God. And that is what I am trying to give to these poor women here. I have been privileged to form a little Bible class for the convalescent patients. We are permitted to meet one evening each week in this very room. Usually as many as twenty women are present; they are so hungry for spiritual food. My praise to God is great that He graciously has used me to bring a few of these dear fellow prisoners to the Savior. This is by reason of the fact that we have a deep fellowship of suffering."

But at this point Dr. Steele suddenly cut short the sad narrative with gravest solicitude.

"Dear Mrs. Rothschild," he admonished her gently, "do not dwell upon these horrors any longer. Try, by God's grace, to *forget*!"

"I can never forget! The agony of it all is seared into my very soul. But—please do not misunderstand me, Dr. Steele—I am truly thankful that I have been able to bring even a fraction of warmth and cheer into their tragic little lives. By His all-sufficient grace I am content to remain—yes, even here in Dachau—until it is His good pleasure to grant me merciful release."

Dr. Steele regarded Gretel with wonder amounting almost to awe. She was her father's own daughter. She possessed, as truly did he, a sublime faith in God and entire consecration. Above every other consideration and at whatever cost, truly her chief delight, like her Savior's, was to do the Father's will.

And now, to Dr. Steele's great gladness, it was clearly His will to lead her out from this present fearful valley of the shadow of death into what he fervently hoped would be for her, henceforth, green pastures beside the still waters. Therefore it was with inward exulting that, very cautiously, he began to break to her the thrilling news that the "merciful release" was near at hand.

"You are content to *remain*? *Here?*" he asked in astonishment. "That is truly amazing—nothing less than a miracle of God's mercy, of His *all*-sufficient grace. It reminds me of Mme. Guyon in her imprisonment in France. Do you recall her lovely verse?

"When place we see or place we shun,
The soul finds happiness in none.
But with our God to lead the way,
'Tis equal joy to go or stay.

"And *you* have come to this same strong conviction—to this same sublime degree of trust! That is very wonderful!"

"Yes, Dr. Steele, I believe I can truly echo Mme. Guyon's testimony: 'Tis equal joy to go or stay'—whichever our Lord may appoint. With her I have learned to desire supremely, above all else, the 'sweet will of God.' That is the chief result which He has wrought in my soul through the refining fires of Dachau."

"Praise Him for such a triumph! Well, from all you have told me, I can perceive that assuredly it has been God's will—which is always perfect wisdom, perfect love—for you to be here thus long in this notorious concentration camp, where He has used your ministry among the women and the little children with such signal fruitfulness. But just as surely it is *now* His will for you to go forth—to leave this dreadful place forever! My dear friend, I have today the great privilege and happiness of telling you that your *Entlassungsschein*—the official order for your release—has come!"

"Dr. Steele! What do you *mean*?" Gretel's agitation—her reaction to the tremendous announcement—was intense. She almost swooned from intermingled incredulity and joy. "Whatever do you *mean*?" she repeated in high excitement, a wonderful new light of hope shining in her eyes.

"I mean," Dr. Steele replied, "that God has marvelously blessed *my* Dachau mission. I told you He had sent me all the way from America to find you and your father and Dr. Rothschild. But I have not yet told you for what purpose. That purpose—*His* purpose—was that I might accomplish your deliverance. And, God be praised, He has, thus far, wondrously fulfilled His own design. Tomorrow, by order of Heinrich Starkmann himself, I am to have the high privilege, the unspeakable joy, of leading you and Dr. Rothschild out of Dachau—out of *Germany*. And then—" He paused. However could he tell the beloved daughter the rest of the story? That her beloved father was to be left behind, alone? How could he possibly tell her *that*? While Gretel was trying to recover her breath from the stunning news of her own near departure, Dr. Steele was feverishly trying to recover his self-command, as he sought for the exact words of approach to this most painful task.

Gretel herself precipitated the crisis. Squarely she propounded the fateful question. "You say, Dr. Steele, that Dr. Rothschild and I are to be released tomorrow. But what about my father? Is he not going too?"

Swiftly Dr. Steele invoked his faith. "Your dear father does not go tomorrow, but he will be following you and Dr. Rothschild very soon."

"How soon?"

"I—I do not know exactly, but it will be *soon*."

"Very well, then. I shall wait until he goes with us. I cannot leave my father."

The messenger of mercy was nonplussed. Here was a sudden, definite impasse. The way of Gretel's deliverance had so wonderfully opened up before her. And now she herself was blocking it!

He looked swiftly at his watch. Five minutes to two! And he was under orders to meet the *kommandant* in his office at exactly two o'clock! But how could he leave Gretel thus? What final word should he say to her?

He extended his hand in parting. "I am so very sorry, dear friend. I have to leave at once for an appointment with the *kommandant*. And then I must go on to Berlin. But I shall be seeing you again tomorrow morning. Think everything through very carefully before then. But remember this. You will have to act in accordance with the *kommandant*'s instructions, as he must act in accordance with Herr Starkmann's. And it is not merely Herr Starkmann's permission, but his *command* that you and Dr. Rothschild leave with me tomorrow. But he absolutely assured that your father *will* follow you both very shortly. *Have faith in God!*"

Thus was Dr. Steele's own faith challenged by the seemingly impossible, as he left Gretel in what was now deep bewilderment and distress, and hurried to the office of the *kommandant*. What would be his mood this time? Fortunately for the visitor, the mood was a cordial one—almost affable. And the dreaded interview was brief.

"Well, my good friend"—the *kommandant* smiled his greeting—"I am glad to be able to tell you that everything is now moving ahead smoothly and swiftly. This *Entlassungsschein,* together with the happy word from Berlin this morning that you have paid the ransom money in full, paves the way for the discharge of our two esteemed prisoners tomorrow. They will leave with you at noon. Herr Starkmann has phoned me again from Berlin, just a few moments ago, to give his final orders concerning this whole *exceptional* affair. He himself will come down with you to Dachau tomorrow morning. He intends personally to make sure that you all are safely over the border and out of Germany forever.

"He has instructed me to tell you that you are to meet him at the Tempelhof at seven o'clock. He will bring you here in his own private plane; and then, after their discharge from our camp is effectively completed, he will fly the Rothschilds and yourself all the way to Rotterdam. From there you can go by plane or boat wherever you wish.

"I have not yet told the Rothschilds they are leaving. I shall see both of them this evening and give them orders to be ready by ten o'clock tomorrow morning. All the papers can be signed and other preparations finished after Herr Starkmann and you arrive. Everything should be in complete readiness for you all to get away at noon."

Suddenly, from the courtyard outside, the two men heard the shrieking of a siren. The *kommandant* rose instantly from his desk, pulling out of the long top drawer a revolver and a sword.

"I am sorry," he apologized, "but I must leave you at once. That siren is an imperative summons. But I shall see you soon again for our final talk. *Entschuldigen sie mir!* Auf Wiedersehen! HEIL HITLER!"

He rushed to the doorway and disappeared through it, leaving his astonished visitor behind. Dr. Steele quickly followed him out of the building in wondering alarm as the siren kept up its shrill shrieking.

Chapter 27

Let My People Go!

Dr. Rothschild was the first of the two prisoners to arrive at the front office for processing. He entered the *kommandant*'s large office held as in a vise between two guards. He appeared bewildered and dazed. There seemed to be about him an apathy comprised half of dullness, half of fear. Even the sight of his cherished friend, Dr. Steele, failed to rouse him. He stood captive between his guards, silent and abashed.

Not so Gretel. When *she* entered, five minutes later, she was wide-awake, electric with excitement. She, too, was flanked by guards, a cruel, cold-eyed *aufseherin* on either side of her, holding her grimly by her arms. But vigorously and decisively she tore herself loose from them and rushed first to her father-in-law and then to Dr. Steele in ecstatic greeting. She completely ignored both the director-general and the *kommandant*.

Angered by this perceived misconduct, one of the two burly camp guards grabbed Gretel's arm and roughly yanked her away from her loved ones. Dr. Steele looked on in wide-eyed wonder. Though every bit as female as Gretel, and his own lovely wife, the hard-faced *aufseherin* before him lacked even the scantest trace of grace or femininity. Her features were harsh, her expression severe, as she jutted out her lower lip in irritation. *"Nein! Stehenbleiben!"* she spat crossly, cuffing Gretel on the side of the head. The other female guard joined in then, yammering angrily in her guttural tongue. But Gretel was not intimidated. Turning on the guard, she snapped back with equal fury, proving to all present that she was a force to be reckoned with. The first *aufseherin* raised her hand as if to administer another blow, when the director-general shouted impatiently, "*Aufenthalt! Im Augenblick!*" Dr. Steele watched as fear entered the guard's chilly, azure eyes and she lowered her hand slowly. Triumphantly, Gretel once again wrenched herself free of her oppressors and stormed indignantly toward Herr Starkmann. "Where is my father?" She was met only with smug silence. "I said, 'Where is my father?' *Where—is—he*?" she hissed, courageously punctuating her last question with three irritated pokes of her finger in the director-general's puffed-out chest.

Instantly, rage replaced smugness. "Silence!" Herr Starkmann shouted back at her, his eyes blazing fire and his booming voice seemingly shaking even the very walls. Dr. Steele winced at the volume. All four guards, male and female alike, cringed in terror. And Dr. Rothschild began quaking uncontrollably.

But Gretel held her ground, undaunted. Utterly defying the order of the director-general, she whirled angrily upon the *kommandant*. "*Where* is my father?" she demanded. "You told me last night that I could see him this morning. But I have *not* seen him! Where is he?"

"Your honorable father is where he belongs!" was the brutal reply. "In his work squad!"

"But you told me I could see him! You promised!"

The henchman of Adolf Hitler admirably exemplified his high calling and his high commander-in-chief. He shrugged his shoulders with complete disdain. "I'm sorry," he replied callously, "but I changed my mind overnight. You have seen your sire for the last time! You will now leave here with these gentlemen. Go! At once!"

Instantly Gretel confronted her adversary with blazing eyes. In a voice trembling with rage, she flung in his face her ultimatum.

"No! I shall *not* go! I absolutely refuse to leave this office until I have seen my father!"

Shamefacedly taken aback for the moment by such an unprecedented show of opposition from a prisoner, the *kommandant* looked limply to Herr Starkmann for his implementation of the order for immediate departure. That haughty dignitary swiftly complied. Drawing himself up in his most impressive military grandeur, he thundered out his imperious command: "Forward to the airplane! Everybody, forward *march*!"

But before even he himself could take the first step in that direction, at that very instant, there was a sharp knock on the office door. Cautiously, in obedience to a directing glance from the *kommandant*, a guard opened it. And suddenly into the office there calmly walked, with majestic tread, Gretel's father himself—Pastor Martin Luther von Ludwig.

Everyone within the room was electrified. Gretel, overwhelmed with sudden joy, screamed out her ecstatic welcome. "My father! Oh, my father!" she cried deliriously. Again she tried to wrench herself free from the *aufseherinnen*, but this time they held her pinioned inexorably.

At the sudden sight of him, the *kommandant* was, for the moment, badly shaken; but quickly he recovered his accustomed firm control. "Von Ludwig!" he queried sternly, "whatever are *you* doing here? By what possible right have you dared intrude within my office? Explain yourself, sir!"

In vain did the *kommandant* and even the director-general himself try to gain ascendancy over their prisoner. In vain did they try to terrify and overmaster him and silence him when he began to speak. But his presence towered over both of theirs as, irresistibly, he was strengthened with might by the Spirit in the inner man.

Both Herr Starkmann and the *kommandant* felt a swift urge to lunge at him and strike him to the floor, but instinctively they realized they dare not touch him. He was invested with an invisible aura of protection that kept them both cringingly at bay. As he replied to the *kommandant*'s inquisition, there was a ringing tone of authority in his voice, a fire in his words—a fire of such force as could enflame a world.

"I am here," he retorted deliberately, "to see and talk with my daughter before she leaves the concentration camp. I have learned that she and Dr. Rothschild are scheduled to leave this morning. I wish to assure both of you gentlemen that, insofar as I can recall, during all these months of my incarceration here in Dachau, this is my first instance of insubordination. I sincerely trust that it may be my last.

"But one thing, gentlemen, I cannot and will not accept: your denial of my right, as Gretel's father, to have fellowship with my own child before you send her forth. You are forbidding me the right and the opportunity even to say to her my last farewell, and to bestow upon her a father's blessing. That opportunity, that right, I now *insist* upon—I now *demand*!"

As he thus declared his irrevocable purpose, the pastor's face was ashen white and sharply contorted with pain, by reason of the intensity of his emotion. But his bearing was magnificent. Majestically he dominated the entire scene. Visibly and powerfully he was under the complete control of the Holy Spirit. "Do you accede, gentlemen," he questioned them compellingly, "to this, my rightful claim?"

"No!" roared the *kommandant*. "We do *not*! You have seen and talked with your daughter for the last time on earth! Leave this office at once! Go back to your work! Go, I said. At *once*!"

Totally ignoring the double order from both *kommandant* and director-general for his immediately return to the work squad, Pastor von Ludwig wheeled squarely away from the two of them and rushed over to his distracted child. As she saw him approach, she screamed out with still more penetrating anguish, "Oh, Father! *Father!*"

So tremendeous was the impact of the pastor's Spirit-filled personality upon them, that the two *aufseherinnen* holding Gretel cowered before him and unconsciously relaxed their grip upon their prisoner—his beloved daughter. Firmly he drew her away from them and enfolded her tenderly within his strong embrace. Flinging her arms around his neck and dropping her head upon his breast, Gretel sobbed convulsively. "Stop that noise at once!" Herr Starkmann shouted savagely. "No hysterics are permitted in this concentration camp!" And then he lunged at Pastor von Ludwig's collar and shook him violently. "Von Ludwig, you dog!" he roared. "You will do as you are told! Go to your work squad *immediately*! And *you,* madame, you will go with *me*! Herr Steele! Rothschild! Start at once! We all are going to my airplane. Right now! This very moment! Go, I tell you, go!"

With white-hot fury Gretel whirled upon him. "No!" she gasped between her sobs. "I will *not* go! I will not leave my father! You cannot *make* me leave him! *No,* I tell you, I will not go! I—will—not—go!"

Very gently her father tried to admonish her. "Yes, my precious daughter, you must go. And I must go. But have no fear, darling, and have no sorrow. God will go with us both, and soon we shall be reunited in that Better Land."

But Gretel still held unyieldingly to her determination. Still she protested vehemently. "No, dearest Father, *no*! I cannot go! I cannot leave you! I will *never* leave you!"

Dr. Rothschild and Dr. Steele had both been silent witnesses of the whole tremendous drama. Dr. Rothschild seemed to be completely uncomprehending of the import of the entire terrifying situation. But the silence of Dr. Steele, on the other hand, was one of wide-awake awareness and of keenest consternation. He was appalled, aghast at the tragic turn of events the totalitarian sentence of doom had precipitated.

He was suddenly conscious, for his own part, of a sense of frustration, of a fear of utter failure of his whole beneficent mission of deliverance. Was it all to end *thus*? In the diabolical murder of Pastor von Ludwig and, quite possibly, of Gretel also? Even though his primary purpose in coming to Germany—the rescue of Dr. Rothschild—would, very soon now, be successfully achieved, the loss of these two other precious lives would haunt Dr. Steele to his grave.

As countless times before in a critical moment he had implored God's undertaking, even so did he now send up an importunate, swift prayer in but two brief words: *Help, Lord!*

And, as always before, the help was swiftly given. This time it came in the form of but *one* word—one magic name flashed instantaneously into his consciousness: *Joseph!*

Immediately his mind was illuminated; the turmoil of his heart was still. It was revealed to him clearly: he himself must right here and now tell Gretel that her husband was alive. That he had been found. That he was safe and well. That even now he was on his way to Palestine to await her there. Yes, assuredly, Gretel, Joseph's father, her father, the Nazi officers: they all must learn at once the startling news: *Joseph Rothschild was alive!*

"Go, woman, go!" Again the director-general thundered at her his command, as savagely he began to shove her toward the door.

Instantly Dr. Steele, with a new sense of conscious strength—inspired by the strength and example of the intrepid pastor—blocked the doorway and held up a detaining hand. In a ringing tone of authority, dominant above even the angry outcry of the director, he voiced *his* command:

"Wait, Herr Starkmann! Before this young woman leaves—before you take her out of Germany—I must be permitted to have a word with her. Listen attentively! Yes, *you*, Herr Starkmann! And *you*, Herr *Kommandant*! Everyone within this room! You all must hear what I am about to say to Frau Joseph Rothschild."

There was a tense silence in that Dachau office as every eye was fixed sharply upon Dr. Steele. He stood before them all—erect, fearless, impressive. "Frau Rothschild"—he confronted her squarely as still she writhed under the harsh grip of her captor's hand upon her shoulder—"my dear friend, I have astounding, wonderful, glorious news for you! Listen. Listen quietly. Your husband, Joseph, has been found in Holland! He is *alive*! And he is well and safe! And right now, even at this very hour, he is aboard a ship that is taking him to Palestine! And he will be waiting there for *you*!"

As Dr. Steele had feared might be the case, Gretel's reaction to his disclosure was indeed a precarious one. She almost swooned, so tremendous was the impact upon her of the thrilling tidings. In a near delirium, an ecstasy of intermingled joy and incredulity and fear, she screamed out, "Joseph! Oh, my beloved! Joseph! *Joseph!*" And then, swiftly wrenching herself free from the director's detaining hand, again she flew into her father's arms and there gave way to a flood of wild hysteria.

Under his soothing influence and his gentle caresses, gradually she became quieted. But soon there arose tempestuously another emotional storm: the storm of indecision. Her heart was literally torn two ways: the urgent impulse of love to rush immediately to her husband; but, countering that longing, her firm resolve never to leave her father. To go with him, if need must be, to his awful death.

Pastor von Ludwig's response to Dr. Steele's dramatic announcement had been a fervent "Praise God! Praise God!" As for Dr. Rothschild, on the other hand, he still appeared dazed, uncomprehending. The two Nazi officers, completely overpowered by the forcefulness of Dr. Steele, stood abashed and motionless.

Gretel continued to cling to her father in a desperate embrace, moaning intermittently, "Joseph, oh, my Joseph!" and then, "Father! My own precious father! No, no! I will never leave you, never, never!"

With utmost tenderness and love, but with wisdom and compelling authority, her father himself broke the deadlock. His own heart torn with anguish, he made his great renunciation.

"No, my child," he thus admonished her, "you must not try to stay with me. God has mercifully given you a wonderful release; you must go, my darling, to your husband. Your place is by his side.

"And it will not be long, my darling, before you, too, will join me in the house of the Lord. For I truly believe that the day of Christ's return is drawing near, when 'the Lord himself shall descend from heaven with a shout, with the voice of the archangel, and with the trump of God . . . Then we . . . shall be caught up together . . . in the clouds, to meet the Lord in the air: and so shall we ever be with the Lord.

"In the meantime, Margarete, it is His command that you occupy until He come. And your occupation will be a joyful one indeed: within the promised land! The Jewish homeland! *Palestine!*

"And now," he continued with holy boldness, "*this* is what I have to say for all to hear!"

Directing his words ostensibly toward Dr. Steele, the fearless man of God, with carefully calculated intent, hurled them with the force of a cannonball, definitely and accusingly, straight at the seared consciences of the director-general and his companion in evil, the Dachau *kommandant*.

"Dr. Steele," he began his invective, "you are returning to America. You will tell your people there exactly what you have seen in this iniquitous concentration camp. You will tell them what your own eyes have beheld during the past week in this abode of Satan.

"You must warn your country—you must warn the world—of what assuredly it can expect if the power of Adolf

Hitler and his wicked cohorts and of the whole nefarious National Socialist Government of Germany is not curtailed—if the tide of Nazi totalitarianism is not stemmed and utterly destroyed before it further destroys the bodies and the souls of men.

"And now to *you*, my fellow citizens of our fair Germany, I give this most solemn warning: Unless the present regime within our beautiful Fatherland,—this once-so-godly land of Martin Luther—unless this hellish regime is completely overthrown, we will be plunged irrevocably into another world war of such magnitude and of such atrocity and horror as will, eventually, wreck and devastate the entire earth."

During the whole time that Pastor von Ludwig had been giving his charge to Dr. Steele, his two tormentors tried again and again, one after another or both together, in a frenzy of desperation, to silence him. But entirely in vain. He continued to stand before them and before all the other astounded auditors within the office, with the calm assurance of one who, consciously, is more than conqueror.

His messages to his daughter and to Dr. Steele at last concluded, he wheeled suddenly and sharply upon the two disconcerted Nazis.

"And now, gentlemen,"—sternly he commanded their fixed attention—"my final word of all is addressed to *you*. Herr Starkmann! Herr *Kommandant*! You both will give most solemn consideration to this which I am compelled to say to you. As the servant of almighty God, and as His emissary to this evil place, I am directly charged by Him to deliver this, His Word of dire warning to you both. Hearken diligently! And may it strike terror to your hearts!"

As Moses before Pharaoh, as Elijah before Ahab, as Paul before Agrippa—even as the Master Himself before Pontius Pilate—so also did Martin Luther von Ludwig stand fearlessly, triumphant in spirit, before his adversaries. Their positions, respectively, as accusers and accused, were entirely reversed. Pastor von Ludwig was the judge; the director-general and the *kommandant* were prisoners at the bar of justice. Visibly trembling before his scorching denunciation, they remained cowering and silent to its conclusion.

"You may elude the judgment of men," he began. "You

may escape human retribution for your wicked deeds. You may continue long upon your sinful course. But do not deceive yourselves; do not entertain a false delusion, a vain hope. You cannot elude the final and inevitable judgment. You cannot escape the final, awful wrath of *God* upon all the monstrous evil that you both have wrought. Every drop of blood that you have spilled, God will require at your hands. Every agony that you have made your fellow men to suffer, that agony will receive from the divine Avenger its just recompense of reward.

"Particularly for the infinitude of agony that you have inflicted upon God's beloved chosen people—His Israel—His retribution against you will be terrible. Hear His own most dreadful word of condemnation to all who hate and harm the Jews.

"Therefore in utmost compassion, Herr Starkmann, Herr *Kommandant*, I plead with you to repent. *Repent!* Repent of your awful sin against God and against His beloved Israel—your sin against all humanity. Repent and turn to God and implore Him for His mercy and forgiveness before it is too late. Before his fearful wrath shall fall upon you! Repent, I beg of you! Repent! For *except ye repent, ye shall all likewise perish.*

"For the last time, I give you both most solemn warning: You may escape an earthly tribunal—you probably will. But you *cannot* escape the judgment seat of God. One day you shall stand before it and render up account of all your evil deeds—unless, first, you have confessed them and have been forgiven. But if you have *not* confessed, if you have *not* received forgiveness, you must then—surely and inescapably—receive God's sentence of eternal doom. As His messenger and mouthpiece, that is my final word of admonition."

Bestowing a last caress—tender, yet infinitely grave—upon his precious child, who again in a flood of weeping clung to him desperately, he gently but firmly released her hold upon him and turned toward the doorway to make his exit. Fervently grasping the hand of Dr. Steele who stood before it, he repeated to him his stern commission.

"Dr. Steele, you will not forget your solemn charge. You

will not fail to publish abroad the terrible evil that exists in this Dachau Concentration Camp. The whole world must be told that Adolf Hitler is the *enemy of all mankind*! That he and all his cohorts here and elsewhere are *direct emissaries* of the devil!

"And remember, especially, Dr. Steele, at your first opportunity after you reach home, you must inform your American government of the exact situation that obtains today in Germany. Your government must be warned! All Americans must be warned!"

"I promise you indeed! I shall most gladly do everything within my power for them all," Dr. Steele responded fervently.

"Thank you, my beloved friend, with all my heart! Now I can go in perfect peace. Farewell. God be with you till we meet again—within our Father's house. Farewell!"

He started to pass through the doorway. But immediately Dr. Steele blocked his exit. "Wait!" he cried in ringing tone of authoritative command. "It is now *my* turn to speak. Dear friend, before you leave, before anyone leaves this office, there is something *I* must say for all to hear. Listen to me carefully!

"Pastor von Ludwig, you have charged me to inform the world of all I know concerning Dachau. In all good faith and conscience, with God as my witness, I accept that charge. Particularly do I accept the challenge to inform my American government. But I want you to know that the American government, representatively, already has been informed. I want every one of you to understand—you especially, Herr Starkmann and Herr *Kommandant*—that all the facts in my possession, which I have obtained right here in this concentration camp during the past week by personal experience and observation—the whole stupendous catalogue of evil deeds of which I myself have been a horrified eyewitness, particularly yesterday's mass murder in the gas chamber—all these facts already are in the hands of the United States ambassador to Germany. I took the utmost care to send them before I left Berlin. And you may be very sure he will relay them promptly to Washington. Within a week they will be spread upon the front page of every newspaper in America and, by Associated Press, throughout the world."

During the whole of Dr. Steele's astounding declaration, Pastor von Ludwig had remained in perfect quietness before him to its conclusion. With his arm again encircling his daughter protectingly, he very gently held her turbulent spirit in restraint also. Dr. Rothschild appeared dazed and apathetic still—almost lifeless indeed—completely oblivious to the entire dramatic scene taking place so vividly before his very eyes.

The two Nazi officers, the director-general and the *kommandant* had listened in speechless, stony anger. But with Dr. Steele's threat of publication to the whole world of all the Dachau outrage, their wrath exploded into a violent torrent of curses.

"You *viper*! You will die for this!" the director-general hissed in fury.

"No, Herr Starkmann," Dr. Steele retorted calmly, "I will *not* die. You do not dare to lay one finger upon me. I claim immunity as a citizen of the United States. If you harm me in any way whatsoever, you will answer for it to the United States government. I am confident that I am under its protection at this very moment. For I made our embassy aware of the fact also that I would be here in Dachau today; and I have no doubt that its intelligence already has this place under close surveillance, with precautionary intent."

Again the director-general, ably supported by the *kommandant*, hissed his venom. "That's a lie!" he screamed shrilly. "The American intelligence will *never* get into Dachau! And *you* will never get out of here alive. I tell you, my friend, you are a doomed man. You will *die*! You will go tomorrow morning with von Ludwig to the *gas chamber*!"

Still did Dr. Steele remain calm and unperturbed. Looking his assailant squarely in the face, he replied quietly, "And I tell *you* I will *not* die. I will *not* go to the gas chamber. And what is more—" Here he paused dramatically for a full moment. And then, as a wave of tensest excitement and suspense swept through the office, he continued incisively: "What is more, Pastor von Ludwig will not die! God's honored minister will *never* go to the gas chamber! For were you to execute him—I warn you emphatically and insistently—it would precipitate revolution within all Germany immediately. It would rend your Fatherland apart in civil war. For the whole Confessional Church of which he is the acknowledged leader would rise in such a fury as to tear Germany in pieces.

"This is an absolute certainty. I have it upon the authority of a prominent and influential German citizen who has kept in close touch with the entire totalitarian situation—a man who was one of the foremost physicians of Berlin, and who also was one of the highest officers in the Confessional Church. That man was Dr. Gustave Eisenleben. He told me, just three nights ago, that the whole church is on the verge of revolt against the National Socialist Government for its iniquitous imprisonment and hideous treatment of their beloved pastor within this hellish concentration camp. If ever it hears that Martin Luther von Ludwig has been exterminated, nothing on earth will hold back its awful vengeance."

And then, drawing himself up to fullest height and confronting the director-general and the *kommandant* accusingly as they both cringed witheringly before him, Dr. Steele, in a crescendo of command, cried out with holy boldness, for all to hear, his stunning ultimatum.

Even as Moses confronted Pharaoh and declared fearlessly unto him, *"Thus saith the LORD God of Israel, Let my people go"*—even so now did God's messenger to Dachau stand fearlessly before the two Nazi officers and daringly demand of them, *"Let this prisoner go!"*

Silencing their instant outcry of rage with his sternly uplifted hand, continued challengingly: "As servant of almighty God and upon His authority, I command you: *Release His minister at once!* You will let him *go*! You will take him with you, Herr Starkmann, together with his daughter and Dr. Rothschild and myself, to Holland immediately.

"And now, as the mouthpiece of the Lord, by His order and in the power of His Holy Spirit—I give to both of you gentlemen this solemn, final warning: There will be dire consequences for yourself and for *all Germany* if you refuse to obey—right now at once—this, His most imperative command: *Let Martin Luther von Ludwig go!"*

The reaction of the Nazis was terrific. They almost frothed at the mouth in their fury. The air was fairly blue with their fierce cursing. But they were helpless. They fully realized their danger and the danger to their nation if they ignored the warning. They were baffled, frustrated, defeated—caught as rats in a trap.

With no alternative but to obey the stern command, the immediate problem now confronting the director-general and his equally crestfallen *kommandant* was how best they could "save face" in so desperate a situation.

The solution of their dilemma came to them quickly. Even in the selfsame manner as Pharaoh had reacted to his impasse before Moses and Aaron, even so now, immediately, did these two replicas of Adolf Hilter react before their antagonists, Dr. Steele and Pastor von Ludwig.

In anger fully as violent as ancient Pharaoh's, the Nazis swiftly poured their wrath upon their prisoner and Dr. Steele. "Very well, then, von Ludwig," Herr Starkmann roared at him, "*go*! We wash our hands of you completely. I myself will see to it that you get out of Germany speedily—this very day! And you will *stay* out, Martin Luther von Ludwig! Never let us see your face again.

"Never mind about his clothing! He will go out exactly as he is—in his prison garments. And with his foolscap on his head. As for his *Entlassungsschein* and other papers, these are entirely unnecessary in his case. He is not being deservedly or mercifully released. He is being disgracefully expelled—disgorged—expunged—to our *unspeakable* joy."

The director-general expressed his contempt for Pastor von Ludwig with a final snarl. And then he gave official orders for departure:

"Forward! To the Airdrome! Guards, hold your prisoners securely: Rothschild and Frau Joseph Rothschild—until they are safely aboard the plane. I myself will secure von Ludwig. He need not think he can get away from *me*! Dr. Steele, follow after us. All ready? Forward *march*!"

The *kommandant* flung the office door wide open, and the strange procession filed out—Herr Starkmann, tightly grasping Pastor von Ludwig, at the forefront, the others coming behind them. The *kommandant* then drew up in the rear by himself.

Forward they all went toward the Airdrome and the waiting plane—across the camp enclosure and onward through the exit gate—Dr. Steele and his three rescued friends leaving forever the horrors of Dachau.

Chapter 28

A New Vision

In the heart of London, in stately Grosvenor Square, the stately Trevelyan house stood waiting for the quartet of émigrés. The British family had earlier welcomed their beloved son Reginald and his affianced bride, along with Elinor Steele, and now made every effort to extend the finest tradition of true English hospitality toward Dr. Steele and those so recently released from the grip of death in Nazi Germany.

Reginald had been dispatched to meet the ship and to collect the guests. Exactly on time, the beautiful SS *Majestic* glided proudly into her moorings at Southampton and, shortly thereafter, the eagerly awaited trio descended the gangplank.

They endured the bothersome demands of the immigration and customs authorities, but, fortunately for them all, they were neither arduous nor prolonged.

And then, without further delay, the passengers boarded the train for London. Soon they were all comfortably settled in the transverse compartment of their railway carriage, where they enjoyed happiest fellowship with one another during the entire two-hour journey.

At Victoria Station, Dr. Steele took his three treasured friends directly to the Windsor Hotel, where they could find rest, good food, and the care of a physician for several days. The excited Reginald then rushed Dr. Steele to the beautiful Trevelyan home and the loved ones joyfully awaiting their coming.

In the course of the conversation, eager inquiry was made of Dr. Steele by all the others concerning his trip to Germany and the welfare of the Rothschilds and Pastor von Ludwig—Reginald having previously written his parents all about Dr. Steele's mission of mercy to Dachau.

Carefully avoiding any mention whatsoever of the more extreme horrors he had encountered in the concentration camp, he gave a general description of the infamous abode and the condition of its unhappy inmates. And then he outlined briefly the events of his tremendous week in Germany, stressing particularly God's wonderful guidance of his way into Dachau and his still more wonderful deliverance therefrom of his three imprisoned friends.

"And where are they now, Dr. Steele?" Mr. Trevelyan asked eagerly.

"They are right here in London, all three of them," his American guest replied proudly. "Right here in the Windsor Hotel. I took them there at once on our arrival from Holland." And therewith Dr. Steele proceeded to describe to all the intently listening company their thrilling departure from the Nazi stronghold, their flight from Dachau to Rotterdam, and thence, also by airplane, to England.

"In Holland," so he told his eager audience, "we had two wonderful days. We were amazed and overwhelmed at the great kindness shown us by the Dutch people. In the hotel where we stayed and in the shops where our friends procured their very necessary new garments, everyone who served us was most sympathetic and cooperative.

"For myself, the crowning experience of our Holland sojourn was my contact with the Dutch Red Cross. On Monday afternoon, while Pastor von Ludwig and the Rothschilds were resting in the hotel, I went to their Rotterdam headquarters. There I had the most valuable opportunity of conferring with two of their highest officers, who confirmed all the information concerning Joseph, Dr. Rothschild's son, which had been given me by a friend in Berlin.

"It's a long and intensely dramatic story, but in brief it is this: Joseph, immediately following his marriage to Pastor von Ludwig's daughter, had been forced by reason of Nazi fury to flee for his life into Holland. There, in the city of Nijmegen, he was hidden for months in the garret of Dutch people friendly to the Jews. Eventually their home was raided by German and Dutch Nazis working in collusion, and the family and a dozen or so Jews they were sheltering were all rushed off in vans to a concentration camp.

"Mercifully Joseph escaped the raid and came under the protection of the Red Cross. Through them, arrangements happily were made for him to be transported to Palestine by agents of the *Mossad Aliyah Bet*, an organization of Palestinian Jews devoted to the rescue, from all over Europe, of oppressed fellow Jews. Their ship, the *Dawn of Freedom*, with Joseph aboard, together with about two hundred other rescued Jews, left Rotterdam last Saturday morning and is now on the high seas on its way to Haifa."

At this point Mrs. Trevelyan interposed an anxious question. "You say, Dr. Steele, your friends who escaped Dachau are now here in London, in the Windsor?"

"Yes."

"Oh, but they should not be in a cheerless hotel all alone! They need warmth of heart and comfort. They need friends and sympathy and love. Why do you not bring them all here?"

"*Here?* To your beautiful home?" Dr. Steele questioned in frank astonishment. "But there are three of them—and with our three that would make *six*!"

"Well, what of it? Six is a delightful number of guests."

"But dear Mrs. Trevelyan," Mrs. Steele protested, "that would be an imposition, I am sure!"

"No imposition whatsoever. To all of us Trevelyans it would be a delight. And we could easily accommodate sixteen," she added as all the Steeles looked incredulous. "In this rambling old house of ours, there is plenty of room. And besides,"—she smiled sweetly—"it would be such a privilege to us to help these dear friends in any way we could. They surely do need comforting after all they have been through."

"Oh, quite!" Reginald agreed sympathetically.

"Well," Dr. Steele responded warmly, "your generous hospitality is truly overwhelming. I do accept it most gratefully for all of us."

"That is settled, then," Mr. Trevelyan concluded the discussion decisively. "It is too late to bring our friends tonight, but please go for them, Dr. Steele, tomorrow morning."

"I shall be most happy to do so. Thank you, Mr. Trevelyan and Mrs. Trevelyan—and you, too, Reginald—with all my heart. I cannot conceive of what it will mean to these dear people to be in your beautiful home after all their terrible suffering. For Dr. Rothschild particularly it will be invaluable. As a Jew, he has had to endure even more frightful atrocities than Pastor von Ludwig and his daughter experienced. I must prepare you in advance for shock when you see him. You will find him a completely broken man."

"Indeed? How very sad! In just what way is he broken, Dr. Steele?" Mr. Trevelyan queried compassionately.

"In every way. Physically he has deteriorated appallingly. The body has been too heavily assailed. And I greatly fear the mind is on the verge of complete derangement. It is a marvel to me that he has retained one shred of sanity, so awful has been his mental anguish.

"But what is infinitely worse is the almost total wrecking of his faith. Before the Nazi inroads upon it, his faith was so vigorous, so staunch, so beautiful in its childlike simplicity. 'Thus saith the Lord' was sufficient answer for him to every question, every problem, every argument. But *now* the one predominating quality in all his outlook is doubt—doubt of himself, doubt of his fellow men, and, what is unutterably tragic, doubt even of God."

"That *is* tragic, absolutely so!" Mr. Trevelyan exclaimed in consternation, his wife and his son sadly echoing his conviction.

"Do you not have hope, Dr. Steele, of his recovery?" Reginald asked anxiously.

"I hardly know what to say, Reg. If only Dr. Rothschild were ten years younger—"

"But he is not old, is he?" Mrs. Trevelyan's question expressed surprise.

"In years, Mrs. Trevelyan, no, he is by no means old. He is not yet fifty-five. But one would take him today to be a man of eighty. In terms of suffering and grief he has outlived Methuselah."

"But might he not even yet make a comeback, Dr. Steele?" Mr. Trevelyan queried hopefully.

"Physically, I doubt it. He has suffered too greatly from actual bodily violence. Besides this, his spirit has been too heavily pressured. Grief takes a fearful toll of the human frame, and Dr. Rothschild's grief has been colossal.

"There may be a measure of recovery, provided there is no organic impairment. This I have not yet ascertained. I hope to have opportunity for a full examination soon. Should we find no vital disorder, in due time with proper care, Dr. Rothschild might acquire a reasonable degree of returning strength—though even of this I am not too optimistic. But never again will there be the vigor of only eight years ago. That is gone forever. His erstwhile magnificent physique has been wrecked—completely and hopelessly."

"Assuredly, Dr. Steele!" Mr. Trevelyan spoke eagerly. "We shall most gladly pledge our faithful supplication for his complete healing."

"We shall indeed," Mrs. Trevelyan echoed earnestly.

"And you can certainly count upon me," Reginald added with prompt and enthusiastic agreement.

"I thank you all most gratefully," Dr. Steele replied, deeply moved. "This gives me fullest confidence for our dear friend. God will answer our united prayer abundantly—above all that we ask or think."

Noon of the next day found the Dachau escapees safely and happily sheltered within the hospitable Trevelyan home. The effect upon all three of them was immediate. The contrast between the hideous environment of the concentration camp and the delicious restfulness of the luxurious English abode; between all the terrible sufferings they had endured in Dachau and the wealth of loving ministrations now outpoured upon them by the Trevelyans and the Steeles alike was striking in the extreme, and their reaction was correspondingly joyful.

To Dr. Rothschild, in particular, the exchange was electrifying. Amid the surroundings of high refinement, among these delightful new English friends with their culture and surpassing charm, the former brilliant Hebrew surgeon was in his native environment. Almost at once, after the first strangeness had worn off, he felt himself at home. Even with the formidable butler he was at ease. Within but an hour of his heartwarming welcome by his gracious host and hostess and their well-bred children, his apathy, his dreadful daze, had completely lifted, even as fog before the rising sun.

Physically, he was very weak. There was visible exhaustion. Under orders from Dr. Steele he spent the greater part of the twenty-four hours in bed. But when he came down to dinner, as he always did every evening, he joined freely and with very evident delight in the stimulating table conversation—led, largely, by Pastor von Ludwig—and even contributed to it in appreciable and valuable degree.

The London days were golden ones indeed—for Reginald and Elinor, certainly, and for all the others, as well. During the mornings the ladies—Mrs. Trevelyan, Mrs. Steele, Gretel Rothschild, and Elinor Steele—usually spent many happy hours browsing through the fascinating English shops and art exhibits. Frequently they remained downtown for lunch in one of the delightful London eating places, a different one each day.

Between Gretel and Elinor there was, from the first moment of their meeting, mutually strong attraction. Each became keenly interested in the romance of the other—Gretel in Elinor's approaching marriage to Reginald; and Elinor in Gretel's soon-coming reunion with her lost husband. As they paired off from the older women, many a sweet half hour did the two young girls spend together in mutual exchange of happy confidences. On the Monday morning following their arrival, the previous Wednesday in London, Dr. Steele, by prearrangement with staff officials, took Dr. Rothschild to the famous St. Bartholomew Hospital for two days of complete physical and psychological examination.

The official report, after thorough exploration, was, on the whole, fairly optimistic. Organically—so the men of highest professional skill concurred in their opinion—their distinguished patient was completely sound. Nowhere had they been able to find any trace whatever of malignancy or of vital disorder otherwise. However, they gave it as their unanimous verdict—with very evident sorrow—that his constitution in general had been irreparably undermined. There was marked deterioration of strength. Whether there would be sufficient resiliency to recapture it was dubious.

But on the other hand, and they all rejoiced in this, his mind was completely clear and alert and vigorous; and his depleted nerves, with prolonged rest under favorable circumstances, assuredly could be restored.

"As for his emotional disturbance—his so terribly damaged morale—if only he could get some challenging new interest in life, some absorbing new activity that would keep him from brooding over the past, this would effect his rehabilitation more quickly and completely than anything else. Thus did the head of the great hospital confide his opinion to Dr. Steele.

"That confirms my own impression entirely," Dr. Steele replied with vast relief.

"The first step toward his restoration," Dr. Steele explained to the examining physicians, "the most imperative step—was getting him released from Dachau. Apart from that, I greatly fear his case would have been absolutely hopeless. Twenty-four hours more of the agonies he had to endure would have sealed his doom as surely as the gas oven would have done.

"At present, for a fortnight, we are together here in London in the home of most sympathetic and helpful friends. Already Dr. Rothschild has shown marked improvement in every area. And from here the way appears to be opening for him to go to the exact place, I believe, where he will have the environment and the opportunities you prescribe as most conducive to his full recovery."

"Yes? And that place is—? We are most profoundly interested, Dr. Steele," a surgeon asked.

"That place is *Palestine*—his own Jewish Homeland! There, I am confident, wonders will be wrought for Dr. Benjamin Rothschild. The thrilling appeal of the land, the new opportunities for rewarding service that it may provide for him: all this will be veritable elixir to his spirit. And once his *spirit* is quickened and reinvigorated, the rehabilitation of all the other areas of his being will naturally follow."

"Excellent! Nothing possible could be better! Just when will he go, Dr. Steele? Have arrangements yet been made?"

"Not fully. But I am hoping they will be completed within a very few days."

"Admirable! I can conceive of nothing more truly wonderful for this so cruelly treated man. But just *how* will Dr. Rothschild get to Palestine, Dr. Steele? I am curious. Entrance for the Jews is difficult, is it not?"

"Yes, extremely difficult, ordinarily. But it is my purpose to enlist the good offices and the most efficient service of the Jewish Christian Fellowship in this regard. I intend to confer with their leaders tomorrow. They will be most sympathetic and cooperative in every way possible, I have no doubt. For in Germany Dr. Rothschild was one of their most distinguished members."

Dr. Steele was as good as his word. Dr. Rothschild had returned from the hospital on Tuesday evening; and early Wednesday morning his angel of mercy from America, continuing his merciful mission, visited the Jewish Christian Fellowship in their London headquarters.

And there he met with most enthusiastic welcome. When he identified himself as the friend and rescuer of their so highly revered fellow Jewish Christian—the very man for whom they had been so tremendously concerned, ever since hearing of his capture and of his imprisonment in Dachau by Hitler's nefarious cohorts—two of the officials of the Fellowship, a Mr. Weiss and a Mr. Shapiro, received him with open arms.

"You are here at exactly the right time," they told him eagerly. "Your plea for Dr. Rothschild could not have been more opportunely presented. For we have visiting us this week, as our most distinguished guest, Miss Keturah Zelde, a member of our Zionist Executive and honorary president of our Zionist women's organization, Hadassah."

"Miss Keturah Zelde!" Dr. Steele replied in astonishment. "Is Miss Zelde *here*?"

"Yes. Do you know her?" Mr. Weiss inquired with surprise.

"I do indeed!"

"She came to London from Palestine last Wednesday, for just a couple of weeks, with the express purpose of arousing interest in her work for these refugee Jewish children. That is what I meant when I said your plea for Dr. Rothschild's transportation to the Land could not have been more timely. Miss Zelde is returning to Palestine just one week from today—Wednesday, July 28—sailing on the British-Palestinian SS *Magen David*. She is taking with her twenty Jewish children from the Continent that she has been instrumental in rescuing only this past week. That would be a perfect opportunity for sending Dr. Rothschild also—providing the funds for his passage could be supplied. I trust we may be able to help somewhat in that regard."

"Full provision has already been made," Dr. Steele said quietly without further explanation. "What is required now is his visa, steamship accommodation, trustworthy escort, and assurance of welcome reception and necessary assistance within the Land. It is for all of these that I have felt constrained to come here and enlist the aid of your Fellowship."

"You have come to the right place, Dr. Steele. We can and most gladly will arrange for all of these requirements."

"Praise God!" Dr. Steele responded fervently, with deep emotion. "I thank you, gentlemen, with all my heart! But I have not yet told you, we also require transportation to Palestine for one more friend. Possibly for two more. The first is Dr. Rothschild's daughter-in-law, the wife of his son Joseph. She, definitely, will go with Dr. Rothschild to meet her husband who has preceded them. The second is Mrs. Joseph's father—Pastor Martin Luther von Ludwig."

"*Pastor Martin Luther von Ludwig!*" was the instantaneous astounded reply. "Is *he* here?"

"Yes, right here in London. You, of course, know him?"

"Undoubtedly! The last we heard of him was a month ago. He was in a concentration camp. And what of Pastor von Ludwig's future? What is ahead for him?" The question was eagerly asked by Mr. Weiss with almost bated breath.

"That is our immediate and pressing problem. We do not yet know what lies ahead. He has been unequivocally expelled from Germany. Warned never to return. I had thought of taking him back with me to America, but in his condition and with all his family gone from him, I decided it would be too precarious. The happiest solution—what appears to be the most beneficent plan—would be for him to be with his daughter and her husband and his very close friend Dr. Rothschild, in Palestine. But I am not yet sure if this is God's will for him—"

"Oh, assuredly it *must* be God's will!" came the enthusiastic sudden interruption. "Certainly he must remain with his daughter! And Palestine would be exactly the right place for him!"

And thus it came about that this same Wednesday evening found the Steeles and the Rothschilds and Pastor von Ludwig—together with all the Trevelyans, seated in the auditorium of the Jewish Christian Fellowship headquarters in London, among some two hundred other guests, for the meeting honoring, and presenting as special speaker, Miss Keturah Zelde of Palestine.

"A memorable evening, a truly auspicious occasion"—as Mr. Weiss had predicted—it proved to be indeed for all who were privileged to be present. For Dr. Rothschild particularly, as Palestine was brought vividly before him, it was a positive elixir, infusing him happily with new life, new hope. Pastor von Ludwig and Gretel and Dr. and Mrs. Steele, and Mr. and Mrs. Trevelyan, as well, all received a wealth of new information and of deepest inspiration.

But it was upon the two youngest members of their party—Reginald Trevelyan and Elinor Steele, his bride-to-be, that the most tremendous impact of all was made. They came, a bit reluctantly, it certainly must be admitted,in response to Dr. Steele's urging that they attend the gathering called by "this wonderful organization of Jews who have accepted the Lord Jesus Christ as their Messiah and Savior, and have banded themselves together for mutual strengthening, and have dedicated their lives for the propagation of their Christian faith among their Hebrew brethren in many countries throughout the world." Little did either of these two dear young people or anyone else dream, that this evening and their meeting with Miss Keturah Zelde would precipitate a major crisis, a veritable revolution in their lives!

Miss Zelde spoke with her usual fire and force, her impassioned words making vital impression upon her hearers. Graphically she described the thrilling work currently being accomplished by Hadassah, the Women's Zionist Organization.

As vividly, with tremendous emotional appeal, she conveyed to the spellbound audience the burden upon her own great heart of love, she struck a responsive chord in the heart of every listener. Many eyes throughout the audience were wet with tears as the noble mother in Israel brought poignantly before them pictures of little ones cruelly snatched from their parents and homes, and driven off into lonely woods where, terrified, they wandered—sometimes for weeks or even months—in a frenzied daze throughout the daylight hours.

More than once Reginald and Elinor were conscious of a lump within the throat and a surge of anger through their hearts as the tragic story proceeded. But they shared joyously in Miss Zelde's elation, and in the elation of the entire audience, as she gave the contrasting picture: the same little Jewish children safely rescued and securely sheltered in the Homeland—surrounded by the love and tender care of foster mothers, warmly and comfortably housed, neatly clothed and abundantly fed—enjoying the happy companionship of other rescued Jewish children as, together with them, they learned anew how to play, how to smile and laugh, how to study, how to work: in short, how to *forget*. How to rejoice in the new life of peace and gladness and security. How to glory in the rich opportunity that now lay before them in Palestine!

Following the public meeting and a brief reception for Miss Zelde, a score of specially invited people withdrew at ten o'clock to the fellowship hall upstairs for a private informal visit with the distinguished guest. Among the fortunate ones thus invited were all the members of Dr. Steele's party, including Reginald and Elinor.

By special request of Miss Zelde herself, Reginald and Elinor remained behind for further conversation with her after all the other guests had departed.

They seated themselves comfortably, and then, with her characteristic direct approach, Miss Zelde came swiftly to the subject that now was uppermost in her consideration.

Already she had been strongly drawn toward this attractive young couple. As they had sat near the front of the auditorium during her meeting, she had been quick to observe their rapt attention and their very evident deep emotion throughout her address—and quick to admire also their culture and their charm.

And so it transpired that when they became, now, thus

closely engaged in conference, with her native ability quickly to win the confidence of everyone with whom she talked, Miss Zelde lost no time in winning theirs. With her affable, forthright manner, albeit with exquisite tact, she asked them a number of searching personal questions. "Tell me," the brilliant Zionist asked Reginald, "what is ahead for you now? Where are you going to locate for your practice?"

"As yet, I am not quite sure. It will be either here in London or in Baltimore. Miss Steele and I are to be married in Baltimore in September, and we may decide to remain there near her parents."

Miss Zelde looked fixedly at the winsome young couple seated before her. And then in compassionate tones, but with her characteristic straight-from-the-shoulder directness, she challenged Reginald's assertion—her dark, piercing eyes seeming to search his very soul.

"Young man, listen to me! Your professional career must not be either in Baltimore or in London—not anywhere either in America or in England. *We need you in Palestine!*"

If a bombshell had suddenly been dropped into their midst, Reginald and Elinor could not have been more startled. Before they could recover breath, Miss Zelde continued quickly:

"Dr. Trevelyan, England and America—London and Baltimore particularly—do not need more physicians and surgeons. They both are full of them. But we do need them desperately in Jerusalem, in our own Berachah Hospital. Since the tragic death of Dr. Baum, one of our most brilliant doctors—murdered by the Arabs, you may recall—and the loss of two others—we have had an acute shortage. In consequence, the main objective of my visit to London at this time—next to presenting the claims of the refugee children, as I have tried to do tonight—is to relieve that shortage. I am here purposely to find two young doctors to take back with me to the Land."

"You two young doctors—you, Dr. Trevelyan, and Dr. Joseph Rothschild—could at once be placed upon the staff of our Berachah Hospital, in charge of its children's department. And Dr. Benjamin Rothschild—in my carefully considered judgment the foremost surgeon in the world—will become our honorary president. And Pastor von Ludwig will be our deeply spiritual chaplain. And *you*, Miss Elinor Steele—dear little girl—you and your fine friend, Mrs. Margarete von Ludwig Rothschild—daughter and daughter-in-law of two of the grandest men on earth—you two young women will fit most beautifully into various divisions of our ministry among children.

"Now, both of you think it over carefully. You have until noon tomorrow to make your decision. Dr. Steele is bringing Dr. Rothschild and Pastor von Ludwig and his daughter here then to discuss all our plans. Will you go to Palestine or will you not? We sail, remember, next Wednesday morning."

"Next Wednesday morning!" Elinor exclaimed in consternation. "Oh, dear Miss Zelde, we could not possibly go then! Why, next Wednesday is the very day that Daddy and Mother and I sail for New York. We have to hurry home to Baltimore, you see," she added, blushing very prettily, "to get ready for my wedding. Reginald and I are going to be married in September."

"Why must you be married in Baltimore in September? Why can you not be married in London in July? Why not this week?"

"Oh, no! We *couldn't* be! Not *possibly*!" Elinor was almost in tears. "You see," she explained painstakingly, "we have our plans all made. We are to have a large wedding in the university chapel, and . . . "

Miss Zelde looked at Elinor in shocked amazement. Her voice and face alike were stern as she answered her with quick reproof. At times, especially if her precious Jewish children were in any way involved, Keturah Zelde could be ruthless.

"You foolish girl! What are ornate weddings and bridesmaids and honeymoons in comparison with rescuing hundreds—yes, thousands, perhaps—of little children from such suffering as you have heard about tonight? Of what account are these glamorous transient joys when weighed in the balance with the eternal joy of such service as stands wide open before you?"

Abashed, Elinor hung her head. The deeply experienced older woman had stirred a terrific emotional storm within her breast. Reginald was quick to quell it. "Let's go home, honey," he admonished her gently, "and sleep over the whole tremendous problem. You are very tired tonight, dear. Things will look clearer to you in the morning."

"Very well, let's do that," Elinor replied falteringly. "But before we go, tell me, Reg, what *you* think about it all?"

"I think it would be wonderful!" Reginald responded with eager alacrity. "It would mean everything in the world for us to have such an opportunity."

Elinor's reaction was swift contrition. Her tears were flowing freely now. "Oh, Reggie! Dear Miss Zelde! I'm so sorry! Do please forgive me! I didn't mean it really—what I said. Of course there is no comparison between our elaborate wedding plans and the wonderful service you so graciously offer us in your own homeland. And I did feel badly about losing our honeymoon in the lovely Canadian Rockies. We have been planning it so happily and for so long." There was still a wistful note in Elinor's brave voice.

Again Reginald came manfully to the rescue and poured in the oil of healing for the wounded spirit, true physician that he was. "Don't you mind about the fancy wedding, sweetheart. We will get married anyway, and that's all that matters. And don't feel disappointed either about the Canadian Rockies. We can go there some other time—perhaps next summer. And we will certainly have our honeymoon, even if it has to be in a different place. How about Paris? How would you like to go there?"

"Paris! *Paris!*" Elinor's response was electric, ecstatic. "Oh, Reggie darling!" she cried jubilantly, her eyes shining radiantly through her now happy tears, "that would be *heavenly*! I've always longed to go to Paris!"

"Fine!" Reginald echoed enthusiastically. "Now, there *is* an idea, really! Miss Zelde, if we do decide to sail with you next Wednesday for Palestine—and I'm sure we *have* decided already," he added, with an understanding, tender glance at his beloved—"couldn't we be married this Saturday and fly over to Paris for a three-day honeymoon there? We could get back to London the next Tuesday evening and be ready to embark on the *Magen David* Wednesday. What do you think?"

She gazed intently upon the winsome young couple seated before her. Her rigid sternness toward Elinor had completely melted into her natural tenderness and warmth of heart. "Dear young people," she murmured softly in tones of mingle exultation and compassion, "you have crowned my journey to London with complete success. I shall return to Palestine and to our beloved hospital greatly enriched by your addition to our staff. God bless you both in fullest measure and maintain your future service in my homeland with honor and success and joy."

Before nine o'clock on Thursday morning it was fully decided to everybody's satisfaction: the marriage of Reginald and Elinor would take place—right there in the Trevelyans' drawing room—at high noon on Saturday. All the details were most carefully discussed and planned.

There would be no music, no entourage, no wedding finery, and only the simplest of floral decorations. The Trevelyans' excellent butler—for this, to him, most auspicious occasion—would devise and serve the tasteful but purposely simple wedding breakfast.

And there would be no ornate display of wedding gifts. Indeed the only gifts received up to the very hour of the glad event were two cheques: a munificent one from the parents of the bridegroom and a quite modest cheque—vastly abbreviated from the originally intended dowry—lovingly bestowed by the parents of the bride. The bulk of the purposed dowry—so carefully saved and set aside through Elinor's girlhood years toward the establishment of her future home with the husband of her choice—that largess was now swelling the already bulging coffers of the National Socialist Government of Germany.

At last it was Saturday noon in the Trevelyan drawing room, and Reginald Trevelyan and Elinor Steele, standing before Pastor von Ludwig in the presence of the small company of loving relatives and friends, were exchanging their marriage vows, each plighting to the other eternal troth.

"I, Reginald, take thee, Elinor—"

"I, Elinor, take thee, Reginald—"

And within the hearts of the bridegroom and the bride themselves there were strangely intermingled agitations of joy and of distress. There was inevitable sadness in the thought of the swiftly approaching farewell to their youthful homes and all their dear ones; but at the same time there was awe-inspiring joy in anticipation of all the unfolding and enlarging wonders of the future pathway now lying golden before them.

And finally there came the soul-thrilling fateful words: "I pronounce Reginald and Elinor husband and wife."

Then followed the joyous felicitations from all the assembled witnesses, the delectable wedding breakfast, the boisterous excitement of the bride and groom's departure and—at last—the happy newlyweds were off for Croydon Airport whence, at three o'clock, they took flight for their three-day honeymoon in Elinor's so eagerly coveted Paris.

Only three days! But they were as days of heaven upon earth. When the blissful young couple returned to London and the Trevelyan home on the following Tuesday evening, the "effervescent Elinor" was more effervescent than ever she had been before in all her life. "Oh, Daddy," she exclaimed rapturously, flinging her arms around his neck in a swift outburst of her usual high-spirited youthful joy, "Oh, Daddy darling! It is all so sudden! Just think of it, in only one week: my wedding, my honeymoon in Paris, and my trip to Palestine! Oh, Daddy, Daddy, it is all so terribly *exciting*!"

And then, with her characteristic kaleidoscopic variation of mood, she turned swiftly to her mother and buried her face upon her breast with a low moan.

"Oh, Mother, darling little Mother! I'm so happy, so happy—but I can't leave you and Daddy! I can't, oh, I *can't*! I won't go to Palestine at all! Reggie and I are going back with you to Baltimore! Oh, we are, we *are*!"

Mother and daughter wept in each other's arms in a strong, convulsive embrace. But the wise and loving father intervened. Tenderly placing one arm around each of them, he expostulated with them bravely.

"Come, come, girls, you must not cry. We must all be glad! And we *are* glad! We shall all be together again soon. For I promise you, little daughter, next summer, if all is well,

Mother and I will come to see you and Reginald in your own new home in Jerusalem! Won't that be wonderful?

"But now, Elinor darling, you must go with your *husband*. Remember God's command: *Speak unto the children of Israel, that they go forward*. Forward! To the land of Palestine!"

Chapter 29

Home—at Last!

Joseph waited eagerly at the Haifa dock for the inbound *Magen David*, a gallant ship bearing homeward Israel's idolized Miss Keturah Zelde and her twenty rescued children.

Finally it was sighted and a great cheer went up from the excited crowd. Fifteen minutes—half an hour—three-quarters of an hour of restless, impatient waiting. And then at last the noble vessel swung gracefully to her mooring amid still more tremendous cheering by the welcoming loved ones. Brass bands played lustily, and children and elders alike sang and shouted and screamed.

Then came the grand climax of all the joyous excitement. The passengers began to descend the gangplank. There were Jewish men and women, Jewish youths and maidens, and the little Jewish children—all clearly agitated with unsuppressed emotion. Quickly they were fairly swallowed up by the throng of fellow Jews awaiting them below. The children, dazed and bewildered—and some of them frightened and crying—were promptly seized upon by members of the official reception committee appointed by Hadassah, and sorted out for distribution among the several previously appointed *kibbutzim* with their respective foster parents ready and eager to receive them into homes and hearts of love.

Amid all the hurrying and scurrying, amid all the clamor and confusion, one name above all others had repeatedly been shouted forth: "Miss Zelde! Miss Zelde! Miss Keturah Zelde!" to which eager cry was added frequently and joyfully: "Welcome home! Welcome home! Our own dear mother, Miss Keturah Zelde! Welcome *home*!"

But not even Miss Zelde engaged the attention of Joseph. He was looking for one face only; he was hearkening for but one beloved voice: *Gretel's*! And at long, long last, suddenly she appeared in view at the top of the gangplank. She stood still for a moment, gracefully poised, as the rising sun beamed its golden rays upon her face, illumining it with peculiarly resplendent beauty.

And then—instantaneously—her eyes met Joseph's! And Joseph's eyes met *hers*!

As swiftly as possible she descended the gangplank. Even more swiftly Joseph rushed forward to its foot to meet her. One instant more of straining both pairs of eyes. Only one instant—and *then*! With a low, glad cry—with a joy beyond all power to express—Joseph Rothschild, the Hebrew bridegroom, and Margarete von Ludwig, his Aryan bride, after six long months of anguished separation—were rapturously reunited.

The others of Miss Zelde's party followed shortly: Miss Zelde herself, Dr. Rothschild, Pastor von Ludwig, Reginald and Elinor Trevelyan—and all in turn were given joyful welcome, not alone by Joseph, but by several other members of the hospital staff and even by leaders in government. Soon the whole company was driven to the King David Hotel for the festive breakfast, purposely arranged in honor of the newcomers by Dr. Rubinoff and a couple of his colleagues.

And there in this beautiful hostelry Dr. Rothschild and Pastor von Ludwig remained in temporary residence. The Trevelyans, together with Joseph and Gretel, were to have their abode right within the hospital—during the period of their adjustment to the respective positions which Miss Zelde, in fulfillment of her promise, made to them at the Jewish Christian Fellowship meeting in London.

But within a week she found for them all, the two fathers and the four young people, a charming permanent home—a munificent gift from the Zionist Organization and Hadassah, welcoming the distinguished families to Palestine. This beautiful dwelling was high up on Mount Scopus, near her own home, and within but five minutes' walk of the hospital.

The house was of ranch-type construction—cream stucco with red tiled roof and broad patios front and rear. It was ideally divided into two spacious apartments, one for Dr. Rothschild, Dr. and Mrs. Joseph, and Pastor von Ludwig; and the other for the Trevelyans. Between the two apartments, one at either end of the broad building, were extensive and beautiful cooperative living quarters, consisting of a large living-and-dining room, and a kitchen that was the last word in modern design, equipment, and efficiency.

And here, in this lovely residence, the six members of the graciously assembled family—miraculously brought together from Germany, from England, from America—lived in sweetest tranquility. Despite all the Arab-Jewish enmity and fury that raged below them throughout the city—and throughout many other areas of Palestine, as well—their hearts and minds were garrisoned by the peace of God, which truly passeth all understanding.

Despite even the vast previous suffering and grief of the four refugees from Nazi horror—in that beautiful abode high aloft on Mount Scopus, the souls it now sheltered so securely were filled with overflowing joy. For all six of them were indissolubly united in the strong bond of mutual love and complete accord of spirit and of understanding.

In the days that followed, many wonderful things transpired for them all. Through mysterious but ever more and more shining pathways were their footsteps led. Great indeed was God's faithfulness.

The two young surgeons, Dr. Joseph and Dr. Reginald, rapidly and most commendably fitted into their new field of service in the positions promised them by Miss Zelde in London. Dr. Rubinoff was quick to recognize their superior skill and, therefore, entrusted to them ever enlarging responsibility.

As for their two young wives, Gretel and Elinor, they, too, adjusted very promptly to their respective assignments. Gretel's remarkable ability as a nurse was at once apparent to all, and her services were eagerly welcomed by every surgeon and doctor fortunate enough to secure them.

Gretel had grieved deeply when she was ignominiously discharged by von Wolfmacht from the Sharon Rothschild Hospital in Berlin. Especially did she grieve that she had failed to win her coveted RN. But to her great delight, she was more than compensated in Jerusalem. Within a week of her appointment to her position upon the staff, she was fully accredited as a registered nurse by the Berachah Hospital.

At the same time Elinor found her sphere of activity among the refugee children completely absorbing. Her vivacious spirit and her untiring efforts to help the little ones in every way possible endeared her to them all.

Thus all four of the young people—Joseph and Gretel, and Reginald and Elinor—were supremely happy as new recruits within the hospital and as new residents in Jerusalem, happy in one another and happy in their varied and wonderful opportunities for rewarding work.

And Pastor von Ludwig was exceedingly happy. For that saintly man of God, though shorn forever of his lengthy and fruitful pulpit ministry in Germany, and released from his amazing soul-healing ministry among his despairing fellow prisoners in the Dachau Concentration Camp, was given still another field of beneficent service. No longer did he hold a pulpit; no longer did he preach to throngs; but his erstwhile saddened heart was comforted and his praise to God was fervent for the new door of fruitful Christian ministry which now stood wide open before him even in Jerusalem. And this was the sweet ministration of individual shepherding . . . of giving aid and counsel and comfort to distressed and anxious souls who came to him with sorrows and burdens and problems of every sort.

For Martin Luther von Ludwig had not been long in Jerusalem before he was recognized and acclaimed as the wonderful pastor of the strong Confessional Church in Germany who fearlessly had dared to defy and denounce Adolf Hitler to his very face; and who, because of that daring, had suffered untold agonies in reprisal. Therefore it was that many fellow refugees in Palestine, and many other souls, as well, sought his presence and his powerful pastoral support, which was always freely given.

But of all the happy hearts within that lovely Mount Scopus dwelling, none was more joyful than that of Dr. Rothschild. When his presence in Jerusalem became known, the city was deeply stirred—so great was his fame, so strong had been his influence worldwide, so true was the compassion felt by multitudes for the sufferings he had endured in Germany.

And particularly was he revered and loved by his fellow Jews within the Zionist Organization and Berachah Hospital. It was not to be wondered at, therefore, that they determined to give him illustrious recognition.

The occasion they chose for conferring this upon him, within but two months of his arrival in Palestine, was his fifty-third birthday. Only fifty-three, but easily he looked seventy-three, so tremendously had been the onslaughts upon him and the outrages he had experienced at the hands of the Nazis.

For his birthday celebration, so he was informed by Dr. Rubinoff, a few of his friends wanted to entertain him, together with all the other members of his family, at a little dinner in the King David Hotel. He accepted the invitation with a high degree of pleasure. It was exceedingly gratifying. It was kind indeed of these new friends thus to remember him on his first birthday in the Homeland.

Accompanied by Joseph and Gretel—the others following a little later—he went to the famous hostelry at the appointed hour. Wondering who the "few friends" might be—Dr. Rubinoff had not told him—he entered the lobby, where Miss Keturah Zelde and a couple of the Berachah doctors were awaiting him. He followed curiously as they escorted him up the elevator and into the grand banqueting hall of the hotel, to be confronted immediately with a number of long tables set in lavish array. And there, to his dumbfounded amazement, suddenly he realized that he was in the center of a throng of guests, numbering at least one hundred, all of whom greeted him with most eager and warmhearted welcome. Among the number were some of the most distinguished residents of Jerusalem—Zionist officers and members of government.

Almost dazed with delighted surprise, he was led to the seat of honor at the head table, between Dr. Rubinoff and Miss Zelde, and the festivities of the auspicious evening began.

Following the sumptuous banquet, which was served by an imposing array of the King David staff, the intended purpose of the whole magnificent affair was gradually unfolded before his astounded eyes.

"We are gathered here tonight, dear friends," Dr. Rubinoff began after a number of preliminaries, "to honor a man who recently has come to our shores. He is a colleague who needs no introduction, for his name is a household word in every land where there are hospitals; his brilliant career in surgery is known to the ends of the earth. He has come to us from Germany, where, as you all know, he established in Berlin and for many years directed the world-famous Sharon Rothschild Memorial Hospital, which has brought healing and new hope to thousands of children.

"And now he has come to us here in Jerusalem, and we are signally honored by his presence. We covet the immeasurable privilege of having close association with him in both our professional and personal interests. For he is a man whom we all love and whom we all delight to honor: our most distinguished guest of this evening, Dr. Benjamin Rothschild—late of Berlin, Germany. But now we are happy to acclaim him 'Dr. Benjamin Rothschild of Jerusalem, Palestine.'"

After the tumult of applause had died down, Dr. Rubinoff continued:

"And now, my friends, as this banquet celebrates Dr. Rothschild's birthday, we desire to bestow upon him a little birthday gift. Miss Zelde, it is our pleasure to call upon you kindly to make the presentation."

Miss Zelde stood up—very charming in her formal black evening gown adorned with gold of Ophir roses—and after a few words of welcome and appreciation of their celebrated visitor, she approached Dr. Rothschild reverently, standing directly before him. With both love and admiration beaming from her eyes, she bent down, taking the esteemed doctor by both hands and looking into his face.

"Dr. Rothschild, in honor of, not only your fifty-third birthday, but your work, your contributions to medicine, your love for children, your exemplary fortitude in the face of suffering, your heart—indeed, your very *life,*"—she squeezed his hands fondly, then released them, turned, and made her way slowly toward a wide, sheet-covered table that he had not seen until now—"it brings me intense delight to present to you"—she paused for effect, as all present held their breath—"the Rothschild Memorial Hospital of Jerusalem for Sick Children!" Then, grabbing the sheet deftly at the corner, she whisked it from the table, to reveal a scale model of an impressive, lofty, white structure that looked startlingly familiar, with its apparent limestone construction, broad exterior steps, and imposing entrance, above which hung . . . a *bronze lamp*.

So excited was the refined Keturah Zelde that she could scarcely control her tremulous voice as she continued. "Oh, Dr. Rothschild, *dear* Dr. Rothschild, this hospital will be state-of-the-art! No hospital like it has existed up to now, and I am unsure that any future one will rival it! Its equipment will be the best and most up-to-date that technology has to offer, its staff the finest that can be recruited." She paused for a moment, to still her enthusiasm a notch before going on. She smiled kindly as she noticed that Dr. Rothschild's lip had begun to quiver and a tear to form in his eye, gathering strength slowly, then coursing down his cheek. Taking a deep breath, Miss Zelde confirmed his memories. "Yes, Dr. Rothschild. In *every aspect* of its construction, it is modeled after the famous Sharon Rothschild Memorial Hospital of Berlin.

"In the lobby of this new building there will be prominently displayed a large and very handsome bronze plaque," she went on. "In clear, raised lettering it will read"—then, reaching behind the table, she produced a large foam visual, crafted to resemble a massive bronze plate. Holding it high, for all to see, she began to read:

"This new house of healing—The Rothschild Memorial Hospital of Jerusalem for Sick Children—will have as its executive staff, when completed, the following distinguished men and women:

"Honorary president, Dr. Benjamin Rothschild; active president, Dr. Joseph Rothschild; executive superintendent, Dr. Reginald Trevelyan; superintendent of nurses, Mrs. Joseph Rothschild; director of refugee children, Mrs. Reginald Trevelyan; chaplain, Pastor Martin Luther von Ludwig."

In conclusion of her address of presentation, Miss Zelde advanced toward Dr. Rothschild, extended her hand to him, and declared with deep earnestness, "Dr. Rothschild, as honorary president of this great new humanitarian institution soon to come into being, we, the members of the Zionist Organization of Palestine, and the officers and staff of Berachah Hospital, pledge you our fullest allegiance and our whole-

THE ROTHSCHILD MEMORIAL HOSPITAL OF JERUSALEM
FOR SICK CHILDREN

THIS HOUSE OF HEALING
WAS ERECTED IN 1937

TO THE GLORY OF GOD
AND IN ESTEEM OF ITS HONORARY PRESIDENT,

DR. BENJAMIN ROTHSCHILD

IN SACRED AND TENDER AND EVER-IMPERISHABLE MEMORY OF
HIS LOVED ONES NOW IN THE HEAVENLY HOME

ROSE
HIS DEARLY BELOVED WIFE

BORN IN DÜSSELDORF JUNE 12 1887
DIED IN DACHAU DURING MAY 1937

X X X

SHARON

THEIR DEARLY BELOVED ONLY DAUGHTER

BORN IN DRESDEN NOVEMBER 17 1913
DIED IN BERLIN DECEMBER 25 1924

X X X

MOISCHE

THEIR DEARLY BELOVED YOUNGER SON

BORN IN BERLIN FEBRUARY 11 1917
DIED IN DACHAU DURING THE EARLY SPRING OF 1937

X X X

THIS THEIR LIVING MEMORIAL IS DEDICATED TO THE ALLEVIATION
OF SUFFERING OF ALL CHILDREN WITHIN PALESTINE—REGARDLESS
OF RACE, CREED, OR CIRCUMSTANCE—BUT PARTICULARLY
TO THE HEALING AND RESTORATION TO THE NORMAL JOYS
OF CHILDHOOD OF

THE REFUGEE JEWISH CHILDREN

RESCUED FROM THE CRUELTIES OF NAZIISM IN GERMANY
AND IN OTHER LANDS OF EUROPE AND BROUGHT TO PALESTINE
LARGELY THROUGH THE EFFORTS OF

H A D A S S A H

X X X

THE LORD GAVE AND THE LORD HATH TAKEN AWAY
BLESSED BE THE NAME OF THE LORD

hearted support. In so doing we count ourselves most highly privileged."

As Miss Zelde sat down and the company broke into further tumultuous applause, Dr. Rothschild was speechless with wonderment and joy. He was almost unnerved, so great was the intensity of his emotion. But he soon, by sheer effort of will, brought himself under control, rose to his feet, and began to speak.

"My kind friends," he began tremulously, "I am overwhelmed. This magnificent plan is the Lord's doing, and it is marvelous in our eyes. I praise Him and thank each one of you with all of my very overflowing heart. May I prove worthy of this highest possible honor which you have given me. God grant that in every way I may indeed prove worthy of your confidence, and that I may abundantly fulfill this exalted trust which, so munificently, you have reposed in me this evening. God bless you all!"

From the summer of 1937 to the summer of 1939, conditions in Europe, particularly in Germany, steadily worsened. Hitler was at the zenith of his power as absolute dictator and, in consequence thereof, the suffering of multitudes reached dire extremity.

After having remilitarized the Rhineland in March 1936—in flagrant violation of the Treaty of Versailles—in his frenzied craving for power and conquest, the "madman of Europe" overran one country after another.

The first to fall before his rapacious might was Austria. In spite of Hitler's solemn avowal—"Germany has neither the wish nor the intention to . . . annex or unite with Austria"—in March of 1938 that once-proud empire of the Hapsburgs was deliberately seized, and seven million Austrians were incorporated into Germany.

During the summer of 1938, Hitler conscripted five hundred thousand men to work at frantic speed for the completion of the Siegfried Line, the impregnable ring of steel and concrete at Germany's western border, designed to prevent encroachment by France.

Next came the dismemberment of Czechoslovakia. In the vain hope of appeasing Germany and restraining her from further depredations—and thus keeping peace in Europe—

Prime Ministers Neville Chamberlain of Great Britain and Édouard Daladier of France overruled the resistance of the Czechs and persuaded them to yield to Hitler's demand for the annexation of the Sudetenland to Germany. By the terms, subsequently, of the famous—or infamous—"Munich Agreement" signed in Munich on September 30, 1938, the Sudetenland thereupon was ceded to the Third Reich and thus became, overnight, a German vassal state. It was reason of this fait accompli that Mr. Chamberlain returned to England with the proud boast that "peace in our time" had been achieved!

Only three weeks later Hitler demanded that Poland relinquish to Germany a strip of territory across the Polish Corridor, and also that she yield Danzig to Germany.

Within but six months—on March 15, 1939—following vicious Nazi attacks upon the Czechs by both radio and press, German troops stormed in and occupied all the remaining territory, after the Sudetenland, of Czechoslovakia. Even by such a ruthless action as this, that staunch little twenty-year-old republic—so constituted after World War I—was taken over in its entirety by the totalitarian Nazi dictator and thus, as a sovereign state, was utterly wiped out.

On March 21 of that same year, the relentless Fuehrer wrenched Memel from Lithuania and forced Roumania to conclude a five-year commercial treaty with Germany, according to the terms of which Roumanian grain would be exchanged for German machinery and armament.

Next in line of the conqueror's march was Poland. By May of 1939 preparations for its seizure were definitely afoot, even though the threatened drastic result was war with Great Britain and France. For Hitler's ruthless invasion and annexation of one coveted territory after another had proved conclusively to both of these great powers that he was determined to control all of Eastern Europe. They knew that his solemn denial of any intention of further conquest beyond the Sudetenland had been completely false. The Munich "appeasement policy" had proved itself to be a lamentable failure.

Therefore, when Hitler claimed overlordship of Poland, both Britain and France rose up in violent protest and befriended the threatened little country. They immediately gave forth their ultimatum: If Adolf Hitler invaded Poland, they—France and Britain—would declare war on Germany.

Thus did it transpire that during the midsummer days of the ominous year 1939, the "status quo" both in Europe and Palestine was one of prevailing tension on every hand—the very atmosphere surcharged with mounting strife and confusion, with unrest and fear.

But within the house of Rehoboth, the hearts of all had peace. They were by no means unmindful of the grave conditions prevailing everywhere; through the press and radio they kept themselves carefully informed of world affairs. And by no means were they indifferent to all the human suffering that was involved. Constantly they were brought into close personal touch with it through their contacts in the hospital and through the steady stream of people who came to them in their home to seek their aid and comfort. But the peace of God which passeth all understanding—even that wonderful peace which can rise triumphant over all opposing circumstances—truly was theirs.

Each morning the four young folks went forth to their respective labors in the hospital, gravely conscious of their responsibilities, but with gladness of heart in their youthful vigor and exuberance and in constant thanksgiving for the opportunities of exalted service that now were theirs.

On Friday, September 1, the crashing news reached Rehoboth. Joseph came home from the hospital at seven o'clock, just as the family was sitting down to supper. His face was white, his voice tense, as he made the startling announcement: "Germany has invaded Poland!"

All day Saturday the ominous reports poured in thick and fast. Hitler was plunging relentlessly, madly forward, devastating one Polish community after another with furious assault.

Finally, at noon on Sunday, the awful climax of the dire tidings came upon the whole Rehoboth household with stunning force. Dr. and Mrs. Steele and the others who had been able to go with them arrived home from church, and at once turned on the radio—just in time to hear Big Ben looming from London. Immediately following the deep sonorous tones pealing forth the hour, there came the fearful proclamation: *"Great Britain and France have declared war on Germany!"*

It was September 3, 1939.

The frightful holocaust—*World War II*—was definitely on.

Onward it raged with mounting fury. Day after day, as the Rehoboth family whenever possible kept closely at the radio, they heard dire reports from Europe.

On September 17 Russia invaded Poland from the east and immediately occupied large areas of eastern Polish territory, while Germany occupied the western portions. Thus was the little country crushed between two great hostile powers.

Among the Jews especially the outrages were most extreme. Thousands of Polish Jews were exterminated. Other thousands were driven into the unspeakable Warsaw Ghetto, where a large proportion of them subsequently were massacred in a frightful manner, while both Britain and France, horrified but powerless to aid them, stood aloof.

At the same time there was much suffering among the Jews of Palestine also, as Arab antagonism against Israel continued.

But despite all the conflict raging around them, near and afar, the peace within the Rehoboth hearts remained deep and abiding. It was a marvel to them all that it could be so while turmoil reigned throughout the world, but it was a glad, undoubted fact.

Meanwhile, Dr. Rothschild, at home, became gradually weaker. But though the frailty of his body slowly yet steadily increased with each passing day and week, his spirit grew more and more effulgent. So much so, indeed, that his loved ones about him persisted in their belief in his ultimate recovery. Joseph and Gretel, in particular, refused to give up hope, even though the sands in the hourglass of the greathearted man were fast draining out.

But miraculously, amazingly, there was a sudden and a strong resurgence of vitality. Even as a candle burning down to its socket will, sometimes, before its extinguishment, have one last flare of brilliant light, so was it given to Benjamin Rothschild to be endued with a supernatural final blaze of light and power—even as he was strengthened with might by

Christ's Spirit in the inner man—for one glowing farewell testimony before his lamp on earth went out.

The occasion and the incentive was the dedication of his new Rothschild Memorial Hospital of Jerusalem. For months Dr. Rothschild had prayed earnestly that he might see the building completed and in operation before God called him home. And God graciously granted his petition.

Up to the very day before the ceremony—Sunday, October 1—it had appeared to be an impossible hope. And all that day the beloved patient was very near the Pearly Gates. But in the evening he rallied and visited for a full hour with different members of the family in turn. And then he had a good night's sleep. On Monday morning he rested and remained very quiet until noon. And then suddenly he electrified everybody by announcing in a triumphant, authoritative voice, "I am going to the children's hospital this evening—to the dedication! Yes, I do feel strong enough. I know that I can make it. God has wonderfully answered all our prayers. Yes, I am *going*!"

The program opened with invocation by Pastor von Ludwig in which he praised God for the life and ministry of Benjamin Rothschild in Berlin, and for the vision which He had given for the carrying forward of Dr. Rothschild's great work through the medium of this new hospital in Jerusalem., It would serve the needs of sick children of all Palestine, particularly of those who were refugees from lands of bitter Nazi oppression.

Pastor von Ludwig then rendered heartfelt thanksgiving to God for the successful completion of the beautiful new building of the Rothschild Memorial Hospital of Jerusalem for Sick Children. Fervently he committed the whole vast enterprise to the protection and guidance and empowering of His Holy Spirit. In conclusion of his prayer, he implored God's blessing upon all who would serve in connection with the hospital and upon every child who would come within its portals.

And then, finally, following music and special acknowledgments, the climax of the program and of the entire auspicious occasion was reached. Dr. Rubinoff introduced the two most important personages present among the whole company: Dr. Benjamin Rothschild, honorary president of the hospital, and his son, Dr. Joseph Rothschild, the active president; and called upon each of them, in turn, to address the gathering.

Dr. Joseph was the first to speak. Profoundly moved, as very ostensibly he was, his words were brief but vividly impressive. He confided to his rapt listeners his heartbreak when his professional career in Germany was so abruptly and ignominiously terminated. And then he told glowingly of his great rejoicing when this wonderful new door of service in Palestine was opened to him.

And then his father, whom everyone present delighted to honor, began to give forth his memorable message. His voice was strong, his whole bearing as he sat upright in his chair, poised and quietly triumphant.

"Dr. Rubinoff—my distinguished colleagues in our noble profession—gracious friends," he said joyously, "my emotions are too profound for utterance. I am moved to the very foundations of my being. Never before in all my life have I been so greatly honored, so greatly blessed—as I am honored and blessed tonight. This new hospital and all it represents is, to me, a veritable resurrection. When, as you all know, my lifework in Germany was laid in ruins, I thought that the end of all things had come. All that I had striven for through many years lay before me a ghastly desolation. I was utterly hopeless and despairing.

"But from that house of death, God Himself has wondrously raised up this miraculous new house of life. From blackest darkness He has brought me to new light and peace and joy. I am fully comforted and compensated. My heart is overwhelmed with praise as I behold this night the realization of my fondest dreams. My Berlin hospital ministered to the children of Germany. This house of healing in Jerusalem will minister to refugee children from all over the world.

"I know full well that I myself will not be here to share in this wonderful work—in the complete fulfillment of this God-given vision. For I am solemnly aware that *'the time of my departure is at hand. I have fought a good fight. I have finished my course, I have kept the faith. Henceforth there is laid up for me a crown of righteousness, which the Lord, the righteous judge, shall give me at that day: and not to me only, but unto them also that love his appearing.'*

"Yes, dear friends, it is the truth. I must lay down my armor. I must pass on the torch. But I am well content to leave the leadership of my cherished lifework in the strong hands of my beloved son. I go in the glad assurance that it will be carried forward magnificently by him. What God has so graciously begun in Benjamin Rothschild, He will perform—He will complete—He will perfect—in Joseph Rothschild."

Bibliography

Frank, Anne. *Anne Frank: The Diary of a Young Girl.* New York: Pocket Books, 1953.

Hull, William L. *Israel—Key to Prophecy: The Story of Israel from the Regathering to the Millennium as Told by the Prophets.* Grand Rapids: Zondervan, 1957.

Mille, Madeleine. *Footsteps in Palestine.* Publisher unknown.

Miller, Basil. *Martin Niemoller, Hero of the Concentration Camp.* Grand Rapids: Zondervan, 1942.

Stein, Leo. *I Was in Hell with Niemoller.* New York: Fleming H. Revell, 1942.

Taylor, Kressman. *Until That Day.* New York: Duell, Sloan & Pearce, 1942.

Uris, Leon. *Exodus.* Double Day, 1958.

Ten Boom, Corrie. *A Prisoner and Yet.* Toronto: Christian Literature Crusade, 1958.

Wilkinson, John. *God's Plan for the Jew,* 2nd edition. Carlisle, England: Paternoster Press, 1946.

Excerpts from:

Brennecke, Fritz. *The Nazi Primer: Official Handbook for Schooling the Hitler Youth.* 1938 (the textbook prepared by the National Socialist Government of Germany for the indoctrination of the 7 million German youths in the ideology and purposed activities of Nazi totalitarianism).

Digest of the United States Congressional Report on the Nazi Concentration Camps of Germany. Publication data unknown.

Hitler, Adolf. *Mein Kampf.* Germany, Zentralverlag der N.S.D.A.P, 1937.

Shirer, William L. *The Rise and Fall of the Third Reich,* 1st Touchstone edition. New York: Simon & Schuster, 1990.

Acknowledgments

In order to establish authentic historical foundation and background for this story, and to present confirming evidence that the many tragic events related therein are not the figments of lugubrious imagination, but represent factual experiences in the lives of tens and hundreds of thousands of unhappy Jewish victims of Nazi venomous hate and outrage, voluminous research has been required.

Among the books and pamphlets carefully studied, the ones listed in the bibliography are the most important. We gratefully acknowledge to their respective authors our indebtedness for the information and inspiration they have afforded us.

Immeasurable contribution toward the development of *Ben-Oni* has also been given us by several friends who have helped in various ways. It would be impossible to name all who have encouraged and cooperated. To an outstanding few, however, particular recognition must be accorded. First and foremost, I would pay grateful tribute to the cherished memory of my beloved brother, Edward, apart from whose faithful and devoted material sustaining over many years of the writing of this book, its production would have been impossible.

Next in order of gratitude is my precious friend and nurse-companion, Mrs. Carl C. Meitz, RN, now of the San Manuel Hospital, San Manuel, Arizona, to whom, literally, I owe the prolongation of my life as, during the period of writing, her skillful and loving ministry of healing twice wrought recovery from critical illness.

Many other cherished friends have sustained me in various ways: by their unwearied and inspiring encouragement, by valuable literary criticism, and, above all else, by faithful prayer-upholding. Conspicuous among these and therefore worthy of special appreciative remembrance are the following:

In the Southland: Mr. and Mrs. Joseph Raffa of Atlanta, Georgia; Mrs. Frank E. White, Mrs. C. B. Conner, Mrs. Sue Harrison, Mrs. Lois Ragon, Mrs. S. R. Stanbury, the late Miss Jesse I. Holtzclaw, the late Mrs. Howard McCall, and Miss Blanche Silvia; all of Chattanooga, Tennessee.

The Misses Ruth and Esther Angel of the New York Gospel Mission to the Jews and—among the faithful Canadian friends—Mrs. Laura G. Hamilton and Miss Florence Glazier of the Biblical Research Society, Toronto; Mr. Denis G. West, past president of the Toronto Branch of the Hebrew Christian Alliance, and his devoted wife—my oft-times most gracious hostess. It was in their hospitable Toronto home—as the hand of our God was upon us all for good—that the concluding chapters of the book were written and the arduous task of revision was at length achieved.

And, in the roster of valued collaborators, last but not least are my long-time beloved friends, Mr. and Mrs. Hugh Douglas Millman, originally of London, England, but now of Fort William, Ontario. To them I owe an incalculable debt of appreciative thanks for their persistent urging and sustaining, and for their unremitting ministry of intercession on my behalf.

To each and every one of these cherished friends I would express my deepest gratitude for the immeasurable blessing they have been to me down all the many years. I praise God for them all, as I count each of them, to me, one of His most precious gifts.

But above and beyond all the human helpers, I owe the completion of *Ben-Oni* supremely to our faithful Lord Himself, as He has furnished alike the command and the supernatural empowering, the inspiration and encouragement for the appointed task. He it is who has been, literally, the Author and Finisher of my faith for its completion. From His first charge to His servant—in the words of David to Solomon for the building of the temple: *Be strong and of good courage and do it: fear not, nor be dismayed: for the LORD God, even my God, will be with thee; he will not fail thee, nor forsake thee, until thou hast finished all the work for the service of the LORD*—even to the conclusion of the writing, He has, over and over again, held before her by His Holy Spirit many other promises of His Word, among them such as these:

Hath he said, and shall he not do it? Or hath he spoken and shall he not make it good?

The Lord *of hosts hath sworn, saying, Surely as I have thought, so shall it come to pass; and as I have purposed, so shall it stand . . . For the* Lord *of hosts hath purposed, and who shall disannul it? And his hand is stretched out, and who shall turn it back?*

Yea, I have spoken it, I will also bring it to pass; I have purposed it, I will also do it.

And blessed is she that believeth: for there shall be a performance of those things which were told her from the Lord.

Our wonderful God has now abundantly fulfilled all these His own wonderful promises. To Him be our eternal adoration, our thanksgiving, and our praise.

We lay *Ben-Oni* at His feet. *It is the Lord*['s]: *let him do* [with it] *what seemeth him good. May God indeed use it fruitfully according to the good pleasure of his will . . . according to the purpose of him who worketh all things after the counsel of his own will* to the blessing of His beloved chosen people, Israel—for the glory of Israel's Messiah, our Lord and Savior Jesus Christ.

—A.S.K.

Toronto, Canada
June 1964